M000274918

Praise for Anna Castle's *Murder by Misrule*

Murder by Misrule was selected as one of Kirkus Review's Best Indie Books of 2014.

"Castle's characters brim with zest and real feeling... Though the plot keeps the pages turning, the characters, major and minor, and the well-wrought historical details will make readers want to linger in the 16th century. A laugh-out loud mystery that will delight fans of the genre."
— Kirkus, starred review

"*Murder by Misrule* is a delightful debut with characters that leap off the page, especially the brilliant if unwilling detective Francis Bacon and his street smart man Tom Clarady. Elizabeth Tudor rules, but Anna Castle triumphs." — Karen Harper, NY Times best-selling author of *The Queen's Governess*

"Well-researched... *Murder by Misrule* is also enormously entertaining; a mystery shot through with a series of misadventures, misunderstandings, and mendacity worthy of a Shakespearian comedy." — M. Louisa Locke, author of the Victorian San Francisco Mystery Series

"Castle's period research is thorough but unobtrusive, and her delight in the clashing personalities of her crime-fighting duo is palpable: this is the winning fictional odd couple of the year, with Bacon's near-omniscience being effectively grounded by Clarady's street smarts. The book builds effectively to its climax, and a last-minute revelation that is particularly well-handled, but readers will most appreciate the wry humor. An extremely promising debut."
— Steve Donoghue, Historical Novel Society

"Historical mystery readers take note: *Murder by Misrule* is a wonderful example of Elizabethan times brought to life...a blend of Sherlock Holmes and history." — D. Donovan, eBook Reviewer, Midwest Book Review

"I love when I love a book! *Murder by Misrule* by Anna Castle was a fantastic read. Overall, I really liked this story and highly recommend it." — Book Nerds

Praise for *Death by Disputation*

Death by Disputation won the 2015 Chaucer Awards First In Category Award for the Elizabethan/Tudor period.

"Castle's style shines ... as she weaves a complex web of scenarios and firmly centers them in Elizabethan culture and times." — D. Donovan, eBook Reviewer, Midwest Book Review

" I would recommend *Death by Disputation* to any fan of historical mysteries, or to anyone interested in what went on in Elizabethan England outside the royal court." — E. Stephenson, Historical Novel Society

"Accurate historical details, page turning plot, bodacious, lovable and believable characters, gorgeous depictions and bewitching use of language will transfer you through time and space back to Elizabethan England." — Edi's Book Lighthouse

"This second book in the Francis Bacon mystery series is as strong as the first. At times bawdy and rowdy, at times thought-provoking ... Castle weaves religious-political intrigue, murder mystery, and Tom's colorful friendships and love life into a tightly-paced plot." — Amber Foxx, Indies Who Publish Everywhere

Praise for *The Widows Guild*

The Widows Guild was longlisted for the 2017 Historical Novel Society's Indie Award.

"As in Castle's earlier book, *Murder by Misrule*, she brings the Elizabethan world wonderfully to life, and if Francis Bacon himself seems a bit overshadowed at times in this novel, it's because the great, fun creation of the Widow's Guild itself easily steals the spotlight. Strongly Recommended." — Editor's Choice, Historical Novel Society.

Praise for *Publish and Perish*

Won an Honorable Mention for Mysteries in Library Journal's 2017 Indie Ebook Awards.

"In this aptly titled fourth book in the Francis Bacon series, Castle combines her impressive knowledge of English religion and politics during the period with masterly creativity. The result is a lively, clever story that will leave mystery fans delighted.**—Emilie Hancock, Mount Pleasant Regional Lib., SC, for Library Journal.**

Also by Anna Castle

The Francis Bacon Mystery Series

Murder by Misrule
Death by Disputation
The Widow's Guild
Publish and Perish
Let Slip the Dogs

The Professor & Mrs. Moriarty Mystery Series

Moriarty Meets His Match
Moriarty Takes His Medicine
Moriarty Brings Down the House

The Lost Hat, Texas Mystery Series

Black & White & Dead All Over
Flash Memory

THE SPYMASTER'S BROTHER

A Francis Bacon Mystery — Book 6

ANNA CASTLE

The Spymaster's Brother
A Francis Bacon Mystery — #6

Print Edition | June 2019
Discover more works by Anna Castle at www.annacastle.com

Copyright © 2019 by Anna Castle
Cover design by Jennifer Quinlan   10916771-1002
Editorial services by Jennifer Quinlan, Historical Editorial
Chapter ornaments created by Alvaro_cabrera at Freepik.com.

ISBN-10: 1-945382-23-6
ISBN-13: 978-1-945382-23-9
Library of Congress Control Number: 2019905320
Produced in the United States of America

ONE

17 March, 1592, Gray's Inn, London

"Keep that frame up," Francis Bacon scolded his young servant. He'd placed the lad on a stool about six feet from the windows in his study chamber, holding the frame of a burning glass at arm's length. He didn't want a human shadow interfering with his experiment. Now if only the fickle March sun would come out from behind that drift of clouds, he could note the result and let the lad step down.

Francis had embarked on a comprehensive exploration of the property of heat. Everyone knew a burning glass could induce heat to the point of flame. They'd tested that earlier this morning. Now he wanted to see if reversing the lens would induce a reduction in temperature. Would it cool a well heated quantity of wool, for example?

"My arms are falling off," Pinnock whined.

"Just a few more minutes. Think of all the lives you'll save."

"By setting balls of wool on fire?"

Francis didn't deign to answer. Pinnock clearly lacked the soul of a philosopher, but he'd have to get used to this work. Now that Francis's older brother, Anthony, had returned after thirteen years in France, things were going to change.

First and foremost, Francis would be spending a lot less time at court, just as soon as Anthony's gout subsided enough for him to leave the house. Anthony was the true politician in the family. Francis's talents lay in the realm of philosophy. He believed in his heart that his best destiny lay in teasing the veil from Nature's secrets to improve the lot of all humanity.

"Ah, here comes our friend the sun! Now we'll see what effect the concave lens has."

Francis stooped to lay his hand on the uncarded mass of wool he'd placed in a wooden bowl on the floor. He'd heated it earlier in a clay pot. Yes, it was still quite warm.

"Mr. Bacon, the books!" Pinnock cried.

"What?" Francis looked first at Pinnock, who was aiming his glass frame at the shelves. Following the gesture, Francis spotted flames leaping up from one of the topmost books. "God save us!"

He leapt up and snatched the book from the shelf. He dropped it on the floor and stamped out the small fire. Only then did he seek the cause, and he could've kicked himself. He'd left his other burning glass — with the original convex lens — on his desk. Purest accident had placed it where its beam would strike the nearest inflammable materials.

"Is it ruined?" Pinnock asked.

"I'm afraid so." Francis picked up the charred book to see which one it was. Just an old copy of Ralph Lever's *The Art of Reason*. He couldn't imagine how it happened to be on top. "It doesn't matter. I borrowed this months ago. Its owner must not value it much."

He tossed the ruined volume into the fireplace and kicked at the ashes on the rush mat. Pinnock could clean that up later. "Shall we make another attempt before the wool cools on its own?"

"Oh, Mr. Bacon. Haven't we—"

Shouts arose from outside the door. Someone was crying for help!

Francis and his servant stared at one another, then both charged for the door at once. "Stay back!" Francis commanded as he hurried down the stairs. He rounded the second landing and saw Anthony sprawled on the last few steps.

"What's happened? Are you all right?" He bounded down to kneel on the step beside his brother.

"I'm all right, Frank. I just lost my footing."

Francis helped his brother raise himself and plant his bottom on the wooden step. His poor gout-afflicted legs twisted uselessly to one side.

The door to Anthony's ground-floor chambers flew open, and his young servant, Jacques Petit, rushed out. *"Mon dieu! Mon cher maître! Que s'est-il passé?"*

"I thought I'd give the stairs a try." Anthony summoned a wan smile. "It appears I'm not quite up to it."

"I should say not!" Francis patted his brother's shoulder.

"Quelle idée!" Jacques wagged a finger at his master, scolding him in the soft twang of his southern dialect.

One of Anthony's secretaries appeared on the flight above, peering over the bannister. "God's mercy, Anthony! What happened?" He trotted down to the bottom step.

"I'm all right, Lawly," Anthony said. "Just a bit of a spill."

Lawson, the secretary, nudged Francis out of the way so he and Jacques could grasp Anthony's arms and hoist him up. The victim protested unconvincingly that he could manage on his own while they carried him into the ground-floor chamber.

Francis stepped out of the way. He had a sudden sense of unreality, as if he were watching a scene from a play being performed on his staircase. He shook his head to clear the illusion and stooped to collect the ebony walking

10

stick lying a few feet from the stairs. The handle was a round ivory knob set into a band of silver tracery.

The men got Anthony settled in his cushioned armchair before the hearth. Lawson said, "I'll leave you, then, if you're really all right. Work to do." On his way to the door, he flicked a wry smile at Francis. "At first, I thought the shouting was coming from your room. Thought you'd set something else on fire. Good thing I came down to check, eh?"

Lawson had lived with Anthony for many years. No doubt he was able to distinguish one brother's muffled cry from the other.

Francis took his customary seat on the other side of the hearth. Jacques offered him a blanket for his legs, but he waved it off. Poor Anthony could no longer tolerate the slightest chill; hence his servant's vigilance. Though Jacques had somehow failed to notice when his master went doddering out the door.

Jacques served each brother a cup of warm spiced wine. Then he continued to fuss over his master, lifting the weak legs onto a padded stool and pressing each one lightly to test for bruises. Anthony allowed the handling without comment, hardly flinching, even when the lad's strong hands probed to the innermost top of his thigh.

A strapping youth of sixteen, Jacques was strong enough to lift the invalid out of bed and carry him across the room. He'd entered Anthony's service at the tender age of eleven as a page and still retained the doe-eyed beauty that had won him that post.

Anthony leaned his head back against a pillow and closed his eyes. Francis sipped his fragrant wine and studied the features that had once been more familiar than his own. Only thirty-five, Anthony looked at least ten years older. His color was poor, even by the warm light of the fire. Chronic illness had etched lines across his forehead and withered his cheeks. He carried too many pounds and limped, even with a cane — when he could walk. His black curls and pointed beard remained unsalted with gray, and his brown eyes shone with intelligence. But the handsome courtier who had wielded both lute and tennis racquet with equal skill had vanished.

Anthony sighed and opened his eyes. He smiled at Francis. "Do I pass inspection, Doctor?" Getting only a roll of the eyes in response, he nodded. "Have I mentioned how much I like your beard?"

Francis had been a dewy youth of eighteen when Anthony left for France. He'd added a crease above his nose from too much reading and lost that arrogant smirk, according to his mother, but was otherwise not much changed. He asked his brother, "Whatever possessed you to attempt the stairs?"

"I wanted to see how far I could get. My cane caught on a baluster, and down I went."

"But why? Can't you send Jacques up to fetch your secretary?"

"It wasn't that," Anthony said. "I wanted to test myself, to see if I'm ready to pay my respects to Her Majesty. The Presence Chamber at Whitehall is on the first floor. That's two flights of stairs, followed by a longish walk."

Francis sighed. "She does ask after you whenever she notices me. You've been gone so long a personal visit is virtually required for persons of our rank." Elizabeth Tudor did not like to be ignored. Then again, what monarch did?

"I know, I know." Anthony echoed the sigh. "I long to go, I truly do. Perhaps in a few weeks I'll be able to manage it."

"You could be carried up in a chair. Everyone knows you suffer from the gout."

"Never!" Anthony swatted away Jacques's hand as he tried to wipe his neck under his ruff with a moist cloth.

"*C'est assez, mon cher.* I am quite uninjured." He turned a scowl toward his brother. "I will *not* be carried into Her Majesty's presence like some Turkish *altezza.* Imagine the talk! People will think I've grown above my station. No, until I can walk into her presence on my own two feet, I will stay home and build my strength."

"As you wish." Francis heard more than fear of embarrassment in Anthony's heated protest. True, his legs were unreliable, but there was some other reason as well. What terror lurked in Queen Elizabeth's Presence Chamber that could outweigh his duty to pay homage?

Anthony had spent many weeks at the court of Henri de Navarre — now King Henry the Fourth of all France. They said Henry's courtiers were far more licentious and addicted to intrigue than the English, who were paragons of virtue by comparison.

Well, thirteen years was a long time. The two brothers had much to learn — and relearn — about one another.

"You're mending well enough," Francis said. "If you refrain from falling again, you'll be walking across the yard before you know it." He gave his brother a tentative smile. "I have rather hoped you'd take my place at court one of these days. You're so much better at small talk than I am. The little lies, the flattery . . . saying the right word at the right time to the right person. I haven't the knack. With you to represent the Bacon family, I could retire to Twickenham and devote myself to philosophy."

He hoped for an answering smile, but Anthony rolled his eyes, impatient. "It's a skill like any other, Frank. Something to be learned. You'll do better, now you have me as your tutor."

That wasn't at all what Francis wanted. "But I'm so bad at it. I don't remember things that don't interest me, which includes most of what transpires at court. Dalliances, for example. It's a major topic about which I would prefer to know nothing. And you're so much more diplomatic than

I am. I have the awkward habit of answering questions directly and saying what I mean, which never turns out well."

"I'm sure you're better than you think." Anthony took a sip of wine and smacked his lips, heedless of his brother's souring humor. "But in truth, your talents do lie elsewhere. You should be Solicitor General by now."

"Our lord uncle has convinced the queen that I'm too young." Lord Burghley's increasingly ill health kept him from court most days, but he still held the post of Lord Treasurer, and the queen still relied on his judgment — especially where his gifted nephews were concerned.

"It might help if you argued a *few* cases in court first," Anthony said, then added hastily, "But I agree. His Lordship has treated you as shabbily as he has me. He's never paid me in full for my services nor helped with my messengers' expenses. It would serve him right if you retired to the countryside to weigh pots of pond scum."

Francis had to laugh at that notion. "Perhaps not the *first* inquiry upon which I would embark. But even if you can't yet go to court, Anthony, I'll still have more time for my studies. Now that you're here, physically present in England, I won't be needed to decrypt and disseminate your correspondence. Your letters were my principal stock in trade, after all. Without them, my shop is empty."

Anthony granted the witticism a small smile but evaded the main point. "We'll have more work than ever, now that I'm back on my native soil."

"But you won't need me—"

"Oh, there'll be plenty of work for you, Frank, never fear. No one has your capacity for concentration. It'd take three men to replace you. Speaking of which, we must hire another secretary. I want one fluent in German and Russian, and Polish, if we can find such a man."

"Another secretary?" Francis frowned. He'd already enlarged his house, raising the roof to add a full story and a more habitable attic. He'd expected some additions to the household, but Anthony had brought his entire retinue.

Most senior members of Gray's Inn had a clerk and a personal servant. Anthony had two secretaries, two clerks, a body servant, a wardrobe minder, a cook, a potboy, a page, and a coachman, most of whom now lodged under this roof. Add that to Francis, Pinnock, and Thomas Clarady, and the house was already full to bursting.

Anthony seemed oblivious to that dull, domestic problem. "We'll want at least two more scriveners. We shouldn't waste the talents of our multilingual secretaries on mere copying. Of course, the most sensitive materials will be handled exclusively by you and me."

Another skilled secretary, educated at Cambridge or Oxford, presumably, and thus expected to dress — and dine and travel — like a gentleman. Two copyists needing desks, candles, ink, food, and somewhere to sleep. They'd have to find another house, perhaps somewhere nearby in Holborn.

"How are we planning to pay for this stable of intelligencers?" Francis asked.

"We need a patron, obviously. Preferably the queen." Anthony's eyes sparkled with delight at the reaction to that blast.

"*Our* queen?" Francis was stunned. England's monarch was notoriously parsimonious. "One doesn't simply ask Her Majesty to pay one's secretaries, however useful one's work might be in furthering her aims." He took several sips from his cup to restore his balance.

"One does if one is the Secretary of State." Anthony's lips curved in a smug smile.

Francis nearly choked on his wine. "Ambitious, aren't we?"

"It makes sense. Think about it. It's been two years since Sir Francis Walsingham died, and she still hasn't named a replacement. Meanwhile, his best agents are

15

scattering to the four winds — or coming to me to ask for a position. They don't trust our lord uncle to pay them anymore than we do."

"You may in fact be the best candidate, but you're simply not strong enough. That's the most demanding job in England." Francis's mind whirled at the impossible notion. Anthony would need a large house of his own to perform that office. Sir Francis had kept something like seventy horses, ready to ride at a moment's notice. The benchers at Gray's Inn would never allow that much tumult inside their studious enclave, even if space could be found.

"Nonsense." Anthony flapped his hand, a foppish gesture that drew attention to the wealth of lace around his wrists. "Sir Francis was housebound for the last years of his life. And I've hardly been idle this past week, in spite of being largely confined to my bed. We're digging into those documents I brought home, thinking about how best to organize them."

"That's a valuable resource." Francis hadn't yet peeked inside the enormous black chest. It had taken two men to carry it up to the second floor, where the secretaries lived. They couldn't keep it down here for fear of light-fingered visitors. Locks on that sort of chest were easily picked, and the letters stored within could cause serious damage to persons and reputations if they fell into the wrong hands.

Anthony had spent his thirteen years in the south of France building the most valuable intelligence service in Europe. He knew who had served whom for how long — or pretended to do so. He'd kept records of alliances and dalliances, both rumored and proven. He had informants in every major port and intelligencers sending him observations even from the depths of Italy and Spain. He knew more about political affairs in Europe than any man in England, now that Sir Francis was gone.

16

Anthony said, "I've started a master list of everyone with whom I've ever corresponded. Eventually, the names will be sorted by country and rank."

Francis chuckled. "You're taking a leaf from my commonplace book."

"You see, I do pay attention. Don't worry, dear brother. There will always be time for your philosophical investigations. You wouldn't be Francis Bacon if you weren't pondering one of Nature's mysteries."

"True knowledge is the foundation of all beneficial applications," Francis said. "Without it, how can we determine which remedies will be most effective?"

"*Précisément, mon frère.* Solid intelligence is the foundation of all policy." That was not what Francis meant, but Anthony sailed on past it.

"The first step," he said, "is to get a good rumor rumbling about my years of experience and the breadth of my knowledge. I know everyone of importance from Rome to Riga."

Francis surrendered to his brother's single-mindedness — for the moment. "How do we initiate this rumbling?"

"We need a friend or two, people of influence." Anthony snapped his fingers. Jacques rose from the stool by the front window, where he'd been watching Graysians crossing the yard through a gap in the curtains. Anthony gestured for him to sit down, then poked Francis in the arm. "Didn't you tell me you were friends with Lady Dorchester? Isn't she a gentlewoman of the Privy Chamber? She must know everyone."

"I can't see her for a few weeks. She's in confinement." Lady Dorchester, née Alice Trumpington, had once spent a year at Gray's under Francis's tutelage, disguised as a young gentleman. He had never once suspected she was anything other than what she'd pretended to be. He still chided himself for his poor observational skills. What kind of natural philosopher could fail to distinguish a boy from a girl?

"Confinement?" Anthony asked. "Whatever for? Oh, of course. She's expecting a child. Well, may God preserve her."

Francis silently echoed that prayer. "We could ask Tom to tell some tales about you in the local taverns. We're between legal terms. He has nothing better to do."

"The *très beau* Thomas Clarady?" Anthony gave a sensuous little wriggle. "Alas, for the vigor of my youth!"

"He's not that kind," Francis said. He did like the idea of dropping this business into his clerk's idle hands. Tom liked intelligencing; he'd said so more than once. Perhaps he could be guided into Anthony's service, taking over the tedious bits to leave Francis more time for his own pursuits.

"A pity," Anthony said. "But that is a good idea. No one loves gossip more than an Inns of Court man. Word will drift up the social ladder as they visit their clients. Let's craft a little story for Clarady to spread. Something praiseful yet slightly droll. A lively anecdote about my weighty chest full of Continental secrets, perhaps."

"I'll see what I can conjure up."

"We still need a patron rather urgently," Anthony said. "We can't count on support from our uncle, but perhaps we ought to offer him the right of first refusal, if only for appearance's sake. People will wonder if we skip past our own relation."

"Any offers from that source will have to be made in very concrete terms. I've had nothing but vague promises and hollow honors in all these years."

"Who else might desire our services?"

Francis noted that "our" with a sinking heart. "My lord of Essex has been very kind to me. He'll expect to be first on the list, or at least co-first, if there can be such a thing. He's eager to meet you when he returns from Rouen."

"As I am to meet him! *Le Roi Henri* likes him quite well, which can be a good sign. It could also mean the man is just good company at a feast."

Francis shook his head. Essex was much more than that. "His Lordship is charming, well-read, and accomplished in all the manly arts. I'm not surprised your king likes him."

"Co-first, then. Although if he's not here . . ."

"We'll write to his sister, Lady Rich. She's living in Essex House in his absence. Lady Dorchester is there as well, as it happens, for her confinement."

"Isn't *that* convenient?" Anthony gave Francis a smile of approval. "You see, Frank. You *are* good at this."

Francis frowned. Two friends did not make him a master of political negotiations.

"You must be sure to attend the christening, Frank, once her ladyship is delivered of her child. Bring a handsome present. She'll ask about me, and then you can slip in some odd facts for her to pass along. How long will it be, do you reckon?"

"A matter of weeks. Days, perhaps." Francis had no idea, but Tom probably knew since he was the child's father — a deep secret not to be shared with the Master of Secrets sitting right here in this room.

When had Anthony become such a Machiavellian schemer? And when had he stopped caring about Francis's philosophical investigations? Apart from a few placating words, he'd shown no interest. He used to listen avidly to each new theory, sometimes helping obtain and measure samples. Those pots of pond scum, for example. Francis remembered the day they'd collected them, ruining two good shirts in the process. He'd been trying to work out whether the stuff was a substance, like oil or mercury, or some sort of vegetable matter.

"Who else, Frank? We should have more than two. Another Privy Council member? Think, man! Our future's at stake." Anthony grinned.

Francis did not return his enthusiasm. "Let's be clear, Anthony. I'll help you get on your feet, figuratively and literally. I'll work to get those rumors started and solicit bids for your services — with the uttermost subtlety, of course. If you like, I'll have a sign painted to hang outside that window" — he jerked his chin at the red brocade curtains — "reading *Bacon Brothers House of Secrets*. But once the wheels are in motion, I'll step back. I'll slip away to a quiet place where I can read and think and write."

"Quelle absurdité!" Anthony puffed in disdain. "If you really wanted to retire to Twickenham to study philosophy, you'd have done it already. Your two little manors are enough to support that simple life. You wouldn't need new clothes every year nor have to buy gifts for courtiers who already own three of everything. You could even continue at Gray's during legal terms, if you dined in commons and took on a few paying clients. You don't need my permission or our lord uncle's. You could just go do it. You don't because it isn't what you really want. You like hearing the latest news before anyone else here. You like being received in the libraries and private parlors of earls and privy councilors. You love having the queen's ear now and then, and you *adore* writing advice letters that are read by everyone who matters. You couldn't give any of that up for a month, much less a lifetime. Besides, our father bred us for this service. You can't turn your back on that. You'll be struggling for a higher position until you go to meet your Maker. In your heart of hearts, you know it too."

Francis cast him a bitter look, lips pressed tight. His gaze shifted to the fire, crackling with fragrant wood instead of smoky coal. He stroked the rolled rim of his Venetian glass cup, filled with the rich wine of Bordeaux and flavored with Caribbean sugar and Indian spices. His two paltry manors wouldn't support *this* level of luxury. He'd have to get by with one man of all work and depend on friends to bring him books. No more popping into the City to read the latest works fresh from the press. He'd be lucky to get news from court once a month. Who among those with entrée to the centers of power would have time to visit him? He'd gradually slip out of touch and out of mind, forgotten in his pastoral retreat, pottering about the garden in a shabby doublet and patched hose, muttering to himself.

Hard truths, but ones he'd needed to hear. He turned to Anthony with a rueful look. "You're right. In part." He sighed loudly. "Well, let's get those rumors rolling. Then we'll make sure our prospects know what we have on offer. To wit" — he ticked each item off on his fingers — "one experienced spymaster, slightly damaged but on the mend; one *infinitely* patient brother with a not inconsiderable skill with a pen; a cadre of multilingual secretaries, each supplied with a swift-fingered copyist; and one large oaken chest, laden with priceless confidential correspondence going back twelve years."

Anthony giggled. "They'll be beating a path to our door."

Francis didn't like the sound of that. "On second thought, perhaps we should start with a few discreetly placed words. We don't want these rumors taking on a life of their own."

TWO

Thomas Clarady pressed his broad thumb into the smooth white instep, relishing the guttural groan that followed. He kneaded the base of each alabaster toe, savoring each low grunt.

"You sound just like a little pig."

Trumpet shrieked and threw a hard pillow, catching him squarely on the forehead.

"Ow!"

Eight and three-quarter months of pregnancy hadn't affected her aim, though nearly every inch of her body had been altered. Even her feet were puffed into lumpy oblongs. Her fingers were puffy too, and her once-slender ankles. Her belly had grown enormous.

How could such a small woman bear such a giant child? It didn't seem possible. Tom's fears about the impending delivery clenched his heart, as it did every time he thought of it, which was every other minute. Childbirth was dangerous; everybody knew it.

"Do my ankles," the lady commanded. "And my legs. My legs have been achy all day."

Tom was used to the bearish tone. He'd been dropping by Essex House every afternoon to rub Trumpet's feet since she'd come back to London. She'd decided to spend the weeks of her confinement with her friend Lady Rich, who had several children and could advise her from experience. London also had the best midwives and physicians in the country. Trumpet's husband, the Earl of

Dorchester, had gone to France with Lady Rich's brother, the Earl of Essex. Thus the plan made sense to everyone.

In truth, Trumpet just wanted to be near Tom. Male visitors were barred during a woman's confinement, but Lady Rich turned a blind eye. She had her own secret lover, who had fathered at least one of her children, so she understood their plight. Thus every afternoon Tom went for a walk along the Strand, passed through the gate, and slipped around to the rear stairs with as much notice from the staff as one of the household cats.

Trumpet had a suite of two rooms and every conceivable luxury, including piles of pillows, fur coverlets, quilted coverlets, and coverlets made of woven lambswool. Red curtains hung around the bed and across the narrow window to ward off plague, demons, and other sources of harm. One snap of the fingers and her every wish was granted — within the bounds of reason. No power on earth could bring her fresh raspberries in March, and no right-minded servant would give a pregnant woman spirituous liquor or a bowl of crushed chalk.

Tom shifted his position, setting her foot flat against his chest to apply long strokes to her ankles and calves, smoothing away the swellings, digging into her calf muscles with his strong fingers. He grinned as little grunts issued from her white throat.

He chuckled. "I love those piggy snorts. *Oof. Oof. Oof.*"

She kicked him, hard. "I am NOT a pig!"

"I didn't say you—"

"*Pig!* Pig, he calls me! After all my months of suffering to give him the child he craves —"

"You're the one who —"

"Now he's blaming *me!*" She glared at her maidservant, who sat placidly beside the bed embroidering a shirt.

Catalina Luna, a Spanish actress who'd come to England with a troupe of street performers, smiled and shook her head. "Pig is not so nice, Mr. Tom."

23

"I apologize, my lady, most humbly and sincerely. Now give me back that leg."

He massaged her limbs in silence for a while. She spread her arms wide across the heap of pillows raising her upper body. "I'll be glad when I can lie on my back again," she said.

She looked like she'd been beached on that dune of pillows, which reminded him . . . "I found a pamphlet in the jakes yesterday about a huge fish that washed up on the shore in Cornwall. It took fifteen men to roll the beast back into the water."

He peered around the belly to shoot Trumpet a grin, only to find her levering herself up onto her elbows, fury blazing in her emerald eyes.

"Not that the story in any way reminded me of you," he amended. "Not in the slightest. It's merely a curiosity —"

"I'm a *whale!*" she moaned. Her humor had shifted from choleric to melancholy in the blink of an eye. He'd grown used to that too. "I'm a hideous, whale-sized pig."

"Fiddle-faddle." He kissed the sole of her foot and set it back on the bed, pulling her woolen petticoat down to cover her bare legs. Then he scooted up to plant a kiss on her forehead and another on her lips. He met her eyes and spoke from the heart. "You're the most beautiful woman in the world, beloved, whatever your condition and whatever your shape. I love you more every day, and that's just the way it is."

She regarded him with a mournful gaze, but he detected a faint curve on her lips. "Whale," she pouted.

"No." He kissed her forehead again.

"Pig."

"Never."

"I meant you that time," she said. They both laughed, humors restored. But then she moaned again. "I'm so tired of being pregnant. Get this baby out of me!"

"I would if I could, sweetling." Tom turned to Catalina. "When will it be?"

She shrugged, an eloquent gesture. "Only God knows that, Mr. Tom. Any day, they say."

"They've been saying that for two weeks," Trumpet grumbled. She poked Tom in the chest. "*You* put it in here. You get it out!"

"Patience, my lady," he said, laughing. "It can't be long now."

"It's an eternity! I'm miserable. I'm enormous. I can't roll over. I can't lie flat. I can't get up without help. My back aches. Twice I've had these horrible clenching pains and everyone thinks, 'It's here! It's here!' but then the pains pass and all I do is burp for one whole minute."

Clenching pains sounded alarming. Tom shot a glance at Catalina, who shook her head. "Normal, they say. A good sign, they say."

"They can stuff their cursed signs up their great, flabby arses," Trumpet said. "I haven't slept for days. I can't get comfortable."

"Oh, my poor Trumplekins! Here, I'll make you comfortable." Tom climbed up behind her so she could use him as a pillow, her weight resting warm against his chest. He wasn't sleeping all that well himself these days, what with worrying about the birth and the whole fraught business of fatherhood. But his main role now was to absorb her grumbles and soothe her little aches.

They lay like that a while, breathing together. Then she stirred and said, "Tell me something about the world. I miss it. What's happening at Gray's?"

"Nothing since Hilary term ended. You know how quiet it gets. Most Graysians have gone home."

"How's Anthony? Is he walking?"

"A little. He has to use a stick, and his servant walks close beside him in case he stumbles. But he crossed the yard to the kitchen yesterday to speak with his cook."

"He has his own cook? I thought that was against the rules."

"Rules don't apply to the sons of Sir Nicholas Bacon, at least not to Anthony. He seems to do as he pleases."

"He should be careful," Trumpet said. "Penelope told me to warn you that she's caught wind of some unpleasant rumors about him. Whispers that he's a sodomite and that he took bribes from Catholics. She thinks the Bacons should be on their guard."

Tom shrugged. "The first part's true enough, or it was when he was healthy. But nobody cares about men loving men, especially not people at Lady Rich's level."

"But it isn't something you want talked about. And it can add to other charges, like the bribes."

"That part doesn't sound likely unless he really needed money." Tom caught himself. "Which is quite possible. Anthony's worse than Francis when it comes to living beyond his means. You should see his chambers. Everything is silk or silver or Venetian glass. He lives like a lord."

"But he isn't one," Trumpet said. "He can't be that rich, can he? Francis wouldn't be constantly scrambling for money if Anthony had more lands."

"They both seem to believe a big pot of money lies somewhere just beyond their present reach. But the same could be said for half of Her Majesty's courtiers."

"True enough," Trumpet said. "All the same, those rumors could cause trouble if they spread too far. The Bacons should find that blabberer and stop his mouth. Tell them the warning comes from Lady Rich."

"I will. She seems to be on their side already, which is a step in the right direction."

"That's thanks to me," Trumpet said. "I do more than lie here grousing, you know. I passed along the word about what a marvelous spymaster Anthony is and how effective he would be as Secretary of State, just like you asked me to do."

"Have you convinced her?"

"She agrees already. I think Essex does too. We'll see when he comes home." Trumpet yawned hugely, throwing her head back and cracking her skull against his chin. She snuggled into him, covered his hands with hers, and fell asleep, just like that.

He bent his head to hers, breathing in the scent of rose oil in her ebony hair, willing his strength into her small body to help her survive the ordeal to come. He felt a kick inside the belly under his hand and marveled at the miracle. His heart swelled with love and pride, almost more than he could bear.

Trumpet insisted the child was a boy, though Catalina said no one could predict that with confidence. A boy would satisfy the principal requirement of a countess: producing an heir. Tom would love to have a son. What man wouldn't? But secretly he hoped for a girl, a spirited minx with ink-black hair and bright green eyes in a heart-shaped face, just like her mother.

* * *

"Mr. Tom," Catalina's soft Spanish voice murmured in his ear. "Wake up. It is time to go."

Tom opened his eyes and yawned. The light had fallen outside the window with the sun gone down behind Somerset House. It would be dark soon.

He eased himself out from under his lady, who continued to snore lightly. He slung his cloak around his shoulders and put on his hat. Catalina walked him to the door.

"You'll send for me the minute anything happens."

She nodded. "We have a stable boy ready to run to your window. I showed it to him already."

27

"Thanks. For everything."

He jogged down the stairs and walked out onto the Strand. It wasn't far from Essex House to Holborn Road, but the narrow lanes sloping northward grew dark early, thanks to the jettied upper stories crowding out the light. Tom put a hand on the knife at the small of his back but met no cutpurses. On the high road, shopkeepers were gathering in their wares while their apprentices closed up the shutters. Tom aimed for the yellow glow of the lanterns outside the Antelope Inn.

This was Tom's home away from home. Popular with clerks and lawyers, the Antelope offered good food, excellent ale, and a decent selection of wines. The crowd was far smaller between terms, which made the long room feel homier. A good fire blazed at one end, and a friendly barman smiled behind the counter at the other.

Tom stood at the door for a moment while his eyes adjusted to the light, relishing the welcome stink of tobacco and beer. He spotted Thomas Lawson, Anthony's secretary and close friend, waving at him from a table near the counter and made his way over. If they were going to live under the same roof, they might as well get to know each other.

"Here's the third Tom," Lawson crowed. "The set is now complete." A handsome man, he always dressed well and kept his dark red beard and moustache closely trimmed. He had an easy manner and an attractive grace of movement. He gestured freely with both hands when he talked.

"I consider myself the first Tom," he said, pulling up a stool, "since you're the newcomers."

The second or third Tom, depending on where you started, was Phelippes, the cryptographer. He was neither comely nor graceful. His straw-colored hair hung limply under his battered hat. He must have cut his own beard with a dull blade and no mirror. Lawson had doubtless dragged him out of the house to give him an airing.

A strikingly beautiful woman sat between the two men. As fair as a summer afternoon, her almond-shaped eyes looked dark in the candlelight but were probably the color of cornflowers or bluebells. Possibly sapphires, in the right light. She was precisely the type Tom used to fall in love with on a monthly basis, back before Trumpet claimed his heart.

A man could still look, however. He recognized her, though they hadn't met. He'd seen her when crossing through the garden at Essex House. She'd seen him too, though Lady Rich had instructed everyone in her household to ignore him.

Lawson caught his admiring gaze and grinned. "Thomas Clarady, meet Elsa Moreau, the beauty of Bordeaux."

The beauty rolled her eyes and extended her hand for a kiss. The amused smile that flickered across her lips acknowledged she recognized him too. "Do you also live at Gray's Inn?"

"Unlike these two, I'm actually a member." Tom accepted a mug of beer from the serving wench, who didn't need to hear his order. He asked Moreau, "How do you know these two rogues?"

"I've only just met Mr. Phelippes," she said. Her voice was as mellow as a well-turned recorder and flavored with an alluring French accent. "For me, it is a great honor to meet the most renowned linguist in all Europe."

Phelippes blushed and spluttered. Tom vowed to take the poor chub in hand and teach him how to talk to women. A visit to the Two Bells brothel in Smithfield might be in order.

Moreau smiled as if at a witty remark. Then she wrinkled her nose at Lawson, taking his hand and giving it a little shake. "I've known *this* fellow for more years than I care to admit."

"We met in Bordeaux," Lawson said. "Or was it Montaubon?"

"One of the two." She rattled off something in French that made them laugh. Phelippes's ears turned pink. She noticed Tom's lack of comprehension. "Don't you speak French, Monsieur Clarady?"

"Only Law French. Doesn't seem much like the real thing."

"Not the sounds," Phelippes said, "but the grammar is similar. Law French is founded on Old French with an admixture of Latin, pronounced in the English fashion."

"I cannot imagine it," Moreau said, cocking her head as if intrigued.

Tom performed a sample, winning a delighted laugh.

"Quel barbarisme!" she exclaimed.

They continued to trade snippets of barbaric language gleaned from Tom's travels with his privateering father and from Moreau's and Lawson's years in France. Phelippes had the funniest bits, but not the slightest notion how to deliver a jest. He would spout his offering into the middle of someone else's turn, then clamp his lips together in such a droll expression they all roared. Then he would beam, thinking his linguistic sally had earned him the laugh.

Tom ordered a bowl of mutton stew and another mug of ale, enjoying the company. He didn't have close friends at Gray's anymore. In spite of his excellent clothes and his tutelage at Francis Bacon's feet, he still didn't fit in with the sons of knights and county justices. His late father had not been a gentleman, however great his wealth.

Tom didn't mind usually. He meant to become one of England's foremost barristers — possibly even a judge. During court terms and learning vacations, he spent most of his time studying. Between terms, he took in copy work, saving his pennies. He planned to sue his guardian for control of his estates on the day he passed the bar, and the Court of Wards charged very steep fees.

He spent little time in the company of women anymore, apart from the proprietress of the Antelope and her barmaids. He no longer had the coin for brothels; besides, Trumpet would gut him like a fish if he fell back into that habit.

He dined every Sunday at his guardian's house, but Lady Russell grilled him on his studies more intensely than the senior barristers at Gray's. He doubted she had ever been winsome or girlish. She'd won the bidding for his wardship after his father died and kept him on short rations, even though his estate was worth eight hundred pounds per annum. But she'd taken a liking to him and wanted him to rise in his legal career. Things could be worse.

The conversation ranged from language to customs, each contributing a lively anecdote. Even Phelippes, who had never set foot out of Middlesex, could offer droll examples of courtesies gone awry from the letters he'd translated. His stories always highlighted some interesting cultural difference. Lawson's always made someone look like a fool. Moreau, like a good Frenchwoman, told tales with an element of romance.

She'd come to England in the service of Lady Rich, who'd hired her on Anthony's recommendation. Her former mistress was a fashionable Protestant gentlewoman in Montaubon. Moreau desired to improve her English; Lady Rich desired to improve her wardrobe. And thus the match was made.

Trumpet had probably suggested the Antelope to her as a respectable place for a woman of her class. She and Catalina Luna used to dress as tradesmen's daughters and meet Tom here for a quiet supper from time to time.

Moreau and Lawson seemed to have more in mind than a mug of beer and some lively conversation. She never let go of his hand, and they'd inched their stools closer together. Tom knew that game. He'd wager their ankles had twined beneath the table, or someone's foot had shed its shoe to play toesies with the other's calf.

Lawson and Anthony had been lovers back in France, or so Tom believed. Anthony wasn't up to much anymore, poor sod. Now the two men were just good friends, with Lawson serving as Anthony's personal secretary. He must be one of those men who was attracted to comely, willing persons of either sex. Any port in a storm, as the sailor once said.

Phelippes launched into a detailed explanation of a new encryption scheme he and Francis were developing, addressing most of his remarks to the much-scrubbed tabletop. Tom gave him his full attention to encourage the man to practice speaking aloud. Lawson and Moreau began talking quietly in French, their heads bent together.

Tom kept his eyes on Phelippes but lent half an ear to the other two. She said something that startled Lawson. He pulled back and gave her a long, considering look. Then he crooked a half-smile at her and shrugged. She smiled warmly, giving him a look under her long lashes that promised good times to come.

Tom wasn't sure which had been the wooer and which the wooed. They'd both won, he supposed. Perversely, he felt the pang of a competition lost, though he hadn't been a contestant. Moreau hadn't so much as batted her thick lashes at him.

And why not, now he thought of it? Had his fair curls wilted? Had his legs grown stumpy? Women had once been drawn to him like bees to a blossoming apple tree. Trumpet must have cast a spell over him so other women saw a warty nose and a second chin.

A commotion at the door drew their attention. Even Phelippes faltered to a halt. A group of three men had entered from the darkened street, or more like one man followed by two unrelated gentlemen. The followers wore legal robes, marking them as Inns of Court men. Tom didn't recognize them. Not Graysians, then; probably Lincoln's Inn. It was the closest.

They moved toward an empty table, still grinning at the man who'd preceded them. That one had been laughing loudly enough to silence nearby conversations. He now stopped to pose with one hand on his hip, tossing a last jest toward the Lincoln's men. The pose pushed his cloak behind his elbow, displaying a costume designed to impress: a well-fitted gray suit trimmed in black, with short round hose and an expensively slashed doublet. Glossy black hair curled under a tall gray hat. He'd trained his moustaches to curl up at the ends, framing the triangle of his pointed black beard.

Clearly a man of fashion. Tom had been one too, once upon a time. He'd executed that very pose and knew exactly what it meant. *Notice me, I beg you, for I am desperate to be seen.*

Everyone saw; most returned to their own conversations. Lawson, however, blew out a vigorous lip fart and said, "What brings that whoreson dolt here?"

Moreau shrugged. "He is an Englishman, is he not? He has come home, just like you."

"Not like me." Lawson's tone was contemptuous.

"Who is he?" Tom asked.

"A ruddy, dog-hearted rascal," Lawson said.

Moreau shot him a look. Questioning? Silencing? "His name is Raffe Ridley," she told Tom.

"So that's Ridley," Phelippes said with interest. "He writes well. A clear hand and straightforward syntax. Copious descriptions, useful for context." To Tom, he added, "He's the Privy Council's emissary in Bordeaux. Official correspondence flows through his hands, along with unofficial messages. His job is to watch, listen, and report periodically."

"Wasn't that Anthony Bacon's job?" Tom asked.

"Anthony acted unofficially, as far as the French were concerned. He built his own network of intelligencers and reported to his uncle, Sir Francis Walsingham, and a few others. But his position was irregular, one might say."

"One might!" Ridley loomed up behind them. His tone was challenging, thick with scorn. Tom smelled trouble.

"Irregular position." Ridley turned his smirk toward Lawson. "Is that what you're calling it now?"

"Mind your own business, Ridley," Lawson said. "No one wants your lies here."

"Tush, tush! Such rudeness! Who can resist the attraction of *la belle* Moreau?" He bowed from the waist, then spouted off a stream of French.

Moreau responded in the same language, her tone crisp. Tom caught the names Rich and Bacon but otherwise understood not a syllable. But something Ridley said widened Phelippes's eyes and narrowed Lawson's.

Lawson snapped something that sounded insulting. Moreau held up her fair hands and said, "This is all in the past, Messieurs. Let us make peace and be friends again. And we are being very rude to Monsieur Clarady. When in England, we must speak the English."

Lawson and Ridley glared at one another long enough to show they weren't letting a woman tell them what to do, then curled their lips and let it go, whatever it was.

"Raffe Ridley." The emissary extended a hand to Tom, which he shook, half rising from his stool. "Another one of Bacon's *mignons*, I presume."

"Bah!" Lawson spat.

Tom sat down and crossed his arms. "I'm a member of Gray's Inn, if you must know. I clerk for Mr. Francis Bacon, but I'm nobody's servant."

"Go find another place to drink, Ridley," Lawson said. "I can show you the door, if you need help." He shifted on his stool as if about to get up.

Ridley shot him a sneer before answering Tom. "Francis, eh? Never met him. He's the one hawking Anthony's overrated services, isn't he? Let the haggling begin! Who will win? More importantly, who will lose once they find out what it costs to tangle with Anthony Bacon."

"You're drunk," Moreau said. "You're talking nonsense."

"Am I?" Ridley drew himself up and puffed out his chest, causing him to stagger back a step. Lion drunk, Tom judged, and ripe for a brawl.

Ridley raised his voice to address his next remarks to the room at large. "You English don't know Anthony Bacon anymore, if you ever did. Don't you wonder what drove him out of his sunny manor in the south of France?"

Lawson shot off another French insult, by his tone. Ridley bent forward to laugh in his face.

Moreau leaned across Phelippes to hiss at Tom. "You must stop them. Trust me; I know these men. They despise each other, and not without reason. This contestation, this is no good for your friends the Bacons."

Ridley raised his voice again. "Anthony's not the only one with secrets. How much could I get for mine, I wonder? I'd settle for a fraction of what he's received. He must be flush after dipping into that bishop's purse."

Lawson jumped to his feet, fists clenched. "You shut your fat mouth before I shut it for you."

"Gentlemen, please." Tom rose as well, holding up both hands, palms out. "Let's all calm down and have a drink. My treat. If there's one thing we English know how to do better than the French, it's brew a jolly good barrel of beer."

They ignored him, squaring off. Ridley said something in French that darkened Lawson's handsome face. Then he pushed Lawson on the shoulder, and that was that.

Lawson swung his arm and landed his fist squarely on Ridley's nose, knocking him backward. Two helpful bystanders righted him and turned him to face his opponent. Lawson raised a fist, and Ridley punched him in the gut. In a trice, they were clenched together, pounding on each other for all they were worth.

"Fight! Fight!" shouted someone with a taste for the obvious.

Tom tried to grab Lawson's shoulder to pull him away, but Ridley's fists kept blocking him. Then Moreau thrust herself between the battling men, scolding them in rapid French, pressing at their chests with her flat hands until they separated. They stood a few feet apart, panting.

Tom whistled under his breath. There was a woman of no mean courage!

"Go home, Lawly," she said to Lawson, using Anthony's nickname for him. It sounded oddly intimate. "Let me speak with Raffe somewhere more quiet. It is time to settle the past. We start fresh in England, yes?"

She held Lawson's gaze until he relented with a grunt. He picked up his hat from where it had fallen and dusted it before setting it back on his head. He took his time about it, letting his anger cool.

"We'll walk with you." Tom wanted to make sure Lawson went straight home. He'd never seen any sign of temper in the man, but then he hadn't spent much time with him yet. He'd joined the newcomers for supper a few times in Anthony's chambers. Afterward, they'd entertained each other with music and stories. It was all very congenial. No one had ever broken down and confessed his innermost secrets, or even an outermost one.

Tom had learned two new things about Lawson tonight. He liked women as well as men, and he hated Raffe Ridley.

The three Toms slung on their cloaks and touched their hats to Elsa Moreau, who stood with her arm laced through Ridley's, clasping his hand as if to prevent it from curling back into a fist. She crooned something at him in French and tugged him toward the barman's counter.

Tom and Phelippes herded Lawson toward the front door. Before they could reach it, he stopped and turned to stab a finger at Ridley. "One word, you traitorous son of a lying whore. One word about that thing and I'll stop your mouth for good."

Ridley answered with a derisive bark. "Try it, you squawking jailbird!"

Lawson lunged at him, but Tom and Phelippes each grabbed an arm and dragged him bodily outside.

"Let it go, Lawson," Tom said. "You're done for tonight."

They walked up Holborn Road toward the path to Gray's Inn, turning their faces into the brisk March wind. That would cool Lawson's temper fast enough. What a night this had turned out to be! Tom cocked his head at Phelippes. "Tomorrow evening, how about we try the Bear Garden for something a little less exciting?"

THREE

Francis Bacon stood in his favorite spot in the Presence Chamber at Whitehall, under a gilded plaque commemorating the Battle of Verneuil set into the ceiling high over his head. That event had been almost as important to the English as the Battle of Agincourt, whose plaque held pride of place in the center of the room. But the history meant less to him than the location, which enjoyed just the right admixture of fresh air from the guard chamber, drawn in by the constant traffic through the door. Newcomers carried the briskness of the fine morning all the way up the stairs with them, while those leaving bore out a measure of staleness.

The Presence Chamber was always crowded at this hour, and not every courtier wore the cleanest linens or took adequate care of his teeth. Today was especially busy because tomorrow was Good Friday. Her Majesty would be too busy with Easter celebrations for several days to meet her subjects here.

This spot also had the advantage of being a judicious distance from the throne: far enough to be politely unable to overhear Her Majesty's conversations, but near enough to be summoned to supply a quote from Roman literature or answer a question about the law. She enjoyed displaying the erudition of her courtiers to foreign visitors.

Standing and waiting, the duty of a courtier. Francis had performed that duty for years. Soon it would be

Anthony's turn, toward which end he must watch for every opportunity to promote his brother's cause.

He watched with little interest as Her Majesty received a cup of intricate design from a master in the pewterers guild. Then she spent many minutes speaking with two gentlemen dressed in the French fashion, their *culottes* fitted to the thigh and extending almost to the knee. The queen spoke right over their sputtering responses. Francis couldn't hear the words, but she seemed to be delivering a rebuke.

Recognizing the gentlemen as King Henry's emissaries, he could guess the content of the rebuke. Her Majesty had sent Lord Essex with a troop of English soldiers to help recapture Rouen from the Catholic League. Instead, King Henry had gone galloping about after lesser targets, leaving the English milling uselessly around the port where they'd landed, doing little more than consuming their victuals and growing discontented.

The scolding ended with a flap of the royal hand. The emissaries made an awkward exit, walking backward while repeatedly bowing forehead-to-knee. The queen ignored them, turning her head to chat with Sir Walter Ralegh, who stood, as always, just behind her left elbow. Something he said made her laugh. Then she returned her gaze toward the supplicants awaiting an audience or enjoying the luster of her presence while exhibiting their finery.

Her eyes lit on Francis, and she crooked a finger at him. He took a few steps and lowered himself to his knees with his head bent low enough to show humility while allowing him to see the open palm inviting him to stand. He took another step closer to the beating heart of England.

"How may I serve you, Madam?"

"How fares your brother Anthony? I hear he has improved enough to leave his mother's house and join you at Gray's, but he has not yet come to visit me. Doesn't he love his queen?" She smiled coyly, but Francis heard the barb within the jest.

"He loves you more than life itself, Madam. Alas, even after six weeks in my lady mother's care, his legs are not as strong as his devotion. He can walk about his chamber and has twice crossed the corner of the yard to the hall, but he must be carried upstairs. He's ashamed to present so weak a spectacle in your august presence. He is also unable to remain standing for more than a minute or two. But he longs to see you, Madame. He's determined to make the attempt within the month."

"I must have my counselors about me in these troublous times. Your brother has a better measure of Henry's character than those blustering ninnies who just left. I want to know what that man can be thinking, squandering my scanty resources in so careless a fashion. Is your brother able to continue his correspondences at all?"

"Oh yes, Madame. He is well accustomed to working from his bed."

"I'm glad to hear it. Let him moderate his diet and have his doctor apply a plaster of horseradish to his knees."

"He is abstinence itself, Madame. In fact, tempting him to eat is one of my challenges. And he is bled weekly by my own physician."

The queen cocked her head as if a novel idea had occurred to her. "You know, my lord Burghley suffers from the gout and has been similarly bedridden in recent years. Perhaps Anthony would be better cared for under his uncle's roof."

Francis blinked at her, at a loss, which he struggled not to show. Her Majesty was possessed of preternaturally acute perceptions. He caught a flicker of amusement cross Sir Walter's face and understood they had passed from concern for Anthony's health to the disposition of Anthony's intelligencing services.

40

The queen would know of their frustrations with their lord uncle. She knew everything — except the things she chose not to hear. She could guess how little the Bacons would like being placed under the supervision of their younger cousin, Sir Robert Cecil, who did most of the work at Burghley House nowadays. Was this a warning that she expected them to cleave to family and not seek other patrons?

Before he could frame a noncommittal response, she raised a finger toward Sir Walter, as if to consult him on a fresh thought. "Then again, that might create an overconcentration of valuable knowledge in one house. What if there were a fire? Perhaps Anthony is better at Gray's for the time being, where other worthies might contribute to his care."

"That does seem best to us at this time, Madame." Francis repressed a sigh of relief.

She nodded. "My lord of Essex sends me letters from France every day. He's of a martial cast of mind, however, and his reports are drearily preoccupied with supplies and the condition of his men. I could wish for your brother's insights, telling me what is *not* being said."

Francis could wish for those insights as well. Anthony was so much better at this verbal jousting. Did Her Majesty mean to suggest that the Bacon brothers cast in their lot with Essex, adding Anthony's considered interpretations to his factual reports?

"His lordship is wise for one so young," Francis ventured.

Queen Elizabeth's brown eyes twinkled. "Old enough to recognize his own lacks. He needs a wise head to guide him."

Did she mean him? She must know he'd been writing advice letters for the earl for the past year. "As do we all, Madame."

"Give my best love to your brother. Tell him not to delay in presenting himself. I long to speak with him after all these years." She smiled with the slow blink that told Francis he was dismissed.

"We work daily toward that much-desired event, Madame." Francis took off his hat, extended a leg, and bowed nose-to-knee. Then he took a few backward steps and returned to his spot under the Battle of Verneuil. He stared at the dusty floor until his heart stopped racing.

He and Anthony would discuss this conversation at length tonight. Had Her Majesty expressed a preference for the disposition of their services or not? If so, which had she indicated: The Cecils or the Earl of Essex?

He usually remained in the Presence Chamber for an hour or two. He couldn't scurry out and run straight home. He'd have to stand here until the clock chimed the next quarter hour at least. He gave one more moment to divining the queen's wishes, then dismissed it with a private smile. He no longer had to solve such problems on his own. He turned his mind instead to the more interesting question of how fresh air mingled with stale to create a balanced atmosphere. Was the air composed of tiny particles that pushed one another about? Or was it like a fluid, mixing fresh and stale together seamlessly, like water and wine?

"Mr. Bacon?"

Francis startled, looking up to meet the black eyes of Lord Admiral Howard. Tall and slender, His Lordship carried himself with an air of command. All England owed him a debt of gratitude, along with Drake and Ralegh, for unwavering valor during that terrible summer of 1588. As much as anything, Lord Howard's implacable will had held their motley navy together to fend off the vast Spanish armada.

"My lord." Francis bobbed a short bow. "How may I serve you?"

"I understand your brother Anthony is back in London. Not yet well enough to come to court?"

"Not yet, my lord, though he is much improved."

"Is he well enough to work?" The Lord Admiral wasn't one to beat about the bush.

"Yes, my lord. We have two secretaries with two copyists in the house, working apace. And of course his intelligencers are still abroad, still observing and reporting what they learn. The flow of information never ceases."

"Good. Good. If he should learn anything of particular interest to me — unusual traffic in the Bay of Biscay, that sort of thing — I would be grateful if you would pass it along."

"I'll see to it personally."

Anthony would insist on holding out for some sort of payment in advance. Typically, no compensation had even been implied. Lord Admiral Howard, as a member of the Privy Council, might believe he had a right to Anthony's intelligences. But his opinion would carry weight in choosing a new Secretary of State. He might even be persuaded to suggest Anthony's name. That would be worth a few free samples, so to speak.

"Have him visit me when he's up to it. I'd like to hear his views on the French situation. Things you don't put in letters." The Lord Admiral's dark eyes glittered as he looked down his long nose. He was too old a hand not to know the calculations being made at Bacon House. "It might be worth his while."

"Yes, my lord." Francis bowed for the third time as His Lordship walked away.

The six bells at Westminster Abbey tolled the three-quarter hour. If Francis could hold out for fifteen more minutes, he could make a respectable departure at eleven o'clock. He should get home in time to supervise Anthony's dinner anyway, to countermand the rich cream sauces that had no doubt been requested. A simple beef gravy would have to suffice.

His mind presented him with an assortment of sauces, sorting them into classes — cream, clear, vegetable, sweet — while he kept his eyes on the beautifully garbed persons moving around him to avoid another surprise. So he noticed when Sir Walter Ralegh made his obeisance to the queen and stepped down from the dais to circulate among the visitors.

Francis braced himself. He found conversations with Sir Walter a trifle exhausting; the man had too much vigor for an ordinary mortal.

"Ah, Mr. Bacon," Sir Walter said, strolling toward him and coming to a stop about three inches closer than Francis liked. The short distance forced him to tilt his head back, which was wearisome for the neck. "Great things are brewing. A much hoped-for event will soon transpire."

Francis blinked at him, entirely at a loss. "Which event is this?"

Sir Walter dropped a mystifying wink. "I'm reminded to send a gift to Lady Dorchester. And why don't you have that clever clerk of yours — Valentine Clarady's son — come visit me? Toward the end of the month would be suitable."

"Oh. Ah. Of course." Now Francis understood. He was referring to Bess Throckmorton and her soon-to-be-delivered child. Formerly Throckmorton — she was Lady Ralegh now, though few knew it. Tom had told him about the Raleghs' secret marriage, passing along gossip Trumpet had from Lady Rich. He'd shared the news about the secret pregnancy several months ago.

Two secrets concerning the queen's favorite, each capable of destroying the man on its own.

Francis appreciated the informal channel for exchanging news with Lord Essex's sister, but he had no desire to hear about Ralegh's clandestine relationship. This sort of secret was as explosive as a powder keg. "I pray all goes well for you, Sir Walter, and for —" He coughed into his hand to avoid naming the name.

Sir Walter grinned, happy in spite of the danger in which he stood. What if the queen were to probe the reason for his buoyant humor? Then again, the risk would only add to the pleasure for this adventurous gallant.

"I owe you a favor, Mr. Bacon," Sir Walter said.

"Do you?" Francis answered. Then he chided himself. Anthony would've agreed with a smile and prepared himself to negotiate.

Sir Walter chuckled at his ineptitude. "You've favored me with your discretion these many months. I'd like to repay you in similar coin, with a discreet word."

"You have me at a loss, Sir Walter."

"I've caught wind of an ugly rumor going around about your brother. My source is Sir Horatio Palavicino, who came to see me yesterday about a ship of his being held up in Plymouth. A simple matter; but while we were waiting for my secretary to draw up a document, Sir Horatio confided that he had heard from his lawyer that Anthony left France under a cloud. They're saying he was obliged to leave in order to evade official censure. Perhaps even criminal charges."

Criminal charges? Francis tucked his chin in dismay. "Who is this lawyer?"

"A member of Lincoln's, I believe."

"It's nonsense. I would know of any such thing." But would he? Anthony had sent him a letter at least once a week for the past thirteen years, but letters could be opened and read. They never wrote anything they wouldn't want someone else to read. They hadn't time to work through all those years, catching each other up on the details. And Anthony was so skilled at keeping secrets.

Sir Walter lowered his voice. "The rumor concerns unsavory practices involving the young pages in his employ. You know what I mean." Disgust twisted his handsome features. Ralegh's disdain for affairs between men was well-known. Francis suspected the queen didn't care — or care to know — as long as it didn't create factions. Men couldn't marry men, after all, so such relationships could not bear fruit that might one day claim the throne.

There had been one episode back in 1586, shortly after Anthony had moved to Montaubon. He'd written a panicked letter, hand-delivered by Thomas Lawson, warning Francis that he might need a large infusion of funds on short notice. Then another letter had come a few weeks later blithely informing him that the difficulty had been resolved.

Some short-lived local scandal, Francis had assumed. A great ado about nothing. He'd forgotten about it.

"Ugly rumors do rise up now and then," Sir Walter said. "Remember the foul things that were written about Leicester over the years? Your brother's success as a spymaster is not unknown. Some persons must fear his return to England with his fabled chestful of secrets. But if the rumor spreads and someone credible emerges to lend it their support . . ."

"Impossible," Francis said. "There can't be any such person because no such events took place."

Sir Walter gave him a studied look. "It's troublesome, nevertheless. Rumors can take on a life of their own. They could impair your brother's ability to continue his work. His intelligencers might be constrained or expelled from wherever they are. A dark enough stain on Anthony Bacon's reputation could endanger our whole campaign in France. I strongly suggest you identify that blabber and shut his mouth."

FOUR

lack-clack! Clack-clack!

That crisp rapping pulled Tom out of a lush dream. He'd been swimming in the Gulf of Mexico with Trumpet, whose naked breasts and belly shone as white and round as pufferfish. He'd bounced her up and down in the warm surf as she giggled.

He tried to go back to it, but the rapping sounded again. *Clack-clack! Clack-clack!*

Tom's eyes opened into his moonlit room at Gray's. A dark figure stood outside his window with its fist raised, rapping on the glass.

"Clarady, wake up!"

Francis Bacon, backlit by the bright half-moon. Tom sat up, the chill of an English spring replacing the sun-warmed seas of Florida. "What do you want?" It came out in a yawning roar.

"I need your help. You must come with me."

"God's bollocks." Tom collapsed back onto his pillows and groaned at the dark ceiling. It could only be one thing at this hour. Bacon had found a corpse out there somewhere and for some reason had decided it was his business. Or someone else at Gray's had found one and come to Bacon for help, who would naturally hand the going-and-looking off to Tom. They'd become the unofficial coroners of Gray's Inn.

Tom got all the way up this time and stuffed his feet into a pair of worn leather slippers. Rising, he grabbed his cloak from its peg. His room was almost small enough to span with both arms outspread. He wrapped the wool around his naked body, then flipped the latch and pulled open the window, turning back to dress without bothering to help his master clamber over the sill.

He found the puffs and grunts behind his back gratifying.

He fished up the shirt he'd worn yesterday and gave the underarm a sniff. Good enough for present purposes. "It's a body, isn't it? Male or female?"

"A man. I didn't recognize him, but I didn't look too closely."

"Where?" Tom pulled the shirt over his head and sat on the bed to roll his stockings up his legs.

"On Gray's Inn Road, just below the juncture with Theobalds."

"What possessed you go foraging for corpses at this ungodly hour?"

Bacon clucked his tongue. "I went out to freshen my wits. Something Anthony said got me thinking about pond scum again."

Tom bit back a laugh. Only Francis Bacon could utter that sentence without humorous intent.

"I used to think it must be some sort of substance," Bacon continued, "oozing into the pond like the springs of black oil described by Herodotus. Of course, that's boyish nonsense, but the constitution of the mass, which grows larger in summer and . . ."

Tom stopped listening. He respected Bacon's brain beyond that of any other man — or woman — but philosophy could lead him down some very odd paths. Tom stepped into his galligaskins, stuffed his arms into his doublet, and stared out at the moonlit field west of Gray's while he laced himself up. By the height of the moon, it couldn't be much past midnight. He'd only been asleep for a couple of hours.

Maybe this would turn out to be some poor carter, dead drunk instead of actually dead. They could send a stableman out to take the man home. Tom could be snug in his bed again in a matter of minutes, diving back into that tropical sea with his bouncy Trumpet.

"Ready." He waited while Bacon struggled back out the window, then stepped out himself, swinging it shut behind him. They angled southwest across the field, then curved north to Theobald's. Tom's shoes were soaked with dew by the time they reached the hard-packed earth of the King's Way. It ran all the way north to Theobalds House, one of the palaces built by the Lord Treasurer, Bacon's uncle. The man was so rich he even had his own roads.

"What did you decide about the scum?" Tom asked. Worry wafted from his master like an odor; some distraction might help as they approached the body. "Is it animal, vegetable, or — Hoi! Isn't that Anthony's coach?"

A richly ornamented box suspended between four large wheels stood at the edge of Gray's Inn Road. Its gilt paint shone pale in the moonlight. The dark curtains were drawn. The two black horses, still in harness, stood on the verge, heads down, cropping at the new spring grass.

"Yes, it's Anthony's." Bacon's tone was crisp. "I said that already. Didn't I?"

"You did not." Tom hastened toward it, clucking at the horses as they lifted their heads. They knew him and gave a soft whicker of recognition before going back to their browsing. He gripped the handle of the door and found it unlatched. The coach's angled position held it closed. "Did you open this?"

"He — it — isn't there."

Tom looked anyway, straining to see into the dark interior. He'd get the lantern from the coachman's seat to have a better look in a minute. He closed the latch firmly this time. "Where is it?"

"Over there." Bacon gestured at a dark form lying a few yards back. A figure in men's garb lay sprawled in the weeds, his arm over his head. The legs lay at odd angles. Tom studied the situation with his hands on his hips, gathering his courage to move forward to look at the face. "It looks like he was dragged into these weeds here."

He walked back to peer at the dirt of the road. The moon shone brightly enough to reveal dents and tracks. "There could've been a scuffle here. Maybe he was pushed out and then dragged. Whoever did it seems to be long gone."

"I suppose he expected the horses to go straight home."

"He doesn't know much about horses, then. Greedy beasts. They won't leave this nice, fresh grass without prodding." Tom drew in a breath and let it out in a big puff. "All right. Let's find out who it is."

He had an inkling already, one he didn't like. He'd seen that doublet before, and recently. Everything looked gray in the moonlight, but he would bet it was gray in truth. There'd be a tall gray hat with a black silk bow in the grass hereabouts or in the coach.

The face was distorted, the mouth twisted and half-open, but he recognized the man: Raffe Ridley, the lout who'd started a fight with Lawson at the Antelope. The costume was identical, apart from the strap tied around his neck. He must've offended someone else last night and gotten himself strangled for it.

"It's Raffe Ridley," Tom said.

"The Bordeaux emissary? What on earth is he doing here?"

"How would I know?"

"But what happened to him?"

"He's been strangled." Tom looked from the body to the coach and back again. "It must've been someone in the coach. They strangled him, dragged him into the weeds, and ran off."

"Anthony could never do this. He isn't strong enough."

"Unlikely to have been Anthony, I agree. It is his coach though."

"He couldn't even walk all the way home," Bacon said, arguing a point that had already been conceded. He frowned at the horses. "Where's the coachman? Are we imagining he did this?"

"I'm not imagining anything," Tom said. "I'm making observations and noting the facts as they stand." How often had he heard that lecture from this very man?

A short silence followed that rejoinder. Then Bacon said softly, "It's different when it's your brother."

"I know. What should we do?"

Bacon rubbed his mouth with the palm of his hand. "I don't know. I don't know."

"There's something in his mouth." Tom gritted his teeth and reached for it, pulling out a wadded handkerchief. He flapped the foul thing open. "It's fine cambric. Not cheap. And it's got initials on it."

"Whose?"

"Can't read them in this light." Tom stuffed it into his pocket to look at later, hating the dampness of the thing but not knowing what else to do. He knelt in the grass to touch the strap around the man's neck. "This is a belt, figured leather. Supple. Good quality." Standing up again, he added, "The design might give us a clue about its owner. More initials, maybe."

"What can Raffe Ridley be doing here, almost at our doorstep? I thought he was in France."

Tom could answer some of that. "He's been here at least a week. He got into a squabble with Thomas Lawson at the Antelope on Monday."

"What sort of squabble?"

"Ridley was insinuating something about Anthony, something that happened in France. Lawson took offense. They mostly spoke in French, so I didn't get much of it. Phelippes was there. You could ask him. Also, a woman from Bordeaux named Elsa Moreau. She's Lady Rich's maidservant."

"What was she doing there?" Bacon took a step back as if distancing himself from any hint of conflict that might involve a person of rank.

"Having a drink, enjoying an evening out. Like me. Lawson had been drinking a fair bit, and Ridley was drunk, at the argumentative stage."

"This past Monday? Then why is he here now? Why is he dead?"

"I don't know, Mr. Bacon. We've got another question to answer first. What are we going to do? We can't leave his body lying here, can we? And what about the coach?"

Bacon sighed, shoulders collapsing. He turned his head to take in the coach, the horses, and the looming shape of Gray's gatehouse down the road, rising above the fruit trees in Pannier's Close. "Farmers will be out in a few hours, coming in to the markets. The coach has our coat of arms on the door." He lifted his hat to run his hand over his head. "What are our options?"

"I can think of three." Tom held up his thumb. "One. I run fetch the sheriff while you wait with the coach."

Bacon shook his head. "Impossible. Everyone will assume Anthony did this, however weak he appears to be."

Tom nodded and held up his forefinger. "Two. We leave things as they are and let the first passing farmer alert the stablemen at Gray's that a coach has been abandoned on the road. They'll see the body straight off and fetch a constable."

"Intolerable. It's Anthony's coach, and Ridley is known to many in positions of authority. Once he's identified, they'll link him to Anthony through Bordeaux. If the story about that tavern conflict comes out, he'll appear to have a motive."

"It's out already, I'd wager. Ridley wanted to be heard." Tom extended his middle finger. "Third option. I shove the body in the coach and drive a couple of miles west. I dump it in a field and bring the coach back to Gray's without comment. Then we keep our lips sealed and wait to see what happens."

Tom watched Bacon work it through. He knew his master to be a fundamentally moral man but also a pragmatic one. He would weigh his obligations against the possible outcomes and find the solution that struck the best balance between truth and necessity.

Bacon gazed sadly at the man on the ground. "What would you do if it were Trumpet's coach?"

Tom snorted. "Bury the body deep in the woods, along with anyone who asked too many questions." It would do permanent damage to his opinion of himself as a man, but he would learn to live with it.

"Hmm." Bacon smoothed his moustache with his forefinger. "I propose a fourth alternative. You drive the coach back to Gray's without comment, as you suggested. I'll go home and wake Anthony. We must discuss this with him. We'll leave the body here for now. It's nearly invisible in the grass. We can decide later about the . . . about the woods." He pressed a hand to his chest as if to keep his heart from falling out.

"I understand," Tom said. "He's your family. You do whatever you have to do."

Bacon nodded, not looking at him. "Let's remove that belt first, shall we? Anthony and I both have belts of Spanish leather with the family crest embossed on each end."

"We," of course, meant Tom. The belt had been twisted tightly in back, but not knotted, for a mercy. He substituted his own black wool garter. A plain, utilitarian

53

item — every man in England had one like it. Tying that strip of cloth around Ridley's cold neck was the most sorrowful and disgusting thing he'd ever done. He silently begged forgiveness of God and prayed never to have to do anything like it again.

Bacon had the decency to stand by while Tom performed the grisly deed. He waited with his head bowed, his slender figure a silhouette in the moonlight. Then he walked back across the field without another word, leaving Tom to take care of the coach.

He walked to the front and stood by the lantern to read the initials on the handkerchief. *T.L.* Thomas Lawson. He'd had an inkling about that too. Like Francis, Lawson enjoyed free use of Anthony's coach.

He took the lantern off its hook and shone it into the interior, searching for anything incriminating. He found Ridley's hat on the forward bench. It seemed unharmed. He threw it into the weeds beside the body. Let the coroner make what he would of its condition.

Then he ran both hands over the brocaded seats, probing into the creases, turning over every cushion. No earrings, no brooches. He found a shilling and kept it; scant wages for mean work. Then he smoothed the fabric and restored the pillows. He shook out the curtains as he drew them closed to be sure nothing had snagged on them.

Sour bile rose in his throat. He spat it into the grass. He'd done some questionable things in Bacon's service, though this was by far the worst. But he couldn't refuse; he never even considered it. Bacon had proven himself a true friend over the years, in his peculiar way. A man didn't turn his back on a friend — or a friend's brother.

The friend's brother's quarrelsome former lover was another matter, but he'd keep his doubts about Lawson under his hat for the time being.

Tom hung up the lantern and cajoled the horses back into line with the carriage. He climbed into the driver's seat and clucked them into motion. Reaching the stable, he hallooed the barred oak doors, pulling the hood of his cloak low over his brow as they opened. He grumbled, "Leavin' me out till all hours waitin' for nuffink," as he tossed the reins to the yawning groom. Further conversation was not required.

He crunched across the silent yard and entered the house to find Anthony's door open a crack, a band of candlelight streaming out, along with the inviting aroma of nutmeg and warming ale. But he had one thing to do before joining the brothers.

He ran up the stairs on his toes, silent as a cat. He listened outside the door to Lawson and Phelippes's chamber and heard only snoring, soft and rhythmic, on two different notes. He gently pressed the handle to open the door. It was too dark to distinguish features, but he could make out the shapes of two men under blankets. The odds favored them being the proper occupants of this room. Anything else would require a conspiracy that included the blameless Phelippes and some unknown snorer.

Tom judged the snores to be genuine, though that was easily faked. Would Phelippes notice if his chambermate went out for a while? Tom cast his memory back to his first year at Gray's, when he'd shared a bed with two other men. You got to where you barely felt it when your chum got up to piss out the window. You'd roll over and be dreaming again by the time he climbed back into bed.

A man could doubt the ground under his feet if he let his imagination run wild. Tom closed the door and slipped back down the stairs.

At his knock, Anthony called, *"Intro,"* and he went in. A backed stool had been drawn up for him between the brothers, each of whom was already snuggled into an armchair with a blanket around his knees. Tom shed his cloak and took his seat.

Jacques handed him a wooden cup of spiced ale. The youth wore a dove-blue woolen robe with loose sleeves and a hood draping down the back. Anthony wore a similar garment, but his was black. The robes seemed practical, if a shade monkish, for men who spent most days in their bedchamber.

The scene was cozy enough for Tom to abandon his effort to refer to each brother as "Mr. Bacon." He couldn't keep them straight even in his own mind. It would be Francis and Anthony henceforward, and heaven help him if any of the elder stepbrothers turned up.

"I've described the situation as we found it," Francis told him. "More or less."

"I can scarce believe it," Anthony said, shaking his head. "Raffe Ridley, of all people!"

Tom asked, "Did you know him well?"

"We were friends once, or so I thought." Anthony shrugged. "He arrived in Bordeaux around the time I moved to Montaubon. That would have been in 1585." He glanced at Francis, who kept his eyes on the fire. Anthony turned toward Tom. "They're a hundred miles apart, but I was still able to ride a horse in those days. We met in Bordeaux, at the house of the mayor, Monsignor Michel de Montaigne."

"The man who wrote those little prose pieces Mr. Bacon likes so much?" Tom asked.

"The very same." Anthony smiled at the memory. "We were all friends then. I even took Raffe into my home when he was sick."

"When was this?" Francis sounded aggrieved, as if it were an important fact of which he had not been informed. But there must many such gaps in their decade-long correspondence.

"Eighty-eight," Anthony said. "That endless, terrible summer. Everyone was desperate for reliable information about the Spanish fleet while we were scrambling to find secure means of sending what little we knew. Monsieur du Plessis, our governor at the time, sent Raffe to the coast to talk to merchants. He picked up a nasty case of quartan fever. He had no one to care for him, so I had him brought to me in Montaubon. He stayed with us for three months. We all got along beautifully, apart from a bit of rivalry between Lawly and Ridley over Elsa Moreau. She's quite a beautiful woman. She was employed in du Plessis's house back then."

"I've met her," Tom said. "She was at the Antelope when Ridley turned up."

"Was she?" Anthony asked. "But of course. She'll be living at Essex House, I suppose, if Lady Rich is there."

"What changed him?" Tom asked. "Ridley, I mean. Friends don't spread vile rumors about friends."

Anthony blinked at him, eyes wide. "I have no idea."

Tom doubted that. Whatever happened must have happened in France — an argument, a debt. It might have been one of those minor slights that only starts to rankle after one's fortunes change. You look back for someone to blame and remember that old offense.

Anthony added, "I did know Ridley was back in England, however. Lawly told me about the *contretemps* in the tavern. Quite unpleasant, he said."

"Ridley came in looking for trouble. But speaking of Lawson . . ." Tom drew the handkerchief from his pocket. He offered it to Francis, who shrank away from it. So he shook it out and held it up where both men could see. "This was stuffed into the victim's mouth. It must be Lawson's. Those initials read *T.L.* Occam's Razor prevents us from postulating another man with those initials popping up in our midst."

Francis rolled his eyes but said nothing.

Anthony raised his cup to Tom. "Well reasoned, Mr. Clarady. You've acquired a good grounding in logic, I see. But the handkerchief signifies nothing. Lawly has a dozen of them, and he leaves them everywhere. I've scolded him about it. That could've been in the coach for days."

"I haven't looked at the belt yet." Tom drew it from his other pocket and held it toward the fire to examine the engravings. He found a tiny boar — an element of the Bacon coat of arms — on each end with the initials *F.B.* "Ah."

He grasped it in both hands to display the initials to each brother in turn. Pink spots bloomed on Francis's cheeks. "That's mine. I must have left it last week when I went for a drive with Henry."

Henry Percy was Francis's current *amour*. They were usually discreet, and it was unlikely that Percy, who had been in the north until recently, had anything to do with Ridley.

"Careless of you," Anthony said, smiling. "Then the killer didn't bring his weapon with him. That suggests he didn't plan to murder Ridley when they met."

"Or that he found this belt under a cushion and decided to use it instead of whatever he brought. He'd have his own knife, of course. Though strangling's neater." Tom coiled the belt up and handed it to Jacques, who took it gingerly between thumb and forefinger and carried it into the bedchamber. Tom hoped he would clean it before returning it to Francis.

Anthony's eyes widened. "*Bon Dieu!* You are quite good at this game!" He shot an impressed frown at his brother.

"It isn't a game," Francis snapped.

He seemed determined to suppress further discussion. He'd barely blinked at the mention of Occam's Razor, a lesson he'd drilled into his students' heads. *Simpler solutions are more likely to be correct than complex ones.* And he usually took the lead in walking through the evidence after they discovered a body.

He'd also taught Tom not to draw conclusions before all the facts had been considered. No matter. Tom could do it himself this time. He'd had plenty of lessons over the years.

Ignoring his obstinate master, he spoke to Anthony. "Did you order your coach tonight or send it out for anyone?"

"No, but I don't keep close track of it. Lawly and Frank use it whenever they like."

"Do you lend the coach to friends? Members of Gray's?"

"Sometimes," Anthony said. "Why leave it idle? But they would ask first, as a matter of courtesy."

"Not if they were planning to murder someone in it." Now Tom had to consider the possibility that anyone at Gray's, or any friend of the Bacons — or anyone who could convince the coachman of that status — could take the coach out at any time. "Who drives it besides Peter Widhope?"

"No one," Anthony said, "and he's completely reliable. He's worked for my mother most of his life. Frank tells me the coach was abandoned with the horses straying into the grass. Widhope would never do such a thing. He cares for those Friesians too much to place them at risk. They might have been stolen out there in the dark."

"Either he left them alone," Tom said, "or someone else drove the coach out last night. Or he let someone take his place along the way. He must know something. I'll question him and the stablemen first thing in the morning."

"Toward what end?" Francis asked, his tone sharp. "We've gone to great pains to remove anything that might implicate us. Why stir things up by asking questions?"

Tom gaped at him. "We have to find out what happened. Don't we? I want to know for my own peace of mind." He had no desire to share a house with a man who could perform this cold-blooded deed — or one who could order it done for him.

"I agree," Anthony said. "Ridley served as an emissary of Her Majesty's Privy Council for many years. Whatever afflicted him last week, we can't let his murder go unsolved, especially not when my coach was evidently used to entrap him."

Tom gave him a short nod of acknowledgment. Either Anthony was innocent or he was a superlative dissembler. Which he probably was, being such a famous spymaster, which brought Tom back around to his original doubts. On the other hand, Lawson could have acted on his master's behalf without telling him about it. He seemed like a loose cannon, capable of starting something without a clear notion of how it would end and then scrambling to cover up the damage.

And yet those snores had sounded so real.

Francis crossed his arms and glared at the space between the other two men. "We can't investigate without provoking curiosity about our interest. Contrary to popular opinion at Gray's, I do *not* poke my nose into every death that occurs in this vicinity. We must have a reason to act, and it can't involve Anthony."

The way he avoided his brother's eyes told Tom he harbored the same unhappy doubts. The coach, the handkerchief, and the rumors that could block Anthony's rise to power, even if he escaped formal prosecution.

They sat in silence for a few moments. Tom drank some of his lukewarm ale. What reason could they dream up to poke their noses into this death, to use Francis's unsavory phrase?

Anthony broke the silence. "We can't leave that poor man lying out there, soaking in the dew. He's been in France for so many years. How will they identify him?"

Tom snapped his fingers. "That's it! That's how we do it."

"Do what?" Francis asked irritably.

"How we get involved." He met Anthony's inquiring look. "We have to discover the body again. I'll do it. I can say the moon woke me up and I couldn't get back to sleep."

"It is very bright," Anthony said, going along with the tale.

"I find the body and run back to raise the hue. The gatekeeper wakes the benchers, who send for the sheriff or the coroner, or both. They'll say, 'Who is it?' And I'll say, 'Some knave by the name of Raffe Ridley. I met him at the Antelope the other night.'"

Anthony raised a doubtful finger. "It might be best not to bring that evening into focus, at least not so early on. It leads directly to the rumors that give me a motive."

"Good point," Tom said, glad for the help. "Well, we can do it this way. I don't recognize him. Now everyone's milling around saying, 'Who is it? Who is it?' Everyone's awake by this time, thanks to all the hubbub. And trust me, half the inn will want to go out and have a look for themselves. Lawson could go out with them. Why wouldn't he? He's wide awake and as curious as the next man. He could cry, 'God's mercy! That's Raffe Ridley, the Privy Council's emissary from Bordeaux!' That'll worry the benchers, never fear. They'll come knocking on Mr. Bacon's door, begging him to take charge."

Anthony chuckled, a rich sound. "Well crafted, Mr. Clarady, and very well told. Thank you. I have no doubt your prediction is correct. Don't you agree, Frank?"

Francis grumbled under his breath. "That's exactly what will happen." He gave an exaggerated sigh, raising his eyes to heaven. "But we must make sure Lawson knows not to mention that business at the tavern."

"I'll tell him. Jacques can wake him and bring him down. Then I suppose everyone but Mr. Clarady should hop back into bed. We'll await the tumult in the yard huddled into our pillows."

Francis frowned. "There's no reason two brothers shouldn't stay up late, talking by the fire. I doubt it will take long to get into our nightgowns. You should go right away, Tom. We don't want anyone else to stumble over the body."

"I'm on my way." Tom swilled the last of his ale and set the cup on the table at Anthony's elbow. He nodded at the brothers and left, crossing the entry passage to go through his own room and out the back window to avoid being seen by the gatekeeper. He strolled at the pace of a sleepless man, in case any other sleepless men should happen to look out their windows, back up to Theobalds Road. He walked the few yards to Ridley's corpse, which remained undisturbed. Then he performed a dumb show of discovery, throwing up his hands, turning in a wide circle, shouting, "Oh, lackaday! Oh, woe is me!" at the top of his lungs.

He saw candlelight bloom in an upper window at Gray's and jogged toward the gatehouse, thinking, *You do whatever you have to do.*

FIVE

Trumpet awoke with a start, her eyes popping open. She blinked at the brightness of the moon and closed them tight. Where were the kindly clouds that usually covered the sky in this season? In fairness, it wasn't the moon that had woken her. She needed to piss for the third time that night, and the blessed baby had just kicked her again.

She threw back the covers and grunted as she struggled sideways. Catalina was at her side before her feet found the floor, helping her to and from the close stool. As Trumpet snuggled into her featherbed, she remembered that the same westering moon shone into Tom's window at this very moment. She fell back into sleep with a smile on her lips.

The next time she woke, sunshine lit the whole room. "Is it late?"

"Not too late, my lady."

"But we have a visitor this morning. We'll need more time to get me dressed."

"We have time."

Trumpet was more excited about this change of pace than the visitor deserved. She was some French Protestant lady who wanted to curry favor with prominent Englishwomen. They would mouth platitudes at one another for half an hour. Perhaps she'd ask some favor, which Penelope would gracefully refuse.

Trumpet would've scorned such a dull chore in the past, but after three weeks in confinement, the mere novelty of a new face was something to look forward to. And it gave her a chance to watch a skilled courtier in action. Though only twenty-nine, Penelope had already become a person of influence, through diligent service to her brother. As the earl's star rose, so did her own. Essex had married a mousy woman, so he was happy to let his sister act as one of his gatekeepers. If you wanted to communicate anything of a delicate nature to the queen's favorite, you'd do well to confide in Penelope first.

Trumpet intended to achieve that status herself. Stephen would never be the queen's favorite himself, but he was swiftly becoming one of Essex's dearest friends. And he had power in his own right, or would, once she figured out how best to exploit his talents. Then she would be the gatekeeper to his favor and a woman of influence in her own right.

It wouldn't happen in a day, but she'd get there. This stay in Essex House was a worthy part of her apprenticeship.

Catalina helped her mistress to the stool again. Then Trumpet washed her face and hands and rubbed the fuzz from her teeth with a finger cloth dipped in sage and salt. Her nightdress was replaced by a clean chemise. Catalina pulled a loose gown over her head, shaking its folds over her pregnant belly. No farthingale, no bumroll. It almost felt like a nightdress, but it was made of a rich brocade lined in heavy linen for warmth. This gown abandoned the whole idea of a waist, falling straight from the small bodice to the floor. The wide, puffed sleeves laced into the short bodice in the usual fashion.

Trumpet held her arms out while Catalina finished tying on the embroidered shoulder rolls. She tucked the last strings out of sight and stood back. Trumpet revolved slowly in front of the mirror, studying her bloated image. "These huge sleeves help balance the enormity of my belly, don't you think?"

Catalina nodded. "You look very elegant, my lady."

A rap sounded on the door, followed by Penelope's head. "Almost ready?"

"Almost." Trumpet turned a full circle to show off her costume. "What do you think?"

"Very becoming. And comfortable too, isn't it?" She had recommended the style and the tailor who made it. She knew everything about pregnancy, having borne three children herself. The last had been the gift of her lover, Sir Charles Blount, boldly named after his true father. Trumpet didn't know how she managed it, although being the elder sister of the queen's favorite undoubtedly helped.

"Almost as good as my fur-lined robe." Trumpet moved toward a chair and let Catalina help her sink into it.

Penelope perched on the chest at the foot of the bed. "How are you feeling?"

"Fat," Trumpet said. "Tom called me a whale!"

Penelope laughed. "Well, he is extraordinarily handsome. And he comes every day to rub your feet. Charles never did that for me."

Trumpet smiled complacently. She lifted a long strand of pearls from her jewelry box and draped them over her head.

"Oh no, Alice," Penelope said. "They emphasize the roundness of your belly. Simpler is better."

"Ha! I didn't realize Occam's Razor applied to fashion."

"What's that?"

"Oh, nothing," Trumpet said, wishing she could call back the revealing quip. "It's just a silly philosophical principle."

Penelope regarded her with a curious look. "You do know the oddest things. But then you lived with Lady Russell for a whole year. You've probably had a complete humanist education."

"We did spend most evenings reading."

"Apart from the whale-ishness, how are you? Any changes?"

"Nothing. I swear to you, my dear friend, if this infant does not emerge of his own volition soon, I will call for a surgeon to cut the cursed thing out!"

Penelope laughed, a musical trill. "Bess said the same thing, almost word for word, when I saw her yesterday. If it weren't such a secret, I'd be taking bets as to which of you will reach the finish first."

"Who would you bet on?"

"Bess. I can't imagine any child of Sir Walter's consenting to second place."

"Nor can I," Trumpet said. "Besides, they started sooner than Tom and me." She bent her head to allow Catalina to pin her headdress to her hair, a dark red billiment trimmed in gold with a black veil that fell to her shoulders.

"What's more," Penelope said, "her midwife seems to think the birth is imminent. She's moved into the adjoining room and had the birthing chair brought up."

"That's exciting!" Trumpet clapped her hands together. "Perhaps it'll be tomorrow. *He who is born on an Easter morn, shall never know want, or care, or harm.*"

"I hope you're right. They'll need all the luck they can get when the queen finds out about it."

They traded dark looks. "How have they kept it secret for so long?" Trumpet adjusted the drape of her veil.

"Her maidservant's dressmaking talents. Sir Walter's consummate acting. And you know how skilled Her Majesty is at not seeing or hearing things she doesn't want to know."

Penelope scooted sideways so she could view herself in the mirror. She smoothed the fair hair exposed beneath her mannish hat. She'd dressed with care this morning too, in black velvet with white silk linings and pinked sleeves puffed to a full two feet in diameter.

She spoke to her reflection. "Bess says they'll delay the inevitable for as long as possible. Let the babe be born, give herself a little time to recover. But she plans to go back to court within a few weeks."

"Is that possible?"

Penelope lifted one shoulder. "One does what one must. I did it."

"Where will she keep the baby?"

"With a wet nurse. Her sister-in-law recommends one in Enfield." Penelope gave Trumpet an amused smile. "You won't be walking around with a babe in your arms all day either, my dear friend. Your mother-in-law has probably already hired a suitable nurse."

Trumpet nodded. That was an impending tussle she kept pushing to the back of her mind. Everyone at Delabere House was excited about the impending birth of the ninth Earl of Dorchester. Somehow everyone assumed it would be a boy. "Why does Bess want to go back so soon?"

"She left without leave; she must return as soon as she can. You had Her Majesty's blessing after a wedding at court, so you can take your time. But I went back within a month after each of my children. If you want to be a lady of consequence, it's the only place to be. My lord brother loves adventure. That helps build his reputation, but it also takes him abroad for long stretches. It falls on me to keep his image fresh in Her Majesty's mind, sharing bits of news from letters and seeking her advice. You should be doing the same for your husband. You build your influence on his standing at court."

Trumpet nodded. She understood the concept and fully endorsed it, but she and Stephen were young. They had time to explore a variety of paths. And she had Tom to consider. He was vastly less biddable than her husband. "I won't go back to Dorset, whatever the dowager countess wants. When Stephen comes home, we'll take a house on the Strand. Perhaps that nurse in Enfield has a sister."

Penelope nodded. "Since Her Majesty's favorite palaces range along the Thames, serving her gives us a good excuse to stay in London. Otherwise we'd be buried in the country."

"Anything but that." Trumpet shuddered. "I love the city. Tom refuses to budge from Gray's Inn, but there are long vacations when he has nothing to do. He could spend some time at court. Francis Bacon does it."

The two ladies exchanged worldly-wise smiles in the mirror. The foundation of their friendship was the shared determination to deny the limitations of their sex and a mutual willingness to skirt the bounds of propriety to achieve their aims.

The churches on the Strand tolled the hour: ten o'clock. Their guest was due. "Who is this lady?" Trumpet asked. "Madame du Splashy-Plashy, or whatever she's called."

"Don't mock her!" Penelope pretended to be shocked. "She's possessed of a *towering* self-regard. It's du Plessis-Mornay. Du Plessis alone is also acceptable. Her husband is — or was — the governor of Montaubon, which is a Protestant stronghold in the south of France."

"Anthony Bacon lived there."

"That's right. They must have known each other." Penelope's eyes narrowed, taking on the inward gleam that meant she was rearranging pieces on some mental chessboard. Everything she did, apart from her *affaire du coeur* with Sir Charles Blount, served her brother's political aspirations. She knew nothing whatsoever about law, literature, or philosophy, but she had a map of Europe in her mind. "She and her husband both write Calvinist tracts in their spare time, I understand."

"Ugh." Trumpet grimaced. "I had enough of that in Lady Russell's house."

"Even so, Madame considers herself a woman of fashion and her husband has the ear of the king. My brother encouraged me to receive her and take her measure."

"Then measure her we shall." Trumpet was glad to spend an hour doing something other than contemplating her belly.

An usher knocked on the door. "My lady? Madame du Plessis-Mornay is here. I escorted her to the gallery, as you requested."

"Thank you, Mr. Hutley. We're on our way." Penelope rose effortlessly to her feet.

Trumpet could barely remember being able to perform that simple feat. Catalina stood before her, presenting her strong arms to use as supports. Once they got her out of the chair, Trumpet set her palm in the small of her back. "Whoo!" Then she nodded at Penelope, who had waited beside the open door.

"Any day now," the seasoned mother predicted.

They passed through Trumpet's unused reception chamber to the short passage that led to the stairs. Catalina and Mr. Hutley each took an arm to help Trumpet down to the first floor.

The gallery ran across the front of the house overlooking the Strand. A strip of garden along the wall gave a bit of distance, so one didn't peer straight down into the street. The endless procession of carts, carriages, horses, and persons on foot afforded a variable vista. Trumpet strolled to and fro before these windows several times a day. It was her only source of exercise and entertainment now.

The ceiling curved to meet the walls, giving the long, narrow room the feel of a tunnel made of oak and plaster. The span was lined with portraits in gilt frames and dotted with chairs and benches. A bank of windows at the east end flooded the space with morning light and kept it from feeling too enclosed. The windows on the Strand side projected out, so one could lean one's elbows on the polished ledge to contemplate the scene.

A woman dressed in court clothes strolled toward the far end of the gallery, studying each portrait as if seeking a resemblance to her own relations— or acquainting herself with notable Englishmen. She lingered longest in front of a large portrait of Robert Dudley, the late Earl of Leicester. It was a magnificent work, showing the man in his prime. He had once been handsome enough to capture the heart of a queen.

He'd built this house, leaving it to his stepson, the Earl of Essex, in his will. It had a private wharf, making it easy to travel up and down the Thames to wait upon Her Majesty in any of her favorite palaces.

Trumpet's assistants guided her a few steps past the top of the stairs before releasing her arms. She reached out to set one palm on the wall and the other into the small of her back. "Whoo!"

At the sound, the woman turned, dropped a shallow curtsy, and moved toward them. Her shimmering skirts extended a full foot from either side of her torso. She must be wearing one of the new great farthingales, as they were called — a flat oval wheel tied about the waist, supported underneath by a thin bumroll. The fabric hung straight down from the edge of the wheel, creating an oval, like a draped table. The wheel tilted down in front to allow for the pointed hem of the doublet. It gave the effect of a narrow waist and focused the eye upward to the woman's bust and face.

Trumpet liked the traditional bell-shaped farthingale, though this new device did create an impressive silhouette. If it was the coming fashion, she'd have to get used to it. She loved the tall, slanted collar the Frenchwoman wore. It looked like a sheer ruff, tilted steeply up at the back to frame the whole head. The lower band plunged into the bodice, creating a long, dramatic V. Du Plessis had covered her bosom with a modest partlet, though she probably left her chest exposed in France, where standards were looser.

An elaborate coiffure furthered the elongating effect. The woman's light brown hair had been shaped into two high mounds on either side of a central part, which was covered with the point of a lace-trimmed coif. A single pearl dripped from the point, emphasizing the heart shape of the whole structure. Her real hair must be augmented by pads of wool or wire to create such perfect forms.

Trumpet's father had given her a heart-shaped face at birth. She didn't like hairpieces pinned to her scalp, but she liked the detail of the single pearl and admired the V-shaped ruff. The elongation would make a short woman, such as herself, look taller.

The woman stopped a few feet away. "My ladies." She sank into a curtsy of respectable depth for a woman her age. She managed to rise with only a slight wobble.

Penelope said, "Lady Dorchester, allow me to present Madame Charlotte du Plessis-Mornay of Montaubon."

"Madame." Trumpet granted the visitor a nod. Her rank released her from an obligation to return the courtesy, and her condition made her unbendable anyway.

"My lady," du Plessis replied. "I am honored to meet you. I hear your lord husband has joined his support to our cause, for which I am profoundly grateful."

"A Protestant France is England's best defense against the Catholic League," Trumpet uttered the stock phrase with a bland smile.

"Would that your queen shared that view," du Plessis said, clasping her hands to her breast. Her pudgy fingers bore several rings with different colored stones in them.

Trumpet blinked at the impolitic response. One didn't greet a new acquaintance by insulting her sovereign.

Penelope said, "Her Majesty's first concern is for her own subjects, as it should be. She feels each soldier's loss as if it were her own sweet son left lying on a foreign shore."

"*Naturellement,*" du Plessis said, "for she is a woman, like us." Her lips formed a simpering smile.

Trumpet repressed a sharp cluck of her tongue. She despised this sort of person, who insulted you in one breath and pretended it was a compliment in the next.

"Shall we sit?" Penelope said.

The usher, who had remained standing nearby with his hands folded, set two armless chairs before a bench under a window. Catalina helped Trumpet onto the bench while the other ladies seated themselves.

Du Plessis aimed her simper at Trumpet. "I see you're soon to be delivered, my lady. Will this be your first?"

Trumpet nodded, rubbing her belly. "It's a boy, I think. Everyone says the signs are there."

Du Plessis wagged her finger to correct such hubris. "Only God knows that, my lady."

"Speculation is a human trait, I think," Trumpet retorted. "Which God gave to us, so why not exercise it?" She was loosely paraphrasing Francis Bacon — very loosely — but this French cow wouldn't know it.

Penelope asked, "Do you have children, Madame?"

"One daughter only, Suzanne de Paz, the child of my first marriage." She sighed. "Girls are *so* much more difficult than boys, are they not? Arranging a suitable marriage is as difficult as negotiating a territorial treaty, I can assure you."

An obvious remark, if there ever was one. Trumpet said, "That's what marriage contracts are for, if both parties have estates."

"Well, yes," du Plessis allowed. "That is *part* of it. But there are other considerations, are there not? Both parties must practice the same religion, I believe. In my country, that poses a greater challenge than here in England."

"We are fortunate in that regard," Penelope said. "Although with luck, perhaps your King Henry will ease that challenge for you."

"We need more than luck, my ladies." Du Plessis pursed her thin lips. "We need the support of the English, the greatest Protestant nation in the world, if we are even to survive. My husband was sent here by *le Roi Henri*, whom we are proud to name our friend as well as our king, to plead our cause."

"Your plea has been heard," Penelope said. "Or do you count the Earls of Essex and Dorchester as nothing?"

The barb struck home. "*Mais non*, my lady!" du Plessis cried. "We are the very souls of gratitude! France has not seen such noble English warriors since Your Majesty's father graced our shores."

Penelope granted the apology a gracious nod, shooting a nearly invisible wink at Trumpet. It was fun, bandying veiled insults with this French pomposity.

Du Plessis took their smiles as a license to press her case. "I have not met your *puissant* husbands myself, to my sorrow. This is why I was so eager to come here today to make the acquaintance of your ladyships." The simpering smile reappeared. "We ladies of influence, if I may be so bold as to include myself among your number, weave the threads that bind our worlds together."

"So we do," Penelope said. One fine eyebrow rose at the awkward metaphor.

"My husband attends each day upon your queen," du Plessis said. "Ready to assist should she require his knowledge of France. While I, for my part, offer the same service to your ladyships. Some things cannot be said at court, as you know. Observations of a personal nature, if you comprehend me."

"I believe we do, Madame," Penelope said, shooting another tiny wink at Trumpet.

"We women hear things, do we not?" du Plessis continued. "The sorts of things men do not speak to other men. The little observations we make sitting quietly in the corner while they make their great debates."

"I suspect you have some such tidbit for us today, Madame." Penelope clasped her hands in her lap, ready for the treat.

Du Plessis's pink tongue ran across her narrow lip. "Perhaps, my ladies, you have received news from your good lords about the happenings in my country."

"We receive letters every day," Penelope said. "We're better informed than the Privy Council."

"Exactement," du Plessis said. "Then you know there has been a small misunderstanding recently between my king and your great lords."

"Misunderstanding!" Trumpet scoffed. "My lord of Dorchester is half-mad with boredom. He went to France to help your king lay siege to Rouen, not idle about in Dieppe playing cards."

"Alas, my lady, you have it in an eggshell. I am certain my king had excellent reasons, but your queen, she has taken offense. She will no longer listen to my husband's explanations. In fact, most lamentably, she has banished him from her sight."

Penelope hummed in a way that might convey either sympathy or disapproval. "Her Majesty is very intelligent and has excellent hearing. She understands things the first time around, as a rule."

"One does not nag a queen," Trumpet added. "It tends to bring about a result contrary to the one you desire."

"I am gratified by your instruction, my ladies," du Plessis said. "Though I hope my husband knows better than to be this nag. I knew I was right to come to you."

"Mmm." That neutral sound meant Penelope was ready to bargain. "I will be celebrating Easter with Her Majesty tomorrow, as it happens."

"You might murmur a word or two," Trumpet said. "Though perhaps it would be better to wait until Monday, or later in the week." She smiled sweetly at the Frenchwoman. "Even the mildest suggestion might be taken amiss if Her Majesty is not in the mood to hear it. There is always a risk."

"I appreciate that. *Absolument*." Du Plessis's tongue flicked across her lips again. "I do not come to you as a mere supplicant. We ladies must stand by one another, must we not? I am capable of reciprocation. I have heard some things perhaps you have not."

"We *love* gossip." Penelope grinned at Trumpet, batting her lashes in girlish glee. "Especially when no one else knows anything about it."

Du Plessis attempted a waggish smile. "This would be more in the nature of a warning. A word to the wise."

"We are agog," Trumpet said. She'd been wanting to use that word for years.

"Well. As you may not know, Montaubon is a small city, with a limited society. Everyone knows everyone, you see, perhaps better than one might wish. One hears things which one might prefer not to know." Du Plessis paused.

"Such as?" Penelope asked.

"Such as things relating to Mr. Anthony Bacon." Du Plessis's eyes darted from one lady to the other, gauging the effect of that name. "Perhaps you know him?"

"We know his brother," Trumpet said. "We hold him in the highest regard." She knew what was coming now: more of the rumors Tom had heard at the Antelope.

"My husband has met that gentleman at court," du Plessis said. "But perhaps he does not know how his brother lived, so far away in the south. We knew, *naturellement*. A house with no wife?" She wagged her finger and clucked her tongue. "So many feasts and musical evenings, always with only men. And worse, with young boys. We ladies know better than to trust in such a man as that."

Penelope leaned away with a curled lip, as if evading a huge fart. "That sort of scurrilous rumor surrounds every man of importance, particularly if he refrains from marrying too soon. Often such men are too busy serving their country for such trivial matters. My lord brother and I — and Lady Dorchester, I am sure — consider that sort of foolish tale slander of the lowest kind."

Du Plessis's mouth dropped open at the unexpected response. She scrambled to recover. "As do I, my lady, I assure you. Poof! It is gone. I merely mention it as the sort of thing other, lesser persons might spread about. And yet I do feel a duty to warn you that Mr. Bacon accepted a substantial sum of money from a Catholic agent last year."

Trumpet was glad she'd already heard this one. It would've startled her otherwise, and she wanted to show this woman nothing but coolness. Penelope was so good at schooling her features. It was clearly an important skill. Perhaps Trumpet could get Catalina to tell her amazing stories in front of the mirror so she could practice.

"Another routine rumor," Penelope said. "Even Sir Walter Ralegh has been accused of that. No one credits it."

"I do not invent this charge, my lady," du Plessis said. "It is known to be true in my region. Your emissary of Bordeaux, Mr. Ridley, he knows it. And my husband's good friend, Monsieur Antoine du Pin, a very respected wine merchant, he knows it too. His family has been prominent in Bordeaux since Louis the Prudent was king."

"Louis the Prudent?" Trumpet burst out. Penelope shot her a quelling look.

Du Plessis failed to notice the disdain in the others' expressions. "The Catholic League does not dispense money out of mere sympathy. There is always an expectation of services to be rendered. Since Mr. Bacon has a specialty in the dissemination of news . . ." She lifted her shoulders in an exaggerated shrug. "Well. I have given you my words of caution. Your ladyships will know best what to make of them."

"Indeed we shall." Penelope offered no smile with that short reply.

The story was undoubtedly overblown, like everything else about this fawning harpy. There were Catholics, and then there were Catholics, for one thing. Tom had said Anthony was as great a spendthrift as his brother. He'd probably racked up so many debts he couldn't scrounge up the coin to travel home. Like any drowning man, he'd reached for the nearest rope.

Trumpet's father, the Earl of Orford, had taken money from Spain too. At sword point on the high seas after a few rounds of cannon fire, but the source remained the same. Perhaps Anthony had taken that money in the privateering spirit, never intending to repay it.

Penelope turned abruptly toward the window. "Mercy! Look how dark it's getting! A storm must be coming. I fear you'll be drenched, Madame du Plessis." She rose and gestured toward the stairs. "Do allow me to summon our coach for your convenience."

The meeting was over. She rose and strode down the gallery to speak with her servant. Du Plessis got up to stand near Trumpet's bench. "May I assist you, Lady Dorchester?"

"No need." Trumpet let Catalina haul her to her feet. It seemed more arduous than it had half an hour ago.

Du Plessis smirked at Trumpet's round belly. "You're close to term, I perceive."

"Any day now, they say." Trumpet smiled.

"You'll want to lay in a good supply of the sweet wine of Jerez and have the kitchen prepare a quantity of strong beef broth."

"What for?"

"To keep up your strength during the ordeal. It's beyond the endurance of many women, especially small ones like yourself. They often do not survive it." Du Plessis's small eyes gleamed. "One of my neighbors in Montaubon suffered in labor for three full days. I could hear the screams all the way down the street. It was *terrifiante*, I can assure you. She lived, but the babe was lost. She has never fully recovered her strength."

Trumpet gaped at her in horror. She'd been told to expect something like seven or eight hours of travail at most. From what she'd heard, she doubted she could endure two whole days.

"I need to sit down," she whispered to Catalina, who helped lower her back onto the bench. She wrapped both hands around her belly, rubbing it to reassure the babe — and herself — that no such calamity would ever befall them.

Catalina stood between her and the Frenchwoman, bristling with outrage. "You are a very cruel woman, Madame! I spit upon your wicked lies! My mistress is strong, like a mountain pony. Her labor will be like this — " She snapped her fingers over her head. "And her baby will be as healthy and beautiful as its mother."

Du Plessis cared nothing for a scolding from a servant. Her eyes gleamed with satisfaction. "That is in God's hands." She dropped a small curtsy and moved toward Penelope, who was beckoning for her to come along.

"She lies, my lady," Catalina said. "She is full of spite. Two days — that never happens. Never!"

Trumpet nodded, wiping away the tears that had sprung into her eyes. She knew the venomous cow only wanted to hurt her, in revenge for the small humiliation of Penelope's scolding. She was too cowardly to attack Lady Rich, a woman of known importance without the cumbrance of an unborn babe. So she had attacked the smaller, weaker opponent.

Trumpet knew this with her mind, but a seed of fear had been planted in her heart. "That stupid bitch," Trumpet muttered. She met Catalina's warm, brown eyes and felt strongly comforted. "She came here to make new friends. Well, now she has two new enemies."

"Three," Catalina said.

SIX

Tom went to speak with Anthony Bacon's coachman first thing after breakfast on Saturday morning. Maybe he slept in a little; it had been a late night. By the time he reached the stables, the carriage was gone. Anthony had sent it — and Lawson — out to Wapping to catch the long ferry to Gravesend. He wanted his secretary to interview an intelligencer before the churl set sail for Hamburg.

How was a man supposed to investigate a murder when the chief suspect could send the major witnesses away whenever he liked?

Tom couldn't even complain about it to Francis Bacon, who wouldn't emerge from his chambers before dinner in any case. He'd most likely have the meal in his brother's chambers anyway.

Tom wished for a moment that Trumpet still lived in her aunt's house on Bishopsgate, so she and Catalina could sneak out in boys' garb to meet him in that alehouse on Leadenhall. They could turn the whole problem inside out and sideways, like a clothing reseller examining a secondhand doublet.

If the courts were in session, his old chum Benjamin Whitt would be here. He loved the pies from that vendor near Newgate as much as he loved his own mother. They could buy a couple and amble up to the churchyard at St. Sepulchre to perch on a tombstone while they chewed over the case. His wits were nearly as good as Francis Bacon's, and he didn't care one way or another about Anthony.

Never had Tom felt so alone, bereft not only of his confidantes, but also of his master's guidance. Francis had given him no instructions last night. Tom suspected there might not be any in the offing. But Anthony had said he wanted to know the truth, and Tom couldn't bear not knowing, not now that he'd tied his garter around that poor sod's neck. He meant to find out, even if he had to shake the whole Bacon family tree down to do it.

He asked the stableman what time Mr. Bacon's coach had left the stables last night. "Round about ten o'clock," he answered. "The chapel bell was tolling as the coach rolled out the door." He pushed his cap back to scratch his sparse hair. "A mite late, I'll grant you, but Mr. Lawson don't keep hours like our regular gentlemen. Comes and goes as he pleases. But there was a good moon, and I suppose he knows his own business."

Tom thanked him, then had his own horse saddled to get out for a trot down Theobalds Road. They could both use the exercise, and he might spot something useful. No luck. He stopped for dinner at the Red Lion and asked if they'd seen a coach with the Bacon coat of arms on the doors. "Bars of gold and azure with red stars on a white field and a boar at the top. It's got kind of a toothy grin. You'd remember it."

The harried alewife laughed out loud at that. "Can't be running out to look at every coach that rattles past, now can I? This road leads to Westminster, in case you don't know it."

He hadn't hoped for much. The ale was worse than he remembered, and the mutton stew was barely edible. At least Tristan enjoyed the outing.

By the time he got back to Gray's, Anthony's carriage had returned. Tom handed Tristan's reins to a groom and went to find Peter Widhope, who was rubbing down one of the matched Friesian mares. Tom leaned his elbows on the half-door and watched for a while, like a man with nothing better to do. He loved stables, with the soft whickering of horses and the warm smells of horse shit and oiled leather. After a while, he said, "That truly is a handsome animal."

"Nothing but the best for Lady Bacon," Widhope replied. He gave Tom a friendly smile without pausing in his work. "How are you this morning, Mr. Clarady?"

"I'm well, Widhope, though a bit short on sleep."

"You gentlemen stay up too late reading. 'Tisn't good for the digestion, my lady says."

The hazards of staying up too late was one of Lady Bacon's favorite themes. Another was lending the coach to all and sundry or using it for unseemly purposes. Tom had wondered how she knew so much about the daily doings of her sons. Now he knew.

Tom had visited Gorhambury a few times, sometimes with Francis and sometimes on his own to fetch or deliver some special item. Lady Bacon ran her household on strict Calvinist principles, gathering everyone for prayers twice a day. But she took excellent care of her people, finding their children good jobs and good marriages. Not a sparrow fell under her watchful eyes. They would gladly answer her questions about the young masters. It wouldn't even occur to them to think of it as spying.

But Widhope knew something about last night's events — something more than the general gossip that must have spread throughout the inn. He kept shooting anxious looks at Tom before ducking back behind the horse.

Tom kept his tone light. "Have you heard about that poor knave I found out in the field last night?"

"Seems to be all anyone can talk about." Widhope exchanged his brush for a comb. He stood behind the mare's neck to tease invisible tangles from her black mane. "It's a mystery how he got there, isn't it? May God rest his soul."

"Less of a mystery than most people know." Tom leaned to the right and clucked. The mare turned her head, exposing her driver's woebegone face. "We found Mr. Anthony's coach standing by the verge while this fine pair stuffed themselves with grass. No driver, no passengers; just an empty coach with two hungry horses."

Widhope closed both eyes and pressed his lips together.

But he couldn't make it go away that easily. Tom needed answers. "I drove it in myself, so nobody else knows about that part. But we can't leave it like that, can we? A man's been murdered. Justice must be done."

He waited. The coachman opened his eyes but kept his lips sealed.

"Come on, Widhope. You know as well as I do that only you can take this coach out of these stables without comment. You left with Mr. Lawson at ten o'clock. We found the coach abandoned a little after one. What happened in between?"

"You should ask Mr. Lawson."

"I will, never fear. Right now I'm asking you. I don't believe for a minute you're the one who left these beauties to fend for themselves. It must've been some other driver. Why not tell me who it was and why you gave him the reins?"

Widhope glowered at the straw-covered floor, scratching the back of his neck. He muttered, "I'm not supposed to say anything."

"Who told you that? Mr. Anthony?"

"Not him. Nor Mr. Francis neither."

"Mr. Lawson?"

He shook his head.

This nut was harder to crack than a year-old walnut. Tom set both elbows on the half-door of the stall and treated the man to a doubtful frown. "You know, I hate to think what Lady Bacon will say when she hears about her expensive Friesian mares being left unattended on the road in the dead of night. We're lucky they weren't stolen or attacked by wild dogs. You're new to London, but I could tell you —"

"No, Mr. Clarady! There's no reason to go worrying Her Ladyship! None whatsoever!"

Widhope's distress made the mare whinny and turn a wide eye at Tom. The coachman stroked her neck to soothe her.

"Now you're upsetting the horse," Tom said unfairly. "I'll get to the bottom of this one way or another, you know. It's what I do. You have my word I won't tell anyone but Mr. Francis. Start from the beginning and say it straight out. You'll feel better once you get it off your chest."

Widhope sighed, his broad shoulders slumping. Then he patted the mare and came around to face Tom. "I'll say you made me do it, threatening to tell Her Ladyship and all."

"That's no more than the plain truth." Tom nodded as if they'd struck a deal. "You left the stable at ten o'clock with Mr. Lawson inside the coach."

"That's right. He told me to stop at the Antelope to pick up a friend and then drive around, someplace quiet. No need to go far, he said. They wouldn't be more than half an hour, he said."

"Who was the friend?"

"Never saw him. Mr. Lawson said they were going to have a rapper-shmal. Some French thing, I reckon." His nose wrinkled, giving his opinion of all things French.

Tom muttered, "Rapper-shmal, rapper-shmal," and then he caught it. Thanks to his years of wrestling with Law French, he could guess it meant *rapprochement*. A reconciliation, eh? That explained why Ridley was there.

"Then what happened?" he prompted.

"When we reached the corner at Holborn Road" — Widhope tilted his head in that direction — "I stopped to let another carriage go by, taking its sweet time. While I was waiting, a young fellow jumped up beside me and said I was to give him the reins and take myself off."

There was a twist! Tom had expected to hear Lawson let him go to take the driver's seat himself. "Who was it?"

Widhope shrugged. "A youngster, by the sprightly way he hopped up."

Someone under fifty, then. Widhope couldn't be a day less. "Go on."

"He had a raspy sort of voice, like this." Widhope grated out the next words. "My master sent me to take your place tonight."

"Who was his master?"

"That's the first thing I asked. I wouldn't give up my post to just anybody, Mr. Clarady. The fellow said his master knew all about the rapper-shmal and wanted to be sure they weren't interrupted. He said it was all arranged with Mr. Anthony, so I shouldn't fret myself about it. He said his master wanted to know what was said without Mr. Lawson and his friend knowing that he knew. He gave me a shiny gold angel — ten shillings! Then he told me not to come home till morning."

"The master's name." Tom met Widhope's eyes. "Or perhaps I should write Lady —"

"No! She wouldn't fault me, I swear it! It was them down there, after all." He tilted his head again, but backward this time, pointing southwest.

"Down where? Westminster?"

"Not that far. Just down the hill."

"*What hill?*" Tom was ready to drag the man over the half-door and shake the name out of him.

"Down on the Strand." Widhope's eyes cut to the side. "Her Ladyship's brother-in-law."

"Burghley House." Now Tom understood the man's reluctance. "Lord Burghley's servant wanted to spy on

Anthony Bacon's private secretary's private conversation, so he paid you to let him take your place."

Widhope winced at the word *spy*. "Not His Lordship. Her Ladyship's nephew, Sir Robert. The fellow showed me a letter with Sir Robert's seal on it. What was I supposed to do?"

"Nothing, I guess." Poor Widhope had been caught between a rock and a hard place. "Where'd you go?"

Widhope's eyes cut to the side again, his lips pressed together.

But Tom could guess that part easily enough. "I know every brothel from here to Hackney. Don't think I won't ask around."

"It wasn't a brothel, Mr. Clarady. I beg you not to tell Her Ladyship. Some of the grooms here talk about a little house on Shoe Lane. Nice girls, they say. Clean. It's never been my habit. In truth, Mr. Clarady, I've never really —"

"I just want to know who was where at what time, Widhope. What you did after you left that coach is no concern of mine — nor anyone else's. You left the coach at the corner of Holborn Road. Did you see it stop at the Antelope?"

"I saw it stop. I didn't see who got in. They went on the other way, toward Broad St. Giles."

"Would you recognize the young fellow if you saw him again?"

Widhope hummed, turning his face toward the rough wooden slats of the ceiling and tapping his lips. Then he shook his head. "He was all wrapped up with a scarf around his face and a big hat."

"Of course he was." Tom couldn't think of anything else to ask. "All right, then. I'll tell Mr. Francis you sneaked upstairs without anybody noticing and slept the sleep of the just."

Relief washed over Widhope's round face. "Thank you, Mr. Clarady. I owe you one."

"I'll remember it." He bade the man good day and left the stables, walking slowly across the yard to Bacon House and his own room.

Everyone knew Sir Robert had his fingers in all the important pies and his ears pricked for the juiciest gossip. Ever since Lord Burghley's health had taken a turn for the worse — permanently, it would seem — Sir Robert had been the acting Secretary of State. The queen refused to name another one, so he did everything under his father's guidance. It was right and proper for him to send intelligencers into the courts of Europe and keep an eye on the wealthier Catholics here at home.

But to bribe his own cousin's driver so his man could eavesdrop on a private conversation? Tom wouldn't have credited such a story in less-compelling circumstances. Weren't they all working on the same side?

SEVEN

"Did you walk?" Francis peered out the window of Anthony's chamber into the Chapel Court. He saw no sign of coach or horses in rich trappings milling near the gatehouse.

Robert Cecil shrugged his thin eyebrows, a gesture he'd taught himself to avoid shrugging his misshapen shoulders. "I spend so much time sitting that it feels good to get out for a stretch. And it is a beautiful afternoon."

More likely he'd walked the quarter mile from Burghley House to demonstrate his possession of two good legs, in contrast with Anthony's gout-crippled limbs.

Anthony had been the most active of the three cousins in their boyhood days, roaming the grounds at Gorhambury or Theobalds. They'd rambled all about, exploring the woods, ponds, and meadows. Sometimes they rode, sometimes they set limed nets in tree branches to catch birds. Sometimes they had the servants set up butts to practice archery, although only Anthony enjoyed that sport. He could hit the target three times out of five, while Francis's arrows either fell short or flew off in the wrong direction. Robert's twisted shoulder prevented him from even drawing a bow.

"Where are your men?" Francis asked. Privy Council members, however young, didn't stroll about unescorted. They had the dignity of their office to uphold — and Robert held up so many these days. Her Majesty had knighted him last year, for no discernible reason. Then she'd seated him on her Privy Council. He was Master of the Court of Wards in all but name and de facto Secretary of State.

Robert said, "They're in the hall, having some refreshment. Don't worry; I won't disturb your afternoon rest for long. But I haven't seen Cousin Anthony for thirteen years. I wanted to respond to your letter in person instead of sending a messenger."

That was plausible enough. He must be curious to see what changes time had wrought on his once-admired older cousin.

Anthony merely nodded at his entrance, seemingly intent upon finishing his letter. He'd spent a full half hour before this appointment getting dressed. He looked distinctly French, with a sheer lace collar falling over his velvet-clad shoulders and a light sheen of oil shaping his moustache into pointed curves. Was the foreign effect intentional, meant to impress his worldly experience on his stay-at-home cousin? Or was this the way he dressed now when company was expected?

Robert's keen brown eyes took in every detail of the richly appointed chamber, doubtless attaching a value to each item before cataloguing it into in his fact-stuffed mind. Silk tassels dangled from the cushions on the armchairs. Silver plate and glass cups gleamed on the polished cupboard. His gaze lingered longest on the silk tapestry hanging over the cupboard. It was small but old and valuable, depicting a hunting scene with the towers of Fontainebleau rising in the background.

Anthony signed his letter with a flourish and shook sand over the page. He poured the sand back into its tray, folded the letter in four parts, and sealed it with the large ring he wore on his left index finger. *"Eh, bien."* He handed it to Jacques with a brief instruction in French to make sure it went out immediately.

Then, at last, Anthony turned to his cousin. "*Alors,*
Robert. I am sorry to keep you waiting. But time and tide
wait for no man. I'm sure you understand."

"Of course." Robert's dry tone made clear that he
understood quite well the trick of making visitors wait.

"Do sit," Anthony said. "Since Jacques is out, perhaps
Frank could offer you some wine?"

"It's right over there." Francis pointed at the bottle and
cups laid ready on the cupboard. He had no intention of
playing the servant. Robert was the youngest. Let him pour
the wine.

"To be honest," Robert said, "I'd rather have a mug of
good English beer. I worked up a thirst walking over here."

"For that, I fear we must wait for Jacques. He'll have
to fetch it from the buttery. *Je suis très désolée.*"

Robert accepted the apology with a smirk and settled
himself in Francis's usual chair. Francis served himself and
his brother full cups of delicious Bordeaux wine, inwardly
pleased that Robert had deprived himself of the fine drink
in his petty attempt to snub Anthony's overplayed
Frenchness.

Robert set his elbows on the arms of his chair and
steepled his fingers, studying Anthony as if reading the
years written on his face. Anthony returned the candid
assessment. Seeing his cousin through his brother's eyes,
Francis noticed the lines etched across the high forehead
and the hollows under the watchful eyes — too many
hours hunched over difficult documents or listening to his
elderly father instruct him in the art of giving counsel to a
queen.

The Cecils, both father and son, bore most of the cares
of England on their weak shoulders, but they had only
themselves to blame if the burden wore them down. They
could share some of it with the members of their own
family — close relations who had long since proven their
trustworthiness and skill. Instead, they kept Francis at

arm's length, year after endless year, denying him any meaningful position. He wrote advice letters. He entertained foreign visitors by showing them the treasures of Whitehall or conversing in the Presence Chamber in French, German, or Latin. Sometimes they granted him a place on a commission charged with some unpleasant chore, like interviewing recusant Catholics in London's jails. Short-lived, unpaid assignments for which he received scant thanks.

Nothing but empty promises and faint praise. He'd been a stalwart member of Parliament for eight years; important work with no pay. He was Dean of the Chapel at Gray's Inn; essential work, also without pay. He'd been granted the reversion of Clerk of the Counsel in Star Chamber; interesting work that would pay handsomely, if and when the current clerk died. Since the man was barely fifty and enjoyed the best of health, Francis couldn't even borrow on the strength of the grant.

Anthony had fared little better, in spite of the wealth of intelligence he had supplied his uncle during his years in France. But now that he was back in England, things would change, one way or another.

Robert said, "I'm glad you're home, Anthony. France is too dangerous, especially for an invalid. You're not able move swiftly if danger should arise."

Anthony chuckled in mild amusement. "The danger seems greater from a distance, I suppose. Especially for those who've done little traveling and fail to appreciate the local context. I was never in harm's way in Montauban, deep in the heart of the Protestant region."

He took a sip of wine, making a show of savoring its quality. "The conflict in the north did make it more difficult to transfer funds, or so I was given to understand by your father. If I'm to exhaust my own wealth in Her Majesty's service, it is better for me to be here to manage my own estates."

Anna Castle

A well-aimed barb! Francis smiled into his cup. How many thousands of pounds did their uncle owe Anthony for his years of service, or would owe, if he were fairly paid?

Robert blinked, not quite smiling. He'd learned long ago to discipline his face and rarely exhibited hurt or surprise. A mild smile, a thoughtful frown, and a watchful gaze constituted his entire repertoire. "That's a wise policy in any case. A grown man shouldn't leave his affairs in the hands of his aging mother."

Francis winced. A heavy shot, which, judging by Anthony's narrowed eyes, struck home.

"Besides, dear cousin," Robert continued, "however safe the south of France may be for the ordinary visitor, I fear your reputation has grown so great you've become a particular target. We had a warning in January of a Spanish plot to kidnap you at sea on your way home. The conspirators planned to trade you for Don Pedro de Valdés, I believe. An officer of the Spanish fleet languishing in our prison in Torbay."

"Bah!" Anthony waved that away with a flap of his lace-cuffed hand. "One hears such rumors. They fly about in great flocks, like the swallows returning from Africa each spring."

"And yet some threats are real," Robert said. "It's my sorry task to weigh them, one by one, and sort the true from the false. I've negotiated several prison exchanges since the dire events of '88. You're lucky to have missed all that."

"I was in the thick of it," Anthony said, "using everything I've learned in my long years abroad to winnow precious grains of truth from the clouds of misinformation blowing across the seas."

Robert offered his not-quite smile again. "Your letters were a useful addition to our resources, adding a correction here and a confirmation there. You should take pride in having done your part. My lord father and I hope you'll be

92

able to continue at least some portion of your correspondences, in spite of your infirmities."

Anthony lifted his chin to look down his nose at his shorter cousin. "Weak legs are no hindrance to the labor of the mind, as your father can attest. He serves the queen as ably from his bed as he ever did from the Privy Chamber. I can manage my intelligencers from this house as effectively as Sir Francis Walsingham managed his from Seething Lane. And I might add without self-flattery that no one knows Europe as well as I do, now that Sir Francis is gone."

That's thrown down the gauntlet. Walsingham's footsteps led straight to the position of Secretary of State. Now Robert knew what they wanted.

A small tension around the eyes betrayed Robert's defensive posture. "You may know Europe, Cousin, but you do not know the queen. Her Majesty expects her counselors to attend upon her personally, day and night."

"Your lord father is as much an invalid as I am," Anthony said.

"Tush," Robert said. "At his advanced age, our gracious monarch makes allowances. And must I remind you that he stood beside her for some thirty-five years? Years that included her most desperate months of imprisonment. Now he has me to act as his surrogate — a seamless change, from her perspective."

Anthony flicked a glance at Francis, whose heart sank. He had no desire to be Anthony's surrogate at court. But Robert had put his finger on the nub. If Anthony could not appear before her to hear her unspoken wishes, Her Majesty would never entrust him with important decisions.

A silence developed while they mulled over this hard truth. Francis spoke first. "Anthony's health improves daily. He'll be able to present himself at Whitehall in a week or two."

"Her Majesty often asks after my health, I hear," Anthony said. "I'm in her thoughts, if not her august presence."

Robert refused to grant even that small concession. "I suppose in two or three weeks the rumors going around about you will have died down. There's always some fresh scandal to titillate the court." He smiled at Francis, a fellow courtier, but the gesture held no real feeling of kinship.

Still, it reminded Francis of another matter. "Perhaps those two French emissaries will be gone by then. I suspect Her Majesty grows weary of their nagging, and thus of the whole subject of the French wars."

"Do you mean du Plessis and du Pin?" Robert asked. "They do seem to have overstayed their welcome."

"Oh, *those* two!" Anthony rolled his eyes. "All they do is nag, usually about their own affairs. I often think my king sent them here to rid himself of their constant nattering."

Francis cut his eyes toward Robert at that revealing turn of phrase. Whose king? Where did Anthony's allegiance lie after thirteen years in France? He caught the faint smile of satisfaction — fleeting, but real — on his cousin's lips and knew he'd caught the slip. Nothing escaped him.

Whatever Robert made of it, he kept to himself. "Your man seems to have gotten lost. Perhaps I will have a cup of wine." He hopped up and went to serve himself. "May I refresh your cup, Anthony?" His tone was a shade too solicitous. Anthony smiled and shook his head.

Robert took a sip, nodding at the taste. Then he strolled over to a set of bookshelves leaning against the wall and turned his head to read the titles. "A nice collection." A compliment so weak as to be an insult. His father's library was the second largest in London and Westminster combined.

But the library at Essex House was the largest, and Francis had free rein there.

Robert resumed his seat. "I mustn't keep you out of bed for too long. Though I've been eager to see you, I am sorry for the proximate cause of this visit. Has anything more been learned about Raffe Ridley's death?"

Anthony sighed as if in sorrow. "Nothing substantive, I fear."

"There's been a great deal of stir," Francis said, adding detail to flesh out their empty answers. "Messengers going out and sheriff's men coming in, most of them knocking on my door to hear the same brief story over and again. We've had very little sleep. Nothing has been found beyond the man's hat."

Robert had undoubtedly been given full reports by the sheriff and the coroner. But not from Tom, who had told the Bacon brothers about the second coachman only a few hours ago.

"I understand your man Clarady discovered the body." Robert had once tried to recruit Tom as a sometime informer. Tom had taken the money, just that once, but made it clear he would never share anything without Francis's explicit permission.

"It was my secretary, Thomas Lawson, who identified the poor man." Anthony spoke as if offering something new. "We were all friends in the south of France."

"Yes, I know." Robert plainly suspected they were holding something back, but then he would even if they had nothing.

"Why was Ridley sent to Bordeaux?" Francis asked. "Who recommended him as emissary, do you know?"

"I asked my father this morning," Robert said. "He proposed him for the post, as a favor to his father, Lancelot Ridley. He was a prominent clergyman in Cambridgeshire. My father owed him a favor at the time. Raffe was personable, fluent in French, and willing to live abroad."

"Sufficient qualifications," Anthony agreed. "An emissary's main task is picking up local gossip, after all."

"He did more than that," Robert said. "He facilitated the exchange of news with merchants and kept an eye on who was shipping what under which flag down there."

"Only half an eye!" Anthony laughed. "He spent more time in Madame du Plessis's parlor than he did on the coast."

Robert dismissed that with a flick of his eyebrows. "I'm told there was an altercation between Ridley and your man Lawson in a tavern the other night. Could that have any bearing on this murder?"

"I honestly don't think so," Anthony said, meeting his cousin's eyes. "That was a bit of chest-beating, I understand. Meant to impress a pretty girl. *Très française*, I'm afraid. A lamentable habit picked up in the south."

"Mr. Clarady was there too," Francis offered. "You could ask him."

Robert gave him a weary look. He knew Tom would stick to whatever story the Bacons had concocted.

"Lawly *was* out that night," Anthony said in a helpful tone. "He tapped at my door on his way up to bed, around midnight. He'd taken the coach out for a breath of air, but he saw nothing worthy of note. He was sound asleep when the hubbub arose in the yard."

"We were here, chatting by the fire." Francis admired his brother's ability to make a vacuous statement sound like honest testimony. *Worthy of note* indeed.

After Tom reported his conversation with Peter Widhope, they'd agreed to admit to Lawson taking out the coach. It had been driven up Holborn Road, after all, past the windows of the Antelope Inn. Someone must have seen the elegant vehicle drawn by its matched pair of exceptional horses.

Francis didn't believe Robert had sent the substitute driver. Why would he bother? As a Privy Council member, he could summon Ridley and ask him whatever he liked — assuming he knew about the *rapprochement*. He obviously knew about the conflict at the Antelope, but then so had Sir Walter Ralegh, indirectly.

Anthony considered nothing too sly for their younger cousin; not if it afforded him any advantage. Robert stored up bits of gossip like a squirrel preparing for a long winter.

In truth, the brothers knew little more than their cousin at this moment since Anthony had sent Lawson off first thing that morning. He claimed the trip had been arranged days before and couldn't be postponed. Francis had privately instructed Tom to interview Lawson before he got back to Gray's and had a chance to talk to Anthony again.

He hated all this tiptoeing and avoidance, but he saw no way around it as yet.

Robert regarded Anthony with a cool gaze. "My source said Ridley was flinging around some unpleasant accusations — about you, Anthony. They managed to find their way to the court, as these things do. Only a few seem to have heard them, fortunately." He turned to Francis. "You must have."

Francis sniffed. "The usual sort of fiddle-faddle that crops up when someone returns from a long absence. Sordid behaviors, bribes from Catholics. Similar charges have been hurled at every Englishman of note who has ever spent time in France or Italy. Remember the villainy published about the Earl of Leicester? You should know better than to credit such tales, Robert."

"Of course, I know there's no real fire. But the smoke is foul, and the scandal alone causes trouble. It's liable to obstruct your, ah, aspirations."

"Empty gossip," Anthony said with another wave of his hand. "Soon to be overtaken, as you say, by the next excitement."

"What could have provoked Ridley's enmity toward you, I wonder?" Robert asked.

Francis wanted to hear the answer to that question himself.

Anthony's eyes widened as he shook his head. "I've thought about it all day long, in among the fuss and bother. If you'd asked me yesterday, I would have said we were friends, Raffe and I. We visited one another, we stayed in each other's homes, we dined at each other's tables. Somehow he must have formed some resentment toward me, perhaps because I succeeded where he failed. I'm honored to count King Henry as a friend. I'm an intimate of most of the leaders of Protestant Europe. Raffe really had only the du Plessis-Mornays, and Madame more than Monsieur. I fear he was never taken very seriously."

Robert didn't appear satisfied with that explanation, though he didn't offer a better one. If he had sent the second coachman, he would already have heard about the conversation between Ridley and Lawson and would thus know more than the Bacons did. He'd always kept his secrets close, hiding them up his sleeve to pull out at precisely the right moment.

But he probably hadn't sent him. It would be inefficient, for one thing. For another, honest Peter Widhope would've told him whatever he knew, if pressed. Francis believed Robert was most likely blameless in the matter of the second coachman. That meant someone else had sent him, in which case Robert was better placed to find out who.

"There is one odd thing about last night," Francis began, ignoring Anthony's creased brow. "Lawson knows nothing of this, but our coachman says another driver took charge of the horses last night at the corner of Holborn Road. He claimed to have been sent by you, Robert. He showed our driver a letter with your seal on it as proof."

"God's breath!" Robert declared. His chin tucked into his ruff as he frowned. Francis had truly surprised him.

That rare event was worth the risk of sharing their morsel of intelligence.

Robert recovered with a shake of his head. "There must be hundreds of letters in this city with my seal on them. That story proves only that your driver is a credulous man. Why, in heaven's name, would I want to eavesdrop on Thomas Lawson?"

"To find out about me," Anthony said. "I'll grant it sounds a bit extreme, but it's well within your scope."

"Spying on my own cousin?" Robert's tone was derisive. "I would never stoop so low."

Anthony barked a scoffing laugh. "Your memory must be failing. Pressure of work, one supposes. I remember vividly the summer you persuaded your under-steward to follow me and let you know whenever I went round to the kitchens."

"You got more sweets than the rest of us," Robert retorted. "It wasn't fair."

"I'm five years older than you, may I remind you. The bigger child always gets more treats. Besides, sweets made you bilious. And you can't deny that it's evidence of your *penchant* for spying."

Robert sputtered some objection, which Anthony countered with the disdain of an older child for a younger one's fumbling excuses. Francis listened to their bickering without interest. Old grievances, best forgotten. But Robert always had been a bit of a sneak. He loved finding out secrets — just to possess them, not necessarily to use them.

Francis's sally had won them nothing. He'd never been able to tell when his cousin was lying. The only thing he'd learned today was that he could no longer tell when his brother was lying either.

EIGHT

On Easter Sunday, all work ceased. All sleep too, thanks to the merry ringing of church bells from Whitechapel to Westminster. The gentlemen of Gray's Inn — apart from a few scowling Puritans — would put aside their quills and don their finery to walk together down to St. Clement Danes to take communion.

Tom pulled on his yellow silk stockings and tied a new yellow ribbon around the crown of his best hat. The colorful touches on his lawyerly black garb reminded him of the peacock he had once been. That cheeky lad had almost disappeared after his father died. Only Trumpet could coax him out now.

After the service, they trooped back to the hall for a holiday feast. Sunday was a fish day — even this Sunday, when Lent officially ended — but oh, what delicious dishes of marvelous fishes were set before them! They had grilled beaver tails, even at the student tables, crisp fried whiting, and salmon with spring-fresh dill in dollops of cream. Tom ate so much he could barely stuff in his piece of Simnel cake. He waddled back to his room and slept for two hours.

A mighty thunderclap woke him with a start. He threw on his cloak, grabbed his lute, and raced across to the hall just before the rain came lashing down. If he was to be trapped by foul weather, better to be in a place with food, wine, and company. He and a group of jolly lads whiled away the afternoon and evening improvising scurrilous ballads, playing cards, and devising a masque mocking the senior barristers.

A day of rest refreshed a man in mind, body, and spirit. Tom woke Monday morning with a renewed sense of purpose. The courts of law would resume on April 15, which gave him two weeks to find out who killed Raffe Ridley.

First step: question Thomas Lawson. Francis had warned him to catch the man before he got home. "Not that I suspect my brother, mind you," he'd said, staring fixedly at his inkpot. "But Anthony's presence might alter the tale, causing some details to be understated or left out altogether."

That hint made Tom wonder about the nature of Ridley and Lawson's past friendship. Maybe they'd been part of a love triangle with arrows pointing in all three directions. Both men wanted Elsa Moreau. She hadn't seemed partial to either of them, but perhaps she was playing it coy. The men might have been lovers too, back in France, where all the trouble began.

Widhope had been told to collect Lawson at Wapping, so Tom went out to the stables after breakfast and begged to ride along. He climbed up on the bench with a hearty thanks and an eager grin. He wanted to talk, but he also wanted a turn at the reins. He'd never driven a coach before.

They took the long way around the northern edge of the sprawling metropolis — three times the distance but faster than slogging through the morning clog on Cheapside. Widhope let Tom drive for a while as they passed along the outskirts of Shoreditch. He'd driven an assortment of carts and wagons back home in Dorset, but nothing pulled by such a pair of well-trained, high-stepping beauties as these Friesian mares. Yesterday's storm had blown the air clean, stirring up the scents of new grass and blossoming trees. With the sun on his cheeks and a breeze ruffling his hair, Tom felt about as contented as a man could be.

They chatted about horses and roads for a while, then Tom steered the conversation to the subject of masters, the Bacon brothers in particular. He allowed that Francis had his flaws, including irregular habits, but given the range of human nature, he could be worse. Tom had learned buckets from him in the past six years, and not just about the law.

Widhope confessed that he enjoyed the pleasures of the capital more than the simpler life at Gorhambury. And Anthony Bacon was a well-spoken man who treated him with dignity, like a young master ought to treat a man of his age and experience. Lady Bacon, being nigh on as old as the Almighty himself, tended to treat her staff like children.

Tom suggested that Widhope might consider which individual deserved his first loyalty: the generous, easygoing Anthony, or the strict, suspicious Lady Bacon. He couldn't in all honesty serve both, not when it came to the carrying of tales. As to the activities that might take place inside the coach behind him, well, it was a driver's duty to mind the horses and not the passengers.

Widhope reckoned his life would surely be easier if he followed that rule.

That was good enough for Tom. He didn't like telltales on general principles. And the last thing they needed at Bacon House was a visit from the dowager, bent on setting her boys to rights.

As they approached a wide spot in the road, Tom decided to conduct a little test. He brought the horses to a tidy stop and persuaded Widhope to climb down and get inside. "I want to see what I can hear. Just pretend you're having a conversation with somebody."

Bafflement crumpled the coachman's homely features. "How in heaven's name can I do that, Mr. Clarady?"

Tom had a ready solution for that conundrum. The man had grown up in Lady Bacon's religious household. "Pretend you're being catechized by Her Ladyship."

It worked. Widhope settled himself on the cushions and began to teach himself his ABCs. Tom clucked the horses into motion, keeping the pace slow. If your passenger wanted to drive around an empty road to have a private conversation, you wouldn't hurry.

At first, he couldn't hear much more than the rumble of Widhope's voice. But when he reached behind him to twitch the curtains open, he could catch most of the words. And when Widhope raised his voice in a creditable imitation of Lady Bacon's quavery tones, every word came through clear as a bell, in spite of the noise of a passing wagon. At night, with nothing stirring but owls and mice, a level conversation between two men would carry well enough for the driver to catch most of it.

Tom pulled over again and traded places to let Widhope navigate the increasing traffic along the eastern edge of the city wall. He'd never ridden inside a coach either. He spread across the back bench, which was padded and covered in red brocade. He measured the width with his outstretched arms: a few inches shy of six feet. There was room for two sets of knees between the facing benches. Red curtains hung on strings above the windows on both sides and across the narrow opening at the front that allowed communication with the driver.

This miniature chamber would be cold on a winter day and damp on a rainy one, but otherwise it was fairly comfortable — once you got used to the rocking. Tom contemplated the possibilities for him and Trumpet in such a moveable, private room. As soon as she found a house in London, she'd buy a coach. Stephen would insist on it. She could use it to change clothes easily. Enter as a lady, exit as a lord. And in between, well . . .

He grinned and turned his face toward the window to distract him from a vision of Trumpet in a thin chemise lolling on the seat before him. He spotted the masts of tall ships rising up beyond the bridge. A welter of feelings rose in his breast: sorrow, longing, love, gratitude. Loss. The sight of ships and the smell of salt water always had that effect on him now.

He loved the sea and the mighty ships that plied its waves. He'd spent one glorious year sailing to the New World with his father when he was a stripling youth of nineteen. He hadn't loved every part of that journey at the time — far from it — but now he cherished every memory.

As they neared the wharf, he scanned the largest ships, half hoping, as always, that one would bear the name *Susannah*. But none ever would. She'd been blasted into splinters by the gunpowder explosion that had taken his father's life. Tears welled in Tom's eyes. He let them stand for a few moments in honor of the man who'd made him before wiping them away with his sleeve.

He took a deep breath as the coach slowed to a halt behind the Bell Inn. This prosperous tavern stood at the end of Execution Dock. Pirates were hung from a low gibbet at the end of the dock until the tide had drowned their rotting corpses three times. Then they'd be cut down and buried. One sorry wretch dangled at the end of the pier today, but fortunately the tide was rising, so not much was visible.

Thomas Lawson must have been watching the road from an upper window. He came out before they could signal for him, striding across the planked walkway. "Here you are, Widhope! I was beginning to think you'd gotten lost." He pulled the door open and startled to see Tom. "Clarady? What the devil?" Then his brown eyes lit with a speculative gleam as a smile curved on his wide lips.

Tom held up a flat palm to nip that notion in the bud. "I just wanted a little chat away from the prying ears at

104

Gray's. And I got to drive for a bit. That's a sprightly pair of horses." He shifted his arse to the rearward-facing bench, yielding the better seat to the other man.

Lawson stretched his arms across the back of the bench and cocked his head to give Tom an insolent appraisal. "You know, you're not bad-looking, Clarady."

Tom shook his head in mock sorrow. "People used to say I was pretty. I must be going downhill."

They chuckled. Both were comely men long accustomed to being judged on their looks.

Tom returned the blatant assessment. Fair was fair. Lawson was tall and clean-limbed, with an easy grace. He had well-balanced features with an expressive mouth habitually quirked in a half-smile, as if every passing moment held some wry amusement.

Lawson accepted the scrutiny, then pointed his chin at Tom. "You're handsome, educated, and not lacking in wit. I'm surprised Anthony hasn't recruited you yet, in one form or another."

"I'm not available in any form. First, I'm a man who likes women. End of story. Second, I'll pass the bar in a year or two. Then I mean to practice law until someone makes me a judge."

"Sounds dull."

"Not to me." Tom planned to be knighted somewhere along the way so he could marry Trumpet if Stephen should happen to die. He didn't wish the man any harm, but following the Earl of Essex meant fighting, which often resulted in death. If that dire chance should occur, Tom wanted to be first in line for the widow's hand.

Lawson lifted one uncaring shoulder. The coach lurched sideways, rocking them both against the padded walls. Lawson lifted the corner of a curtain to peer outside. "Looks like we're taking the long way around."

"Less traffic outside the city."

"I like the city," Lawson said. "I missed Paris during our years in Montaubon, and Paris is small compared to London."

"Is that where you met Anthony? In Paris?"

Lawson nodded. "My father served Sir Edward Stafford while he was the queen's ambassador there. We lived in Paris for some fifteen years or so." His eyes flashed at some exciting memory. "It's a wonderful place to spend your youth. The French are so much more flexible about so many things. But you couldn't fully appreciate it, given your limitations." He flashed a lecherous grin.

Tom ignored it. "Have you ever been anywhere other than Paris and Montaubon?"

"Lots of places. I was born in Kent, so I'm as English as you are, but my first nursery maid spoke Polish, or so I'm told."

"Polish? What does your father do?"

"Nothing now. He died three years ago. He was an embassy secretary. He studied civil law at Cambridge and had a knack for languages, so he was much in demand. My mother loved travel, so we *enfants* were dragged along in their train."

"Sounds like a lively childhood," Tom said, a trifle envious. Until he turned eighteen, his dad had never taken him farther than the Isle of Wight. "Do you speak Polish?"

"*Niewiele.*" Lawson flashed a challenging grin. "That means 'not much.'" His eyes danced with amusement, ready to play a game — any game he could win. Which seemed to sum up his general outlook on life.

"I don't speak any foreign languages," Tom said, "apart from Latin and Law French, which doesn't count. Now that you and Phelippes are in the house, I'm feeling a bit behindhand."

Stephen had spent a year touring the Protestant states and came home perfectly fluent in German. Trumpet spoke adequate French, like all Her Majesty's gentlewomen. How had Tom reached the ripe old age of twenty-five without acquiring a single modern tongue?

"Better get busy," Lawson said. "Anthony's pouring coals into the letter-writing forge. I speak German too. We moved from Krakow to Vienna when I was eight. Now that's a beautiful city!"

"How fluent are you?"

Lawson shrugged. "I get along well enough on the street, and my written language is improving." He winked. "Not enough for Anthony's purposes. We're looking for a skilled German translator."

"Don't look at me." Vienna was a Catholic city, Tom thought, part of the Holy Roman Empire. Poland was Catholic too. Had Lawson's father been one of that kind? Anthony seemed to be more broad-minded than most Englishmen about religious matters, perhaps from having spent so much time abroad. He must have Catholic intelligencers, come to think of it, working in Italy or Spain. They wouldn't last long in those places if they didn't conform to local practices.

Tom didn't know where Lawson stood with respect to religion. These days, it always mattered. The Bacons must know, but since they weren't sharing much with him, he decided to do a little probing on his own. "Poland, Vienna, Paris. Did your father only work in Catholic countries?"

Lawson's face flushed dark red. He shrank into the corner of the coach, arms crossed, and glowered at Tom. "Damn you down to hell, Clarady. I've done my penance for having the wrong parents. Isn't ten months in Newgate Prison enough for you people?"

Tom was nonplussed. "What are you talking about? When were you in Newgate?"

Lawson stared at him, a muscle pulsing along his clenched jaw. Then he shook his head and sank into the cushions. "You don't know?" He blew out a contemptuous breath and offered Tom a tired sneer. "They don't tell you much, do they?"

"If you mean the Bacon brothers, they haven't told me anything about you. I haven't asked. Why were you in Newgate?"

"Because Lady Bacon thinks I'm a bad influence on her son." Lawson's voice dripped with bitterness.

"Ah." Tom nodded. "You have my sympathies. I spent four days and four nights in Newgate a while back. Enough for a lifetime. I can't imagine surviving ten months in that stink hole."

"Four nights," Lawson scoffed. "And you had friends, I'll wager, bringing you all the little comforts. Wine, food, blankets . . ."

"It didn't seem like enough at the time." In retrospect, Tom owed apologies to both Francis and Ben. He'd been furious with them over his unjust imprisonment and how long it took to gain his release. But his years of legal studies had taught him that the authorities would have been grossly remiss if they hadn't arrested him, given the circumstances.

He'd earned his week in jail through his own bad judgment. Maybe Lawson had too. "I wasn't aware Lady Bacon had so much influence with the sheriffs of Middlesex."

Lawson blew out a long lip fart. "You can't possibly be that innocent! The lady has a brother-in-law you may have heard of. Lord Burghley? The Lord Treasurer, Master of the Court of Wards, Chancellor of Cambridge University, and ruler of everything except the queen herself. Lady Bacon put *him* up to it."

"He doesn't grant her every wish," Tom said. "If he did, Francis would be on the Privy Council."

"He'll never give the Bacons real power, either of them. Too much competition for the little hunchback, Robert. Burghley throws them a sop now and then, but mark my words. If you're planning to rise through Francis Bacon, you'd better find another ladder."

Tom poked a tongue into his cheek as he digested the truth of that observation. He knew Francis felt obstructed, but he had only just turned thirty-one. Tom assumed he would gain higher positions sooner or later. If Francis were Solicitor General, for example, he'd be a powerful aid to Tom's aspirations. He wouldn't jump ship, not for years yet.

"What does Lady Bacon have against you?" he asked.

"What do you think?" Lawson's lip curled. "She got an inkling about the nature of my friendship with Anthony. She seems to have a nose for these things."

"The servants tell her. Anthony should send the Gorhambury people back and hire Londoners. They won't care, and they won't be loyal to Her Ladyship."

"Thanks, Clarady." Lawson snapped his fingers at him. "I'll pass that along. She couldn't bear to think such things about her own son, or speak them out loud, so she told Lord Burghley I was a Catholic."

"Are you?"

"Nominally, I guess. I was baptized in Poland. Catholic churches are the only kind they have there. We attended Catholic churches everywhere we went. It's a diplomatic courtesy. My father did what was expected. I think my mother liked the popery. You know — the incense and the mystery. I'm more like my dad. I follow whoever I'm with to whichever church they like and don't think much about it either way."

That fit Tom's sense of him. It also sounded like a practical stance for a man who traveled through many countries. He couldn't very well insist on an English church wherever he might find himself on a Sunday morning.

Tom was convinced. Lawson was no Catholic. "I believe you."

"Thanks." Lawson's narrowed eyes measured Tom anew. He didn't say it, but Tom knew he'd earned a small favor.

"How did you get out?" he asked.

"Anthony came home. He didn't even know I was in jail until he left France. They arrested me in Dover the minute my feet touched English soil. Anthony was furious when he found out and demanded my immediate release. They let me go, but I doubt he'll ever forgive them, either of them. Especially not Lord Burghley."

"Did Francis know?"

"He must have, but he wouldn't use up a favor on my behalf." Lawson's eyes went flat. "He's nothing like as generous as his brother."

"He has his moments." Tom knew Francis wouldn't care a fig about the sexual side of Lawson's history nor about his shallow Catholicism. But he didn't seem to trust Lawson, in spite of Anthony's favor. There must be a reason.

They jolted along in silence for a while, each gazing out a window. Then Lawson turned toward Tom with that mocking half-smile on his lips. "I doubt you sacrificed a whole morning of copy-work just to learn my personal history. You want to ask me about Ridley, don't you?"

Tom smiled. "Did you kill him?"

Lawson sighed, a defeated sound. "I'll admit I had reason to wish him gone — or his mouth stoppered. But strangling a man in a coach is not my style."

Not exactly a denial. "You were the last person to speak with him, as far as we know."

"*We?* You mean you and Francis." Another sneer. "Anthony thinks this morbid by-work is *quintessentially Frank*, as he put it. Using his own special form of logic to track down murderers."

"I do most of the actual tracking," Tom said. "And it isn't morbid. It's necessary. We've prevented more than a few deaths and brought some dangerous individuals to justice. I'm proud of our work."

"You can't be very good at tracking if you think I'm the last one to speak to Raffe." Lawson jerked his chin toward the front curtain. "Widhope drove him home. He must've asked him where he lived. I didn't know and didn't care. I just wanted to talk to him, someplace quiet. If he had a grudge against Anthony, why not come to us about it first?"

"Good question. So what happened?"

Lawson raised both hands in a wide Gallic shrug. "I tried to reason with him. Anthony would've found him a post — a good one — once he was named Secretary of State. Raffe was cutting off his own nose to spite his face by undermining Anthony's reputation."

"Makes sense to me," Tom said. "What did Ridley say?"

"He laughed in my face. Said I was trying to bribe him with an empty purse. He said the Cecils would never let so important a position slip from their grasp. He said if Anthony thought he would ever see another penny from his uncle, he was a fool. He said he personally didn't blame him for taking money from the bishop, but others might think differently, especially here in England."

Tom frowned. "What bishop?"

"You'll have to ask Anthony." Lawson quirked his lips. "At bottom, I suspect it's plain old envy. Anthony's father was an important man. Raffe's was a preacher, and not a rich one. Anthony's mother is one of the most respected Calvinist writers in Europe. Raffe's was, I don't know — a nobody. A wife. Anthony is a close friend of the king of France. Raffe?" Lawson blew out a dismissive breath. "He doesn't have many friends, apart from that ridiculous Madame du Plessis."

"A man that hath no virtue in himself ever envieth virtue in others," Tom quoted.

"What's that?"

"A line from one of Francis's essays. He says envy is the attribute of the devil because the envious man seeks to work evil against his fellows."

"You see?" Lawson held out flat palms to ask for agreement. "Green-eyed jealousy, that's what killed Raffe Ridley. Anthony can't be the only one he offended. Whoever the other whoreson knave was, he must've got into the coach Friday night and stopped Ridley's tongue from wagging once and for all."

"What about the handkerchief?" Tom asked.

"Don't you have one?" Lawson seemed puzzled at the abrupt change of subject. "A well-dressed Inns of Court man like yourself?" He pulled a pristine linen square from his sleeve and held it out. "Have mine, then."

The simple, unthinking gesture gave Tom pause. The man seemed to have no idea what role a handkerchief had played in Ridley's death. He waved away the offer. "I meant the one I found stuffed into Ridley's mouth."

Lawson collapsed into the cushions as if Tom had pushed him back. "*My* handkerchief? Are you sure?"

"It had your initials embroidered on it. Didn't Anthony mention it?"

Lawson shook his head, his face the portrait of disgust. He wiped his lips with the back of his hand. "He didn't tell me everything, it would seem."

And why was that? Tom wondered. Didn't Anthony trust his dear old chum? Or perhaps Francis had persuaded him to hold it back. He'd want to Tom to be watching while that detail was dropped in Lawson's lap. Now, seeing the convincing expressions of surprise and disgust, he believed the man might truly be innocent.

"How do you explain your handkerchief in Ridley's mouth, then?"

"I can't." Lawson tossed his head, recovering his natural aplomb. "But Anthony gave me a dozen of them,

112

and I don't keep track. They don't clean this coach very well, you may have noticed. It could've been here for days."

Tom nodded. He couldn't account for all his handkerchiefs if pressed, and his were far more richly embroidered. He had two spinster aunts with little else to do. Not to mention a mother, three sisters, and the one-legged bo'sun who had lived with the Claradys since Tom was a baby. As the single cherished son, his linens were a household priority. "How did it end, your *rapprochement?*"

Lawson shook his head. "I could see it was no use before we'd made the first circuit around that road behind the inn. I told Widhope to drop me at home and take Raffe wherever he liked. And that's the last I saw of him."

"Except it wasn't Widhope."

"Who wasn't?"

"The driver. It wasn't Widhope. Some other churl budged him off the bench at the corner of Holborn Road. You didn't notice?"

Lawson scowled at him. "You're not making any sense."

"It's not my story. The fellow claimed Sir Robert Cecil sent him, though Sir Robert has denied it."

"He would, whether it was true or not." Lawson regarded Tom with a steady gaze, though their bodies rocked from side to side with the movement of the coach. "Let me get this straight. You have no idea who was driving this coach — none whatsoever — yet you blame *me* for what happened after I left." He shook his head and turned his face to the window. His eyes seemed more sad than angry, like a man who knows he can never win, whatever he might do.

Tom watched him, sympathy fighting against suspicion. His dejection now was palpable. It cloaked him like a damp fog. Maybe the second coachman had picked up another passenger. Or maybe he had done the deed himself.

Maybe Lawson really was innocent — of murder, at least.

* * *

"How's she doing?" Tom asked Catalina, who opened the door at his knock. He handed her his cloak and crossed to the well-draped bedstead. Trumpet lay in the center of the bed supported by a wall of pillows, her arms and legs splayed on either side of her mountainous midsection. She really did look like some great fish clad in an embroidered chemise and a velvet wrapper, beached in the center of a silken expanse.

Tom knew better than to say that out loud, but she read his face. She always could. "I've grown past whale. I'm turning into a hippopottlemus. Remember that beast in Mr. Bacon's *animalium?*"

The juncture of images shook a laugh out of Tom that wouldn't stop. He bent down to remove his shoes and the laugh abated, but then he looked at her and it started up again. He took a deep breath and kissed her on the forehead. "I'm sorry, sweetling, but it's funny."

She tilted up her chin as if offended, but her eyes sparkled with merriment.

He kissed her belly. "When's my baby coming out to meet its papa?"

"Never. He's too comfortable in there."

Catalina returned to her usual post on the padded bench before the window. "Very soon, we think, Mr. Tom. The baby has dropped."

"Is that good?" It didn't sound good.

"Very good, Mr. Tom. It means he is ready to come out."

Trumpet leveled a weary gaze at him. "I have to piss every ten minutes, and I'm waddling like a duck."

"A hippopottle-duck." Tom grinned but made no dent in the weary look. "All right, I'll stop. You look well, sweetling — pink cheeks, bright eyes. And you're strong enough to be mad at me without just cause."

"She is healthy," Catalina assured him. "The baby is healthy. He kick day and night. We are ready."

"It doesn't matter anyway," Trumpet said. "I've lost the bet."

It took Tom a blink to catch up. "Bess had her baby?"

"Yesterday. A boy. They're both fine."

"Thanks be to God!" Tom cried. "Trust Sir Walter to arrange matters so that his first child is born on Easter Sunday."

"I should've guessed it," Trumpet said, "and saved myself two pounds. Guess what they're going to name him?"

"Walter?"

"No, goose! That's far too simple. They're christening the poor mite Damerei."

"Damn her eye? What kind of a name is that?"

Trumpet shrugged. "Some Plantagenet something-or-other. It's Ralegh's way of reaching for a royal ancestor. Arrant nonsense, if you ask me."

Tom bit back a smile at the unwitting snobbery of a woman possessed of not one, but two of the oldest titles in England. If he could reach a Plantagenet in his family tree, he'd leap for it too.

He took up his position, leaning against a bedpost, and raised Trumpet's left foot, slipping off the thin wool stocking. Once upon a time, this would've led to love play, but there was nothing alluring about his beloved hippopottlemus. The hoyden she'd been was in there still — he could see her in the twitch of the cupid lips and and the sparkle in the emerald eyes. That Trumpet would be back soon enough, if tempered by motherhood, and they could play their old games again. Both the ones in bed and the ones out there in the city.

She closed her eyes with a luxurious moan as he kneaded her swollen foot, stroking the high arch with his strong thumb. He worked in silence, savoring every second — the touch of her skin, the sound of her breath, even the light *snick-snick* of Catalina's needlework. He shifted to the right foot, thinking about that day — not too far off — when she'd be able to get out and about again. She'd want to be part of this Ridley business, if she could.

And she'd be furious if he didn't tell her about it. "We have a new case."

The green eyes popped open. "What, murder? Who? Where? How?"

This was why he loved her, or one of the reasons. What other woman would respond so keenly to such a topic? "Who, is a man named Raffe Ridley. Where, is not far from Gray's, up at the juncture of Theobalds. When, was Friday night, or rather early Saturday morning."

"Friday! Why did you take so long to tell me?" She tried to leverage herself up to a more vertical position but failed, sinking back into her pillows with a grunt. Catalina brought another big pillow over to stuff behind her back so she could see Tom's face as they talked.

"Saturday was full of benchers and coroner's men running hither and yon, half of them wanting to hear my story again for themselves. And yesterday was Easter Sunday, as you may recall. I went to church. Besides, this one's ticklish, worse than usual."

He told her everything, from Francis knocking at his window to the body in the wet grass a few feet from Anthony's abandoned coach. He told her about the handkerchief, which pointed at Thomas Lawson, and the belt, which the murderer might have expected to do the same. Trumpet gave him her rapt attention, oohing and aahing in all the right places. He made a bit of a drama out

116

of going back out into the moonlit night to rediscover the body.

"God's teeth!" she swore. "I wish I could've been there. My first question is, why strangle him instead of stabbing him with your knife? It'd be faster, and you wouldn't have to get around behind him."

Tom ran that through in his mind. Everyone carried a knife, for eating as well as a dozen handy uses. Usually you kept it in a short scabbard at your side or in the small of your back. Some people, himself included, carried a knife that could serve as a weapon if the need arose.

"No." He shook his head. "Stabbing's messy. You'd get blood on your hands and your clothes. More things to explain later. Strangling is trickier, as you so astutely point out, but you can walk away from it without so much as a smudge."

"That makes sense. Have you found the coachman yet?"

"He isn't missing." Tom told her about the second coachman and his putative connection to Sir Robert Cecil.

"Pish, tush! Of course, he'd deny it. Sir Robert would deny the sky was blue if it served his purpose. Although he's more likely to offer a bribe to the regular driver than send in a second one. Less fuss, and you'd never hear about it."

"That's true." Tom grinned at her, giving her the full dimple. "Not even Mr. Bacon thought of that." He appreciated her insights. She'd seen more of Sir Robert than Francis, even, having been a gentlewoman of the Privy Chamber before marrying Stephen.

"You can't imagine Anthony did this," Trumpet said. "I thought he was too frail to walk."

"He can walk a little, but no, we don't think he strangled Ridley with his own two hands. We think Lawson did it, either at Anthony's request or on his own initiative, for his own reasons. Except now I'm not so sure."

He told her about the conversation in the coach on the way home from Wapping. "The upshot is that now I think he could be innocent. Which means I have to start from scratch."

Trumpet studied his face. "You don't like him. Lawson."

Tom waggled one hand from side to side. "He's handsome, sociable, and tells a good tale. He seems like a decent fellow at first blush. But something about his manner always makes me think he's lying or telling half-truths for some ulterior purpose. My gut doesn't trust him."

"Oh, well then." Trumpet had always considered Tom's gut as reliable as the Delphic Oracle.

"On the other hand, it's telling me to keep looking. Lawson's as slippery as an eel, but I didn't get a whiff of violence from him. And I provoked him. I was fishing and caught more than I expected." Tom told her about the ten months in Newgate at Lady Bacon's behest.

Trumpet's pretty face twisted in disgust. "Ten months in prison, ugh! I don't blame him for being unhelpful. That's enough time to build up a very sturdy grudge, but why take it out on Ridley? Lady Bacon's the one who did him the injury."

"He can't get to her," Tom said. "Or Lord Burghley, if he even dreamed of trying. They're both as safe as pontiffs, tucked up in their private palaces with three dozen servants between them and the door."

"He did start that brawl in the Antelope," she pointed out. "That shows some taste for violence."

"True." Tom thought back to that evening. "He'd been drinking fairly steadily. And Ridley practically slapped him in the face to make him throw a punch. I'm not a violent man, but it would've raised my ire."

"I would've pounded him into dust, except you would've stopped me."

118

Tom chuckled. She had a combative streak, all right —
all five feet of her. If she were a large man, she'd be
dangerous. Then again, if she were a large man, she
would've learned to hold herself back.

"Who else are you looking at?" she asked.

Tom shook his head. "Nobody. Lawson's all I've got
so far, but he'd have to be a skit-brained idiot to stuff his
own handkerchief in the victim's mouth. Now that I've laid
it out for you, the whole thing looks false to me. It's too
convenient. Anthony's coach, recognizable from half a
mile off. His secretary's handkerchief in the victim's mouth
and his brother's belt around the neck. Someone
deliberately staged that scene to implicate Anthony
Bacon."

Trumpet hummed her disagreement, shaking her
head. "I wouldn't give up on Lawson so easily. Your gut
doesn't like him, which makes him worth a long, hard look.
All that stupidity could be accounted for by simple panic.
Think about it. Here's two men, enemies, in a small place.
They're arguing. Lawson can't make Ridley see things his
way. Maybe Ridley scoffs at him, maybe he laughs with his
fat mouth open, like this." Trumpet tilted her head back in
an adorable attempt to imitate a fat man emitting a scoffing
laugh.

"Oh yes. I can picture it," Tom said, grinning.

She ignored that. "It's the last straw for Lawson. 'I'll
shut your cursed mouth,' he says, and pulls his
handkerchief out of his sleeve. He stuffs it into Ridley's
mocking mouth. 'Ha!' he says, but Ridley's still scoffing,
even under the handkerchief. So Lawson says, 'Stop that
gabbling, you clamorous, flap-mouthed clodpole, or I'll
shut you up for good!' He grabs the next thing he lays his
hands on, which happens to be Mr. Bacon's belt, and wraps
it around the varlet's neck, pulling it tight until the man
stops squawking. Next thing he knows, there's a dead man
lying limp in his arms. He panics. He flings open the door

and shoves the body out with his feet. Then he jumps out and runs away without a backward glance."

Tom could see it as clearly as if he'd been there. "That all makes sense, more or less. Except the strangler dragged the body into the weeds. There might've been a scuffle outside. It was hard to read the marks in the moonlight. Also, what happened to the driver in your version?"

"He ran off when the shouting started, like a big coward, not wanting to be a party to whatever happened next."

"Not much of a spy, then. You'd think Sir Robert would want to hear about the shouting most of all." Tom scratched his beard, working through her version in his mind. Then he nodded. "It's good, my lady. Plausible."

She preened herself with the little wriggle and the catlike smile that made Tom's heart turn handsprings. "What does Mr. Bacon think?" she asked. "Francis, I mean."

"He thinks Anthony did it, or told Lawson to. It's tying him in knots. He gave serious thought to walking away and letting some farmer find the body after I removed the evidence and took the coach back."

"That's not like him."

"This one's different," Tom said. "I warned you. While we were standing out there considering our options, he asked me what I would do if it were your coach and your enemy lying in the grass."

"What'd you say?" Trumpet's eyes shone. She knew the answer.

"I said I'd bury the body deep in the woods along with anyone who asked too many questions and take the secret to my grave."

Trumpet nodded. "I'd do the same for you." She laid her hands on her huge belly and met Tom's eyes. "But let's not require such favors from one another for a few more weeks, I beg you."

120

NINE

Trumpet turned sideways, smoothing the cascade of pleats running down over her belly, contemplating her profile with a critical eye. "This baby is half as big as I am."

"It will be baby size, my lady. You will see." Catalina sat in her favorite seat by the window, mending something. She could sew, look outside, and watch her mistress all at once. But then, being the personal servant of one lady must be far less demanding than being an actress-cum-garb-maker for a traveling troupe of actors.

Trumpet knew she appreciated the security and comfort of her life now, but she wondered if Catalina ever missed the adventures. Trumpet missed them, all the small ones she'd had thus far. When she became a Lady of Consequence, she intended to do more than write letters and receive nitwits seeking favors.

"You know," she said, turning to view the other side, "this dress will still be useful when I return to normal size." She attempted to span the girth with both hands and failed. "I could smuggle a whole barrel of gunpowder under here."

"A small one, perhaps." Catalina put down her mending to give the idea her full attention. "I could sew a leather covering with straps that go around your back. Then the front would be smooth, like a belly."

Trumpet pointed a finger at her. "Brilliant! It would keep things from falling out too."

"But a barrel would not be comfortable, my lady. The edge is very hard."

"True." Trumpet considered her strength and carrying capacity. "I could fill it with scrolls. I could carry a whole embassy's worth of secret documents. No one would question a pregnant lady. People barely looked at me when we were traveling here from Dorset."

"Women would look."

"But your leather sack would fool them. They wouldn't look *under*. How rude! And the sleeves could be richly embellished to distract them." Trumpet nodded at her reflection. It was a good stratagem. They just needed a reason to deploy it.

Stephen could easily be persuaded to take a turn in an embassy somewhere. Some German-speaking country would be best. Trumpet had never set foot outside of England. She'd never been on a ship, even though her father spent most of his days sailing the wide sea in search of Spanish plunder. She spoke French well enough. She could learn German too. She could learn Italian or Danish if she put her mind to it.

Perhaps she could find a reason for them to conduct a tour of the embassies in the German-speaking countries. Though she couldn't steal documents everywhere they went; someone would catch on. Well, she still had a few knots to untangle.

The largest of which was Tom. She couldn't leave him for any length of time again, not ever. Those six months in exile at Delabere House in Dorset had been enough. She'd done her duty by the estate and the dowager countess, learning the names and roles of everyone in the household. The countryside was beautiful, she had to admit, the rolling hills dotted with dense woods and striped with swift rivers. The house was well tended and supplied with every comfort.

But it wasn't London. Trumpet had grown up on the windy coast of Suffolk in a castle slowly crumbling into ruins. She'd had enough of the pastoral to last her a lifetime. She wanted to dress up like young gents and prowl the city with Catalina, slurping oysters from the shell, trading curses with blue-liveried apprentices, and paying a penny to join the groundlings at the theater. Or hang out her bedroom window to watch boats on the river or people bustling past on some grand street like Bishopsgate.

She loved London and would cling to the bedpost howling at the top of her lungs if they ever tried to drag her back to Dorset. Vienna, on the other hand, or Antwerp . . .

She'd just have to persuade Tom to come with them. If he were one of Stephen's retainers, it would be easy. He would naturally travel with his master. Stephen had offered him a position more than once, with generous terms. But Tom wanted to "stay the course," as he kept saying.

His stubborn streak grew stronger as he got older. But then, she wouldn't love him so much if he weren't so steadfastly his own man.

She gave one more look at her enormous belly. "Please tell me I'm not going to get any bigger. I won't be able to stand up."

"I think your baby is ready, my lady. My heart tells me so."

"Your heart, or the bet you have with Elsa Moreau?"

Catalina rolled her eyes upward in a comically pious expression.

"How much?" Trumpet demanded. "And what day did you pick?"

"One shilling. I say one week. She say three days."

"I hope she wins. If she does, I'll pay that shilling myself in sheer gratitude."

They collected themselves and made their slow way through the adjoining room to join Penelope for a stroll in the gallery. Elsa Moreau and Catalina paced several feet behind them, engaged in their own quiet conversation.

"Did you go to court yesterday?" Trumpet asked Penelope.

"I did. I saw Mr. Bacon — Francis, not Anthony. He seems more unhappy than usual."

"Tom doesn't think Anthony will be well enough to go out for some time. That must be worrisome for everyone in the house."

"It's a pity," Penelope said, tucking Trumpet's hand under her elbow. "I long to meet him. But he can't come here, and I can't go there, thanks to Gray's Inn's absurd rules about women."

"They are a nuisance. Did you put in a good word for La Plashy?"

"I most certainly did not!" Penelope's dark eyes flashed with anger. "Not after what she did to you. Catalina told Elsa, who told me, and rightly so. She offended us both with that wicked lie. No woman has ever spent three tortured days in labor, my dear Alice. Not one."

Trumpet's heart swelled with an uprush of affection. She'd never had a female friend before, not of her own rank. She'd never had any friends, really, until she met Tom. Having this powerful, intelligent, courageous woman on her side, even in so small a matter as scorning the same obnoxious person, made her feel not only protected, but also somehow larger.

"Thank you," she said. "It still upsets me, even though I know she said it only to frighten me. She wanted revenge for our scoffing at her great secrets about Anthony. She didn't dare to come after you, so she struck at me."

"I *loathe* bullies," Penelope said with heat. "Some might think I'm one at times —"

"Never," Trumpet said, smiling. "You only contend with people of your own station."

"I am often haughty." Penelope smiled like a naughty child. "Especially when I dislike a person. I can be peremptory to the point of rudeness, or so my mother says. I can be devious, perhaps even underhanded, in pursuit of my brother's advancement. I will use any tool within my grasp to further the rise of the Devereaux family."

"Of course you will. That is the role of a woman of influence."

"Quite so. But I can honestly say that I am *never* cruel, especially not to those in a weaker position." She cocked her head at Trumpet. "What about you, Alice? You have a few secrets up your sleeve, I'll wager. You're witty and well-read, I have learned, yet you play the ninny so convincingly at court."

"Why, thank you, my lady." Trumpet bobbed a brief curtsy. "I might have played a trick or two in my time." She placed a finger on her cheek as if trying to remember, stalling while she decided what story to tell. Penelope already knew that Tom was her lover. She might have guessed he was the father of her child, but she couldn't be certain of it. She'd proven her friendship though, and she had her own secrets. She knew full well how to keep them.

Besides, Trumpet dearly wanted to show this important person that she had talents beyond the bearing of children.

"Well," she drawled, "I tell the truth — when it suits me. But my real talent lies in long-running deceptions." She paused for effect, then dropped her cannon ball. "For example, when I was sixteen, I disguised myself as a boy and spent three terms living at Gray's Inn, studying the law."

"You *didn't!*" Penelope stopped in her tracks, pressing one hand to her chest and groping for the wall with the other. She regarded Trumpet with sheer amazement emblazoned on her lovely face. "Lady Dorchester, you astonish me! A difficult feat, I might add."

Trumpet grinned at the effect of her revelation. "That's how I met Tom, as a matter of fact."

"Oh, did you?" Penelope laughed. "That explains your special friendship. Few men would come every evening to rub the feet of a woman carrying their rival's babe."

"Tom's not like other men. But yes, we were friends before we became lovers. And Stephen had his own paramour at Richmond last summer. When I found out, it made me jealous. I turned to Tom." She placed a hand on the belly. "The babe may not be his, but my heart is."

"I know how that goes." Penelope hummed three descending notes. "Someday, Alice, you must tell me *everything* about your three terms in that masculine preserve. I suppose that's where you became friends with Francis Bacon. And here I thought Sir Walter Ralegh was the greatest dissembler of my acquaintance."

"Pish, tush!" Trumpet flapped her hand. "All he does is withhold a few particulars of his private life." Then she spluttered a giggle. "Can you imagine Sir Walter in a court gown? All six feet two inches of him?"

"Oh no, you naughty minx! Now you've made me see it." Penelope giggled too, her eyes squinching closed. They clutched one another, laughing helplessly, until a twinge in her belly made Trumpet gasp.

"I think I need to sit down."

Penelope nodded and beckoned to the maidservants. She watched as Catalina reached a strong arm under her mistress's shoulders and guided her to the nearest bench. She stood before her guest with the gleam of fresh appraisal in her black eyes. "Do take good care of yourself, Alice. I suspect we'll find many interesting uses for your talents down the road."

* * *

Trumpet awoke from her midmorning nap thinking, *Somewhere down the road?* She didn't have to wait that long. Women of Influence most commonly worked their wiles by writing letters. Lady Russell advised the Privy Council from her bed; Trumpet could do the same. Not the council, she barely knew those old men. Nor had she anything to say to them — yet. But she could help Tom and Mr. Bacon with the Ridley matter. In fact, she might well work it out before they did.

And wouldn't *that* be a feather in her cap!

"Do we have paper and ink?" she asked Catalina, squirming toward the edge of the bed. "Help me to the desk. I'm going to write some letters."

The most important questions, as she saw it, concerned Raffe Ridley and his actions in France. She also wanted to know why Madame du Plessis-Mornay was spreading gossip about Anthony Bacon. As she smoothed a sheet of linen paper on the leather writing pad, it occurred to her that two people spreading the same two rumors were probably connected. Good old Occam and his ever-handy razor demanded it.

She should learn whatever she could about Ridley. If she could dig up something sordid about the du Plessis cow, so much the better. She knew four people with some knowledge of France, but Lady Russell disapproved of idle gossip. She'd leave her out for now.

First on the list was Aunt Blanche. Her late husband, Lord Chadwick, had amassed a fortune from the iron on his vast lands in Staffordshire. Since he and his wife both enjoyed traveling, he offered his services to Her Majesty as an emissary. They'd lived in Geneva, Venice, Prague, and Paris, venturing as far afield as Constantinople. Blanche's two daughters had married German noblemen. One was the Margrave of Grabowsee or some such place.

Aunt Blanche lived in a big house on Bishopsgate, a mere mile or two away, but she might be visiting relations in Devonshire. Trumpet asked her if she'd ever met or heard of Ridley or the du Plessis-Mornays, and if so, to please tell her everything. She explained that she'd just met the latter and couldn't decide what to think of her. She added a note about her health, sealed the letter, and placed it to one side.

She addressed the next letter to her uncle Nathaniel Welbeck, a barrister and resident of Gray's Inn. He wasn't presently in residence since courts were adjourned, but she had the use of the Essex messengers. It might reach him before Tom and Mr. Bacon worked it all out.

Uncle Nat dabbled in smuggling when not devising clever ways for widows to protect their wealth. He sometimes sailed with the goods himself, especially along the coast of France, and he specialized in items of interest to Catholics. He would know Raffe Ridley, if the man had been a decent emissary.

She was his favorite niece. In fact, he had provided crucial support for her year at Gray's, introducing her as his nephew and letting her live in his chambers. She asked if he knew anything untoward about a Huguenot named du Plessis-Mornay. She also asked him what Raffe Ridley might have against Anthony Bacon. For all she knew, Ridley and her uncle had spent many an evening drinking in some tavern in St. Jean de Luz. If Uncle Nat liked Ridley, he wouldn't tell her anything, but it couldn't hurt to ask.

She added the note about her health and signed the letter. On second thought, she scribbled out a copy to send to Gray's in case he came back early. Signed, sealed, and added to the stack. If he was at Gray's, she'd have an answer tomorrow. If not, it could be weeks.

The last letter was to her newest resource: her husband, Stephen. Here, she could express her wishes with perfect candor. They'd become friends during their months of isolation in Dorset. He'd meekly accepted her ban on conjugal relations during her pregnancy, which simplified things considerably. They got in the habit of spending the last hours of each day together in the small parlor between their bedchambers. Each would report on his or her activities, learning their respective roles on the estate. They discussed the servants, the neighbors, and the many visitors who came to meet the new countess, assessing their clothes and manners in exquisite detail. They shared many opinions, as it turned out. They liked many of the same things, like marzipan, the music of flutes, and strong color pairings.

Stephen had changed since that term at Gray's so many years ago. His year in the German states had seasoned him, and the removal of his late father's heavy hand had allowed him to grow up. Trumpet discovered, to her surprise, that she liked him. She would never admit that to Tom, but there it was.

She told him about the baby and her health and begged him to assure Lord Essex that his sister provided her with every comfort. She told him about the wagers and told him to bet His Lordship ten pounds that the ninth earl would be born either Sunday or Monday of next week. "Our child will certainly be fair of face, so I recommend the Monday."

Then she moved on to the main thrust. She told him about Ridley's death, saying merely that his body had been found in a field. She urged him to find out everything he could about the man. What did he do? Who were his friends? He died holding some kind of grudge against Anthony Bacon that no one here could fathom. Find out why.

"Most importantly," she wrote, "my dearest husband, I want you to uncover every scrap of ill fame and scurrilous gossip about a personage named Madame du Plessis-Mornay. Her vanity <u>knows no bounds.</u> There *will* be something. Gossip about her husband, who affects to be a friend of King Henry, will serve as well. That vicious harpy injured me! Only verbally — I am well — but it still hurt.

<u>Our honor is at stake!</u> I intend to crush her into powder, by means of humiliation. I'm counting on you to send me the munitions I require."

She signed it, "From your loving wife," and sealed it with the new ring he'd given her for New Year's Day. She handed it to Catalina, bidding her to carry it straight down to the steward. Another advantage of living at the center of things: letters were delivered to and from France every day. When she and Stephen had their own establishment, they would keep a stable of fifty horses, with messengers ready to ride at the wave of her hand.

TEN

Francis tapped on his brother's door, opening it when invited. He found Anthony sitting up in his armchair with a writing table set before him.

"Good morning, Frank." He seemed in good spirits.

"You're looking well today."

"I feel well, thank you. And it promises to be a warmish day, which always helps."

Francis nodded. "I wonder if you might feel up to going to court with me, just for a brief visit."

"Mercy, no!" Anthony gawped at him as if he'd suggested they go hunting for wild boar. "I'm feeling better, but that doesn't mean I'm ready to go bounding up and down those stairs."

"I suppose not." Francis sighed. "We could take the coach. You could sit outside. People could come visit you, for a moment or two."

"Sit outside Whitehall in a coach, like some lofty potentate? I think not!" Anthony's expression softened. "I know you're eager for me to be restored to the active brother you remember. I long for that as well. But it will take time, Frank. You must try to be patient."

"I am trying." Francis closed the door. He hadn't really expected a different response. But he couldn't let it go altogether, to be buried under press of work. Anthony must get up one of these days and go pay his respects to the queen — and take Francis's place at court, at least some of the time. They could divide the week between them; that would be fair.

He stopped at Tom's room next, knowing he'd be up and dressed, already hard at work copying out some will or bill of sale. Five years ago, if Francis had found him at his desk with an inky quill in his hand, he would have sent at once for a physician.

Tom greeted him, inviting him to come in and sit on the bed. Francis declined, preferring to stand by the window.

"What can I do for you, Mr. Bacon?"

"I'm on my way to court. How did things go with Lawson yesterday?"

"Ah yes." Tom stuck his quill in the inkpot, tilted his backed stool against the wall, and stretched his long legs under the small desk.

He proceeded to give a nearly verbatim report of the conversation, inserting his impressions of his target's truthfulness where appropriate. His memory had improved mightily over the past few years. Francis would like to give himself credit, but he knew the greater taskmaster was his aunt, Tom's guardian, Lady Russell. Nor should Tom's own desire to attain mastery of the law be underestimated.

Francis listened in silence, reflecting on how much Tom had grown up since they first met. He'd lost the glowing beauty of youth, replaced by a firm-jawed, mature comeliness that would endure for most of his life. Vestiges of the impudent lad still lingered in his ready smile, but his eyes had acquired a somber shadow when his father died.

"I suspected him at first," Tom said at the end of the recitation. "I'm still half convinced he did it — but only half. He was truly surprised about that handkerchief, or I've lost all ability to read men's faces."

Francis nodded, hope rising. If Lawson were innocent, so was Anthony. "What about the second coachman?"

132

"He claims not to have noticed, which brings me back around to thinking he did it. I don't see how it's possible. You'd feel the weight shifting, for one thing, as the new man climbed on and Widhope climbed off. You know how those carriages jiggle about."

"That's true," Francis said, hope sinking again. "I wish I could believe Widhope was lying."

"Impossible. He doesn't have the imagination." Tom wagged a finger at nothing. "I did prompt him to give a thought to his loyalties. He should be bearing fewer tales to your lady mother in future."

Francis's eyebrows rose. "So *that's* who told her about Henry."

"You're welcome," Tom said with the old cheeky grin. "Did you ask Sir Robert about the second coachman?"

"We did. He says it's arrant nonsense, but he would regardless. I suppose we must believe in the man's existence, but I don't know how you'll find him."

"I could find out where the stablemen from Burghley House do their drinking," Tom said. "Go have a few beers, see if I can turn over a few stones."

"I doubt that will work, though I have nothing better to suggest. My lord uncle's servants would never tell tales out of school." Francis sighed. "I fear we are at an impasse."

"Not quite. We have one very good candidate: Thomas Lawson."

"What about the handkerchief? You said he was genuinely surprised."

"I did," Tom said. "On the other hand, he could've forgotten about it, having pulled it out and stuffed it in Ridley's mouth in the heat of anger."

Francis frowned. That didn't seem possible, but he had no experience of violence on which to base his judgment. Tom, on the other hand, had a most active imagination! That was one of the things that made him so useful.

Tom let his stool down with a light thump and set his folded hands on the table, plainly preparing to say something Francis wouldn't like. "Here's the thing, Mr. Bacon. The most plausible explanation is that Lawson invited Ridley out for a drive with the intention of murdering him, with or without your brother's explicit or implicit instruction. Whoever the second coachman was, he must have run off when things got rough. But Lawson did it, whether he remembers the details now or not."

Francis turned his gaze toward the window, seeing nothing. "I refuse to believe that."

Tom let a moment go by in silence, then said, "That's not the same as saying, 'I'm convinced he did no such thing.' Which is what you'd say if you were, so you're not. Not completely."

Francis gave him a sour look. On that note, he went out to spend another fruitless morning bearing the Bacon standard at court.

* * *

Francis barely had time to navigate to his favorite spot in the Presence Chamber before Sir Walter strolled over to speak with him. Not, for a mercy, about his reckless secret marriage, but to request a service. "Her Majesty would be grateful if you would take Monsieur du Pin on a tour of the Privy Garden."

"Now? Is she expelling me from the Presence Chamber?"

"Not you. Him." Sir Walter tilted his head toward the entrance, where Francis belatedly noticed the Frenchman pretending not to mind that everyone was ignoring him. "She can't listen to another word of his relentless pleading, but she can't just toss him out on his ear either."

"I suppose not," Francis said. "He is still a friend of King Henry, as far as we know."

134

"And his family are wine merchants of considerable standing." Sir Walter flashed the smile that had won a queen's heart. "They've supplied the royal cellars for centuries. Her Majesty likes their New Year's gifts."

"I understand." Francis heaved a sigh. "I exist but to serve."

"As do we all, Mr. Bacon. As do we all."

Francis walked over and greeted Monsieur du Pin, gesturing toward the blue sky outside the window. But as they walked together down the wide staircase, he couldn't help thinking that this service was in some degree a form of penance. Her Majesty couldn't openly complain about an invalid failing to visit her, but it galled her nonetheless. So she punished the only Bacon available — him.

On the other hand, it truly was a lovely morning — cool enough to make him glad for his cloak, but warm enough to wear it open. A light breeze tossed the branches of the pear and damask plum trees, whose white blossoms were reflected in the puffy clouds that kept the sun from burning too brightly.

It also occurred to him that he might be able to learn something about Ridley and his conflict with Anthony.

They took the first path leading around the outer edge. Francis liked to start at the boundary and work his way toward the fountain at the center. Their pace was leisurely since there was no need for haste. They paused at the first of the heraldic statues that stood upon painted pillars placed throughout the garden.

"What manner of beast is this fine fellow?" du Pin asked, studying it with his hands behind his back.

"This is a gryphon. You see he has the body of a lion and the head of an eagle." Francis pointed from the curling tail to the sharp beak. "He is the emblem of Edward the Third, who was king of England some two hundred years ago."

"He is magnificent." Du Pin smiled. "Your queen is well defended."

Francis heard a barb in that comment — that she was defended from unwanted visitors by unimportant courtiers like himself. The weather was pleasant, but in other ways this had not been the best of mornings.

Nevertheless, he knew his duty. "I understand you are originally from Bordeaux, Monsieur du Pin. My brother says that is a region of great beauty as well as excellent wine."

"Ah, but they go together, those two, do they not? The grapes must have the best soil, you see, and a sufficiency of sunshine with *precisely* the right amount of rain." He held up finger and thumb as if measuring. "Too much, and all is inundation; too little, and the fruit dries on the vine. Then you have raisins, not grapes."

"I like raisins."

"*Eh, bien.*" Du Pin chuckled. "But you like wine better, *n'est pas?*"

The path curved gently to the left, taking them parallel to the river. Francis turned the conversation in a different direction as well. "You must have known our emissary in Bordeaux, Raffe Ridley."

"*Mais oui.* How not? There are not so very many Englishmen in the south of France."

Francis stopped to face him. "Perhaps you have heard that Mr. Ridley met with a tragic end last week, not far from where I live."

"I have heard this sad news. It is *très tragique*, as you say. He was a young man, much too young. But that is what led to his death, I hear." Du Pin gave his head a world-weary shake. "An older man such as myself would have gone earlier to bed. They say Mr. Ridley left a tavern late at night and was set upon by, ah, *voleurs.*"

"Thieves, yes." Francis was glad to hear that story repeated. They'd pushed it as hard as they dared to the

136

authorities to prevent any serious pursuit of the murderer. Obstructing the course of justice was a bitter pill, but one he was forced to swallow to protect his brother.

"I fear some of our streets can be quite dangerous," he continued. "We are all very sad. My brother and Mr. Ridley were good friends."

"Oh, do you think so?" Du Pin shot him a wry look.

"Weren't they?"

Du Pin made a little frown, accompanied by a little shrug. "After the manner of countrymen living in a foreign land. But there was always the competition, was there not?"

"Anthony never mentioned any competition."

"*Mais non*, why should he? He was always the winner." Du Pin gave him a shrewd look, tapping his temple with one beringed finger. "He is a clever man, your Lord Burghley. He sends this Ridley to play the official role of emissary. *Eh, oui*, he has good hair and good legs. He is well-spoken. He is able to go up and down the coast speaking with merchants to show that the English have their eyes open. But Ridley, he does not always understand what he sees. For that, your clever Lord Burghley has his clever nephew Anthony, sitting in his house in sleepy little Montaubon, writing his many letters."

Francis frowned, taken aback by this speech. It made him feel the fool, for one thing. It never occurred to him that his uncle might have chosen Ridley as a foil for Anthony. It probably had occurred to Anthony, but he'd never shared it with Francis. Did he consider his younger brother too innocent for such a ruse?

Du Pin smiled impishly, wagging his finger at Francis. "We French are not so easily deceived, Monsieur Bacon! We know which is the real intelligencer. The Spanish, they know it too. Do not underestimate them."

"No, never." What did the Spanish have to do with it? They were the subject of most intelligence-seeking, of course, but why bring them into this particular case?

Francis covered his awkward silence by reaching for a branch of a plum tree that fortune had placed ready to hand. He inhaled the rich perfume as if savoring a favorite treat, which it was. Then he remarked, "After the summer of '88, England will never underestimate the Spanish again."

Du Pin availed himself of the fragrant branch in turn, making a show of sampling the scent like a man with an expert nose. Then he nodded at Francis, and they resumed their slow circuit. "Ah yes," he said, "that was a summer of *terreur* for you English. For us, it was a summer of suspense. All of us along the coast asked ourselves, 'How many ships are coming? One hundred? Two hundred? None at all?'"

"No one really knew until they were sighted off the coast of Cornwall."

"Even then, we did not know where they would go. England? The Low Countries? Or some port in France?" He shook his head. "Much fear, much doubt. Much confusion. We did whatever we could to keep our little ships afloat, as in your so lively English expression."

Francis nodded. "Was your family able to continue to trade their wines? That must have been difficult with a mighty fleet obstructing the Bay of Biscay."

Du Pin produced one of those Gallic shrugs that conveyed a whole conversation. "What could one do? All was *tres perturbé*, Monsieur." He broke into a smile of pleasure, pointing ahead a few yards. "But what is that yellow flower? He is all alone among these white trees."

"That's a daffodil," Francis answered, not fooled by the Frenchman's sudden enthusiasm. They'd passed a large patch of the same flowers minutes ago. But he accepted the change of subject, stopping now to explain the white greyhound of Richmond perched on a red-and-white-striped pillar. Then he turned his guest to watch a small ship whose white sails glistened in the sun as it clove the silvery waters of the Thames.

He needed scarcely half his mind to conduct a tour of this familiar garden. With the other half, he wondered what the du Pins had done to keep their little ships afloat in that season of doubt. Something related to Anthony's intelligencing, perhaps? Or some compromise with the Spanish?

ELEVEN

Tom had been mulling over the question of Lawson's guilt or innocence all morning. Today's copy-work was a packet of testimonials taken down by a lawyer with a neat hand. The content was routine, so he only needed half his wits to direct his quill. The rest went to the Ridley matter.

He would've sworn Lawson had been genuinely surprised by the handkerchief. Now Trumpet had made him doubt that again.

Tom couldn't get the knack of the man. He had a changeable humor, like wind in the doldrums; sometimes blowing hard, other times as quiet as a held breath. He worked hard translating and copying Anthony's letters, sitting for long hours at his desk without complaint. Then he might spend weeks riding across Europe to deliver especially sensitive letters. A messenger had to be content with his own company for long stretches. But it also helped to make friends along the way for safety. That demanded a degree of sociability. Lawson had nice manners — when he chose to use them — but he favored a sardonic pose that felt like a challenge.

His loyalty to Anthony seemed to be the only constant thing about him.

Tom set his quill aside and tried to imagine being so furious he could stuff a handkerchief in a man's mouth and not remember it. He thought back to the night he and Trumpet had broken the bed in his little room above the kennels at Richmond Palace. They'd somehow snapped a rope under the thin mattress, spilling them into the straw on the floor. They hadn't noticed a thing until their passion was spent. Then they'd looked around, wondering what had happened. But that passion had been mutual.

He closed his eyes and summoned up the blind rage that had overtaken him once or twice after his father died. He'd maintained a stoic facade in front of other people, but alone in his room at night, he'd given in to grief and anger. He could remember wringing the sheets and hurling curses at the ceiling. He could've wrung someone's neck then, given the chance and someone to blame. And he might've reached for something to stuff in the man's mouth to keep his shouts from rousing the house.

Passion left you feeling dazed, disoriented. You might forget a small thing like a handkerchief in those first few minutes. But Ridley had been dragged into the weeds. That showed caution, not passion. Wouldn't you remember the handkerchief then? And if you were Lawson, wouldn't you take it with you?

Tom dipped his quill and began to write. He needed to talk to someone who knew Lawson well enough to say yea or nay. Anthony could, but wouldn't. He was the master of the art of revealing nothing while seeming all candor and cooperation.

One other person in London had known Lawson back in France: Elsa Moreau. She just happened to live in the house he'd be visiting that evening. Maybe she could shed some light on Ridley's grudge too. Tom scribbled a note to Trumpet, asking her to arrange a meeting. He got up and shouted for Pinnock, promising him another half-hour lute lesson if he would deliver the letter straightaway. And then he went back to work.

* * *

Lady Rich shimmered out of the doorway leading to the gallery as Tom came up the stairs at Essex House. "Good evening, Mr. Clarady."

Tom bowed, head-to-knee. "My lady. How may I serve you?"

"I wondered if you had given any more thought to my lord brother's offer to join his retinue."

"Oh! Ah . . ." Tom kept wishing everyone would forget about that. Fortunately, the earl had not made the offer personally. He doubted he could refuse him, though he'd refused Sir Walter Ralegh. And Ralegh had known his father, which counted in his favor. But Essex was a legend already. No one could withstand his charm.

Trumpet wanted him to enter Stephen's service. Tom told her he would do that on his way down to hell, and not before. She considered Essex his next best option, even though it would mean fighting in France — actual fighting with swords against men who meant to kill him. She said that fighting alongside the Earl of Essex was the shortest path to a knighthood. She said he could practice the law later — assuming he survived — and that being Sir Thomas Clarady would shorten the path to a judgeship as well.

She made a strong case; she always did. But both Francis Bacon and Lady Russell thought he should stay at Gray's, especially now he was a scant two years from passing the bar. And Tom could feel his father's hand on his shoulder and that warm voice in his mind's ear telling him to remain his own man.

"I, ah . . ." He looked at his feet, then found his courage — and his courtesy — and met the lady's famously beautiful eyes. "Alas, my lady. My guardian, Lady Russell, won't allow it. She means for me to pass the bar. Which is what my father wanted as well."

She gave him a dry look, making him feel like a stubborn child. "Let's hope you don't come to regret that decision." She gave him time to bow again, then left the way she'd come.

Tom went the other way. He passed through the anteroom and rapped on Trumpet's door, opening it when invited. He found his beloved ensconced in her nest of coverlets and pillows. She gave him the daily report on her condition, looking bright-eyed and sounding cheerful. For her sake, he hoped the humor would last.

Normally he would kiss her and settle at her feet, but today Elsa Moreau intruded on their intimate gathering. At his request, but still he could wish they'd arranged to send for her after he'd arrived. Seeing Trumpet made him want to touch her so much that, for a moment, he could not take another step. She met his eyes and smiled to show she understood. They would imagine the kiss for now and make it up later.

Moreau sat on the small bench before the dressing table, holding a glass bottle in one hand as she rose to greet him. All of Catalina's paints and pomades were displayed. They must've been discussing the art of disguise, which meant Moreau had been brought deeper into Trumpet's confidence than Tom would have expected.

"Thank you for meeting with me, Mrs. Moreau."

Tom set his hat on a table and moved a chair next to Catalina, where he could easily see Trumpet, but Moreau was obliged to turn toward him, away from the bed. He knew Trumpet would make faces, and he wanted to be the only one to see them.

When they were both seated, he leaned forward, clasping his hands between his knees, and painted a somber expression on his face. "Did Lady Dorchester tell you about Mr. Ridley?"

Moreau nodded, her expression matching his. "Only that he was killed last week on an empty road not far from that place in Holborn where we met. What happened to him?"

"The official story is that he was set upon by thieves in one of those dark alleys branching off the Holborn Road. They strangled him and dumped his body in a field, well away from their accustomed haunts."

Moreau covered her rosy lips with a graceful hand. *"Quelle horreur!"* Sorrow darkened her sky-blue eyes. She really was an extraordinarily lovely woman.

Tom caught Trumpet's narrowed look, promising punishment if he entertained a single warm thought about Elsa Moreau. He returned a weary flutter of his eyelashes. He was well beyond that youthful foolery, and she knew it.

Moreau laid the tip of a white finger on her chin. "You said, 'the *official* story.' Is there another one?"

"I'm afraid so." Tom glanced from side to side, pretending to include the others in his admonition. "What I'm about to tell you must be kept in the strictest confidence."

She nodded, eyes wide. "Not even my Lady Rich."

"You can tell your mistress, but no one else. The truth is that the body was found near Anthony Bacon's coach, which had been abandoned along Gray's Inn Road."

"Mon Dieu! How can this be?"

"That's what I'm trying to find out. I've learned that Thomas Lawson invited Raffe Ridley for a drive that night to discuss their differences."

"Oo la!" she exclaimed. "That would be a long drive. Then did Lawson kill him at last?"

Tom noted that "at last" but put it aside for the moment. "It looks that way, but there are complications."

"Looks may deceive you." She arched her fair eyebrows. "What does the driver say?"

"Alas, the Bacons' driver knows nothing. Lawson claims he left Ridley alive and well when the coach dropped him at Gray's Inn."

"Do you believe him?"

Tom gave her half a smile. "I don't know the man well enough to judge. That's why I wanted to talk to you, Mistress. You knew them both in France and aren't involved in this affair. I'd like to ask you a few questions about the past."

"*Mais non,* I do not mind." She folded her hands neatly in her lap.

"Good. First, how did you come to live in Bordeaux? Or was it Montaubon?"

"I am born in Bordeaux, Monsieur Clarady." She pronounced it the French way, with the accent on the final syllable. "My father is a gentleman, a good Protestant, but with perhaps too many children. I am the youngest daughter. I watch my sisters marry and settle in little houses and have their little children, and I think, oh, this is not for me! I want to travel. I want to see Paris and meet people of importance. So I become the servant of Madame du Plessis-Mornay. Do you know her?"

Tom shook his head. "No, but I've heard about her from my Lady Dorchester."

Amusement lit Moreau's blue eyes. She knew what he had heard. "She is very respectable, so my father, he is happy. He is also happy to have one less dowry, I think. At first, it is all I desire. We go to Paris, we go to Genève. I see Notre Dame, we visit the finest mercers, with silks and laces from the whole world. I learn to style the hair. My mistress is the most fashionable of all the ladies. We are very proud. But then, her husband, he is so important, he is made a governor, and so we must live in Montaubon. The place is nothing. Beautiful, perhaps, but with scarce so much as one slip of lace to be found."

"Sounds like Dorchester," Trumpet said.

Tom had thought it a great capital when he first went there — how many years ago? Now he considered it a muddy hamlet. Compared to London, everything else was dull.

Trumpet had listened to the history with narrowed eyes. She shot several glances toward Catalina during the account, but the Spanish woman's face held the look of courteous attention she wore as a matter of habit. Trumpet tended to assume that Tom would fall in love with any beauteous, fair-haired woman, will he-nill he. He'd just have to make sure that kiss, when he had the chance to deliver it, would alleviate that concern.

Tom continued his interview. "You didn't like Montaubon, I gather."

Moreau shook her head. Strands of golden hair peeked out from beneath her modest coif. "Madame and I, we are unhappy. All is tedium — until Mr. Anthony Bacon arrives. He is not like the others in this town. He loves music, dancing, wine, games in the garden on summer evenings. We love to visit him. My lady spent many hours at his table while I divert myself with his secretary. We play cards and smoke little pipes of tobacco."

"Was Lawson with him from the start?" Tom asked, manfully ignoring the puffing motions she made with her plush lips.

"No. Did he not tell you?" She cocked her head in surprise. When Tom shook his head, she shrugged and went on. "They met in Paris. Lawson was a messenger. You know the sort. He is comely, he speaks Latin and *français*. Also, *allemand*, I think. He is a young man of good parents, but with no money and no plan. He likes to see new places and meet new people." She sighed. "I would do that work if I could."

"Me too," Trumpet said.

"Me? No," Catalina said. "I like sleeping in a warm bed every night and having good food every day." She'd spent twenty years or more living on the road, so she had no romantic illusions about that life.

Tom said, "I've been tempted. But it doesn't lead to anything."

"It led Lawson to Monsieur Bacon," Moreau said. "At first, Monsieur Bacon must send letters through the embassy in Paris, like everyone else. But when he found his house in Montaubon, he wanted his own men. He remembered Lawson and sent for him. They are great friends from the start, if you understand me." She winked broadly.

"We understand." Tom had grown weary of that stale innuendo. He wanted to explore his idea of a triangle between Moreau, Lawson, and Ridley. "I got the sense at the Antelope that you and Lawson might also have been friends. If you understand me."

"You mean lovers." Her eyes flashed. "No. Did he say we were?"

"He didn't say anything. But you two were holding hands and whispering, so I wondered."

"*Non, non,* Monsieur." She wrinkled her nose as if inhaling a bitter memory. "He asked me, many times. But always I say no. He is with Monsieur Bacon. I will not help to deceive so nice a man. But Lawson, he beg me. *Encore,* I say no."

Begging did not seem like Lawson's style. Tom had never done it. A wink and a welcoming smile was usually all it took. He might sing a serenade under the window if he was keen and she was coy. After that, he'd just move on to the next one. Lawson seemed cut from the same cloth. "How did he react to your refusal?"

"At first, he is like so." She performed an uncaring shrug. "But then he tries again, and I am more severe. That makes him angry. Or maybe Monsieur Bacon scolded him. I do not know. But he struck me, here." She turned her head to exhibit a flawless jawline.

Tom frowned at the spot as if he could see the purple bruise from six years past. Lawson hadn't raised a fist to him in the coach, even when provoked. Tom was a good deal larger than this woman, but even so. A cutting insult, rather than a blow, seemed more Lawson's style.

"What about Lawson and Ridley? Was there ever any sort of dalliance there?"

Moreau trilled a laugh so sublimely feminine it made Trumpet lower her head and curl her lip. Tom put a patient smile on his lips, hoping his eyes hadn't flashed or twinkled.

"Monsieur Clarady! What a clever man you are!" She clapped her hands to applaud him. "I saw them once, in the stable." She squeezed her eyes shut to show her feelings about that spectacle.

"Did that affair last long?"

"Me, I do not know. Was it an affair? Or was it only once?"

"Weren't they worried that Mr. Bacon would find out?"

She pursed her lips in the effort of remembering. "Even then, Monsieur Bacon was not always well. He stayed in his bed for days sometimes. But I think if he knew, it might make him unhappy. Do you not agree?"

Tom did. A man could be indulgent with his servants and liberal with his friends yet still expect fidelity from a lover. What would Anthony do if he found out about Lawson's bout with Ridley years later?

"What happened between them — Lawson and Ridley? Did they quarrel?"

"Oh! They always quarrel, those two. Worse as time passed. Over love, perhaps. Over me sometimes." She sang the last word and made a winsome face. Trumpet pretended to stick her finger down her throat. Tom bit the inside of his lip and refused to look at her.

"Did you and Ridley ever . . . ?"

"*Non*, and *non encore*. He is dead, and I am sad for that. But he was a man who always wanted what he did not have. More money, the prettier woman. Other men always have

148

the better thing. He was like a small dog who must bark at the bigger one, even to his peril."

"I saw that," Tom said, remembering the display Ridley had made of himself in the tavern. "But the big dog doesn't bite the little one. It's usually the other way around."

A flash of what — confusion? irritation? — crossed her face. Then she lowered her head as if about to share a secret with Tom alone. "There is another reason. Or, no — two. They go together, these two."

"I'm listening," Tom said.

"Do you know that Anthony Bacon's mother is a very strict Calvinist?"

"That is a well-known fact."

"She has strong ideas about dalliance, especially between men . . . You understand?"

Tom nodded.

"Well, someone told her something about Lawson and her son. Someone also told her Lawson was a Catholic, which he is not. He is nothing in religion. He does not care about churches. Do you know who that someone was?"

"I'll take a wild guess," Tom said. "Raffe Ridley?"

"The very same. He visited her, some time when he is bringing letters to your council. He poisoned her mind against Lawson. And he told her when Lawson would arrive in England so she could send him to the jail."

"Aha." Tom flashed a knowing glance at Trumpet. "So Ridley's the one who peached on him. Lawson didn't know."

"You asked him?"

"It came up."

Moreau shrugged. "He would guess it, I think. He would lie to you to hide his anger."

"How do you know all this?" Tom asked. "Lawson told me Mr. Bacon didn't know he was in jail until he got home."

149

"*Mais non.* Monsieur Bacon was still in France at the time. Me, I am in London with my Lady Rich. Here, in this house. Lawson knows this because Monsieur Bacon sent me to serve her."

"I see," Tom said. He glanced at Trumpet, who had a skeptical look on her face.

This part of the story made sense to him. Trumpet didn't know how desperate those prison walls made you feel. The noise, the stink. The other prisoners, some of whom definitely belonged there. You'd reach for any branch within your grasp. Lawson probably sold one of his pretty handkerchiefs to pay the messenger.

"I could do nothing for him," Moreau said. "I am only a servant. I cannot ask my mistress to do something for him. This is a matter for the great ones."

Tom agreed. Francis had asked his lord uncle to help get Tom out, but in this case Lord Burghley had been one of the people keeping Lawson in.

"How did you find out Ridley was the informer?"

She blinked at him a few times, her long eyelashes fluttering. "He told me himself, Monsieur Clarady. That night at the tavern, when you took Lawson away. He bragged it to me to show he is more clever than Monsieur Bacon. Too cruel, I think. Such a thing would make the big dog bite the little one, do you not agree?"

Tom stroked his beard, nodding. "It might. It very well might." Especially added to a threat to expose that old infidelity to Anthony, from whom all good things flowed into Lawson's life. "But I don't believe he would risk Mr. Bacon being accused along with him."

"This is not possible." Moreau seemed dismayed by the idea. "Monsieur Bacon is an *invalide*. It is a well-known fact." She glared at Tom. "Who is saying this impossible thing? Is it the driver who says it?"

Tom shook his head. "He wasn't there at the end." He wouldn't mention the second coachman outside the inner circle. "But it was Mr. Bacon's coach. It seems a stupid choice of setting if Lawson had planned to murder Ridley for revenge or to keep him quiet."

"Ah, now I understand your problem. But Lawson, he is not so clever. He is a man of moods. He is hungry, he is lusty, he is laughing, he is angry." Moreau performed each of these emotions in a rapid dumb show. "He meant to talk with Raffe, perhaps, but then the little dog bark and bark. Lawson killed him to make him stop. He did not think, *mon Dieu,* but this will look bad for my dear Anthony — until it is too late." She treated him to a bright smile. "This answers your questions, I think. Does it not?"

Trumpet's eyes narrowed again, though she couldn't see the brightness of the Frenchwoman's smile. Perhaps it was the way Moreau straightened her back along with the smile, pressing her breasts forward. The linen of her partlet was just this side of transparent.

Tom leaned back in his chair and scratched his beard with a thoughtful finger. She'd brought him full circle, adding more reasons for Lawson to want Ridley dead. He glanced at Trumpet to see how she liked this new version, but she'd wrapped her hands around her belly and closed her eyes. The baby must be kicking.

Tom turned back to Moreau, who had folded her hands in her lap again, waiting for his next question like any well-trained servant.

She'd given him what he came for: a reason for Lawson and Ridley to hate each other. More than one, in fact, and all good. She'd told him the story he wanted to hear.

Then why couldn't he bring himself to believe it?

TWELVE

T he door opened immediately after a short rap, giving Francis no time to respond. He was kneeling by his hearth, wherein he'd built up a goodly bed of glowing coals.

Thomas Phelippes walked in with a commonplace book in his hand. His eyes were so fixed on the page he barely missed the corner of the small bed set against the inner wall. He glanced up and said, "Say, Frank, I wonder what you'll think of this twist to our cipher. Why not insert a Greek letter into the sequence? Let alpha stand in for a sequence of three a's, for example."

"I'll look at it later. I'm in the middle of an experiment." Francis gestured toward the pair of iron dogs he'd set up to support the objects being tested: a pot made of thick baked clay, a copper pipkin, a block of oak, and two fist-sized balls of round shot, one of iron and one of stone.

"Oh, that does look interesting. But do you think using alpha for the letter A is too obvious? We could make it more opaque, yet still easy to decrypt at the other end, by working the Greek alphabet backward."

Francis surrendered to the linguist's single-mindedness and rose to study the examples in the commonplace book. They discussed the *pro et contra* for several minutes. Then Francis managed to herd Phelippes back out the door.

He pulled the oak door shut with a sigh. He'd never met anyone whose work so perfectly suited his nature. All

Phelippes needed was a room with enough warmth and light for writing, a sturdy desk with plenty of ink and paper, and plain nourishment delivered at regular intervals.

Francis went back to the fire and gingerly tested the top layer of his substances. Another few minutes. Meanwhile, he could inspect the character of the ash produced by burning different materials. He set a flat pan on a trivet to heat, then laid out his samples. He had wool, paper, and wood — the obvious choices — but also some pieces of antler and a few elemental substances from his apothecary: sulphur, mercury, and iron filings.

He was scarcely halfway through that set before another knock sounded on his door. *"Intro!"* he shouted, not getting up.

Tom walked in and took one sniff before crying, "God's teeth, Mr. Bacon! It smells like the bottom of hell in here!" He strode across the room and raised the latches to throw both windows fully open.

"Close them, quick! You'll alter the circumfusing constitution of warmth."

"The what?" Tom ignored his command. Everyone always did. "You can't breathe that stuff, Mr. Bacon. It'll make you sick." He gagged dramatically. "What are you doing? It smells like sulphur."

"It *is* sulphur. That's my base test. Sulphur is one of the two fundamental elements, so the residue left after burning it is simply sulphur."

"If you say so." Tom remained standing by the window with his nose pointing out.

Francis got up and waved him away, closing the windows. He sat at his desk and dipped his quill in the inkpot to jot some notes. "You can help me. Why don't you test the relative heat of those objects facing the coals and tell me which is hottest and which is coolest?"

Tom shrugged and knelt to place his hand on one of the balls of shot. "God's bollocks!" He leapt up, letting loose a stream of colorful curses, and glared at Francis. "Why do I do these things?" He shook his hand and blew on it, wincing.

Without looking up from his notes, Francis exhibited two fingers on his left hand bearing bandages soaked in burn ointment. "Perhaps you have the soul of a philosopher, deep down inside."

"Not me. Although I do like intelligencing. Is that a form of philosophy?"

Francis finished his note and looked up. "In a way." He shoved the pot of ointment toward Tom, who scowled at it but took a scoop to slather on his injured hand. "Intelligencing entails the amassing of information based on observations and testimony, then analyzing it to achieve an understanding of an ongoing state of affairs. The larger goal is formulating strategies to improve the condition of one's nation or polity. So yes, I would put it under the heading of political philosophy." He smiled. "There, you see? You're a philosopher after all."

"As you will," Tom said, his tone devoid of enthusiasm. He wrapped his handkerchief around his injured hand. "Do you want to hear about my conversation with Elsa Moreau?"

"Who?" Francis jotted down a note about his new insight.

"Lady Rich's maidservant. The one who was at the Antelope when Ridley and Lawson had their brawl. She knew them in France. I told you I was going to question her yesterday when I went to visit Trumpet."

"Oh yes." Francis sighed and set down his quill. "Can't we do that later? At supper, perhaps? But no, Anthony will be there. After supper, then. Or tomorrow is soon enough. There's no particular rush, is there?"

"None whatsoever," Tom said, walking to the door. "In fact, why not wait until someone else is strangled? Perhaps they'll do it in Anthony's bed this time."

He left without waiting for an answer. Francis dismissed Tom's exaggerated sense of urgency. This murder seemed clearly to have been motivated by Ridley's slanders. Unless someone else popped up to spread the same tales, there was little likelihood of a second crime.

He decided not to test his objects with his hands again. He'd try an indirect method of measuring using a standard substance known to retain heat: wool. He found a pair of old stockings and layered them over one hand. Then he pulled each object away from the coals with a pair of tongs before placing his protected hand across its face. He strove to clear his mind of prior opinions as he judged the relative heat remaining in each substance. Iron was the hottest; that was quite clear. Clay came next, which surprised him. Then the stone.

He jumped up to write down his judgments, attempting to grasp his quill before remembering to remove the socks.

A series of raps in a jaunty rhythm sounded on his door. *"Exite!"* he called, hoping whoever it was would take the hint and go away.

But no, the door swung wide to reveal Thomas Lawson. He liked to open doors like that, doubtless enjoying the dramatic effect. All it really accomplished was a dent in the plaster on the far side where the handle struck the wall.

"God's mercy, Frank, what a mess you're making." Lawson sniffed the air and made a sour face. He wagged his finger. "You are quite a naughty boy!"

Francis felt warmth in his cheeks, which he had no need to measure. "I'm studying the property of heat." He tried to sound crisp and authoritative but feared a touch of petulance colored his effort. Men like Lawson always put him at a disadvantage. He hoped that wasn't why he didn't trust him.

Lawson smiled indulgently. "Well, if you can spare a moment before burning the house down, Anthony would like a word. Or shall I have a couple of grooms carry him up here?"

"No, no." Francis sighed. "I'll come down."

He called Pinnock out of the bedchamber and told him to clear everything away. "Be careful with the things near the fire. They're still hot."

"I know all about heat," the lad retorted.

"Would that that were true." Francis directed him to open both windows and the door and wave damp towels around to clear the air. "But note the time when you start and finish, please. I have the dimensions of this room. Then I can calculate how long it takes to replace that volume of atmosphere."

* * *

Francis stretched out on his bed after dinner — not to take a nap, but to think about heat and related properties. How did smells get into the air, and how did heat amplify that process? The stink of sulphur had almost completely disappeared, for instance, while the dark undertones of charcoal and hot iron lingered on. Their elemental natures must be heavier.

"Mr. Bacon?" Pinnock's voice startled him. "Sorry to wake you, but there's a message from your lord uncle."

Francis groaned and sat up, swinging his legs onto the floor. "I wasn't asleep," he said, reaching for the note. "Not really."

His Lordship wanted to know how Anthony was doing. His son's report from Saturday must not have been sufficient. Perhaps he thought some change might have transpired in three and a half days. Naturally, he couldn't just write to Anthony and ask. He wanted a firsthand report.

156

Summons from this source could never be refused, not while Francis had two good legs to propel him down the hill. He changed out of his philosophy clothes — a well-worn suit of brown serge — and into something more suitable for the pomp and polish of Burghley Hall.

A short walk later, the usher led him to his uncle's private parlor, where his uncle was sitting in the chair he'd had specially made with an elongated seat that supported his gouty legs. A narrow desk stood near his right hand with ink, quills, paper, and a stack of folded letters. The usher collected those on his way out.

Francis took the chair placed ready for visitors. After the usual greetings concerning Lady Bacon's continuing good health, His Lordship turned to the main topic. "When will Anthony be fit to visit the queen? I fear she may be feeling neglected."

"I am sorry for that," Francis said, "but we're doing what we can. I'm afraid the journey home depleted him severely. It's going to take time."

His uncle put him through the now-familiar catechism about symptoms, remedies, and prognoses. They went on to the more familiar litany of rote excuses. Francis could answer these questions in his sleep at this point and had to struggle not to appear bored. He ought to write them up — he wrote so much more fluently than he spoke — and have Tom make half a dozen fair copies. Then when someone asked him, "How is Anthony?" he could hand them the sheet of paper and think about something interesting while they read.

Although that would be considered rude, however efficient it might be for both parties. Social niceties were meant to be dull.

"You've grown weary of these questions, Nephew." Lord Burghley peered at Francis from beneath his thick gray eyebrows. His eyes seemed smaller, shrunken within deep webs of wrinkles, while his forehead had grown higher, accentuating the steep line of his nose.

Francis acknowledged that truth with a wince. "Not of the questions, my lord, but rather of the need for them. I'll confess I had imagined that when Anthony came home, he would return to the brother I remembered after a few weeks of rest. He would take up his work again, and there would be more time for my philosophical inquiries. So far, that has not been the case."

"I should think you would have less work, now that others can translate and copy his letters. And his correspondence must have abated while he is confined to his bed."

"Oh, nothing stops him." Francis had to smile. "My brother's capacity for work is rivaled only by your own. There are more letters rather than fewer. And though I don't have to translate them myself, I supervise their translation. I carved out this morning specifically to study heat, but not ten minutes went by without someone knocking on my door to ask me something or tell me something or fetch me down to speak with Anthony."

Burghley produced a gravelly chuckle. "That sounds familiar. I set aside an hour to immerse myself in some treat, like one of Seneca's tragedies, but seldom have ten minutes of peace before another urgent message arrives."

Francis marveled at the rare moment of accord. He was loath to ruin it with a request, but he might never get a better chance. He sighed to signal his melancholic state. "Can't you pull some plum out of your pocket, Uncle? A post that will support me and my inquiries at a reasonable standard?"

Burghley shook his head, but he smiled as he did it. "I'm afraid I have nothing sweet enough for your tastes."

"I'm not so very fussy. Vice-chancellor of a university would do. Or even provost of Eton College."

"Oh, Frank." Burghley laughed heartily, ending with a sigh. "Do you really want to be responsible for a herd of restless boys who would rather hunt rabbits than open a book? And you know what a vice-chancellor's day is like. Fielding an unrelenting flood of demands from all quarters: students, parents, faculty, courtiers. You'd hate it."

Francis slumped. "I know."

"You could try the Twickenham approach for a year or two," Burghley said, not unkindly. "It has the advantage of being cheap."

Twickenham was Francis's little hunting box on the Thames, across the river from Richmond Palace. He escaped to that tranquil retreat whenever he could, especially in the summer when plague threatened the city.

"Perhaps I will." For a moment, Francis felt a stirring of possibility in his breast. But only for a moment. "I'll discuss it with Anthony."

"Mmm."

They could both predict the outcome of that conversation. Anthony, like Thomas Phelippes, loved his work and had little interest in anything outside it. He needed Francis's talents too and would bend all his persuasive powers toward keeping his younger brother right where he was.

Francis blurted, "It's just that sometimes I wonder why I don't drop this hubbub of political business and do the work for which I truly believe God made me."

Burghley raised his bushy eyebrows. "Perhaps God expects you to do the work your father bred you for first."

Francis had no argument for that. Both his parents had trained him for government service. Anthony had said more or less the same thing. Perhaps he should start believing it.

Burghley gave him a moment to let the thought sink in. Then he said, "I do wish I were strong enough to visit Anthony myself. Or that he was well enough to come here.

I would very much like to hear the details that were left out of his letters over the years. I understand he kept copies of everything. It would be fascinating to go through them to see how well his intentions and my interpretations marched together."

Fascinating for His Lordship. Time-consuming, unpaid work for Anthony. And since neither man could step foot from his house, Francis would have to play the go-between. Tweedle and thump; the same old pipe and drum, marching him around the same old circle.

No part of *that* could be said out loud. He'd risked enough already. "You two would find a great deal to discuss, I'm sure."

"Perhaps he could be brought here to spend a few days, or even weeks. We'd take very good care of him."

"That sounds sensible," Francis said, "but I can promise you he would never agree. You know how he is. He must be independent, as far as possible. And he's very well taken care of in my house. I enlarged it, you know, to make room for his household servants and his staff of clerks."

Burghley grunted. "He always was a wayward boy."

Francis, sensing that the interview was coming to an end, shifted his weight, ready to rise. But his uncle had another question.

"Has he said anything about those two Frenchmen who have been wearying Her Majesty lately? Du Plessis and du Pin?"

"No. But I had a pleasant conversation with du Pin yesterday, in the Privy Garden."

Another grunt. This one sounded amused. No doubt someone had told him about du Pin's not-so-subtle ejection from the Presence Chamber. "I've been thinking about a letter Anthony sent me back in '88. He said du Plessis and du Pin would be sweating into their doublets — with fear, one assumes — about some information

Anthony had uncovered to their detriment. Nothing ever came of it. I've often wondered what he meant."

"I don't know," Francis said. "I don't remember seeing such a letter. It's a vivid image. I would remember."

"That's why I asked."

"Who delivered it?" Francis asked. "Didn't the messenger elaborate?"

"Lawson, I think. He must not have. I was buried in messages that year." Burghley bent his face to his fingertips, massaging his temple. "But Anthony wouldn't write that sentence without reason. I wonder if it mightn't be of interest still, now that those men are here."

"I'll ask him. I'll ask Lawson too, though I doubt he'd remember the content of any given letter."

Burghley grunted again. This time the sound expressed disapproval. "I don't like that man. No strong reason, I just don't quite trust him. I wish we could find a way to separate him from our family."

Francis nodded, once again in complete accord. "So do I."

THIRTEEN

Trumpet picked at her partridge pie, spooning up only the fleshy bits of mushroom. She couldn't fault the dish — the cooks at Essex House knew their craft — but she had little appetite today. She stirred another spoonful of sugar into her wine and took a goodly swallow.

Catalina twitched her lips. The wine had already been sweetened. But Trumpet didn't care. She craved sweetness, and sugar never hurt anybody, pregnant or no.

"What did you think of Elsa's story?" she asked her maidservant.

"I think she lies about something, but I do not know what."

Trumpet nodded, glad for the confirmation. "The part about the father with too many daughters was certainly a lie. Monsieur Moreau could easily have found a merchant or a thriving farmer to marry her for her pretty face alone. The lucky man would offer a handsome bride-price to boot, most likely."

"She said she wanted to travel. That part I can believe."

"Her father would never allow it. By the time she turned fifteen, that girl would have a line of suitors knocking on the door with their purses open." Trumpet pushed her dish away and leaned back in her chair. "But why tell the story in the first place? Tom didn't ask for her complete history. He just wanted to know how she'd joined the circle around Anthony Bacon."

"She wants Mr. Tom to think she is a gentlewoman." Catalina set aside the silver comb and brush she'd been polishing and came over to remove Trumpet's tray. She set it on a table near the door, where the waiter would collect it.

"If she's not a gentleman's daughter, who is she? Could you tell anything by the way she talked?"

"Not the talk. I do not speak French so well." Catalina returned to her stool. "But I think she is like me."

"I thought that too," Trumpet said, "but I don't know why. What did you see?"

"I think she may be a player, my lady, like I was before I came to you. She acts like Columbina."

"Who?"

"The beautiful servant in Italian *commedia*. When she is surprised, she is like so." Catalina widened her dark eyes and formed a perfect O with her lips. "When she is sad, she is like so." She slumped, rounding her shoulders and turning her wide lips down.

"That's it exactly!" Trumpet cried, slapping her hand on the table. "I wonder if Penelope knows."

Catalina shrugged, lifting both hands and shoulders the way Elsa — and, presumably, Columbina — would do.

"I didn't believe the part about Lawson hitting her either," Trumpet said. "Tom thinks he's more likely to sneer than to strike. And what about her seeing Lawson and Ridley in the stables? She makes him sound like he went around stalking everyone, whipping out his pillicock at every opportunity."

"Why would he risk losing his place with Mr. Anthony?" Catalina asked. "That seems very foolish."

"She wanted us to think the worst of Lawson; that much is clear. But why? Tom said they seemed friendly that night at the Antelope. Would you hold hands with a man who'd punched you in the face?"

"No, my lady. I would think of ways to hurt him."

"Would you wait six years?"

"Yes. Longer."

Trumpet met her servant's eyes and nodded. She would too. "But we don't believe he hit her, so why did she lie?"

"To throw the blame away," Catalina said, tossing an imaginary object over her shoulder. "To make Mr. Tom look at Lawson and not at her."

"But why?" Trumpet drummed her fingers on the oak, considering the possibilities. Penelope should be warned if her maidservant wasn't what she seemed. Let her decide for herself how much it mattered.

Trumpet wouldn't trade Catalina Luna for any other servant in the world. Apart from her skill at creating disguises, the Spanish woman had become her closest friend and ally. It didn't matter where she'd come from; on the contrary, her irregular experiences were a major asset. But Penelope Rich, née Devereux, wasn't the sort to dress in boys' clothes and climb out the window to sport about the city. She'd hired the French woman to maintain her position in the vanguard of fashion at court.

Trumpet had effectively raised herself in her solitary castle, where she'd mostly made her own rules. Penelope had grown up with two parents, a sister, and a brother. Her mother had doubtless taught her how to behave as an earl's daughter and what to expect from those in her service.

"It could be harmless," Trumpet said. "Moreau might just want the comforts of service in a great house. On the other hand, the Earl of Essex is not some minor governor in the south of France. He's among the most important men in England. If she is a spy, she must be exposed. And wouldn't everyone be astonished if we were the ones to do it?" Trumpet grinned. "There must be rumors downstairs, jealousies and desires, swirling around the beauteous newcomer. Find out what you can about this Elsa Moreau from the other servants."

* * *

On awakening from her after-dinner nap, Trumpet found a letter from Lady Elizabeth Russell waiting on her desk. Her Ladyship had been at Bisham Abbey, her house in Berkshire, for several weeks and wanted to know how her apprentice was faring. Trumpet had lived with the redoubtable lady for one whole year. A year of atonement, during which she had labored to rehabilitate her damaged reputation. They'd become friends during that year, as different as they were. Trumpet valued Her Ladyship's advice, even when she had no intention of following it.

Lady Russell had lived in Paris once upon a time. Many years ago — perhaps too many to know La Plashy — but she maintained a correspondence with many notable Protestants abroad. She might have heard something.

Trumpet sharpened her quill and inked a lengthy reply. She lamented that she remained undelivered. Then she supplied a detailed description of her health and the baby's movements, along with her daily diet and exercise regimen. Lady Russell suffered from the chronic pain of a twisted spine and had a great appetite for matters relating to physic.

Finally, she moved on to the most pressing matter — gossip, the worse, the better — about Madame du Plessis-Mornay. "She's a French Protestant. Her husband is important, or *she* thinks he is. Anything, however petty, will be of interest to me." She signed it with affection and ordered it to be sent to Blackfriars at once. Lady Russell might profess to despise gossip, but she often had a good supply of it. And she'd initiated this exchange by asking for *all* the news.

Trumpet had a reply in less than half an hour. Blackfriars stood a scant half mile from Essex House, after all. A boy could run each way in five minutes.

Lady Russell wrote, "Of course I know Madame du Plessis, or rather, I know *of* her. I left France in '66, so we never met. But Monsieur du Plessis-Mornay is prominent in Huguenot circles. He's written some moderately well-received tracts and has always been a staunch defender of the Reformation in France. My sister Anne would know more. She often resorted to Madame du Plessis for a woman's perspective on Anthony's health and the quality of the company he was keeping. Shall I ask her?"

Trumpet clucked her tongue in frustration. It would take more than a day to get a letter back from Gorhambury. Trumpet might give birth at any moment; she could brook no delays.

She wrote back, "I wouldn't credit reports from that source if I were Lady Bacon. Madame has been here attempting to spread unsavory rumors about Mr. Bacon, plainly motivated by personal malice. I don't know what provoked the malice, but it's as clear as the nose on her face. She claims he performed unnatural acts with the boys in his household. Worse, she says he took bribes from Catholics."

Half an hour later, she slit the seal on Lady Russell's reply. She laughed as she displayed the paper to Catalina, whereupon one single word occupied the upper third. *"NEVER!!"*

Lady Russell elaborated. "I'd heard about the woman's vanity but considered those reports mere envy stimulated by her husband's appointment to the governorship. Her slanders are abject lies. They must be <u>crushed</u>. I shall have her visit me here so I can perform the deed myself. I might ask Anne to come down to assist me.

"Meanwhile, I have remembered a probable cause for the woman's animosity toward my stainless nephew. She has a daughter by a previous marriage. I forget the creature's name. The father was a nobody; a lesser French gentleman of no known accomplishments. Madame attempted to arrange a match between this daughter and Anthony, if you can believe it. He rejected it out of hand, naturally. Doubtless he was the soul of courtesy, but a vain woman can tolerate no rejection. She must have been humiliated, and like all who lack inner resources, she let that resentment fester. If the daughter remains unwed, that would add thorns to her crown of mortification. How better to explain the original cause than by accusing the unwilling bridegroom of a preference for his own sex?

"Anthony wasn't ready to marry at that time, but had he been, he could have looked *much* higher than the daughter of a French nonentity. I fear now he will never be well enough to wed, but that is a cause for sorrow, not scandal."

Trumpet clapped her hands in glee. "Now we know," she crowed to Catalina. "We've found the boil on the arse of that overstuffed vulture." She tapped a foot thoughtfully. "The question is, when will it do us the most good to expose it?"

* * *

The early drizzle had turned to rain before she left her room to go up to the gallery for her afternoon walk. As she peered through the gloom at the Strand, she saw beasts and people slipping in the mud, splattering their shins. For once, she was glad to be trapped in a velvet cage.

When Penelope joined her, Trumpet snuggled into her warm cloak and listened to the daily report on Bess Ralegh and baby Damerei. Bess was up and about already, walking daily to restore her figure while her maidservant refashioned her court clothes. She still intended to return to her post as one of the gentlewomen of the Privy Chamber within a month.

"How long can they keep this secret?" Trumpet asked. "I find it incredible they've lasted this long."

167

"Bess said that Sir Walter fears Sir Robert has discovered the marriage."

"Not the child?"

Penelope shrugged.

"How?" Trumpet asked.

"Who knows? He has eyes and ears everywhere." Penelope touched her with one long finger. "Take that as a warning, my dear. Sir Walter denied it, of course."

"I wonder if that was wise. The storm is coming, will he-nill he. He can't hide a growing boy from Her Majesty forever. He won't want to. It isn't like him not to sail straight into the wind and take the bull by the horns."

Penelope chuckled. "I assume you did not mean to compare our sovereign queen to a bull. But I don't blame him. The risk is tremendous. He could lose everything: houses, lands, all his lucrative offices. He isn't like Sir Robert and my lord of Essex, you know. He isn't building his own base of power with a stable of intelligencers and representatives in Scotland and France. He's made no effort to form alliances with other powerful men. Sir Walter stands alone, wholly dependent on Her Majesty."

Trumpet had seen some of it but had not understood it in that way. Sir Walter had shown no interest in Anthony Bacon's services, for example, as far as Tom knew. But Essex and Sir Robert had both made their interest clear. If Anthony couldn't become the queen's Secretary of State, he could still serve in that capacity for a great lord like Essex. Sir Walter didn't seem to want to build that sort of scaffolding for his ambitions.

"He doesn't seem to want power *per se*," Trumpet said. "He has no desire to govern England. He wants money — lots of it — to go forth and conquer a new world, but he doesn't want to compete with the Cecils here at home. That's what Bess told me, anyway." Trumpet and Bess had been chambermates at Richmond Palace. Once each had discovered the other's secret lover affair, they'd shared many a midnight confidence about their men.

"He'll delay as long as possible," Penelope predicted. "Trying to sail in front of the storm, so to speak."

"They'll have to sail very fast to escape Sir Robert. What will he do with his knowledge? Is he waiting for the perfect moment to destroy Sir Walter? He'd remove the only other person who has the queen's ear."

"That's an intriguing question," Penelope said. "He's a great collector of secrets, is Sir Robert. I think he likes possessing them, like a box full of curious shells. He probably wants advance warning of the impending tempest. Mark my words, he'll find a reason to be absent when the storm strikes. Then he'll find a way to turn Her Majesty's wrath to his advantage."

"Won't he blackmail Sir Walter?" Trumpet would if he had something she wanted and there were no better way. "Extortion can be a very useful tool."

Penelope chuckled again. "You continue to surprise me, Alice. I don't believe that's Sir Robert's way, though he's not above letting you know he *could* do something if he wanted to. He's a sly little man. He collects rumors about anything that might affect the queen's temper in order to anticipate her response to whatever he might be trying to put forward."

"I suppose that explains the second coachman," Trumpet said. "He wanted to know what manner of scandal was in the offing while appearing —" She realized that Penelope had stopped moving to stare at her with narrowed eyes.

"What second coachman?"

Trumpet cursed under her breath. That was meant to be a secret. This baby must be muddling her wits as well as making her eat twice as much and sleep three times as much as usual.

Then again, why shouldn't Penelope know? She was a clever plotter. She might have something fresh to contribute to the tangled Ridley matter.

Trumpet told her about the young man who had appeared out of nowhere and taken charge of the horses, claiming to be an agent of Sir Robert Cecil. Everyone assumed he'd learned about the meeting from informants in the taverns around Westminster.

Penelope listened in silence, her slender eyebrows arched and her fingers laced together. "It doesn't surprise me. Consider his behavior toward Sir Walter. He could never have discovered that marriage without bribing clergymen — or grooms and drivers. My lord brother says there is no love lost between the Bacons and their cousin. He would never simply *ask* them anything." Furrows appeared on her brow. "But do the Bacons believe this second driver sat there on the bench while Anthony's secretary strangled that poor man?"

"No one knows what the driver did. He was gone when Francis found the body. The second coachman might have done the murder himself, for all we know. He might not have come from Sir Robert at all, but been a third party altogether."

"You horrify me! I won't dare venture out after dark, with false drivers leaping from street corners to murder their passengers."

"I'm sure that never —"

"I thought the Ridley matter was settled," Penelope said, seeming offended by the intrusion of the violent topic into her sanctuary. "Wasn't Elsa helpful?"

"Oh yes. She gave us a plausible description of what might have happened. But Tom's gut is telling him to keep looking. Until he finds that second coachman, we won't get to the bottom of this affair."

"Oh, men and their precious guts!" Penelope waved that away with a merry laugh.

Trumpet didn't join in. "Tom's gut is almost always right. I place great store by it."

"Ah, well, then." Penelope surrendered with a roll of her eyes. She tucked Trumpet's hand into the crook of her elbow and resumed their stroll. After a minute or two, she said, "I have a new proposal for you to suggest to your friend Tom. See what his gut thinks of my idea. Assume you're right, that the second coachman did murder Raffe Ridley after dropping off Lawson. I think he did it on Sir Robert's orders, planned in advance, to silence the man before his slanders could throw a dozen years of foreign intelligence into the common sewer."

Trumpet shook her head. "Tom said Anthony keeps his old letters in a chest in his bedroom."

"Tush, Alice! Don't be so precise." Penelope showed her the smile of a cat with its prey between its paws. "If Anthony's reputation were destroyed, everything that flowed through his hands would be tainted. Not because of the sodomy; no one but shopkeepers cares about such things. But if he were suspected of being in the pay of the Spanish, nothing he ever reported about Spain could be trusted. His analyses of French affairs would be suspect as well. Everything built on his information, including my lord brother's present campaign, would crumble into ash."

It was Trumpet's turn to stop and stare. "I hadn't thought of it that way. Neither had Tom. Mr. Bacon might have — Francis, I mean. He usually thinks of everything, but he doesn't share much." She rubbed her belly while she imagined what actions had been taken or avoided as a result of Anthony's work. "Then you believe the real motive for killing Raffe Ridley was to *protect* Anthony, not to implicate him. And at the same time" — she shook her finger at her friend in sheer excitement — "to rid him of a troublesome servant by making it look like Lawson did it."

"Now you're catching on." Penelope's dark eyes gleamed.

"God's great blue bollocks!" Trumpet cried. "You are the *wittiest* woman!" She rose on her toes to plant a kiss on Penelope's cheek.

She had an explanation for the murder that took all the facts into account. The best one so far. What's more, neither Tom nor Francis Bacon had even considered it. *Ha!*

FOURTEEN

Tom inked the words *le fitz serra enherité* for the third time in as many paragraphs. Mr. Trotte's wills were wordy and repetitive, but he paid five shillings per copy, and each copy only took about four hours. But Tom's mind wasn't on his work this morning. Yesterday's drizzle and gloom had blown off, replaced by sparkling sunshine, dancing green leaves, and twittering birds. How could a man concentrate with so much springtime going outside his window?

His mind was as restless as his body. He wanted to discuss Trumpet's new idea with Mr. Bacon, but he'd gone for a drive with Henry Percy. You'd think they'd avoid that cursed coach, although there weren't many alternatives.

Ah, well. He wanted those five shillings, so he bent his head to his labor. Not a quarter of an hour later, Pinnock bounced in to drop a letter on his desk. "That's an hour you owe me."

"We'll do it tonight." Tom didn't mind giving lute lessons to a willing pupil, and now that Anthony was here with his collection of musical instruments, Pinnock had something and somewhere to play. Things were much livelier in Bacon House nowadays, what with music in the afternoon and guests for supper every other night. Tom wondered how long Gray's benchers would tolerate the disturbances.

The boy left. Tom smiled at the signature scrawled across the fold as he slit the seal with his penknife.

Trumpet's normal writing was impeccable, if a trifle tight, but her signature had grown more fanciful with her advance in rank.

She skipped the salutation, picking up as if they were still in the same room. "Remember the package our mutual friend delivered on Easter day? Go visit the supplier. That's a connection worth maintaining, even if you don't want to work for his firm. I hear he often meets customers at the Mermaid, especially on days like today. The queen has fittings all morning, so her gentlemen are at liberty. I shouldn't think a gift would be necessary, though some small memento of your father would be appropriate. Your friend, a Woman of Influence."

He kissed the letter, savoring the faint smell of vinegar and marjoram from the concoction she used to treat her itchy scalp. He got up to slide his money chest out from under the bed, adding her letter to the ribbon-tied stack. He should burn them since they declared their illicit intimacy as loudly as a herald's proclamation, but he couldn't do it. What if she died in childbirth? Or what if Stephen found out some other way and penned her up in Dorchester, beyond Tom's reach? He'd need these tokens of her fragrance and spirit.

He closed the box and looked around his tiny room for a gift worthy of the most splendiferous man in England. Sir Walter had five of everything already, each one of the finest quality. Tom's father had brought him a magnificent yellow pearl earring from the Antipodes. He'd stopped wearing it after a withering lecture from Lady Russell, but he wouldn't part with it to save his own life. Nor could he surrender the brass astrolabe the crew had presented to him in the captain's memory. Besides, Sir Walter must have astrolabes of his own — golden ones, made by Persian craftsmen.

He'd have to go with empty hands. He welcomed the excuse to get out and stretch his legs. Besides, Sir Walter had just become the father of a healthy baby boy, and he couldn't even crow about it. Maybe that would be gift enough — congratulations and a celebratory drink.

He donned his hat and walked out the front door. Everything looked brighter after yesterday's cleansing rains, even Newgate. He lifted his hat to the miserable edifice as he passed by. He couldn't blame Lawson for carrying a grudge against the man who'd helped lock him up in that rat-infested hole. But grudges were one thing; murder was another.

Cheapside was an unholy mess, the road well churned by the weight of carts and horses. It might be the widest street in London, but that just meant three times the traffic. The muck didn't bother Tom much. He never wore his best shoes into the City, not even to meet Sir Walter Ralegh. And stockings were easily washed.

The Mermaid Tavern occupied the whole stretch from Bread Street to Friday. Tom had been there been many times with his friends Christopher Marlowe and Thomas Nashe. It had been a while since he'd seen those muddy rascals. But the theaters would open soon, now that the afternoons were warming up. The poets would gather afterward to throw barbs at each other's plays.

Tom had to stop inside the door and blink for a moment, letting his eyes adjust to the dimness. Somehow it was always twilight in a tavern, whatever the weather outside. The low ceilings spanned by heavy beams allowed little light to enter through the short front windows. And the patrons seemed to like the gloom.

He asked a wench if Sir Walter was there. She directed him to a table against the east wall. Tom walked toward it but saw the knight had company, so he hoved to a few yards off to let himself be spotted. Sir Walter saw him and tilted his chin in greeting, then held up a finger to bid him wait. Tom folded his hands to show compliance.

He looked at the other man — not rudely, just noticing — then flinched as he realized what manner of man he was. The blackness of his hair, the ornateness of his doublet, but more damning still, the silver cross around his neck. *A Spaniard!* A filthy, traitorous, pope-loving Spaniard, sitting in an English tavern as if he had a right to be here instead of lying five fathoms under the sea. Drinking English beer, no doubt, and eyeing the English wenches who served it with his beady black Spanish eyes.

Tom's lip curled and his fists clenched. If it weren't for the Spanish and their lust for conquest, his father wouldn't have filled his hold with the gunpowder that claimed his life.

The man got up, bowed to Sir Walter, and walked toward the door. Tom's eyes bored holes in his forehead. The Spaniard raised his black eyebrows, unperturbed. Tom stood his ground, forcing him to turn sideways to get by. Tom spat into the straw as the blackguard passed him.

Ralegh beckoned to him and he went, bowing before taking the offered stool. "Forgive me, Sir Walter, but what was that cursed Spaniardo doing here? How can you bear to talk to them?"

"I don't do it for pleasure, Mr. Clarady, I assure you." Ralegh drew a long pipe from his purse and tapped it against the table to be sure the bowl was empty. "I share your loathing, but it's a job that must be done. We're negotiating for an exchange of prisoners. We have more of their officers than they have of our merchants, but it's still rough sailing."

"Officers captured in '88? That was four years ago."

"It can take a long time to sort out the aftermath of such momentous events." Sir Walter patted his round hose and found a pouch of tobacco. He gave Tom an indulgent smile as he filled his pipe. "You didn't come here to spit at Spaniards. What's on your mind?"

"My lady sent me. Lady Dorchester. She thought you might appreciate a kind word about what a happy day Easter Sunday turned out to be this year." He flashed a grin. "I thought you might let me buy you a drink."

A broad smile split Ralegh's handsome face. "Your father to the life! Not just the looks, but the sauce too." He pointed his pipe at Tom's chin. "I'll wager you keep that beard short so as not to hide the famous Clarady dimple."

Tom made a droll imitation of a pious face. "The benchers have rules about beards, and I try to obey the rules, when I'm able." He waved at the wench, who sailed over to take his order. "Two dragon's milks, if you please."

Ralegh caught her sleeve before she left. "Make mine a beer. And bring me a bit of flame, won't you?"

"Make mine a beer too, then," Tom said. "I thought a stronger brew seemed more festive, but it's too early. I have work waiting for me."

"I'll be dining at my desk today," Ralegh said. "Some letters must be sent immediately. I'm not certain all the officers I was just bartering with are still alive."

"That could be a mite awkward." Tom tapped a short rhythm on the edge of the table, looking about the tavern as if seeing it for the first time. The smoke-stained ceiling, the floorboards covered with broken straw, the motley stools and scuffed tables all seemed lit with an inner glow this morning. Six years ago, he would've turned cartwheels in the street to attract Sir Walter Ralegh's notice. Now here he sat, having a drink with the queen's favorite, chatting about work as if they were the best of old friends.

He did feel a kinship with this man, though they stood at opposite ends of the scale. They were both forced to love their women in secret and hide the one thing in this world that made a man gladdest — a son. Although Tom's babe might turn out to be a girl. He lowered his voice and ventured a personal note. "I hope all turns out well for you. I mean in terms of her, ah — of your mistress's wrath."

Ralegh shook one finger, down at table level, to signal silence while the wench brought their mugs. She set them down and handed Ralegh a glowing splint. He lit his pipe, puffing up the smoke with little smacking sounds, then crushed the splint under his shoe. He waited for the wench to be well away before answering. "She'll forgive me eventually. In her heart, she'll understand. And they can't get along without me serving the crown's interests in the West Country." He took a long draft of smoke and blew it out in neat rings.

Tom admired the display but could sense unease under the arrogance. Ralegh stood on the forecastle eyeing an oncoming storm, gauging the distance, but refusing to give way. He didn't deserve any punishment, in Tom's view, not for seeking what every man wants — someone to love him and an heir to carry on his name. And all he had to defend himself *was* himself — his wits and his courage. He didn't have a house full of spies and assassins ready to do his bidding like Sir Rob —

Wait a minute! Tom did have a gift to offer. He had Trumpet's new explanation for the Ridley murder. She'd told him that Penelope said that Bess believed Sir Robert had discovered the secret marriage. This would serve as a handy counterweight.

Tom lifted his cup to hide his face while he pondered the rights and wrongs of the thing. Mr. Bacon would consider any disclosure a breach of confidence. But he hadn't even heard the new version, thanks to running away whenever Tom tried to report it. And he hadn't told Tom everything he knew, not by a fair stretch. He knew something about whatever lay behind those rumors, but he'd stitched his lips together on that topic.

Furthermore, Sir Walter knew how to keep a secret better than most. He was second only to Francis Bacon in terms of wits and impartial in regard to Anthony's intelligence services. He might be able to help Tom cut the

Gordian knot of spying and lying and sort the Ridley matter out once and for all.

He licked his lips and looked up to find Sir Walter watching him with a patient expression in his brown eyes. "Spit it out, lad. What's stuck in your craw?"

"I may have a gift for you after all, sir. Do you know about a man named Raffe Ridley?"

"The emissary from Bordeaux? Of course. I knew him. He was murdered recently in Holborn." As the captain of the guard, Sir Walter received daily reports from the coroner about serious crimes within twelve miles of the court. "Strangled, as I recall, by ruffians in an alley after midnight. Sad business."

"Sad is right, but the rest isn't." Tom smiled grimly at Ralegh's surprise. He told him the whole story, including the part about driving the coach back to Gray's with his face hidden by the hood of his cloak. He'd told it so many times now that it didn't take long.

"I don't know this Lawson," Ralegh said. "Though my Lord Burghley doesn't seem to like him."

"Nobody seems to like him but Anthony. Something about about him rings false, but more in the way of small lies told to gain a small advantage, in my view. I don't get any sense of threat from him. But we have a solid explanation at last, thanks to my Lady Dorchester. Sir Robert found out about the meeting, doubtless from someone at the Antelope. He sent his own man to replace our coachman and eavesdrop on Ridley and Lawson. Maybe this man acted on his own impulse, or maybe this was Sir Robert's plan all along. Whichever way, the second man dropped Lawson at Gray's, drove back to the empty road, and murdered Ridley. Then he ran off, knowing the coach, the belt, and the handkerchief would implicate Lawson. Sir Robert protects the value of Anthony's work and rids them all of the untrustworthy Lawson in a single stroke. Nice and neat, just the way Sir Robert likes it."

He nodded at Ralegh, who sat smoking and listening without expression.

His silence provoked Tom to add a few caveats and underscore the main import. "None of us will do anything about this, obviously. I mean, the Bacons won't. Nor would I expect you to. Not that I would. Expect anything, I mean. I wouldn't dream of it! But you could keep it up your sleeve, to balance out Sir Robert's knowledge of your, uh . . . your, uh . . ." He faltered to a halt at the flash in Ralegh's eyes. He'd overstepped.

But no, Ralegh's judgment came in the form of a wry chuckle. He pointed his pipe at Tom again. "Your father's son, every inch. That was bold, me boyo, and kindly meant. But wrong on all counts."

"How so, sir, if I may ask?" Tom struggled to contain his disappointment.

"This is Lady Dorchester's idea?" Ralegh asked. At Tom's nod, he chuckled again. "She certainly has a lively mind." He took a swig of beer and wiped the fringe of his moustache with the back of his forefinger. "It's not implausible in terms of the facts, Clarady, but it's impossible in terms of character. I've spent many long hours working side by side with Robert Cecil. Tiresome work sorting the spoils of a captured ship among a crowd of fractious, greedy men. He never lost his temper once, and we were sorely tried. Sir Robert has no need for murder. If he wanted to stop Ridley's gossip, he would simply order the man to shut his mouth."

"He doesn't seem too fond of his cousins." That sounded feeble even to Tom. How had he ever considered this idea worth so much as a puff of smoke? He'd been the veriest fool.

Ralegh took another drink, giving Tom's bruised feelings time to recover. "I doubt your lady's thinking too clearly these days. I know mine wasn't. I suspect she had help with this story from her hostess. In fact, I suspect that fair lady concocted the whole thing. Any strike against Cecil works to her brother's advantage."

"I should've seen that."

"Not at all," Ralegh said. "You're too honest a man for such dealings. Francis Bacon will say the same thing when you tell him."

"If I bother." Tom sighed and raised his mug. "I guess the drink will have to do for a gift."

Ralegh raised his mug. "To fatherhood." Tom echoed the toast, his heart turning somersaults in his chest, as it always did when he heard that word.

"You meant to do me a good turn, lad," Ralegh said, "so I'll do you one. I know you've had offers to leave Gray's and chart another course. I think you're right to stay where you are, though my own offer stands."

"It's very flattering, Sir Walter."

He waved that off. "I won't press you, but good men are hard to find. You'll be asked again by others. Here's my advice. Don't enter Lord Dorchester's service. He's not yet formed, in my estimation. And you'd be sailing too close to the wind with respect to the lady."

"I know. And I won't. Serve Stephen, I mean." He met Sir Walter's eyes. "But I can no more stop loving Trumpet than I can stop being an Englishman. That ship sailed years ago."

"I understand. But be careful. Dorchester's not the feckless youth he was last year. He's growing up and finding he has teeth." Ralegh drew on his pipe, but it had gone out. He tapped the cold ashes onto the floor and tucked the figured clay piece back into his doublet. "Here's another word of advice. Don't go with Essex either, no matter what the Bacons do. His Lordship isn't altogether seaworthy. That's not envy talking. I have a wide experience of men, all sorts and stations. There's something out of trim about that young man. Some extravagance in his nature or an imbalance of his humors. Beware the sister as well."

"She terrifies me," Tom confessed.

Ralegh laughed. "Then you should be all clear in that quarter." He placed both hands on the table and said, "Duty calls. I thank you for the beer, Mr. Clarady. And give my best wishes to your lady." Then he rose and walked away.

Tom sat for a long moment, enjoying the reflected glow of the famed adventurer's presence. Then he called for another beer and some food as well — roast mutton with spring peas and a heap of mashed turnips. He chewed over Ralegh's advice along with the meal. Was there any use in warning Trumpet about Lady Rich? They'd become great friends, by her account. Perhaps now wasn't the time. She needed peace and good feelings all around.

On the other hand, she would know if he held back any part of his conversation with Sir Walter. She could read him like a child's primer. He couldn't lie to her any more than he could stop loving her.

Tom shook his head as he sopped up gravy with a chunk of bread, marveling at the problems his life held for him these days. Consorting with the great could be as heady as sailing a pinnace in a brisk wind, but it could also be as risky as picking your way through the rocky shoals of the West Indies in a heavy rain.

FIFTEEN

Trumpet added another thick slice of onion to the honeyed slice of bread and took an enormous bite. Yesterday, she could barely eat a thing. Today, she felt ravenous, with a specific hunger for coarse brown bread covered with thickened honey and raw onion. She chewed and swallowed, then smacked her lips, dabbing at a dribble of honey rolling down her chin.

"When is she coming?" she asked her maidservant.

"Soon, my lady." Catalina sat at the dressing table unpacking her box of paints and other theatrical oddments.

They'd invited Elsa Moreau to come have a drink of wine, hoping to cajole her into telling them the truth about her origins. Catalina had asked a few seemingly idle questions among the Essex servants last night. The yeoman of the cellar, himself a native of Bordeaux, had assured her that Elsa had never been brought up in a respectable home. He had been passing through the laundry one day where she was pressing some of Her Ladyship's finer linens. She'd burned her hand on the iron and produced a stream of curses only a child of the meanest streets could know. There were many such around the port of Bordeaux, orphans or the offspring of thieves and prostitutes.

"She's no more a gentlewoman than I am," he'd declared. But he refused to repeat that assertion, even to Lady Dorchester. "Why make trouble for myself? That sort will stick a knife in you just for looking at them the wrong way."

Trumpet wanted more than that anyway. She wanted to know how Elsa had wormed her way into the du Plessis house and why she'd lied about Lawson and Ridley. Two falsehoods in one short interview roused her suspicion. Tom, poor man, had been too busy struggling against his attraction for the golden-haired vixen. It was up to her to remedy his shortcomings.

Elsa had shown an interest in Catalina's costume-making arts the other day and seemed impressed by Trumpet's successful deception at Gray's Inn. Elsa must have achieved nearly as great a transformation to gain her place with Madame du Plessis. She couldn't have leapt in one jump from the streets to the governor's house. She might have other stories as well. Perhaps she could be engaged in a game of *who's the cleverest* and accidentally drop some clue about her real history with Lawson, Ridley, and Anthony Bacon.

Elsa knocked on the door as Trumpet was stuffing the last of her bread-and-honey into her mouth. Elsa chuckled at the remains of the unconventional meal and offered a gift: a length of exquisite Belgian lace.

"My lady thought you might like this for the christening gown."

"Mmph, mmph," Trumpet said, her mouth full.

"It is perfect," Catalina translated. She gestured at the small bench before the dressing table and got up to pour cups of wine for herself and the guest.

"How fares my Lady Dorchester this evening?"

"Hungry." Catalina smiled affectionately at her mistress, who nodded her agreement, honey oozing down her chin.

"That is a good sign, is it not?" Elsa Moreau poked among the jars on display, opening one and dipping her finger into the purplish paint. She turned to the mirror and dabbed the sample on her cheek. "Oh yes. The perfect color. But do you often wear bruises?" She pulled her handkerchief from her sleeve and wiped it off.

Trumpet resisted snapping her fingers. Who would know that but another player on the stage? She washed down the bread with a swallow of wine. "Anything unsightly on the face stops people from looking too closely."

"That's very clever, my lady," Elsa said. She picked up a small vial and removed the stopper to take a sniff. "Mmm, musky. Sir Charles wears something like that."

"A small amount is attractive," Trumpet said. "A large amount makes people sneeze."

Elsa trilled her musical laugh. "You're very skilled at diverting the gaze." She opened a small box and lifted out a tattered strip of hair. "What in heaven's name is this?"

Now Trumpet laughed. She hadn't seen that scrap of her history in years. "I was playing a youth of fifteen. My counselor said a pathetic moustache would make older men feel sorry for me and do their utmost not to stare at the pitiful object." Her uncle had been that clever counselor.

"A wise advisor!" Elsa held the object under her own nose. "But it must be very itchy, is it not?"

"I got used to it. I was more worried that it would come off at an awkward moment, so I used a lot of paste. That was hard to wash off. My upper lip always felt a little raw."

Elsa put it back in its box. "You suffered for your disguise, my lady. I suppose it is much harder in the light of day. At night, you only wear a dark cloak with a big hat and a scarf around your face."

The very words Tom had used to describe the second coachman. Trumpet felt a tingling at the back of her neck and decided to take a gamble. "No one pays any attention to the coachman anyway."

"That is true. Especially not when the horses are so beautiful a pair of black Friesian mares as . . ." She faltered, met Trumpet's leveled gaze, blinked, and looked away. She shot a glance at Catalina, who regarded her with a crooked smile.

"Mercy!" Elsa cried, leaping to her feet. "My lady told me not to dawdle, and here I sit, gossiping away." She sang the last few words and hastened out the door.

"Well, well, well," Trumpet said. "Wasn't *that* an interesting slip?"

"Are those Freezings the horses of Mr. Anthony?" Catalina asked.

"I do believe they are. As a matter of fact, I believe we've found our second coachman. Penelope told me the right story, but with the wrong master."

* * *

Trumpet scarcely had time to wash her hands and face and use the chamber pot — tasks that took infinitely longer in her current state — before the door opened to admit Penelope. She closed it behind her and leaned against it, riveting her obsidian gaze on Trumpet.

The intensity of her glare sent a shiver up Trumpet's spine. She placed a protective hand on her belly as Catalina moved to help her sit down. The faithful servant stood behind her with a comforting hand on her shoulder.

Penelope's lashes fluttered in amusement at their alarm. "Don't worry, I won't eat you. You're far too large a meal." She chuckled, but no one else did. "I want you to do something for me, Alice. When your lover comes to rub your feet this evening, I want you to tell him a new story about how Raffe Ridley met his death."

"I believe I have a new story already." Trumpet didn't like her use of the word "lover." She'd always just said "Tom" before. "Although I'm not sure how it starts."

"Hmm." Penelope crossed the room to gaze out the window at the colorful evening sky, her dark skirts swaying as she moved. "I should think you'd have worked that out by now, sly little fox that you are." She spoke over her shoulder. "That was a stupid slip, about the horses. You lulled her into letting her guard down."

"It's time to tell the truth." Trumpet mustered a smile. "She's led Tom and Francis Bacon on quite a wild goose chase."

"You misunderstand me." Penelope turned her back on the sunset. "That's not the story I want Tom to hear."

"Another fable? I'm willing to listen, though I make no promises."

Penelope unfolded a tale similar to the one about Sir Robert and his overreaching servant. This time, however, Madame du Plessis-Mornay played the role of instigator, while her stableman did the dirty deed.

"It's better than the last one," Trumpet said. "I'll confess I prefer the new villain. But while I might wish it were true, I know it isn't. And I think Tom's had enough nonsense for one week."

Penelope treated her to a derisive smile. "Jest if you like, but not for long. Because I want you to tell this story to Tom this evening. Make sure he believes it. You have no choice in the matter, Alice. You must comply."

"I don't think so." Trumpet returned the smile in full measure. "You underestimate me, Penelope."

Penelope's chilly gaze moved toward Trumpet's belly. "It doesn't take a Francis Bacon to guess who the father of that child is, whatever fiddle-faddle you spout about Tom looking after his friend's family in his absence. What do you think Lord Dorchester will do when he learns the truth?"

Trumpet gasped at the betrayal. It felt like a blow, right under her heart. She mastered the hurt and lifted her chin.

"He can't do much beyond confining me to Delabere House long enough to give him a real heir."

Penelope trilled a high-pitched laugh. "I mean, what will he do to Tom? Stephen's a *lord*. Boyhood retainers mean less than his favorite pair of riding boots. Do you imagine the benchers at Gray's will stand up to the Earl of Dorchester for a student they never wanted in the first place? Do you think Francis Bacon will stick his neck out? Then you *over*estimate him."

All Tom's dreams would be dashed. Destroyed. The vision of her beloved darling being brought to such public humiliation brought tears to Trumpet's eyes. She bit the inside her lip, willing them back.

Penelope smirked. "You know how Her Majesty treats adulterers. You'll end up in the Tower until your bastard is born. Tom will go to prison. Newgate or the Clink. And who will be left to find any mercy for him there?"

He'd hated those four days and nights in Newgate. Not just the foulness and the confinement, but the shame of it. Francis Bacon had pleaded with his lord uncle to free him. But no one would dare cross the queen for a man who'd planted a cuckoo in a nobleman's nest.

Penelope delivered the final blow. "Who knows what will become of the child. It will be an outcast from the day it's born. But you'll never see it again, so you'll never know, will you?"

A tear rolled down Trumpet's cheek. She couldn't stop it. She wrapped both hands around her belly, struggling to suppress her fear, knowing the babe could feel it too. She couldn't fight that evil witch. Someday, but not now, and not for such a cause. She nodded once, surrendering. "Curse your black heart, I'll tell him whatever you want. But to satisfy my own curiosity, I want to know why she did it."

Penelope shook her head. "Suffice it to say the truth would embarrass me. Elsa made the wrong decision and then left things in such a state that blame could fall on Anthony Bacon. That's the last thing I want. I can't be responsible for a rift between him and my brother before they've even met." She licked her lips, as content as a cat with a dead bird between its paws. "Be content. This new version satisfies everyone."

Everyone who cared nothing for the truth, which left out Francis Bacon — and Tom.

Trumpet pressed her lips together, turning her face toward the curtained bed with all its silken comforts, thinking about lying upon it in a short while with Tom at her feet. Thinking about lying through her teeth to him. She didn't know how she could do it, but she had no doubt the implacable Lady Rich would exact her penalty if she failed.

Penelope spoke softly. "You don't have to tell the story yourself, Alice. You just have to support it. Approve it. Elsa can speak the actual words."

"No." Trumpet drew on centuries of inherited hauteur to lift her chin and put steel in her voice. "I would never hide behind a servant. If a lie's to be told on my account, I'll be the one to tell it."

* * *

An hour later, Tom kissed her bare instep and set to work. He sprawled across the foot of the bed, regaling her with tidbits from the wills he'd been copying, knowing she'd enjoy puns based on the assize of *mort d'ancestor*.

Trumpet studied his features with helpless adoration, her love for him too big for her heart to hold. His beauty no longer topped the list of reasons for loving him; in fact, it had fallen nigh to the bottom. Well, maybe somewhere in the middle. But his brightness, his candor, and his ever-blooming zest for life topped the list, just beneath his unquenchable love for her.

They'd never lied to each other; not really. Not even before they knew they loved one another. Not even before he discovered she was a girl. In fact, she'd started dropping hints the minute she lost her heart to him, which was the first time he'd winked and given her that cheeky grin. Six years later, they were bonded to one another more tightly than most husbands and wives, however many months of separation they must endure.

But needs must. She had to break their trust in order to protect his future.

"Tom," she said with a rising lilt. "I've learned something astonishing this afternoon."

"More astonishing than wanting to leave a manor to your cat?" Tom grinned at her.

"Perhaps not. But we have a real solution to the Ridley matter at last."

"What ho, another one?" He'd told her about his meeting with Sir Walter that morning when he first came in. Tom had shrugged off the lost theory without regret. "Not someone who lives in my house, I hope. That was the best part about the last one."

"This one's the truth; I'm sure of it. Elsa had a drink with some friends from France last night, servants of the du Plessis-Mornays. They told her what really happened out there in Anthony's coach."

Her serious tone registered at last. He sat up and said, "Tell me."

She gulped down the bitter taste of lies and spun the tale Penelope had taught her. "The story comes from a groom in the du Plessis stable who had a special friendship with another stableman, a man named Louis Vandame. The groom caught Vandame packing to return to France. Vandame pulled him aside and said, 'If you don't see me again after the masters come home, I want you to know what happened.'"

"Vandame told the groom, who told Elsa Moreau," Tom said. "That's a little indirect."

Trumpet shrugged. "We can't help that. Don't you want to hear the whole thing?"

"I'm listening. But you know how every person in the chain makes their own small adjustments."

"I know." Trumpet got through the rest of her story without interruption.

Madame du Plessis had egged Ridley on to tell those lies about Anthony Bacon. The insult to her daughter still rankled, after all these years. She and Ridley were both envious of the warm welcome Anthony had received, to say nothing of the money he'd been given to travel home. Everyone thought he was some kind of hero, a prodigal son. No one had bothered about Ridley's homecoming, though he'd been gone just as long and had worked just as hard. And Monsieur du Plessis was barely tolerated at court, through no fault of his own.

When Ridley told Madame about Lawson's invitation to a *rapprochement*, she'd urged him to go. She'd had a change of heart about her old friend, it would seem. She wanted him to rein in those rumors. Her husband had caught wind of them, and it wouldn't be long before he worked out where they'd started. And Ridley knew far too much about her personally.

But why not extract some of Anthony's riches first? Madame assumed Lawson arranged the meeting in order to offer a bribe. That was how the world turned, was it not?

They agreed to substitute their own man in the driver's seat. They couldn't have a Bacon man sitting there listening to the negotiations. Madame wanted her cut, so Ridley would have to press for a substantial sum. Fortunately, she had a stableman with his own grudge against Ridley. The man did seem to inspire them.

Things went wrong from the start. Lawson had no money and didn't want to talk about the rumors. All he cared about was Newgate. He left in a huff, telling Ridley to go to the devil. Madame had foreseen this as a possible outcome and had prepared the driver with a plan of last resort. He should silence Ridley once and for all, doing his best to make it look like Lawson had done the deed. Ridley had become too great a liability for her. She promised the driver a comfortable pension, on a nice little farm he could call his own. She gave him money to go home and wait for her to return."

"This sounds a lot like the last story," Tom scoffed. "Except for the ending. Perhaps we should hire Thomas Nashe to write something more original."

She laughed, hating how easy it was. "That silly tale was Penelope's little jest. I was a simpleton to fall for it. You know how much Essex and Sir Robert despise one another. She thought it would be amusing to poke a stick into that anthill."

"Not so amusing for Burghley's coachman, if I'd ever found him."

"You never would have because she invented the whole thing." Trumpet filled her lying eyes with earnestness. "Madame du Plessis is a nasty piece of work, Tom. It doesn't surprise me she'd have servants cut from the same cloth."

He nodded, accepting her conviction without a murmur. Why shouldn't he? They trusted one another implicitly. "Vandame is the driver's name, you said?"

"Louis Vandame. The du Plessis-Mornays are living at the Savoy. Elsa met the other groom at the White Hart on the Strand. She assumes he lives above the stables at the Savoy."

"The second coachman was really a driver, then."

"Very good with horses, Elsa said. She knew him, of course, having worked for Madame in Montaubon."

"What did he have against Ridley?"

"I don't know," Trumpet said, glad to give one honest answer.

Tom dropped to one elbow again. "I'll want to question Moreau myself to get the details. People forget things or tell things out of order." He drew a finger up the bottom of her foot, watching her twitch with a playful grin.

It was all she could do not to burst into tears, but she knew Penelope was listening behind the door. Trumpet reminded herself that this was all for the best, all for Tom's own good. She promised herself that if he found out about it — *when* he found out about it — he'd forgive her. Which was more than she could ever do for herself.

SIXTEEN

Candlelight glowed under the door to Anthony's chamber. Tom heard voices within and decided to make his report. Good news shouldn't wait until morning.

He expected to find the brothers snugged up in their usual chairs before the fire, with Jacques tucking pillows behind them and filling their polished cups with fragrant wine. But tonight only Francis reclined with his feet on a low stool. Anthony limped back and forth across the length of the room, leaning on his ebony cane, grasping the top so tightly his knuckles shone as white as the ivory knob.

"I'm glad to see you feeling better, Mr. Bacon." Tom watched him execute a turn at the end of the room and pause to make a florid gesture to underscore his improvement. Tom had never seen him standing up before. He was taller than he'd thought and had a touch of grace, even with the cane, that his younger brother lacked.

Tom was beginning to understand Francis's frustration. If this man were as whole and hearty as the Earl of Essex or Sir Walter Ralegh, he'd be shouldering his way into the tight circle around the queen to give the others some stiff competition. Francis hated going to court. You could see it in his face every time he left the house to go to Whitehall. He loved Her Majesty and knew his duty, but he hated the standing, the waiting, and the sly maneuvering.

Anthony, on the other hand, belonged there, or else directing affairs of state from some great house on the Strand. Francis belonged in a judge's robes on the dais in

Westminster Hall or pottering around the grounds at Twickenham in his philosophy clothes, discovering how Nature worked.

Gout had stolen those promises, taking two men down with one affliction.

"You look like a man with something to say, Mr. Clarady." Anthony steadied himself with both hands on the stick, balancing his weight on both legs. His lace cuffs shone in the warm light of the many candlesticks placed along his route. He was fully dressed in doublet and hose of black broadcloth, with gold chains hanging from his neck. He wore fine black stockings and polished shoes with bows on the toes. He'd left off his hat. His black hair fell in gleaming waves to his shoulders.

"Are you going out?" Tom asked.

Anthony laughed. "Not yet. Soon, perhaps. I'm hoping to make a small excursion in a week or so."

"That's wonderful! Will you see Her Majesty at last?"

"One step down, for a start." Anthony flicked his dark eyebrows, inviting Tom to guess.

Francis spoiled his little game, fortunately, since Tom hadn't the least idea. "I've had a letter from my lord of Essex. He and the Earl of Dorchester are coming home in a week, weather permitting. Essex has news for the queen, and Dorchester is eager to be here for the birth of his first child."

"Of course he is." Tom's stomach clenched. Stephen's presence in Essex House — to say nothing of Lord Essex — would make it impossible to see Trumpet. Well, she'd deliver the babe any day now and be able to sneak out again soon enough. "I do have news, as it happens. I was visiting — ah, the Antelope this evening."

He met Francis's eyes, widening his slightly to indicate that he'd been with Trumpet. They hadn't told Anthony about their history with her since it wasn't their secret to spill. She could tell him herself someday, if she wanted to.

Tom decided to leave her out of it altogether. The story had originated with Elsa Moreau, who did stop in at the Antelope from time to time. She might well have gone there tonight for the purpose of telling Tom about Madame du Plessis and her vengeful coachman.

"News from the local tippling house?" Anthony smiled. "We must hear it at once. Jacques, bring Mr. Clarady a chair and a drink. Tavern tales are thirsty work."

Francis watched him get settled with a speculative gleam in his hazel eyes. "A new explanation of the Ridley matter, I imagine."

"That's right," Tom said. "I met Elsa Moreau this evening. She heard a very interesting story from a servant of the du Plessis-Mornays. Have you heard of them?"

"Du Plessis," Anthony moaned. "How will I ever escape that troublesome pair? They follow me everywhere I go, like a clot of muddy weeds stuck to the bottom of your shoe."

"You followed them to Montaubon, as I recall," Francis said. "Wasn't it Monsieur du Plessis who recommended the place?"

"He might have done." Anthony hadn't budged from his spot in front of the curtained windows. He appeared to be gathering strength for another tour. "One fails to recall every trivial detail."

"I think this is the truth about what happened last Friday night," Tom said. "My gut tells me Elsa Moreau is a shrewd judge of the persons involved, and the story made sense to her."

"Ah, the gut!" Anthony said. His tone held respect, not mockery. "I understand that's an important factor in our analyses." He began to walk toward the bedchamber again, rebalancing himself at every step.

Tom told them the whole story, just as Trumpet had told it to him. He prided himself on his memory for turns of phrase and nuances of presentation. When he finished,

Francis stared into the fire, petting his moustache with his index finger. He often did that while assimilating new information, matching it up with everything else stored in his outsized brain. Never mind that whoever he'd been talking to was left standing while he lost himself in thought.

Anthony supplied the courteous response. He'd reached the middle of the room, where the other two sat. "You astonish me, Mr. Clarady, once again. That story sounds so contrived as to be utterly fabulous, and yet your own conviction makes it ring true. I assume you questioned Moreau, attempting to catch her out on the details?"

"Of course," Tom said. He had, somewhat. Trumpet had started looking weary, so he'd cut things short. "Also, the groom who told her the story had no reason to lie. She said he seemed glad to share the burden of the secret. And why would either of them invent a story about this, of all things? Neither of them could know anything about the coach, much less the second coachman."

"That's a valid point," Anthony said. "Perhaps the strongest one yet."

Francis sniffed. "It does seem very convenient, doesn't it? That Lady Rich's servant should pop up with an explanation that blames everything on a foreigner whom her mistress despises."

"Does she?" Anthony asked. "How would you know that?"

Francis blinked like an owl caught in the garden after sunrise. Tom scrambled for an explanation. Should he let Anthony think he was sporting with Elsa Moreau?

"I've met Mrs. Moreau once or twice," he ventured. "She is extraordinarily beautiful. One evening, I heard a droll account of Madame du Plessis's visit to the ladies at Essex House. She put the wrong foot forward trying to tattle on you, Mr. Anthony. Lady Rich made it clear such prattle wasn't welcome, especially not about a man she held in high regard."

Anthony paused to regard Tom with a speculative eye. "I'm gratified by Lady Rich's interest. And Lady Dorchester's too, perhaps?"

Tom smiled agreeably but didn't answer. Anthony continued on his labored path.

Francis shot Tom a narrow look. He could easily guess that Tom had shared everything with Trumpet, which she might have passed along to Lady Rich. Their maidservants would likely have been present. He could assume all those women knew everything they knew about Ridley's murder. But he couldn't reveal that to Anthony without making Tom look like the worst sort of babbler, spilling secrets to impress his latest *inamorata*.

What a mess! Tom couldn't see a way out of it — not yet. Let the child be born and the confinement end. Let the lords return so Trumpet could move into her own house and be her own mistress again. Then she could tell Anthony whatever she chose.

Luckily, Francis had an answer. "Lady Rich has always been active in her brother's cause. She's certainly clever enough to connect Ridley to you, especially given a servant who lived inside your circle in Montaubon. Her Ladyship might have asked Moreau to inquire among her former fellows to find out if Ridley and Madame du Plessis's friendship had continued here in London."

"So now you believe it?" Anthony tossed the question over his shoulder.

Francis shrugged, though his brother couldn't see the gesture. "I merely point out that the story's provenance is not beyond the realm of the reasonable."

Anthony chuckled. He reached the bedroom door and turned carefully around. "I think you're disgruntled because you didn't get to exercise your inductive reasoning. You would rather elicit a solution from a curious arrangement of the cushions in my coach, or some such detail that everyone else missed."

Francis gave him a withering look. Anthony licked his bottom lip — or perhaps stuck his tongue out at his brother. Then he turned a skeptical eye toward Tom. "Although it does seem very convenient. What did Elsa want for this juicy tidbit?"

"Nothing," Tom said. "Or, well . . . I paid for her supper."

"A whole supper?" Anthony asked, adding a waggish uptilt to the question. "Mutton or fish?"

Tom stammered, "Ah, well . . . your lady aunt has a tight grip on the purse strings."

"Tsk, tsk." Anthony grinned. "We should send you to France. The ladies at King Henry's court would pay *you* to listen to their stories."

"Perhaps she wanted to do her mistress a favor," Tom said, "as Mr. Francis suggested. She met the groom to ask about Ridley and learned more than she bargained for."

Francis sniffed. "The motivations of both Madame du Plessis and her driver strike me as thin. He holds an old grudge, and she's become worried about some gossip she initiated. It's too flimsy."

"He prefers solid facts," Anthony told Tom, as if imparting a family secret. "You don't know these people, Frank, not the way I do. That driver, for one. Was his name Vandame, perchance?"

"It was," Tom said, surprised. "Louis Vandame."

Anthony nodded. "The man's a thief and a scoundrel, a blight on an otherwise blameless family. He worked for me for a year or so until the stableman caught him stealing bits of silver tackle. I believe du Plessis took him on as a favor to Vandame Senior."

"It's a long way from stealing trinkets to strangling a man," Francis said.

"Which brings me to his mistress. You've never met her, either of you, so you can have no idea. She's a woman of tremendous vanity. I doubt she's ever forgiven the slightest offense, though I can't say offhand what I might have done to warrant such abuse of my coach and my secretary."

"Hoi!" Tom snapped his fingers. "I forgot the whole business of the rejected daughter."

"The daughter," Anthony said. "I'd forgotten all about her. Not a memorable girl, poor lass."

Tom filled Francis in. "Madame du Plessis has a daughter by her first husband. Old enough to wed, I suppose, but still unmarried. Madame tried to hook Mr. Anthony, but he refused. According to Elsa, he made some jest or other that ruffled the mother's feathers."

"Did I?" Anthony frowned at the ceiling. Then he laughed. "Oh dear. I'm afraid I did. The girl's name is Suzanne De Paz. I believe I said something like, 'My life would be de Guerre if I should marry de Paz.' An ill-considered quip. I should know better, but sometimes my wit runs away with me."

Tom knew *guerre* meant "war." He had that much French. "They say nothing offends a woman more than rejecting her daughter when offered."

"Envy," Francis said, "is considered one of the deadliest sins for good reason. It grows in the heart like an inward cancer. I can see wounded vanity inspiring Madame du Plessis to spread rumors about you. We know Ridley had cause to envy you as well. She encouraged him, and he was willing. But then, for no reason, she changed her mind."

Tom had an answer for that. "She didn't so much change her mind as lose her nerve. Ridley was too successful. And too noisy, getting drunk and starting fights in taverns. She feared her husband would trace the rumors back to her and be angry. The groom said that when Madame found out about the *rapprochement*, she feared Ridley would make a private bargain with you, Mr.

Anthony, through your secretary, and leave her twisting in the wind."

"That's a little strained, Mr. Clarady," Anthony said, "but I believe it. Vain persons assume they are the center of every conversation and the target of every plot."

Francis nodded. "And dishonest people assume everyone else is taking bribes. Yes, that supports the story. She sent her criminous driver to find out what terms were being offered. Then, when Lawson left without offering anything at all, the driver executed the alternative plan. One assumes he was well paid."

"I'm sure she had the measure of her man." Anthony cast his gaze toward the front windows. "I'm going to make one more round."

Tom sipped some wine — now cooled, but still spicy and rich. "It's the only explanation we have that cuts the Gordian knot."

Both Bacons smiled at his allusion, as if they had sole authority in old Greek tales. He'd read a book or two on his own initiative. He'd graduated Bachelor of Arts from Cambridge University, after all.

"You know what I mean," he persisted. "The conundrum. Someone supposedly killing Ridley to stop his slandering, thereby benefitting Anthony, but using his coach and pointing all the clues at his secretary, thereby ruining him."

"Poor Lawley!" Anthony said as he huffed past them.

"That was a conundrum," Francis said, approving Tom's use of the term. "The sheer nonsensicality of it was enough to rule out Robert on the spot."

"He had better ways of making Ridley stop," Tom said. "He could just call the man into his office and say, 'Desist.'" He hadn't told Francis about his drink with Sir Walter and didn't mean to, so he might as well make use of the man's words.

"Indeed." Francis watched his brother reach the windows and pause, head hanging as if spent. "It's time to sit down, Anthony."

"I'm going to walk back to my chair." He turned around, his face drawn with the effort.

Tom said, "There's a library on the first floor at Essex House. Jacques and I can carry you straight in from the coach. No stairs at all, and no one standing around watching."

"You've become quite familiar with His Lordship's house." Anthony gave Tom a knowing smile.

Tom winced, pretending to be rueful. Let him think he and Elsa Moreau had explored the house in their search for trysting places.

"Let's hope I can manage on my own by then." Anthony focused on his feet as he made the distance from window to hearth. "I want to make a good impression."

Francis said nothing. He watched his brother's faltering progress with a critical eye and a quirk on his lips. It looked like disbelief, although anyone could see Anthony was genuinely struggling to walk, even with the cane. He should have two of them, with stronger handles.

What provoked the quirk, then? Surely Francis didn't think Anthony had invented the du Plessis story, teaching it to Lawson to carry to Elsa Moreau, to be told to Tom. That would be too tangled a web even for so crafty a spider as Anthony Bacon. Or would it?

The spider staggered back to its nest, sinking onto the cushions with a groan of relief. Jacques rushed to wipe beads of sweat from his master's brow and lift the weary legs to a padded stool. He draped a coverlet over the legs, drew Anthony's hair back from his neck, and set a cup of freshly made spiced wine at his elbow.

"Well," Anthony said after refreshing himself with a long draught, "we have our answer. Now what shall we do with it?"

Tom looked to Francis, who shrugged. "The driver's gone, or we could turn him over to the authorities. Without him to bear witness against his mistress, I don't see any way of bringing her to justice."

"Justice." Anthony spoke as if his brother had told a comic tale ending on that word. "We most certainly cannot turn the driver over to the authorities. Have you forgotten that we've already supplied them with a story, which has been duly recorded as the official explanation?"

Francis still looked disgruntled. He hadn't fully accepted the new story, but he hadn't offered an alternative either. Not one, in all these days.

"You look unhappy, Frank," Anthony said. "I should think you'd be pleased. You can stop suspecting me of ordering a man's death." Anthony winked at Tom. "I must thank *you*, Mr. Clarady, for seeking the truth even after my brother begged you to let it drop."

"I never did any such thing," Francis answered in a supercilious tone. "But I am disappointed to learn that you inspired this vast, overarching antagonism among your neighbors without so much as a whisper of it to me."

"Oh, I see," Anthony said. "You feel left out. I assure you, I had no idea Madame du Plessis harbored such animosity in her prodigious bosom. Nor Raffe, for that matter."

"There are too many gaps," Francis said, ignoring his brother's levity. "Whole chasms are opening up beneath your correspondence of the past thirteen years."

"Chasms?" Anthony asked. "Of course there are. Canyons, abysses, and vast desert wastelands. You know perfectly well one can only write a fraction of what one means to say. Letters are too easily intercepted."

Francis grunted and lowered his nose into his cup. No one could argue with that basic fact. "Someday you and I will sit down and go through that chest of letters. Then you can fill me in on everything I missed."

Anthony laughed. "I've been trying to get you to help sort that mountain of paper for a week. Will tomorrow morning suit you? Or are you planning to burn a few more fingers?"

They traded a few more brotherly barbs. Tom didn't mind. He had three older sisters. Compared to their battles and machinations, these two were amateurs.

"What shall we do, then?" Tom asked. "I don't like the idea of that driver walking free. And trusting a woman like du Plessis to behave herself doesn't make much sense either."

"Here's what I suggest," Anthony said. "English law may not be able to touch them, but we can expect Monsieur du Plessis to discipline both wife and servant. There's a war in France; let Vandame go help fight it. His family's honor will be preserved, but his life will be as harsh as that in any prison, for as long as he manages to hold on to it."

"That sounds fair," Tom said. If the man did his part and survived, he'd redeem himself.

Francis sighed. "I suppose it's the best we can do."

"That's not all," Anthony said. "Let us use our knowledge to expel the du Plessis-Mornays from England once and for all." He flashed a smile at Tom. "No punishment could be greater than sending that queen of vanity back to Montaubon, where the draper's wife is her only follower." He turned the smile toward Francis, who returned it with a flat gaze.

"That's scant justice for Raffe Ridley," he said, "lately an English gentleman. You gave him a house room once upon a time. Don't you want his murderer to hang?"

"I do not possess such power. Perhaps I should challenge Madame du Plessis to a duel?"

Jacques giggled loudly, clapping his hand over his mouth.

Anthony smiled at him. "Lawly would find it amusing too. And we do owe him something after all the hard thoughts that have been sent his way." Then he shrugged. "We take the remedy within our grasp, Frank. That's all we can ever do."

Francis grumbled into his cup, "You used to tell me everything."

"We used to be children," Anthony said.

Sending the murderer off to war seemed fair enough to Tom, as did confining a vain woman in a narrow sphere. But dissatisfaction hung thick in this spice-perfumed chamber. They'd solved a thorny problem in their favor. They'd gotten what they wanted. Then why did everyone seem so out of sorts?

SEVENTEEN

"No, no. I can't sit down. My back aches. I feel like I slept in a barrel." Trumpet pushed Tom's helping hands away and continued on her path across her bedchamber.

"Then come sit on the bed and let me massage the ache away." Tom's eyes and voice were so filled with loving concern it made her heart sick after the lie she'd told him yesterday. Guilt propelled her from end to end of her prison.

"Walking is better." It let her turn her face away from him most of the time.

"As you wish." He perched on the end of the bed, his usual place. Catalina sat on her usual stool by the window. She'd set her sewing aside to keep both eyes on her mistress, evidently sharing Tom's concern for this vagrant humor.

Or she might think the restlessness was caused by the baby wanting to be born. Trumpet couldn't think about that, not with Tom here. She couldn't stretch out on the bed to let him rub her feet. She couldn't sit on the dressing-table bench to let him rub her shoulders. She couldn't bear for him to touch her, great falsificator that she was.

"Are you worried about Madame du Plessis finding out you helped us point the finger at her?" Tom asked. "Because the Bacons are going to confront Monsieur with his wife's crimes tomorrow. Anthony intends to send them back to France. She'll never trouble you again."

"I don't care one fat fig about Madame du Plessis." Though that wasn't true. She hated the woman, which was a form of caring. She still felt a clench of terror whenever that terrifying childbirth story crossed her mind.

That answer had been evasive, not false. Evasion might not be the truth, but in truth, it wasn't a lie. She would count it as a half-truth. Perhaps a hundred of them could compensate for one big lie. She should keep score to know when she could face those candid blue eyes again.

To people like Penelope — now revealed to have the moral foundation of a feral cat — her lie was nothing. Less than nothing. Penelope doubtless told lies that big six times a day, just to maintain the craft. But such people did not know what it meant to love a man like Tom.

"What's wrong with you this evening, sweetling?" he asked. "Is it the baby?"

"The baby's fine." Another evasion; the babe was as restless as she was. "Let's go walk in the gallery. There's no one in the house but servants, and they're used to you."

She had something to share with him anyway — more evidence against Madame du Plessis. Perhaps the Bacons would find it useful in making their case tomorrow. Stephen, bless him, had sent her a delightful story about La Plashy, straight from the French court. And there was a portrait in the gallery that would supply the perfect illustration.

Two days ago, she would've been dancing on her toes with glee over Stephen's story. He'd given her the winning card to throw on the table at the height of the game. But now she knew this was no game. The gossip, the stories, the manipulations could mean life or death for someone. Another lesson learned at Lady Rich's feet.

When they topped the stairs and entered the gallery, Tom's jaw dropped in admiration. The opulent chamber looked its best at this hour. The north-facing windows showed faint streaks of pink behind the thatched roofs across the road. Errant beams of sunlight picked out golden edges on gilded frames.

Lover of life and true mate of her soul, Tom moved instinctively to her favorite window. He leaned his elbows on the stone sill and gazed down at the busy thoroughfare. "Now *this* is a view!" He turned around to lean his elbows on the sill, beaming with that irresistible grin. "If you stood here long enough, I'll wager you'd see everyone you've ever known pass by."

Trumpet summoned a smile. "You might see them and not know it. People look different from this angle. Mostly what you see are their hats and their horses."

"A fair point." He turned his attention to the long expanse of polished oak panels, the silk-covered benches, and the double row of portraits stretching back for what felt like a quarter of a mile. He gave a low whistle, awed. "This is the sort of place you deserve, my lady."

She hated when he called her that — unless his intent was ironical. Then she rather liked it. He only used it *in veritas* when he felt humbled by her status, which happened whenever he was confronted with the imposing grandeur of a great house. Someday she'd have to show him Orford Castle. It had been a long time since anyone had polished anything there since her father had sold of most of the things worth polishing.

Tom had grown accustomed to the hall at Gray's Inn, which had been substantially rebuilt in Francis Bacon's father's day, but in the ancient style. Its lofty hammerbeam ceiling and the stained glass displaying seals of prominent members were meant to impress, like this gallery. But that hall was also a place of active work. Hundreds of men ranging in age from fifteen to eighty gathered there every day to eat their meals, carry out legal exercises, play cards, and practice dancing. The place was thus marvelous and quotidian at once.

Essex House had been built by the Earl of Leicester twenty years ago. He'd needed a place to live and house his retinue, handy to Her Majesty's palaces. He'd also needed a house grand enough to proclaim his status and awe his rivals. Trumpet didn't want Tom to be awed. She wanted him always to be Tom.

His eyes searched hers as he asked, "Do you want me to enter Essex's service, Trumpet? I mean, do you honestly think I should?"

Two days ago, she would've said *yes*. Today, she knew better. She met his eyes and spoke the truth. "No, I don't. Stay your course, Tom. Be your own man. Be a barrister — be a great one." The ache in her heart eased a little. She would do anything to protect Tom and help him reach his dreams. Once he passed the bar, he would be safer.

"I thought you wanted us to align ourselves with the Essex faction. Isn't that why Stephen's in France?"

She puffed that away. "I couldn't pry Stephen from Essex's side with a wherryman's long-handled oar."

That made Tom laugh, restoring him to his normal bouyant spirits. "We could try, if we could get him to stand still for a moment. You hold him down, while I —"

"Stephen!" She'd forgotten the letter. She couldn't hold a thought in her head for more than a few minutes, not with the guilt thrumming in the back of her mind. And the baby kicking, and Tom grinning at her with that relentless dimple.

Tom whirled around, as if expecting to see him coming up the stairs. She shook her head at his alarm. "He's not here — not yet. The wind is so fickle it could be a week before they can cross with all their horses. But I have a letter from him."

"Oh, a letter." Tom sounded jealous. "I can write you letters."

"You've written me dozens, and I love them all. I keep them hidden in Catalina's costume box. But this is different. Last week, I asked him to find out what he could about the odious du Plessis. Gossip. Anything that will prick her monstrous vanity."

"Sounds like a good job for Stephen. What did he find?"

"Something wonderful." She cocked her head. "But first I have to show you an example." She held out her hand. Tom took it and tucked it under his elbow. She led him to a darkish area and pointed at a small portrait placed below eye level — a position of dishonor. "See that woman?"

"The one in the red gown with that red what-d'ye-call-'em on her head?"

"That's the one."

"Friend of yours, is she?"

"Hardly. She's Margaret of Valois, wife of King Henry the Fourth. But she doesn't live with him anymore. She's gone over to the Catholic League. Her brother's the Duke of Anjou, which is why she's hanging down here in the shadows."

Tom studied the portrait. "Her eyes are too small, and her nose is too long. Look at how it sort of drips off there at the end."

"It's a vile nose. *Our* child will have a beautiful nose, whoever it takes after."

"I'm hoping for green eyes," Tom said. "Fewer complications."

"Me too. But Stephen's maternal grandmother had blue eyes. They have a portrait in their gallery."

"I've seen it. Her nose is just like Stephen's. That long triangle with the narrow tip. But do you know, my mother has brown eyes. I get these blue ones from my father."

Trumpet smiled. She loved those eyes, but one pair was enough. "I pray every night that there be no dimple"

"Me too." Their eyes met in a communion of anticipation and trepidation, along with the knowledge they'd stand together, whatever happened.

"Why are we studying the nose of the queen of France?" Tom asked.

"We don't care about the nose. It's her hair that concerns us. That's what the letter's about."

Tom pursed his lips and looked down at her with his senior barrister face. It usually made her laugh. Today, it made her heart turn somersaults — or maybe that was the baby. She'd better get on with the letter. She'd have to sit down in a minute.

Tom nodded, frowning, then issued a ruling. "I agree with my lord of Dorchester. The hair is dreadful. What's under those mounds? Mice? Packets of sweets?"

"No, but how perfect! Now attend, if you please. This is the queen, yes? Where she goes, fashion follows, even all the way to insignificant places like Montaubon."

"Ah, I begin to understand. Your favorite Frenchwoman, La Plashy, styles her hair in this overbuilt mode."

"*Exactement.* And that hair is the reason Raffe Ridley was strangled."

"You've lost me again."

Trumpet nodded. "It's true. La Plashy considers herself a woman of influence, a status which demands a certain outward appearance. Alas for her, she resides among Calvinists, who despise such false embellishments. One Sunday in church, the minister scolded the women for using pomp and artifice, as he put it, to elevate the hair."

"Looking straight at her, no doubt."

"Madame was aghast. Humiliated. She rallied the townswomen to defend their hair. But then the resident Englishman, a son of Lady Bacon, the well-known pillar of that strict religion, spoke against the puffed-up hair. Spoke dismissively. Spoke *derisively*. In short, he scoffed at it, thereby scoffing at Madame herself."

"I am my hair, and my hair is me." Tom shook his head in mock dismay. "I would consider that a deadly offense. Was there a duel?"

"If she'd been a man, there would have been." Trumpet felt a twinge in her belly and grunted, placing both hands under the great weight to support it. "Let's sit down."

Tom guided her to a bench farther down the gallery. He sat opposite her, far enough not to seem improper if anyone should come in. Although his mere presence was so improper that she might as well be sitting in his lap.

"In all seriousness, sweetling, you can't believe that woman had Raffe Ridley murdered because Anthony Bacon insulted her hair."

"Stephen says she was hugely offended. Her husband too. The story got out, as such tales tend to do. He was mocked at court. She's horribly vain, Tom. Add the public humiliation to the rejection of her daughter, and Anthony made a lifelong enemy. As for Ridley . . ." She shrugged. "Elsa thinks he may have been La Plashy's lover at one time. Her husband is often away at court and cares more for his immortal soul than for his wife. It might not be true, but if it is, it's another reason for her to want him gone."

"It sounds like everyone was dallying with everyone in that little town. I'll tell the Bacons about the Affair of the Hair. We're meeting with Monsieur du Plessis in the morning to deliver Anthony's judgment. He wants them to leave at once and take their friend Antoine du Pin with them. The coachman will be sent to the vanguard of King Henry's troops."

"That sounds fair." And it relieved her of the burden of sending an innocent man to the gallows. That thought had weighed on her conscience too.

Tom gave her an admiring smile. "I must thank you, Trumpleton. You solved the Ridley problem without even leaving the house. Now Anthony can boot his enemies out of England and go back to hawking his services to the lords with the deepest pockets."

"Good luck to him." Trumpet felt the baby moving and struggled to her feet. She needed to walk. She had the strongest feeling that her time was nigh. Tonight, tomorrow, the next morning . . . But she didn't want to alarm Tom, not yet.

Another evasion, but a considerate one. Perhaps the baby would balance out the lie. Once it was born, she could move out of Essex House. Then she would tell him the truth. No one else had to know. They wouldn't upset Anthony's arrangements. Tom could decide for himself what he wanted to do about it. She would accept his ruling.

He wouldn't like it; that much she knew. She'd put him in the unhappy position of lying to the Bacons, for one thing. She hadn't considered the consequences of the lie, but in fairness, Penelope hadn't given her time to think. She'd threatened a woman on the brink of childbirth with harm to both her child and its father, then moved directly to the execution of her demand.

Another lesson learned.

If she'd had one day to reflect, she'd have discussed Penelope's demand with Tom. She knew what he would say. "We'll find a way around it. We'll tell Mr. Bacon, and he'll find a way. But we should never give in to a blackmailer."

And then the solution came to her: she'd just have to turn the tables.

EIGHTEEN

"Anthony, you take longer to get dressed than a noblewoman going to court." Francis plopped down in his chair by the unlit hearth. He wasn't looking forward to this confrontation, but he didn't need Anthony in train. He and Tom could deliver their ultimatum to du Plessis in short order and be home in time for a nice nap before supper.

"What do you know about a woman's toilette?" Anthony sat on a stool while Jacques fussed about him, combing and curling his hair. Both Bacons turned toward Tom, the resident expert on women.

"Don't ask me," Tom said. "My sisters live in Dorset. But I have another story for you while we have time. I've learned another reason for Madame du Plessis to dislike Mr. Anthony." Tom shot Francis a significant look before adding, "I saw Elsa Moreau again last night."

"That woman has considerable liberty for a maidservant," Anthony observed. "I would expect Lady Rich to be a more exacting mistress."

"She just slipped out for a few minutes, hoping she'd catch me at the Antelope again." Tom produced a sheepish smile.

"Oho," Anthony said. "Do I sense a budding romance between the gentleman of Gray's and the humble maid from France? Though I fear Mrs. Moreau is far from a maid."

Tom laughed, though it sounded forced. "Do you want to hear the latest tidbit?"

Francis and Anthony shushed one another and painted attentive expressions on their faces. They were treated to more secondhand gossip.

Moreau said she had suspected that Madame du Plessis and Raffe Ridley had been lovers, as well as gossiping companions. That would make a better motive for the husband than the wife, one would think. But it sounded like something a discontented servant would invent. They could never use it without seeming vulgar.

Anthony wrinkled his hose. "It's possible, I suppose, though I don't think I believe it. Then again, I've known more than a few devout persons who've slipped in that area."

"We could count ourselves among that number," Francis said. "Although neither of us trades on a reputation for rectitude."

"Perhaps not. But I've made good use of our mother's." They grinned at one another.

They were having a cheerful morning. Anthony was about to make a foray beyond his chamber door, they had solved a disturbing crime, and they had an excellent excuse to banish two troublesome persons from their lives once and for all. If only Anthony would stay home and husband his strength today, Francis would be quite content.

Tom said, "There's more," and proceeded to relate an absurd tale involving hairpieces.

"Preposterous!" Francis objected. "No one could hold a grudge for such a thing."

"I'd forgotten all about that." Anthony grinned over his shoulder at Jacques and gave him the gist of the story in French.

"Ooh la!" Jacques laughed and clapped his hand over his mouth.

Anthony smiled at Tom. "Thank you for the timely reminder. That episode was hardly a cause for murder, but add it to the rest . . ." He shrugged. "Du Plessis would certainly set Madame aside if he learned of her adultery. Then she would have nothing. Her father is a minor civil lawyer, I believe. No lands to speak of."

Jacques began fluffing up the layers of his master's sheer lace-trimmed ruff. Anthony pushed his hand away, ready at last. "Is the coach here?"

Both Bacons looked at Tom.

"I'll see to it." He got up and went out, returning in a trice. "I could've just looked out the window. I'm so used to those curtains being closed that I forget you have a clear view of the yard. It's right outside the door."

Jacques helped his master up, but Anthony insisted on making his way outside on his own with his cane. Tom and Jacques lifted him bodily into the coach. Francis hopped in after, giving thanks to God for not inflicting their father's disability on him.

Anthony puffed at the effort, and his face seemed drawn.

Francis chided him. "It isn't necessary for you to make this expedition, Anthony. I've served well enough as your ambassador all these years."

"A post you've grown weary of, as you inform me on a daily basis. I'm making this effort as much for you as for me. It's good practice. Furthermore, that dire woman put my friend Lawly in danger of hanging. She tried to destroy my good name. I want to render this judgment myself."

They glared at one another. Tom broke in to ask, "Will they accept your sentence, just like that?"

"Perhaps not 'just like that,'" Anthony said, "but yes, they must if they want to keep this story from circulating. It would cause great trouble for them here and ruin them in the church at home. And I could create other problems for Monsieur du Plessis, if I so desired."

"What are these mysterious 'other problems'?" Francis asked. "They keep being referenced without being elucidated. How can I negotiate terms when I don't have all the facts?"

Anthony smirked. "That's why I'm here."

Tom and Jacques traded eye rolls at the sniping, so Francis held his peace for the remainder of the short drive down to the Strand. Anthony allowed Tom and Jacques to carry him into the depths of the Savoy. The du Plessis-Mornays had leased a pair of rooms in one of the several houses on the east side. Tom had ascertained that their tenement was on the ground floor, or Anthony would have had to leave this job to Francis.

Lodgings in Westminster were hard to come by, so Francis was not surprised to find a miniscule and scantily furnished habitation. The reception parlor was smaller than Francis's study chamber, with a tiled hearth set into one wall and a narrow window, firmly shut, at one end. The place stank of cold ashes and stale bodies. Doors hung in two walls, making it difficult to place chairs for everyone. Tom and Jacques ended up on a bench blocking one of the doors. The paneling was cracked, and the plaster ceiling showed stains from old water leaks from the floor above.

The du Plessis-Mornays' lodgings might be mediocre, but their clothing was beyond reproach. No wonder Anthony had taken such pains with his toilette. Francis and Tom had dressed as they would for a morning at the Queens' Bench, like professional gentlemen — in other words, in well-tailored, but non-ostentatious, black wool.

Monsieur du Plessis wore a doublet of buff silk liberally slashed to reveal the brown silk lining. His ruff was plain in that it bore no lace, but the cambric pleats were stacked four levels high. He'd combed his thinning, buff-colored hair straight back from his high forehead and trimmed his beard into a narrow wedge that hung down the front of his ruff.

Madame outdid her mate, resplendent in red velvet with yellow pricks and a tall upstanding ruff as sheer and lacy as Anthony's. She wore the newfangled farthingale, which demanded a full yard of space, occupying a bench as wide as that supporting both Tom and Jacques.

Monsieur introduced Francis to Madame, ignoring the retainers. No pretense was made that this was a social engagement. Monsieur said, without preamble, "Your note mentioned a serious matter of importance to us both. What is the nature of this matter?"

Before Francis could respond, Madame interjected, "You've spoken with Lady Rich, I presume. I would expect her to exercise more discretion."

"I've never met her," Anthony said coolly.

"I have," Francis said, "and indirectly, she is the reason we're here."

"She lies, then," Madame said. "She is without scruple, that woman. She stole my maidservant. Now she seeks to embarrass me. It is not enough to humiliate me in her house."

Francis frowned at her. What could she mean? They hadn't mentioned their charges yet.

"What is this reason?" Monsieur raised his pale eyebrows.

"We're here about the murder of Raffe Ridley. An old friend of yours, I believe."

"And of Monsieur Anthony," Madame said. "Of us all, *bien sûr.*"

Her husband shot her a quelling glance. "I thought Mr. Ridley had been set upon by thieves."

"That is the official story," Francis said, "but it is not what happened."

Monsieur folded his hands over the peascod belly of his doublet. "*Eh, bien.* You wish us to hear something. We will listen."

Francis summarized the story told by Elsa Moreau to Tom, omitting the testimonial trail. That might seem deceptive to some, but it was sound legal practice and had the advantage of making a long story short.

Monsieur listened impassively. Madame, in contrast, fixed Anthony with a speculative glint in her eyes. From time to time, her gaze wandered toward Tom. Only to be expected; women's eyes always lingered on Tom.

At the end, Monsieur said, "Then this second coachman killed Mr. Ridley?"

"That is correct," Francis said. "His name, we now know, is Louis Vandame." He had to raise his voice to compete with Madame's expostulations. "He is a servant in your employ, sent by your wife to eavesdrop on the conversation. She hoped Lawson would bribe Ridley to stop his slanders. When that failed, your servant silenced the emissary permanently."

Monsieur du Plessis said nothing, but the way he tugged at his beard betrayed his uncertainty. Had his wife done this thing or not?

Madame bristled, taking a step forward. Her overlarge costume forced the men to take small steps back. "Elsa Moreau, that little viper. She would say anything against me. You know this, Monsieur Bacon."

Then she and Anthony erupted into a furious altercation in French. Or rather, she was furious. He was cool. He leaned back, arms crossed, firing a cannonade of verbal shots. She leaned forward from the waist, flinging both hands about and practically spitting in her fury. They'd engaged in a duel of sorts, after all.

At last, Monsieur could tolerate no more. *"Silence, ma femme!"* He rattled off a scolding command to depart. After she maneuvered her skirts through the door, the room felt larger and considerably calmer.

Du Plessis turned toward Francis. "You can have no proof."

"We are satisfied that this is the truth. I also remind you that our word carries weight here. This was your wife's form of wild justice, Monsieur, for which you must take responsibility, both legally and morally."

"You really ought to keep better control of her," Anthony added unhelpfully.

"I say it is mere speculation." Du Plessis tried to hold his ground, but he must have felt it crumbling beneath his feet. He, more than anyone, must have had his wife's measure: a vain, haughty, impetuous woman. His face showed that he believed her capable of at least setting up that volatile situation, in which Vandame could exact his private revenge against Ridley.

"Not speculation," Francis said. "Ratiocination. We have the testimony of Vandame himself." That was an exaggeration. Neither he nor Tom had spoken to the man, or the groom who bore the tale.

"Impossible!" du Plessis said. "He returned to France three days ago."

Francis blinked, calculating. When had Moreau spoken to him? He glanced at Tom, who held one thumb up, close to his doublet. They must be within that limit.

Anthony said, "It falls upon you to exact his punishment. No good can come from involving the authorities here. I'm willing to keep this whole affair *en famille*, provided that you accept my judgment."

"Agreed," du Plessis said. The case was won.

Anthony laid out his demands. "The murderer will be sent to fight against the Catholic League. You are charged with ensuring that he serves and does not desert his company."

Du Plessis dipped his head. "That is fair. This is not the first time Vandame has brought trouble to my family or his own."

"Now for you and your wife," Anthony said. "You will leave England at once and never return. Furthermore, you will retire from the court of my dear friend *le Roi* Henri. Make whatever excuse you like. Find a little house in the countryside and devote yourself to that Calvinist college you're always talking about. In exchange, I will say nothing of your wife's perfidy to my lord uncle or my sovereign queen."

Du Plessis drew a long breath through his long nose. Then he gave a supercilious shrug. "*Eh, bien.* I grow weary of this cold land. But do not believe your own reputation is untarnished, Monsieur Bacon. Not among the people in Montaubon."

"Feh," Anthony said, seemingly unconcerned. They began dickering over the details, leaving Francis to ponder the import of that last barb. Could du Plessis be harping on that tired old scandal about Anthony's alleged catamites? Or was it the rumor about Catholic bribes?

He listened to the negotiations with half an ear, feeling useless. He'd contributed nothing to the success of this day. Tom had brought home the solution while Anthony served as prosecution, jury, and judge. Francis's presence was utterly superfluous. He couldn't even answer the fundamental questions about the roots of this conflict.

He fumed while the bickering continued. How could he defend his brother if he didn't know the truth?

NINETEEN

"You didn't need me in there at all," Francis told Anthony as they walked through the gatehouse at the Savoy. They stopped on the narrow strip along the edge of the Strand. Tom hovered at Anthony's side, ready to lend an arm. But the invalid seemed steady enough with his cane planted at the vertex of his spindly legs. Jacques ran around to the stables to summon Widhope with the coach.

"You used to like going places with me." Anthony's tone teased, perhaps in an attempt to soothe his brother's irritation.

It didn't work. "When I was ten," Francis said. "I've wasted an hour here that could have been better spent reading Cardano's book on cryptography."

"Haven't you finished that yet? You started it yesterday. Your wits must be rusting with age." Anthony shot a wink at Tom, who had better sense than to return anything other than a polite smile, as if he hadn't been listening.

"Where is that cursed coach?" Francis stepped into the street to scan the oncoming traffic for Anthony's gaudy carriage. A man rushed out of nowhere and shoved him, hard, straight into the path of an oncoming wagon.

Francis screamed. The horses screamed too, their sharp hooves flashing over his head. A hand clutched his belt and hauled him to safety. Tom pressed him against the wall and dragged Anthony right up beside him. He shouted, "Look after him!" and dashed down the street after the ruffian who'd nearly cut the thread of Francis's life.

"God's mercy." He took a grateful breath, and then another one. "Are you all right?" he and Anthony asked each other simultaneously.

"Yes," Anthony said. "Thank God Clarady is so quick-witted. He had your belt before your feet left the ground. And thank God for good Spanish leather!"

"Thank God that driver was awake and had control of his horses." Francis had walked up and down the Strand a hundred times — a thousand — with nothing more than ordinary alertness. He even enjoyed the boisterous scene sometimes, as evidence of a thriving capital. Now the traffic sounded like a nightmarish cacophony of beasts and wheels, crushing and slicing everything in their path.

The two brothers held each other, pressed tight against the wall, until Widhope pulled up in front of them, shielding them from the street. Jacques leapt out, saw their distress, and quickly bundled them into the safety of the curtained carriage. He reassured himself and them with a stream of mild scoldings in French. Francis's laces had come loose all across the back, both hose and stockings. He crouched on the bench while Jacques restored him to dignity.

Soon after that was done, Tom returned, panting. He leaned on the open door to catch his breath. Then he held up a length of dirty linen. "I had him by the ruff, the whoreson knave, but when a mule with a wide load jostled us, the scoundrel pulled the lace and slipped right out of it. What with that mule and the crowd, he got away. I didn't recognize him, but I'd know him again."

"I doubt we'll see him," Francis said. "But thank you for trying. And for —"

Tom nodded. "He meant to kill you, Mr. Bacon. That's the most dangerous stretch of road in Middlesex. Carts and horses are still going fast, coming off the farm roads.

Farther up on Cheapside, it's nose to tail, but here —" He broke off with a whistle.

Francis had a disturbing thought. "I suspect he mistook me for Anthony."

"Or he wanted to break you two apart," Tom said, "and didn't care which one he got. And consider this, gentlemen. No one knew you'd be out here at just this moment except for those du Plessis-Mornays in there." He pointed with his chin.

"Madame's last stab," Anthony said.

He looked pale. Tom saw it too. "Let's get you both home for a nice hot drink." He grinned at them, that famous Clarady grin.

Before climbing in, he faced the westerly breeze and unhooked a few inches of his doublet, opening his shirt to get some breeze on his chest. "Whew! Something cool for me, if it can be found. I worked up a sweat chasing that rampallion."

A looked of longing stole over Anthony's face as he watched from the corner of the coach. Francis had grown accustomed to Tom, but for a moment he saw him through his brother's eyes. Tall, straight, and well-framed, with tawny chest hair peeking out from under his sweat-dampened shirt. Golden curls escaped his hat to fall upon his clear brow, framing the warmth of his cornflower-blue eyes. As he hoisted himself limberly into the coach, he brought in the smell of a healthy man — salty sweat mingled with the sandalwood Pinnock used to wash his rubbing cloths.

Anthony leaned against Francis's shoulder to murmur a quote from the *Iliad* in the original Greek. "Godlike Achilles, valiant as thou art."

"Mm-hmm," Francis answered.

* * *

Jacques and Tom carried Anthony into the house. He'd had enough exercise for one day. Francis gasped as he pushed open the door to the outer chamber. The place had either been ransacked or subjected to a wandering whirlwind. Chairs and stools lay overturned, and chests of papers had been emptied onto the floor. The shelves of books had been swept clean, with the precious volumes lying torn and broken on the floor.

"God's bollocks!" Tom cried. "What happened here?"

He and Jacques brought Anthony straight into the bedchamber and laid him on the bed. Jacques set about making him comfortable, removing his shoes, ruffs, and doublet, while Tom and Francis toured the two rooms, inspecting the damage.

Francis sifted through a chestful of scattered clothing while Tom examined the rear windows.

"This is how he got in," Tom said, jiggling a broken latch. The pane beside it had been broken. "He punched right through this pane, probably with the haft of a knife. Here's the glass on the floor."

"What's missing?" Anthony asked. He lay against his pillows with arms and legs splayed, his body spent but his wits still working.

"Nothing of value," Francis said, "as far as I can see. Your tapestry is undisturbed. Your silver goblets from Geneva are all there too. None of the plate on your cupboard has been disturbed. But everything with paper in it has been scattered to the four winds."

"My chest!" Anthony cried.

"I'll go," Tom said, and ran out of the room.

Francis knelt to search under his brother's bed. "Your money box is still here." He rose and climbed onto the foot of the bed. "How do you feel?"

"Tired, but otherwise all right. How are *you*? You're the one who's been jerked around like a brown trout."

"I'm all in one piece. I could use a drink."

Anna Castle

Jacques pressed a cup of wine into his hand and gave another to his master. "You need one yourself," Anthony told him.

Then Tom came back and accepted a cup. "The chest is safe. I doubt they even went upstairs. If it was a du Plessis man, he wouldn't have had much time. Whoever it was could've been jumping out the window as the coach pulled up in front."

"What about my men?" Anthony said.

"The clerks on the second floor heard nothing," Tom said. "But this sort of thing needn't make much noise. Lawson and Phelippes went out to buy ink and paper half an hour ago." He sat in a chair near the bed and drank thirstily for a moment. "They didn't go into my room, by the way. At least, nothing's disturbed. No one could break in through the front windows; there are too many people crossing the yard."

"Who would do this thing?" Francis asked.

"Who knows about that document chest?" Anthony asked.

"Sir Robert," Tom said. "Doesn't he?"

Francis frowned. "He wouldn't do *this*. Or if he did, his men would know more about their target. They wouldn't shake books around, for instance."

"No member of the Privy Council would resort to such measures," Anthony said. "Who knew we were away from home?"

"Anyone could pay someone who lives here to keep an eye out. Someone in one of the rooms facing the yard," Tom said. "We may be between terms, but there are still fifty men in residence. And the ones who stay during vacations are the ones most likely to need more coin."

"Ugh." Francis hated thinking one of his colleagues could abet such treachery. "But they wouldn't know about the chest."

226

"They could deduce its existence," Anthony said. "Lawyers, especially. They store their correspondence too."

"I can't think of anyone else," Tom said, but he shot Francis a tiny wink.

So Trumpet knew. Then Lady Rich might as well. But would she send men to steal the chest? Her lord brother wanted Anthony's knowledge and wits, not just his documents.

"That brings us back to the du Plessis-Mornays." Francis met his brother's eyes with an implacable look. "It's time for you to tell me what you know about them. What could be so damning it warrants an attempt on our lives?"

Anthony drew in a deep breath and let it out with a long sigh, making a show of surrendering. "Very well. I suppose you should both know, given today's events. I haven't any solid proof, mind you, unless I can locate the sailors who sold us the information in the first place." He paused and added, "Ridley might have known. He never said anything to me, but perhaps it played a part in developing the climate of mistrust that led to his death."

Francis stuck to the main theme. "You wrote our uncle about something that had du Plessis and du Pin sweating into their doublets back in '88." His brother could evade, stall, and prevaricate until everyone else gave up and went home. Except him.

"I'm getting there," Anthony said. "Yes, this was in '88, during the summer, when King Philip turned Europe on its head. Nothing could be shipped through the Bay of Biscay, remember; not with that fearsome armada streaming past. Nothing could get in or out of any English port. So anyone who depended on trade with England found themselves looking toward a frugal winter."

"That would include half of the coastal towns in France," Tom said.

Anthony nodded. "Worse, King Philip paid the Duke of Guise to organize a rebellion in Paris while the armada bottled up the channel. More chaos in France meant less aid for us from our allies. King Henry was deeply frustrated, but at that time he held sway only in tiny Navarre. Even the mayor of Calais, whose town would starve were it not for travelers to and from England, offered support to the Spanish fleet. That did seem to be the way the wind was blowing. So perhaps it is not so odd that a greedy merchant like Antoine du Pin would take advantage of the situation. He spent those months quietly supplying Spanish ships, at twice the usual charge, no doubt."

"Supplying what?" Tom asked, his jaw tense. "Gunpowder?"

Anthony shrugged. "The specific inventories are not known to me. But powder was in great demand that year."

Tom beat his right fist against his left palm. God help du Pin if he should meet that fatherless young man on a deserted street. He'd be wiser to go home with his compatriot.

"What about du Plessis?" Francis asked.

"I wasn't certain of his part until today, although he knew about du Pin's dealings *post facto*. Today's dirty tricks are as close to a confession as I could want." Anthony's eyes flashed. "I know he profited from the collusion. He acquired two fine horses at a time when I had to sell mine to pay messengers. Everyone else in Protestant France was tightening their belts, while Madame du Plessis wore new silk dresses to church on Sunday."

Francis nodded, considering the implications. "If his English customers knew du Pin had supplied Spanish ships with so much as a cup of water, his trade would evaporate in one day. The queen would ban his ships forever, however good the wine might be. Even smugglers are too loyal to touch wares from such a tainted source."

"The family would be ruined," Anthony said. "And when du Plessis-Mornay's part in it came out in France, he would receive harsher treatment from *le Roi Henri* than I dished out this afternoon. Even if all he did was sit quietly by while his friend endangered Henry's allies, he might spend the rest of his life in prison."

"Worth killing to prevent," Tom said. "This is all making more sense to me. Dalliance and a love of gossip are one thing. Harsh words and a blow or two are the usual results of that. Most people survive such insults well enough. But treason, collusion, and life in prison are another kettle of fish altogether."

"Well put, Mr. Clarady," Anthony said. "Have I satisfied your curiosity, Frank?"

"Never," Francis said. "I'll always have more questions, until the day I die. But for you, today, I have just one. What's behind Ridley's claim that you took money from Catholics? Which Catholics?"

"That was a bare-faced lie," Tom said.

Anthony sighed. "Not quite, Mr. Clarady. This was in '88 again — September or October, I think. I was down to my last franc since no one could get money safely out of England. The Bishop of Cahors was kind enough to lend me a thousand marks. All he wanted in return was a letter to Lord Burghley asking for the release of two Welsh Jesuits." He smiled at Tom. "Cahors is a pretty little town not far from Montaubon."

"Jesuits," Tom said, disgust written plain on his face. "How could you?"

"I needed the money. That sort of exchange is more routine than you might guess. Those two priests should not have been in England, I agree. But they were relatively harmless sorts, and no one worries about rebellions in Wales."

"Even so, Mr. Bacon! How is that not the same as what that maggot du Pin did, begging your pardon? Apart from the timing and the matter of scale."

"The Bishop of Cahors is not a member of the Catholic League," Anthony said. "He's a kind and thoughtful man. A good friend in need. He cared about the well-being of his compatriots and was willing to secure their release by going through the proper channels. There are Catholics and there are Catholics, after all, just as there are fanatical Presbyterians who lay waste to Anglican churches. Good men and bad on both sides. It's my job to distinguish among them."

Tom grumbled but had to admit to the truth of that. He'd met some hotheaded Puritans who wouldn't balk at murder if it would further their aims.

"Well," Anthony said, looking now at Francis, "those are my great secrets. Are you satisfied?"

Francis smiled, but the answer was *no*. His fraternal intuition told him that something still lurked unspoken. Nevertheless, they'd both had enough shocks that day. "I'll hold myself content for now."

"Good. More to the point, I fear we won't be safe in our beds until my documents have been catalogued, with several copies made." Anthony leveled a meaningful look at Francis, who groaned. More tedious labor, but he could make a quicker job of sorting a chestful of papers than anyone else. Cardano's book could wait a little longer.

TWENTY

Tom got the note from Catalina on Monday shortly
after dinner. "It's time."

Thank God he was already dressed because he couldn't
have managed it. He turned around three times in his tiny
room, trying to decide which way to go, before
remembering he had every right to walk out the front gate
in the middle of the day. He was halfway across the yard
when he remembered Catalina said a first birth could take
hours. So he jogged back into the house and up the stairs,
bursting into Mr. Bacon's study chamber without
knocking.

"It's here. I mean it's coming. I mean it's time! I'm
going. I may be gone for a while. Could be hours, they say."
He slammed the door without waiting for an answer and
flew down the stairs. He willed himself to cross the yard at
a normal pace, raising his hat to the gatekeeper in the
normal way, then strode briskly down to Holborn Road.
He sprinted the rest of the way, dodging angry passersby
without apology.

Someone had been watching for him because Catalina
met him at the bottom of the tower stairs. She led him to
a small anteroom on the ground floor and told him to wait
there. "I will come to you when I can. The midwife does
not worry and says neither should we. We are in God's
hands."

"Tell her I love her. Not the midwife, my — my
Trumpet." Tears sprang into Tom's eyes. He couldn't help

it. His heart had grown too big for his body, swelling so huge even his skin felt the tremors.

"I will." Catalina clasped his hand in both of hers — a rare gesture. "My lady is strong, Mr. Tom. All will be well."

Tom nodded, his throat choked with emotion. The moment she closed the door, he let it out, collapsing against the wall as gut-deep sobs shook his body. When they were spent, he patted himself on the chest and wiped his eyes on his sleeves. He sighed noisily, alone in this bare room. A man should have friends with him at a time like this, but there was no one within a three-day's ride he trusted. Apart from Mr. Bacon, who was never helpful with this sort of thing.

Some men spent these hours in the nearest tavern, drinking down their hopes and fears. He didn't want that either. He wanted to remember every minute of this day, even the sobbing. And what if Trumpet needed him? For what, he couldn't guess, but if she did, he wanted to be ready, with his wits about him.

No, he was well enough on his own here. He had a window looking toward the outer wall. He had a sturdy chair — two, for variety, straight-backed and solid. He had a square table equipped with a candlestick and a flat box. He opened it to find paper, quills, and a pot of ink. They thought of everything at Essex House.

He began to pace from the outer door to the inner, remembering Trumpet's restless pacing yesterday and Anthony Bacon's labored hobbling across his opulent chamber. A lot of back-and-forthing these days, all told. But Trumpet would soon be back to her normal vigorous self, God grant she survive this day. Poor Mr. Bacon would never be an active man again.

Tom paced from the table to the window for a change, thinking about the day he'd first discovered his friend Trumpet was, in truth, a girl. That day had started out fraught with difficult feelings, he recalled. They'd washed clean away when he saw that beautiful, green-eyed maiden rising from the duck pond he'd thrown her into, thinking she was someone else. Now there was a kick in the gut. For a few minutes, he'd thought he'd gone stark mad.

She'd surprised him time and again since then, not only with her talent for disguises, but with the very essence of who she was. Her boldness, her swiftness of wit, her clownish sense of humor. Her agility, her strength, her passion. He didn't know exactly when he'd discovered that he loved her, though she could tell him — to the minute, most like.

The chapel bell began tolling the hour. He stopped to count. "Three o'clock?" he queried the silent walls. "How can that be? I left my room not much after one."

The door opened, and the boy who'd brought the message entered with a tray. He set a jug, a cup, and a plate of bread and cheese on the little table.

"How is she?" Tom asked.

The boy shrugged. He was only a messenger. After he left, Tom filled the cup with cool beer and drank it down. He hadn't realized how thirsty he was. Time might stand still for his overcrowded mind, but his body still ticked the minutes by, wanting food and drink. And a piss.

He slipped into the patch of garden along the wall and relieved himself in a corner out of sight of any windows. He went back in and took a bite of cheese, then sat down and ate it all, though it lacked flavor. He might need his strength, and who knew how long he would be here?

He got up to pace again, opening the window to admit a breath of air. He'd used up the original supply. He sat for a while, beating out song rhythms with his hands on his thighs. Then he got up and paced again. The bell tolled four o'clock, then the quarter hour, then the half. And then a scream rent the air.

"Trumpet!" Tom tore open the door and barreled up the stairs two at a time. He flung open the door of her room to see her squatting in a low chair, soaked in sweat, her thin chemise and straggling hair plastered to her body. Her eyes were closed and her head hung low while she took short, gasping breaths, like a fighter between rounds. An older woman in a brown dress sat before her, right up between her open knees.

Catalina rushed across to shove him out the door again. "Go away! You cannot be here, Mr. Tom."

"She screamed," he pleaded.

"Yes, yes. All women scream. It is good. The baby is coming!"

He dragged himself back down the stairs, gripping the smooth railing as if he'd aged a hundred years since bounding up. He shut himself back into his pen.

Where were all the servants? This house must have fifty at least, even when the lord was away. But there could have been a troop of women bearing cloths and urns of water in that chamber. He'd only had eyes for Trumpet.

He paced the room, going around in a circle, wearing a path in the bare oak boards. Trumpet screamed again, and he thrust a knuckle between his teeth to keep from screaming with her. Each cry stabbed him like a dagger in the belly.

He'd fought Spaniards to the death on his father's ship. He'd once fended off a crazed murderer with a poisoned blade. He'd broken through a lead-framed window to rescue the woman he loved. He'd been pushed off a cliff and left to die with a broken leg. He'd sweated and struggled to climb the ladder into the gentry, bearing a thousand slights along the way.

But he'd never done anything as hard as waiting at the bottom of that stair.

Finally, a baby wailed far up above, and his heart leapt into his throat. Another sob escaped his lips; this time one of joy. He laughed, then fell on his knees and thanked the Lord. He raised eyes to the ceiling and said, "Dad, wherever you are, I hope you can see this and be happy with me."

After an eternity, Catalina appeared, cradling a bundle of blankets in her arms. She grinned at him and turned down an edge to show him the face of his child.

He marveled at it, unable to form words.

"It's a boy," she said. "Perfect and healthy."

"A perfect boy," Tom echoed, daring to stroke the rose-petal cheek with the tip of his finger. "My lady, how fares she?"

"Tired, but well."

Tom grinned so broadly he thought his face would split, tears streaming down his cheeks. Trumpet lived. Now he could live too.

Catalina's brown eyes also shone wetly. "His name is William."

"William. My boy Will." Tom studied the tiny face, storing it up in his treasure house of memories. The chubby pink cheeks, the round little chin, the button eyes in palest green. "Green eyes." Another thing to be thankful for.

"I must go back," Catalina said.

Tom nodded, full to the top now anyway. "Tell my lady I love her."

Catalina laughed, from happiness, not mockery. "She knows."

* * *

Tom walked on air all the way home. He raised his hat to everyone he passed. They smiled at him, uncertain if they knew him, but he strode right on along. No uncertainty for him today. Today, he was a father.

"I've got work to do," he informed a startled matron. "I must rise, to be worthy of my son."

He would pass the bar in two years, giving a legal performance to rival Francis Bacon's. Then he would sue for his livery and take control of his own estates. A father should not be the ward of the queen.

He'd have quite a bit saved up by then. He would work harder now and earn more. He could take on some intelligencing work for Anthony — but only if it paid him in cool, hard coin. Then he could borrow what money he lacked on the strength of his estate and his nascent legal career. Older women liked him; he would specialize in wills, just as he and Ben used to talk about doing. They should form that partnership once he passed the bar. Clarady and Whitt, legal counsel, all kinds.

Ben! He'd want to know this glorious news as soon as may be. He was the only friend Tom had who knew about him and Trumpet. He could crow about his boy Will to his heart's content in a letter to Ben. Tom strode into Bacon House intending to go straight to his desk to write a good, long letter.

But the door to Anthony's room gaped wide open. Francis stood in the middle, wringing his hands. "Tom! Thank God you're here! Anthony is missing!"

TWENTY-ONE

Francis had never needed Tom more, not even when his own life had been threatened. Anthony was everything to him — more than position, more than philosophy. More than truth.

"He can't be missing, Mr. Bacon." Tom came in and cast a glance around, as if Francis had merely mistaken his elder brother for a joint stool or a length of curtain.

"He's gone, I tell you. He went out and hasn't come back. Look!" Francis strode into the bedchamber with Tom at his heels. He flung up the lid of Anthony's wardrobe chest and pointed into it. "Do you see that?"

"See what?"

"His best doublet and hose are gone — the black velvet with the silver silk lining."

Tom blinked at him uncomprehendingly.

God's teeth, what makes the man so dull today! "He went to court," Francis snapped.

"Are you sure?"

"Of course I'm sure. Jacques is gone. Lawson's gone. I was out for hours, witless fool that I am. I went up to St. Paul's to browse the latest books. I had dinner in an ordinary, for a change of pace." Francis barked a terrified laugh. "What was I thinking? Meanwhile, Anthony got a note from someone, telling him he could find Her Majesty riding in St. James's Park this afternoon. He could approach quite near in his coach, the note said, then walk but a little distance to meet her without having to cope with any stairs."

"A note from who?" The vagueness had cleared from Tom's eyes at last.

"The under-chamberlain, or so it said. I didn't recognize the hand."

"You have the note?"

Francis nodded. "It was on the desk. Phelippes is here, working with the clerks on the second floor. But you know how he is. He barely noticed when Lawson popped up to say they were going out. It might've been two hours, he said. It might've been three."

"Anthony couldn't stay out that long." Tom scratched the back of his neck, his gaze wandering around the room. Then he smiled, as if to himself — a smile of joy. Was he brainsick?

"What *can* you be smiling about?" Francis demanded.

"I'm sorry, Mr. Bacon." Tom flashed that smile again, as if he couldn't make it stop. "My son was born today. William. He has green eyes, like his mother. She's well. Tired, but well. He's perfect. Perfect and well, with green eyes." His eyes glazed over with wonderment.

"Oh. Well. Congratulations." Francis reached out and gave him an awkward pat on the shoulder. At the moment, he could barely remember who the mother of this child was. "I can't think about that now, Tom. I need your help. We must find Anthony. He could be hurt and lying by the road somewhere."

"We'll find him, Mr. Bacon. I'll bet he got tired after the excitement and stopped off at an inn to rest for a bit. The Red Lion's on the road going past St. James's Park. That's a nice place. I could trot down there to see and be back in a matter of minutes."

Relief washed over Francis like a warm summer rain. "Oh, thank God! Yes, go. I'll — I'll wait right here." He walked back into the front room and sat down in his usual chair, his hands planted on the arms.

"Let me get you a drink first," Tom said, moving toward the cupboard.

"No, no. No need. I'll wait for Anthony. I want to hear all about this big adventure."

Tom seemed doubtful about leaving him alone. "I'll call for Pinnock on my way out."

"He's searching through Gray's. He'll be back soon. Go! Go!" Francis showed him a smile. It felt stiff on his lips, like wet wool stretched across tenterhooks.

"All right, then. Back in two shakes of a little lamb's tail." Tom went out, leaving the door partly open.

Before the front door thumped closed, Tom called, "God's teeth, man! What happened to you?" Francis's stomach clenched. He clutched the arms of the chair as if someone were trying to tear him out of it.

Then Tom came in, supporting Lawson, who seemed to have injured his foot or ankle. He had a purple bruise across one temple and scratches on the opposite cheek. Blood had trickled onto his ruff, spreading in a dark stain. His clothes were streaked with mud, his round hose crushed flat. One stocking hung down in back.

"What's happened?" Francis heard his voice spiral up in panic. "Where's Anthony?"

Lawson shook his head. "They took him. I don't know who."

"What do you mean 'took him'?" Francis almost shouted the words.

"Let him sit down, Mr. Bacon," Tom said. "I'll get us all a drink, and then he can tell us what happened from start to finish. That's the way you like it, isn't it? First one thing and then the next, so we can follow the whole chain of events." He moved as he spoke, helping Lawson onto a stool in the circle before the fireplace, then going to the cupboard to pour three cups of wine from the jug Jacques always kept ready.

Francis studied Lawson as if he'd never seen the man before. Nearly six feet tall, broad enough of shoulder and ready enough for action, one would think. He lacked the weekly lessons in the arts of wrestling and sword fighting that Tom enjoyed as a gentleman of the Inns of Court, but surely he would be capable of putting up *some* defense. "Why didn't you help him?"

Lawson shook his head, his face stricken. "I didn't have a chance."

Tom pressed cups into their hands and pulled up another stool, closer to Francis than he usually sat. "Take a good, long drink," he said, "and then start with the note." He'd clearly taken up his master's role, which was good because Francis's wits seemed to be lagging. The words "they took him" still echoed in his ears.

Lawson swallowed a few large gulps, then wiped his mouth on his filthy sleeve. He nodded at Tom. "Thanks." Then he directed his tale to Francis. He might lack training in the martial arts, but he had long since learned to deliver a succinct report.

"Anthony got a letter from a Sir Oliver, one of Her Majesty's under-chamberlains — or so we thought. He didn't recognize the hand. Anthony had written to your cousin Sir Edward Hoby to ask if it might be possible to meet Her Majesty while she was out of doors. Hunting, perhaps, or walking in her garden. That way he wouldn't have to suffer the indignity of being carried upstairs."

"Why wouldn't he tell *me* he was thinking of such a thing?" It wasn't the proper way, but perhaps under Anthony's special circumstances it might be allowed.

Lawson shrugged a weary shoulder. "He knew how much it meant to you. And he wanted to arrange it on his own and not depend on you for this."

"Hmm." Francis understood that part. Anthony always wanted to be the elder brother, the first to discover or do or arrange whatever it was they had going.

Lawson continued, "Also, he feared to miss the chance while his legs felt so good and strong, as he put it. When the letter came, he insisted on going at once. So we hopped to it, donning our finery. Jacques and I carried him to the coach, sparing his legs for the great moment. We avoided the traffic by going through St. Giles. As we came down the Haymarket Road, we heard shouts and a loud cry. Then the coach began jolting over a rough surface. We'd gone off the road. I did my best to protect Anthony from banging against the sides. I shouted to Widhope, 'What are you doing, man?' but got no response. When we stopped, I opened the door to cry, 'What ho?' and got a crack on the head. I woke up some time later lying in the brush under a tree. I sat up and groaned, felt the lump on my head, and heard Widhope groaning nearby. He was lying in the grass along the verge. The horses nudged at him with their noses, trying to wake him. The coach trailed behind them on the slant, both doors hanging open. Anthony and Jacques were gone."

"God's mercy," Tom said. "You're lucky to be alive."

"I know it." Lawson blew out a big breath. "I never even saw them. Widhope says there were three. They wore black masks to hide their faces. They dashed out of the darkness under the trees. They must've been waiting for us. Anthony's coach is so cursed easy to recognize. One of them leapt onto the bench, cracked poor Widhope on the noddle, and pushed him off. The ruffian must've grabbed the reins and driven off the road a bit before stopping to snatch their prizes."

He turned a sorrowful face to Francis. "I'm so sorry, Frank. This is all my fault. I should've been paying attention. I should've opened the curtains and kept an eye out instead of listening to Anthony rehearse his greetings to the queen."

Tom shook that away. "If he wanted you to listen, you would listen. You wouldn't turn your —"

"I should never have let him go in the first place!" Lawson cried. "I should've smelled a rat the minute he slit the seal on that note. It's a basic rule of life. *Never* believe it when something you've been longing for suddenly drops into your lap. Never!"

"Now that's just —"

Francis spoke right over Tom's objection. "No, Lawly, it's all my fault. *I'm* the one who kept scolding him about going to court. If he hadn't been so keen to please me, and stop my endless nagging, he would've seen the falseness of that note at once. Nobody presents themselves to the queen while she's out hunting. It simply isn't done."

"Now, now," Tom said, "your brother is a grown —"

"My fault!" Francis stabbed at his chest with both sets of stiff fingers. "All my fault! I've been happy to exploit Anthony and his correspondence all these years to gain the attention of the powerful and win the respect I crave. Oh yes! All the while pretending that I had *loftier* aims and more *significant* pursuits, if only my pesky brother would leave me in peace to follow my destiny." Tears welled in his eyes. "Now all I want is my truest friend home again, safe and sound."

Lawson's eyes brimmed as well. "Anthony's the only one who ever believed in me. He saw something in me no one else ever did, not even —"

"*Enough!*" Tom bellowed. "Get a grip on yourselves! We've got work to do. We've got to figure out who took Anthony and where they took him. Then we need to come up with a plan for getting him back."

Francis gaped at him. "How can you be so calm at a time like this?"

"Someone has to be," Tom said. "Now stop blubbering and start thinking. Who wants Anthony's intelligences the most? Lord Admiral Howard?"

Francis guffawed. "My lord of Effingham! That's the most —"

"Or what about Sir Robert? You said your lord uncle offered to move him into —"

"That's even more preposterous! They wouldn't send that note, for one —" Francis noticed the gleam in Tom's eyes and realized he'd been played upon. "Oh, I see. Very clever."

Tom flashed an impudent grin. "I knew a truly stupid idea would jolt your wits back into working order."

"It worked." Francis gave Lawson a somber look. "You're not to blame, and neither am I. Nor is my cousin, my uncle, or any member of the Privy Council. We can also rule out the Earl of Essex, safely assuming that he did not slip into England unannounced in order to spirit Anthony off to Chartley Castle in Staffordshire."

"We know who it was," Tom said. "The man we threatened yesterday. Philippe du Plessis-Mornay."

"Don't forget the wife," Lawson said. "That woman is the devil incarnate." He jumped to his feet. "What are we waiting for, Clarady? Let's go pound on their door."

Francis looked up at him, battered and bruised but ready to dive back into the fray. Whatever his flaws, he truly did love Anthony. "Go. Ask. See what you can see."

They grabbed their hats and left. Francis went to the window to watch them cross the yard. They might learn something, but they wouldn't be bringing Anthony home. His heart told him it wouldn't be that simple.

He paced around the room some more. The rich furnishings seemed so purposeless without Anthony's animating presence. His gleaming locks, his personal grace, his knowing eyes and penetrating wit demanded silk and silver as the appropriate setting. Without him, it was all a load of gewgaws and gaudy trifles.

He wished he could do more, but he'd only be in the way at the Savoy. Tom and Lawson could walk faster without him — and issue threats his presence would only negate. He could have another look at that note, however. What if it had come from someone known, someone other than du Plessis? They mustn't waste time pursuing the wrong abductors.

He ran upstairs to the second floor and found Phelippes writing away at the larger desk. Two clerks worked at smaller ones, facing one another beneath the windows at the back of the long, open room. Phelippes raised his head, moving his quill to the side so as not to drip ink on his page. "Has Anthony come home yet? He'll want to read this before I send it off."

Francis shook his head. His throat closed with fear again, but he choked it down. He drew up a stool and spoke quietly, telling Phelippes what had befallen the spymaster.

"God's mercy!" the cryptographer swore softly. No need to alarm the clerks. "I can't fathom it. I thought du Plessis was one of ours. All on the same side."

"Baser conflicts lie beneath the political realm, I fear." Francis asked to see the note again. He stared at it, struggling to find traces of someone he knew, someone reachable, but failed. "Are you sure you've never seen this hand before?"

Phelippes peered at it again, holding it closer to his nose. "I wouldn't bet my life on it, but I don't think so. I've a good memory for this sort of thing." He leaned back, candlelight glinting off the glass in his round spectacles.

His facility for "this sort of thing" was renowned across the Continent. "Could it be du Plessis writing with his left hand?"

"It would be slanted the other way. But we have lots of letters from him here." The small man got up and opened the great document chest, sifting through it, opening some letters, tossing others aside.

The contents seemed wholly without order. Francis vowed to sit up here and sort them out himself, making lists and tying related pieces together in bundles, if only Anthony could be returned to him whole and hale.

"Here's a couple." Phelippes brought his samples over to the desk. He'd already lit two candles against the lowering evening light. "And here's one from du Pin for comparison. You can see they're quite different. Note the length of the *J* and the width of the capital *M* in *Majesty*."

"Are there any from Madame du Plessis?"

"The wife?" Phelippes scratched his chin. "I don't think so. She didn't correspond with Anthony, as far as I know."

Francis gazed bleakly at the scattering of unfolded letters. "Who would do this thing? Steal my invalid brother out of his coach in broad daylight?"

"Had to be daytime," Phelippes said, pedantic as ever. "They'd never tempt him out at night. As for who?" He ran a hand through his thinning yellow hair. "I can think of a dozen people in Spain, France, or Italy who would snatch him out of a coach, a ship, or off the back of a horse if they could." He pointed at the open chest. "That chest is valuable, especially to us if our reports are doubted or challenged. It contains a wealth of dates and places, names of persons in attendance at secret meetings. Powerful men speculating about the intentions of their counterparts in other countries. But your brother has more stored inside his head than a dozen such chests."

Phelippes met Francis's eyes with a look laden with grim warning. "It pains me to say it, but Anthony himself is the most valuable intelligence resource in Europe."

TWENTY-TWO

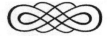

Tom knocked on the door of the du Plessis-Mornays' house. He waited a few moments, then tried again. No answer.

"Are you sure this is the right house?" Lawson asked.

"We were here only yesterday. See the way that vine has peeled off on one side? I noticed the mess of brown stains it left behind."

Lawson scowled at the unkempt wall, then lunged forward to pound on the door with his fist. "Open up, curse you! Open this door or I'll kick it down!" Anger stained his cheeks the color of his red hair.

"Cool down," Tom said. "We'll have to be smart with this pair. Don't forget we have no authority to compel them to cooperate."

The door swung open. A girl of about thirteen years gawked at them, goggle-eyed.

"Is your mistress in?" Tom asked, trying for a friendly smile.

She shot a glance over her shoulder, which was enough for Lawson. He pushed the door full open and barged in past the mute servant.

Tom followed, leaving the door open. The sparsely furnished room of yesterday was even less welcoming today. All the chairs were gone, replaced by chests with open lids heaped with clothing and other oddments. Madame du Plessis stood in the middle of the mess with her hands on her hips and a hostile glare in her brown eyes.

She wore a simple gown of blue wool today with an ordinary farthingale and a shallow ruff.

"Why do you beat upon my door so loudly? The neighbors will hear. And how dare you push yourselves into my home?"

"Where's Anthony?" Lawson demanded.

"Monsieur Bacon?" She shrugged, an elaborate French gesture. "But he is not here. Look, if you desire. We have so small a space." She waved a hand toward the back room, where a man stood with a basket in his arms, watching them.

"Where's your husband?" Tom asked.

She leveled a glare at him. "Gone to arrange our journey. Me, I pack. Monsieur Bacon told us to leave. *Très bien*, we go."

Lawson clenched his fists but held them low. "Don't you know he's fragile? We've got to get him home!"

Tom laid a restraining hand on his arm. "We know your husband took him somewhere, Madame. You'd better tell us where, or we'll . . ." He faltered. Do what, beat it out of her? That would be unthinkable, even without the gaping girl and the man with the basket.

Madame's lip curled in contempt. "Will you call the *gendarmes*, Monsieur? What do you call them in English — the constables? Then you will charge me with what, *précisément?*" She clucked her tongue reprovingly. "My father, he is also a man of the law. I learned enough from him to know you can do nothing to me. Nothing at all."

Lawson shook a fist. "Damn you to hell, you foul excuse for a woman! Tell us where he is!"

Madame eyed the fist with unflinching calm. "Will you strike me, Thomas Lawson? Or perhaps take me out to your coach and strangle me?"

"No, that's your trick," Tom said, but his words were lost as Lawson exploded in a burst of furious French. She answered him in like style.

Tom grabbed Lawson's arm and tugged him toward the door. "This is hopeless, man. Let's get out of here."

"Beware, Monsieur Le Blond!" Madame called. "That scheming whore might make you the guilty one next time."

Which scheming whore? Tom wondered as he ushered Lawson back to the Strand. He would've applied that epithet to her.

* * *

It was nearly dark when they got back to Gray's Inn. Lawson gave Mr. Bacon a brief account of their fruitless mission while Tom asked Pinnock to fetch something light from the kitchen. He filled cups of wine and ushered the other two men toward their seats. Bacon's eyes were wide, like a man who'd come unstrung. He sat plucking at the ruff on his wrist and looking about him as if he'd set something down and now couldn't find it.

Lawson hadn't tended his injuries before they went out. He looked like a wild man who'd scratched his way out of the forest. No wonder Madame du Plessis had treated him with such contempt.

Tom wanted Anthony home and safe as well, but every time he paused, to look for a cup or peer out at the darkening sky, his heart returned to that wellspring of joy — Baby William, his son. He probably lay in his mother's arms at this moment, peaceful and warm, while she gazed at him with love. Trumpet knew they had Tom's love too, and that he would be there if he could. He was there in spirit, his arms around them both.

He drew the curtains closed and turned back to his distraught companions. "Let's get this fire going, shall we?"

He took a stick from the basket and stirred up the banked coals, adding small sticks until they blazed up, and then setting a good-sized faggot on top. He found the lambswool coverlet and draped it over Bacon's knees. His master didn't seem to notice. He just kept staring into the leaping flames. But he drank when Tom pressed the cup into his hand.

Tom took his stool. "We won't get answers from that woman, or her husband, I'll wager. He's with Anthony, wherever that is. We'll have to reason this out ourselves, the way we do, eh, Mr. Bacon?"

"Oh, call me Francis. At least for tonight. 'Mr. Bacon' makes me think of my father for some reason." Doubtless because the man's portrait gazed down on them from over the mantelpiece. "What would he think of me, for letting such a fate befall us?"

"Not your fault, Francis," Tom said. "We settled that. Time to move forward."

"Where do we start?" Lawson asked, equally despairing. He sat on Anthony's footstool, leaving the armchair empty.

"Well," Tom said, "how about motive? What's the purpose of this reckless deed? There's no coming back from a thing like this."

"They mean to kill him!" Bacon cried. "To stop him from telling what he knows."

"I doubt it," Tom said. "For one thing, it would be a great waste. Anthony knows more than just that one bit of treachery. And if they'd wanted to kill him, why not do it on the spot?"

Francis groaned.

"I'm sorry," Tom said, "but it tells me they don't mean to harm him. Think, gentlemen. They took Jacques as well. They intend to keep Anthony alive and taken care of."

Francis fell back in his chair, wrapping his hand across his forehead as he blinked at the plaster ceiling. "Jacques! How could I forget him? Bless the boy! And thanks be to a merciful God for his unstinting devotion to Anthony."

Lawson nodded. "That's the one thing that keeps me from absolute despair. Jacques is smarter than he looks.

He's not a child anymore either, though du Plessis may think him one. He'll defend Anthony tooth and nail if it comes down to that."

Tom said, "What can he mean to do with Anthony? Lock him up in Montaubon or wherever he goes?"

"I don't believe that's possible." Francis sat up straight, his color returning. "I doubt they possess anything larger than an average manor, which wouldn't lend itself to the long-term maintenance of a secret prisoner. Word would get out. King Henry would hear of it and send soldiers to bring Anthony to him straightaway. Du Plessis would be destroyed. He knows that as well as I do."

Lawson added, "Anthony writes to King Henry at least once a week. Two weeks without a letter and the search would begin."

"Good," Tom said. "That sets a limit. They're not bringing him back to their house. Where will they go, then?"

"Something much worse, I fear," Lawson said. "I don't know if he told you this, but we were warned that some Spaniards were threatening to capture Anthony *en route*, to barter him for an officer named Don Pedro de Valdés."

"Sir Robert told us the same thing," Francis said. "Anthony scoffed at the idea. We should have been more on guard."

"We would've been watching for Spaniards," Tom said, "of whom there aren't any in this situation." Except that one at the Mermaid, talking to Sir Walter. How could he track him down?

"I didn't believe it either," Lawson said. "There are always rumors of that sort. People love to tell frightening stories to travelers. I wish I could remember where that particular rumor came from."

"Du Plessis or du Pin, perhaps?" Tom asked. "That might be what put it in their minds. And it makes sense from their perspective. They snatch him off the road and put him on a ship. They take him down to St. Jean de Luz and sell him to a Spaniard for a sack of gold doubloons. They rid themselves of the man who could destroy them and make a profit to boot."

Francis's face crumpled in horror. "Treat my brother like a horse or a cow to be bartered and sold? I can't bear to think about it, but I fear you may be right. What can we do to stop them?"

"Find him," Tom said. "If the wife is here, they won't have sailed yet. We can look for the ship."

"He may not be on a ship," Francis said. "He could be at an inn near the wharves or a house in the city. They might keep him anywhere until they're ready to sail."

"We should keep an eye on the wife." Tom glanced toward the curtains. It was full dark by now, though the moon was just past the half. "We can't do any more tonight though."

Pinnock came in with a tray of food: bread, cheese, cold ham, and a pot of mustard. He put it on the desk and set a small table between Bacon and Lawson. Tom got up to close the door on the empty bedchamber and light candles around the front room. Bacon was jumpy enough without dark nooks and shadowy corners harboring unknown terrors.

He served himself and sat back on his stool, balancing his wooden plate on his knee while he built a tower of bread, cheese, and ham, mortared together with mustard. He was hungry, and the food was good. Gray's might skimp on variety, but never on the quality of such staples as these.

Lawson ate like a man preparing for battle, stuffing chunks of this and that into his mouth and chewing it grimly. Francis picked at a single slice of cheese.

That wouldn't do. He had to eat or he wouldn't sleep, and if he didn't sleep, he'd be useless tomorrow. Better to keep the conversation going. Questions revived him, the way the smell of oats could rouse a weary horse.

Tom said, "I still find it incredible that all this hatred could result from one ill-considered remark about a woman's hair. However foolish the —"

"Hair?" Lawson said. "You don't mean that business about Minister Berault's decree? All that fuss about wigs and wires?"

"That's where it all started, wasn't it?" Tom asked. "Anthony said something tart, Madame du Plessis took offense, and that was the end of the friendship. That woman knows how to carry a grudge; I'll give her that. She and Raffe Ridley became friends in opposition to Anthony, or that's how it looks to me. Nothing like a shared sense of injury to form a bond. Then when they both turned up here, she used him to take another stab at Anthony."

Francis added, "Then Ridley overstepped and became the enemy, so he had to be extinguished. That woman's lust for vengeance cannot —"

"No, no, no," Lawson burst in. "Madame du Plessis never wanted Raffe Ridley dead. Don't believe that for a minute! He was her only friend — of her own sort, anyway. There was the draper's wife and the minister's sister, but —" He stopped himself with a sweep of his hand. "They were thick as thieves, those two."

"Thieves fall out," Francis said. "Anthony believed it."

Lawson shook his head. "He accepted it because it plucked the noose from around my neck. It also gave him an excuse to send du Plessis back to France with his tail between his legs." He set his plate aside and put his elbows on his knees, steepling his fingers and tapping the tips together the way Anthony did. "It's a sorry affair," he said in a creditable imitation of Anthony. "Now what use can we make of it?"

"Was none of it true?" Tom asked with a sinking sensation in his gut. "That servant of theirs, Louis

Vandame. You don't think he could've been the second coachman? Because we know there was one."

"It could've been Vandame," Lawson said. "I believe Madame would send him to back Ridley up. But not to murder him." He set his plate aside and picked up his cup. "Vandame wouldn't do it, even if she wanted it, which I'm telling you she never did. Most thieves avoid violence like the pox."

Tom's shoulders slumped. He shoved the remains of his supper onto the table and grabbed his own cup. "Why didn't you tell us this yesterday, before we went down to the Savoy to threaten those people?"

"That's *my* question," Lawson said. "You two were so busy suspecting me that it never occurred to you I might have something to contribute."

Tom gave him a rueful look. He should at least have taken Lawson out to supper one night to ask him about those days in Montaubon. He could've listened with a skeptical ear. At the very least, he would've gotten a better sense of this difficult man. Get past that mocking pose and see what Anthony saw in him.

No use now.

"How did Anthony know our ploy would succeed?" Francis asked. "It seemed to me that du Plessis honestly did not know what his wife might have done. That was the only reason he agreed to listen to Anthony's terms."

"She tried to throw the blame on Lady Rich at first," Tom said. "Remember? Before she even knew what we were going to tell her husband. Then she switched to Elsa Moreau, calling her 'that little viper.'"

"That's a sign of guilt," Francis said. "Throwing the blame as far as one can. Lady Rich refused to countenance her lies about Anthony, thus making herself a target. And we mentioned Moreau as our original informant. She grasped whatever name was offered."

Tom shot him a warning look. Lawson couldn't know how they knew what was being said in Essex House. But both men moved on without a hiccup.

Francis said, "I have no doubt that Madame du Plessis wanted to ruin Anthony and take revenge for the multiple humiliations he'd inflicted on her."

"If you're still talking about the hair, she had her revenge for that in '86. More than enough, even for her. Monsieur du Plessis played his part in that too."

"What happened in '86?" Francis asked. "Anthony's never told me the whole story. He makes some quip and changes the subject. But if we're going to cut through this tangled mess of secrets, lies, and scandals to bring him home, I must know the truth."

Lawson didn't answer at first. He took a long drink of his wine, plainly deciding what to tell them. "He didn't want you to know."

"Why not?" Francis sounded hurt.

"Shame, mostly. Disgust with himself for letting things get so out of hand."

"What things?" Francis said.

Lawson met his eyes. "Be patient, I beg you. I've never told this story, and it's a long one." He drained his cup and held it out to Tom.

He got up to bring the jug over. He refilled all their cups, then set the jug on the empty cheese plate. "We're listening."

Lawson took one more drink and began. "All right, then. It was in 1586. I joined Anthony's household three or four months before the trouble began. We were madly in love, if you can believe it. Things cooled off after the crisis, and now we're just good friends. Back then, we couldn't get enough of each other. We strove to please one another with all sorts of little treats. Sugared flowers, perfumed gloves, clever entertainments. We competed to see who could hire the prettiest, most accomplished pageboys. We had so much fun on Saturday nights, when all the good Huguenots were confessing their sins around the family Bible. Anthony and I would recline on couches and watch the boys perform for us. They danced and sang and recited poetry."

"Sounds very Roman," Tom said.

"That was the idea. We did the work, writing a pound of letters a day. Anthony dictated; I wrote. Then in the evening, we devoted ourselves to pleasure. We both drank too much. Worse, we let the boys drink too much. Anthony was never much good at disciplining the servants."

"Neither am I," Francis admitted. "And I think I see where this is going. One of the boys was ill-used."

Lawson nodded. "We didn't know about it. Maybe we were blind, but we honestly didn't know."

Francis said, "I knew he was accused of sodomy that year. But I assumed it was in reference to you, not a child. He would never do such a thing. It's not in his nature."

"Nor mine, I assure you. But Pierre was forced by someone, or so he said. The actual incident was never made clear. That's why we didn't credit it at first. When and where did this assault occur? We never heard any details. The boy in question left our house for the du Plessis-Mornays'. We assumed the parents had decided it was a more important post than our house since du Plessis was the governor. Several weeks after he left us, Pierre told the cook about being abused in Mr. Bacon's house. The cook told Madame, Madame told Monsieur, and the fat went into the fire. Before we knew it, du Plessis had lodged a formal complaint with the seneschal of Quercy. Anthony was arrested and carted off to jail."

"God's breath!" Francis cried.

"What's a seneschal?" Tom asked.

Francis answered him. "Something like a sheriff. He administers the king's justice in his designated region." He turned back to Lawson. "I had no idea Anthony had been in jail. None whatsoever."

"No one did," Lawson said, "except for a handful of people. I think everyone knew they were treading on dangerous ground, arresting the son of the late Lord Keeper of England. It never became general gossip in the town, for a mercy."

Tom suspected another cause for the secrecy. "Why didn't du Plessis have a talk with Anthony before rushing off to the authorities? That smells suspicious to me."

"You have a good nose, my friend." Lawson gave him that twisted grin. "You haven't heard what Anthony said after Madame's second reprimand in church for her ridiculous hairpieces. No one could forget it. He said, *De vrai, Madame du Plessis porte la briggaine dans cette maison.*"

"Ay, me!" Francis clapped a hand to his chest, clearly shocked.

"What does that mean?" Tom asked.

Francis translated. "In truth, Madame du Plessis wears the codpiece in that house."

"By my quill and inkpot," Tom said, grinning. "That's hard."

"He was always too clever for his own good," Francis said.

"It caught on," Lawson said, "as these things do. Du Plessis was even mocked at court. King Henry's courtiers are not renowned for their pious behavior, if you follow me. And du Plessis had such an exalted opinion of himself; who could resist taking him down a peg or two?"

"I remember Anthony was desperate for money around that time," Francis said. "More than usual."

"Local tradesmen called in debts when people realized he was gone. For a while, I didn't know if I'd ever see him again." Lawson's eyes grew hard. "You learn who your friends are, don't you? King Henry is a true prince. The instant he found out about it, he demanded Anthony's immediate release. He told his ambassador to England, a fellow named Buzenval, to send five thousand écus at once. Buzenval didn't have the money, or so he said. So the king told du Plessis and du Pin to advance five hundred each without delay. They made excuses too. We were tearing our hair out, selling off plate, wondering if we could scrape together enough to flee to England. Then the king, bless his eternal soul, found a cousin with a thousand écus in his spare purse. Gradually, we pulled our life back together. But *that* was Madame's revenge. She didn't need to murder her favorite drinking companion."

They sat in silence, absorbing the sordid tale. Sodomy was a capital crime in France, as in England, though it was rarely prosecuted here. Here, you would hang. There, you'd be burned alive. Tom took a deep draught of wine to drown that hideous thought.

"Who did it?" Tom asked. "Who hurt the boy?"

"Or did someone put him up to telling the story?" Francis asked.

"That's what I thought at first," Lawson said "The whole thing smelled like spite. I thought Elsa had cooked up the story to get me back for rejecting her. She more or less threw herself at me one night when we were out drinking with a group of upper servants. I turned her down — rudely, perhaps, looking back. At the time, I thought I was being witty. Anyway, I thought the original idea was hers. You know, accuse the man who rejects you of buggery. That'll show him!"

"That's a cautionary tale," Tom said. And yet another reason to be glad he was no longer tempted by fair-haired wenches in taverns.

"Then why aim at Anthony?" Francis asked.

"That must have been Madame's work. Elsa persuaded Pierre to tell the cook, who told Madame, who decided she would rather hook the bigger fish."

Life in a small town. Another good reason to stay in London. At least here people had real things to fuss about. Tom said, "It sounds like you changed your mind. You said, 'at first.'"

Lawson nodded "After Elsa left for England, I heard rumblings about Vandame from one of our grooms. He liked the small ones, this fellow said. That turned the whole thing upside down. We'd fired Vandame for stealing silver bridle ornaments, and he went over to the du Plessis's also. There weren't a lot of choices for servants in that town, and everyone liked Vandame's family. No one knew what he'd been doing with the younger boys. He might have bribed or threatened Pierre to say Anthony hurt him, in revenge for the dismissal. Madame pounced on the story like a cat on a mouse, and the rest we know."

Francis said, "Anthony could have told me all this when he got home."

"It was over and done with." Lawson gave him a sad smile. "He blamed himself for not taking better care of his people. That assault happened in his house. He felt responsible."

Francis nodded, his eyes sad. Tom thought Anthony did have a share of the blame. It's a master's job to maintain order among his people. Lady Bacon, for all her severity, was a kinder mistress in the long run.

"You've changed your mind twice about that story," Tom said. "How sure are you of this last version?"

"As sure as I can be. That groom was passing on an old complaint, but when the name Vandame dropped from his lips, everything fell into place. He used to eye the boys the way some men eye horses or beautiful women. He had his own little room above the stables. The boys slept in a gang. It wouldn't be hard to lure a page who had been dipping into the wine jug up to your warm bed." Lawson nodded, frowning. "The wine was our fault. The rest was Vandame."

"At least he'll deserve his punishment," Tom said. "But if he didn't kill Ridley, who did?"

"I don't know," Lawson said. "I wasn't there, remember?"

"No, you weren't." Tom extended a hand and waited for Lawson to take it. "I apologize for suspecting you."

"Apology accepted. You had every reason to — at first."

"I owe you an apology as well," Francis said. "Not only for suspecting you here, but for not working harder to shorten your stay in Newgate."

Lawson grunted in surprise. "I doubt you could have done much, Frank. Not with both your mother and your uncle ranged against me. But I accept the apology."

"But I'm not convinced by your arguments concerning Ridley," Francis said. "Thieves fall out, as I said before. So do drinking companions. The story of that poor child and all the adults who exploited him tells me that Madame du Plessis is a ruthless woman capable of extreme acts. If she knew Vandame raped the boy, she would have a tremendous threat to hold over him. It's only been six years. She could go home and tell the seneschal she had new information. King Henry wouldn't rescue a stableman. Vandame would be burned at the stake."

"You'd do anything to avoid that fate," Tom said. "Anything at all. And I'm not certain the strangling happened inside the coach. The hat was crushed, but there were those scuffle marks in the road. You could get Ridley out of the coach somehow. You could just say, 'Let's talk outside where we can get a bit of breeze.'"

Lawson nodded. "Then you drop something or kick him in the gut. When he bends over, loop the belt around his neck and pull."

"Even a smaller man could do it that way," Tom said. "He'd have the advantage of surprise."

They grinned at one another, pleased with themselves for working that part out.

"I'm glad to get to the bottom of the Ridley matter," Francis said. "And gladder still to know neither you nor Anthony had anything to do with it." He flicked aside his coverlet and got to his feet. "And now I'm going to bed. I'll take some poppy juice to help me sleep. I'll tell myself that Anthony is asleep too, under Jacques's tender care. Tomorrow, somehow, we'll find out where he is and steal him back."

TWENTY-THREE

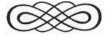

The nurse took Baby William to the nursery to change his linens and wrap him in a clean blanket. Trumpet took advantage of his absence to sit at her desk and read her mail with a cup of warm ale at her elbow. She was far from her old self — it had only been one day, for mercy's sake — but she could see her feet again, and that was well enough for now.

She took the first folded square from the small stack on the silver plate and noted the writing on the front. "This one's from Aunt Blanche." She opened the page and read. "Ah, well. She doesn't know anything about du Plessis or any other Huguenots, for which she thanks her dear Lord. But if I ever have a question about the ladies of Bohemia, she could fill a book."

"Will we go to Bohemia someday, my lady?" Catalina looked hopeful. She must miss getting out and about as much Trumpet did; more, since she wasn't exhausted by pregnancy and the ordeal of childbirth.

"Someday, perhaps. Not soon." Trumpet folded her aunt's letter and dropped it into the small scented box. She picked up the next one. "This is from Uncle Nat."

"Is he in London again, my lady?" Uncle Nat had recommended the former player to his niece after Catalina had grown weary of theater life, which was where he'd discovered her. They still liked to meet from time to time and dally away an afternoon.

"Mm-hmm. He's back at Gray's." Trumpet read the note in silence. "He doesn't know anything about a Madame du Plessis, though he's heard that her husband is an insufferable prig. That report comes from a mutual friend named Antoine du Pin." She frowned at her servant. "Hasn't Tom mentioned him?"

Catalina shrugged. Her eyes had taken on a dreamy look at the mention of Uncle Nat.

She had been tending her mistress day and night for many long weeks. She'd earned a little fun. Baby William had two nurses, and Trumpet could survive for a few hours without constant observation. Uncle Nat could arrange a suitable place.

Trumpet said, "This du Pin sounds like the sort that might interest Anthony Bacon. He's a wine merchant from an old family in Bordeaux. He and Uncle Nat meet from time to time in a tavern near the port in Bordeaux to drink and play cards. Uncle Nat says, 'He's as good a Protestant as I am.'" Trumpet laughed. "I know what that means."

Outwardly, Nathaniel Welbeck conformed to the established religion. Inwardly, he had his own moral code and retained a fondness for the costlier trappings of Catholicism.

"And listen to this: 'What du Pin loves is money and the game of trade. He's not above shipping Spanish wine in French barrels, for instance.'" Trumpet folded up the letter. "Anthony will certainly want to know about that."

Heaping more coals on the heads of du Plessis and his friend lifted another portion of her guilt. These people should not be in England. Their stableman might not have murdered Raffe Ridley, but the emissary wouldn't have gone about spreading those nasty rumors if it weren't for Madame and her never-ending spleen. This du Pin had apparently earned his punishment independently of the rest.

She took a drink of the well-spiced ale. Her lie had had greater consequences than she'd dreamed it would, but they weren't entirely undeserved.

She folded Uncle Nat's letter and added it to the scented box. Then she picked up the last one and smiled at the name inked across the front. Tom's impeccable script; she'd know it from across the room. She held the page to her nose, but it only smelled of ink and something moldy — probably the message boy's cheesy hands. She kissed the seal and slit it with her ivory-handled penknife, then opened the folds and sniffed again. Ah, here was a trace of the indefinable scent of Tom. Perhaps she could persuade him to start wearing some perfume of her choice. Something musky with attar of roses . . .

"Great God above!" she cried, scanning the first line. "Anthony's been taken!"

"Taken where?"

"They don't know." She continued to read, reporting the gist every few lines. "Anthony was snatched out of his coach yesterday afternoon. They took Jacques — that's the boy who tends to him — so they must mean to keep him alive. Oh! They believe du Plessis and du Pin are behind it but have no idea where they're keeping the prisoners. They fear the plan is to sell Anthony to the Spanish." Trumpet gaped at her maidservant. "How appalling!"

"God save the poor man," Catalina said. "He is the one who is so feeble, is he not?"

"How could he survive the journey? But there's more." Trumpet drew in a sharp breath. "You won't believe this. They know the dastards are still in London because Madame has not yet left the house in the Savoy. But Tom writes, 'She won't talk, and we have no means to compel her. Could you and your friend Lady Rich find a way to crack that nut?'"

More consequences of that cursed lie! It caused Anthony to deliver an ultimatum to the Frenchmen, which drove them to this desperate deed. Well, Trumpet had caused all this through her confusion and cowardice. It was up to her to put it right.

"No means to compel La Plashy." She smiled at Catalina. "I'll find the means. She'll babble like a drunken parrot before I'm done."

She drummed her fingers on the polished desktop, gazing out the window. First, she must write to Tom to assure him answers would be forthcoming. Penelope could probably needle the truth out of La Plashy, but Trumpet had a bigger cannon to deploy. Lady Russell knew every Protestant of note in Europe, including France, through decades of voluminous correspondence. One word from her and the Du Plessis-Mornays would have to choose a new religion.

The mere thought of the redoubtable Lady Russell made Trumpet feel stronger. She could brazen out Penelope's revelation about Baby William, if the witch ever dared to utter it. But she wouldn't once Trumpet got through with her.

William had green eyes, like his mother. Everyone said babies' hair darkened as they grew older, so that nearly transparent gold wouldn't last. Catalina could devise a gentle dye to turn it light brown, like Stephen's. Hair was nothing. There was no trace of a dimple; that was what mattered most.

Who did little Charles Rich take after, one might ask? His mother, his father — or his mother's lover?

Cackling to herself, Trumpet snatched a sheet of paper and dipped her quill. She told Tom to warn Mr. Bacon that she had to tell his aunt about Anthony's capture. She'd find out anyway if they never got him back.

She knew Lady Russell would be at home at this hour, reading and writing letters. That was what Women of Influence did in the morning. Her Ladyship would willingly come to Essex House to rescue her nephew — and to see the baby.

"What time should we say?" Trumpet asked her maidservant.

"Two o'clock, my lady. Time for a nap after dinner, which older ladies require."

"Good thought. And it will give Mr. Bacon time to have a word with my uncle. While we're about it, let's get the truth out of Elsa Moreau."

Trumpet told Tom what time to appear. She hinted that he and Mr. Bacon might learn something else of interest, then added a few lines about Uncle Nat and du Pin. She signed and sealed, then kissed the seal before the wax completely hardened. Then she clapped her hands in sheer delight. "This will be my first social event after my confinement. It seems fitting it should have to do with murder and abduction, don't you think? A harbinger of adventures to come."

She pulled out another sheet of paper and thought for a minute before writing to Lady Russell. Best to lay it out as simply as possible. There was just no good way to tell a woman her nephew would be sold to the Spanish unless she could compel a baboon to speak.

She handed the letters to Catalina. "Have the boy deliver these at once. Then tell Lady Rich I wish to speak with her at her earliest convenience, by which I mean now." She drew in a fortifying breath. "It's time to get things sorted out around here."

* * *

"How's our new mother?" Penelope said, sweeping into Trumpet's parlor with an indulgent smile. "Was there something you needed from me?"

"There is." Trumpet sat in the largest armchair, fully dressed in a red wool skirt and doublet with a six-inch ruff around her neck. "You may sit down if you like." Her cool tone signaled the first change in their respective roles.

"I'll stand. What do you want?"

"I want you to have Elsa Moreau present herself at two o'clock in the front parlor to tell Francis Bacon the truth about Raffe Ridley's death."

Penelope scoffed. "I will not. I don't want that story told." She looked down her nose at her guest. "Have you forgotten my conditions so soon, Alice? I hold your lover's future in my grip."

Trumpet levered herself out of the chair with a grunt, strode across the small room, and slapped her hostess smartly across the cheek. "You will address me with respect, *Baroness*. I can protect Tom better than you might think. And you're in no position to threaten me. Does your lawful husband know who the father of your children is? Do *you*?"

She turned her back on the woman to return to her chair but remained standing beside it with one hand on the top rail. She wasn't quite steady on her feet yet.

Penelope's lip curled in preparation to make some pert reply. But Trumpet hadn't finished. She stopped the words with one imperious finger. "How do you think my lord of Essex would respond to the news that his sister threatened to ruin the wife of one of his most stalwart supporters? The Earl of Dorchester has brought both men and money to your brother's cause. That's worth a far sight more than a few coy letters written by an idle lady playing at intrigue. Furthermore, when matters of interest to Essex arise in the House of Lords, I hold two votes" — she raised a cupped hand — "while you have none since your husband regards you as little more than a broodmare. An unfaithful one, at that."

Penelope listened to this in silence, one palm soothing the offended cheek. She regarded Trumpet for a long moment through narrowed eyes. At last she said, "Very well. It appears we are equals now, my lady."

"No," Trumpet said. "I'm greater. But we can be friends of a sort, now that we understand each other."

TWENTY-FOUR

F rancis walked across the yard at Gray's on Wednesday morning, girding himself for a challenging conversation. It was the mark of his determination to do whatever must be done that he was willing to seek assistance from this source. He and Nathaniel Welbeck, Lady Dorchester's uncle, had never liked one another. Welbeck regarded Francis as an overindulged, self-important bore who'd risen only thanks to his father's reputation. Francis considered Welbeck to be little better than a pirate, regardless of his standing as a senior barrister of Gray's Inn.

But the note Trumpet had sent Tom this morning suggested Welbeck might know something useful about Antoine du Pin, so the attempt must be made. Francis knocked on the door on the ground floor of Ellis's Building.

"Intro!"

He entered to find his rival with his feet on his desk, reading some illustrated broadside. The rest of the desk was littered with papers, hats, coins, and handkerchiefs — the sort of oddments one pulls out of one's pockets on returning home. The room reflected the same standard of disorder. Heavy furniture showed the dents and scratches of many moves, one small stack of books burdened a shelf, and a pair of rapiers hung crossed on the wall.

"Ah, Bacon. I've been expecting you." Welbeck gave him a twisted smile. "My niece wouldn't trouble herself about French Protestants unless she was involved in one of your intrigues."

"My brother Anthony has been abducted."

The smile vanished, and the feet dropped to the floor. "How?"

"He was snatched out of his coach on Monday afternoon. Circumstances implicate Philippe du Plessis-Mornay and Antoine du Pin. Anthony, perhaps rashly, revealed that he has damaging information about them." Francis shook his head again at his brother's foolhardiness. "Our hypothesis is that they mean to sell him to the Spanish, to be traded for a prisoner. But he'll never survive the journey. We must find him before they sail."

Welbeck sank back in his chair, rubbing his short brown beard. "God's breath, Bacon. That is *not* what I expected. This isn't one of Alice's games." He gestured at a chair near the desk. "Sit, please. I'll tell you what I can. It won't be much."

Francis gave him a brief account of the conversation at the Savoy and the attempted theft of Anthony's documents. He skirted around the Ridley matter. Fortunately, Welbeck seemed uncurious about the reason for their visit to du Plessis.

"I had no idea du Pin was capable of such a foul act. Selling supplies to the Spanish in '88 is one thing. He's a merchant with stock to sell. Wine doesn't keep very long, you know. Naturally, I disapproved, but I didn't know about it until much later. Besides, it was none of my affair."

"Have you known him long?"

"Years, but not very well. We liked to meet at a tavern near the port whenever I found myself in Bordeaux. I knew he was a greedy rascal, loyal only to his own family. He cared less for religion and politics than I do. He tagged along with du Plessis to court, mainly because noblemen buy a lot of wine." Welbeck shrugged. "He was good

269

company. And he always had the most beautiful women around him."

Francis didn't care about the man's past. "Where can we find him? We have no idea where he's holding Anthony and Jacques. A house in the city? Or farther afield, perhaps some place like Bermondsey? London must have a hundred inns and twice that many lodging houses. We can't search them all."

"You won't have to. He won't be far from his ship."

"Do you know its name?"

Welbeck shook his head. "The family has more than one. He'll have brought a cargo to sell, whether he was here to argue King Henry's case or not. He wouldn't waste the voyage. It'll be a good-sized galleon, something with a big hold."

"East of the bridge, then." Francis felt the tight band of panic around his heart loosen a fraction. The task was not impossible.

"Closer in rather than farther out. He'd have the barrels to unload and an outgoing cargo, I should think. He won't be living on the ship himself. He once told me he couldn't wait to make port to get out of that cramped berth and into a full-sized bed."

"An inn near the river," Francis said. "The better-quality establishments, I suppose."

"That's right. You know how Frenchmen are about food." Welbeck's brown eyes were filled with concern. Francis hadn't known he was capable of that emotion.

"Thank you," he said, getting up to leave. "You've narrowed the field for us considerably. I'm grateful."

To his surprise, Welbeck got up to see him out. "I'm truly sorry for this disaster, Bacon. I was looking forward to meeting the famous Anthony Bacon. I still am. You'll find him. I have every confidence. And if there's anything more I can do, don't hesitate to ask."

He opened the door to find Tom standing outside with his fist raised, ready to knock.

"Clarady," Welbeck said. "You look like a man with a message. Good news, I hope?"

"A step forward, perhaps," Tom said. "Another note from Lady Dorchester. She says our meeting is set for two o'clock."

"Good." Francis nodded at his colleague and stepped out to the entryway.

"Your aunt will arrive a little later," Tom said. "Elsa Moreau has a story to tell us first."

"Another one?" Francis scoffed.

"Elsa Moreau?" Welbeck, who had started to close his chamber door, swung it fully open again. "Is *she* here?"

Francis turned back to him. "She's in Lady Rich's service. Do you know her?"

"Intimately, at one time. She's one of those beautiful women I mentioned. Du Pin's doxies."

"She's no lightskirt now," Tom said. "She's a fine lady's maid, as respectable as —"

"Catalina Luna?" Welbeck smiled. "Their histories are similar in some respects, though Catalina has a good heart. Du Pin told me about her the night I —" He coughed into his fist. "She tried to pick his pocket down by the wharf one day and drew a knife when he caught her hand. He saw the beauty under the dirt and offered her a better position. She'd been scratching a living with a troupe of street players and thieving on the side. Du Pin bragged about transforming her himself. He taught her how to speak, how to dress, and how to use a knife for something other than stabbing."

Tom looked staggered. He prided himself on his ability to sum people up.

"She's had years of practice." Francis offered that slender comfort.

Welbeck cocked his head. "Last I heard, du Pin had agreed to find her a position in a decent household. That was what she wanted, he said. Security. He considered it a challenge, and it sounds like he succeeded. But she couldn't have leapt from the Garonne district straight into Essex House."

"She was in Madame du Plessis's service," Francis said. "I don't know how long."

Welbeck chuckled. "That old dog! I don't know anything about the wife, but du Pin thought his old chum du Plessis could use a little tarnish. I'll wager he expected Elsa to seduce her master, for lack of other entertainment."

"That's not how things turned out," Francis said. "But I'm afraid it's a longer story than we have time for this morning. We have a search to conduct."

"Of course, of course." Welbeck started to pat him on the shoulder but thought better of it. "Let me know what happens." He went back into his room and closed the door.

As they left the building, Tom said, "I'm glad we'll finally get to the truth about the Ridley matter."

Francis scowled at him. "I don't care about the Ridley matter anymore."

"Of course you do, Mr. Bacon." Tom sounded slightly shocked. "You always want to know the truth."

Francis grunted. "Not this time. Not if it hinders our finding my brother."

* * *

He changed into his best doublet after dinner, knowing his lady aunt would be dressed in formal black and probably wearing her great widow's cowl as well. Trumpet, with her shrewd sense of costume, would be dressed in similar vein. Lady Rich always took pains to outshine the other women in the room. The tribunal of three ladies would present an implacable front to the recalcitrant Madame du Plessis.

He devoutly hoped this stratagem would work. Tom could visit every inn from Wapping to Woolwich, but he couldn't enter every room. Few landlords would give up their lodgers, especially not regular customers. Du Pin would doubtless have paid more for privacy.

And how could they hope to identify his ship? Paddle about in a wherry, craning to hear a snatch of French conversation? There could be several French ships in the Thames today, as well as a Belgian one or two.

Francis gave the crown of his hat another whisk with the brush and set it on his head. At least there had been no difficulty luring their victim into the trap. Trumpet's letter said she'd responded to Lady Rich's invitation with alacrity. Even in her current straits, the ambitious woman leapt at the chance to visit Essex House again, eager to gain an introduction to the renowned Lady Russell. In her excitement, she'd apparently forgotten that august personage was Anthony Bacon's aunt.

Francis appreciated the symmetry of using the woman's own vanity to bring her to justice.

Tom knocked at his door. They walked down to Essex House in silence. Francis was surprised when the usher led them around to one of the walled gardens behind the house. He'd forgotten about the maidservant's new story. He couldn't imagine what she could add at this late stage, but perhaps she knew something about her former employers' whereabouts.

Trumpet, Lady Rich, and a fair-haired woman in a gray dress were already there. Trumpet sat on a chair under the arbor. The servant sat on a stool in the path. Francis followed Trumpet's gesture to a bench placed against the brick wall. Tom took up a post behind Trumpet, where he could see over her head. Lady Rich stood beside a weathered gray post.

Francis regarded the servant with only mild interest, noting her exceptional beauty while hoping this wouldn't take long. "What have you to tell us, Mrs. Moreau?"

"First," she said, "I must avow that my lady never instructed me to play the role of coachman or to do away with Raffe Ridley."

Francis gasped, completely taken aback. "*You* killed him. And you were the second coachman."

She nodded. "As I say, all on my own. My lady only wanted to hear what Lawson would offer Raffe to stop his slandering. We thought Mr. Anthony would try to bribe him, you see. My lady wanted to know the terms and also to be certain the terms were accepted."

Francis glanced at Lady Rich. Her expression was unreadable. Trumpet, on the other hand, wore a thin smile. She had known the truth when she let this woman tell Tom the other tale. Tom couldn't see the thin smile, but he must realize she'd deceived him. He was looking down on her dark head with a clenched jaw.

Ah, well. They would sort it out between themselves.

"If Her Ladyship sent you to listen," Francis said, "why not simply invite yourself to the meeting? From what I've heard, that wouldn't have been difficult for you."

"I knew from the start that I would kill him. I knew nothing would ever stop his *babillage idiot* — his stupid talk. He is envious, you understand. He wanted to ruin Mr. Anthony." She paused to lick her bottom lip and shoot a quick glance at her mistress. "And I feared he would enjoy his babbling so much he would tell everything he knew about everyone."

"About you, for instance." Thanks to Nathaniel Welbeck, Francis understood what lay behind that vague remark. "You were afraid Ridley would tell Her Ladyship about your past."

Moreau pressed her lips together and gave him a baleful look. It almost made him shiver, even with the sun-

274

warmed bricks behind his back. "What do you know about my past, Monsieur Bacon?"

"Enough. Your friend — or should I say rescuer? — Monsieur du Pin is an acquaintance of my lady Dorchester's uncle. The world is not so very large, Mrs. Moreau. Or perhaps you simply did not run far enough away."

"What's this about?" Lady Rich asked. "What past? What need had you of rescuing?"

Moreau lowered her gaze to her hands, plainly unwilling to condemn herself. So Francis related the brief history Welbeck had told him. "I'm afraid you've been sadly deceived, my lady. As were my brother and Madame du Plessis."

Lady Rich regarded her maidservant with loathing. "You'd best tell them the rest of your story. Lady Russell will be here soon."

"What will you do with me, my lady?"

"Lock you up while I think about it. Now speak!"

Francis said, "I don't believe there's much more to tell. Lawson never knew you'd taken the reins. Why did you make it look as though he had committed the murder? Did he know about your past as well?"

She shrugged. "I do not think so. But someone must have the blame, you see. The easier it is to see what happened, the less will anyone look. I stole Lawson's handkerchief at the tavern. That gave me the idea. I showed myself to Raffe and said, 'Come out. Walk with me.' He put his head out the door, and I hit him with my sock." When Francis frowned, she added, "My sock full of sand. It always works. Then he fell, and I strangled him. I meant to use my own belt, but I found another one on the floor. I thought it must be Lawson's. I dragged Ridley off the bare road a bit, so white in the moonlight. And then I come home."

She folded her hands like a good pupil who had completed her recitation.

Francis regarded her in some amazement, seeking to reconcile her gentle appearance with the cool savagery of her words. He couldn't do it. "Are you still in communication with Monsieur du Pin?"

"I have not seen Antoine since I leave France. I did not know he was in London."

"Do you know where he is?"

"I do not." She looked at Lady Rich, the first sign of regret coloring her blue eyes. She could feel pity for herself, it would seem. "I would tell you if I knew. I never meant harm to come to Mr. Anthony. You must believe that."

He did believe it. Lady Rich wanted to stop Ridley and didn't mind throwing Lawson under the coach as well, but she wanted Anthony to join her brother's faction. Francis imagined she'd said something like, "That blabbermouth Ridley must go, one way or another." Her unscrupulous servant filled in the rest.

He got to his feet. "I don't need to hear any more." He touched his hat to Lady Rich. "You'll know best how to deal with her." He touched his hat again to Lady Dorchester. "Shall we move on to the next performance?"

* * *

The usher escorted them to the large parlor on the ground floor, where portraits of the late Earl of Leicester and Her Majesty Queen Elizabeth hung in positions of honor on either side of the marble fireplace. The three ladies occupied high-backed armchairs placed like judges' thrones before the hearth. A low seat, almost a footstool, squatted before them at a little distance.

After making their greetings, Francis took the lesser seat appointed to him a few feet to one side of the ladies. Tom went to stand against the far wall. He'd avoided

Trumpet's attempts to speak with him on the way in from the garden.

Moments after they got themselves arranged, the usher announced their visitor. Madame du Plessis had to turn sideways to maneuver her ridiculous farthingale through the door. Her eyes went first to Lady Rich, a smile lighting her plain features. The brightness faded by a candle or two as she met Lady Dorchester's leveled gaze. The light went out altogether as she noticed the stern widow seated in the center and the low stool waiting empty before her.

"I don't believe we've met," Lady Russell said, "though we have corresponded. I am Lady Elizabeth Russell, Dowager Countess of Bedford."

Madame du Plessis sank in a shallow curtsy. She bowed her head and murmured, "I am honored, my lady. My ladies."

"Do sit down," Lady Russell commanded.

Madame du Plessis looked around the room as if seeking an escape, but the usher stood beside the door through which she'd entered, and Tom blocked the one leading farther into the house. Three windows spanned the outer wall, but she'd never get through them in those skirts. She took the seat.

Francis felt no pity for her. She may not have ordered Ridley's death, but she had started this trouble. And he didn't forget the revenge she'd already exacted for Anthony's one brash comment about her hair.

Her red brocade skirts puddled gracelessly around her feet, garish in contrast to the somber garb of her judges. Her hair, piled up on either side of a straight part, seemed clownish. She had evidently not learned that lesson either. She was stubborn as well as vain.

She attempted to fold her hands in her lap but couldn't reach it and ended up resting her elbows on the shelf-like contraption beneath her skirts, letting her hands dangle like the feet of a little dog awaiting a treat.

Lady Russell cleared her throat. As the eldest, she assumed the leadership role. She addressed du Plessis without preamble. "You have information which we require, Madame. Where is my nephew Anthony?"

"Nephew?" Du Plessis began emitting a sort of tremulous whinny.

Lady Russell regarded her with a cold eye. "Surely you know Lady Bacon is my sister and Anthony is her son. How do you think he gained such ready acceptance among the Calvinists in France?"

Du Plessis's mouth opened and closed. She seemed astonished, but she must have known.

The two sisters had threaded the warp on which Anthony had woven his tapestry of informants. From before he was born, they'd committed their formidable educations to advancing the cause of the complete Reformation. They'd woven a vast web of connections throughout Europe, sustaining it through a constant stream of letters, translations, and smuggled religious literature. When Anthony established his base in Montauban, he'd expanded into the political realm. He'd never scorned a useful source on the basis of religion, accepting Catholics into his service as well as Protestants. But the foundation of his great work had been laid by his mother and his aunt.

"I will ask you again," Lady Russell said. Her tone showed that she would brook no further evasions. "Where is my nephew?"

"I can't tell you that, my lady. My husband —"

"You can and you will. If you fail to supply us with every detail, right here and now, I will set to work writing letters to every important Protestant in Europe. My sister Lady Bacon will join me in this effort. We will inform them that neither you nor your husband are to be trusted. We will tell everyone that you, in particular, are a lying, scheming harpy who places her own pride above the Reformation."

Du Plessis quailed, her mouth twisting in dismay.

Lady Bacon added, "We will also warn them that Monsieur du Plessis received money from King Philip of Spain in 1588 while England battled for her survival."

"That was Antoine du Pin!" du Plessis cried, flailing like a fly whose wings were caught in a spider's sticky web.

"You and your husband profited from that exchange," Lady Dorchester put in, "which makes you complicit."

Lady Russell nodded at her. "How many loyal Protestants lie moldering beneath the sea thanks to your treachery? How much blood was spilled to pay for the pearl dangling between those absurd mounds of false hair you're wearing?"

The blood drained from du Plessis's sallow face. She whispered, as if her voice had failed, "How can you know these things?"

"My nephew knows them." Lady Russell spoke with crisp articulation. "Do you think I won't move heaven and earth to bring him home?" Her voice rose to a thunder.

Madame du Plessis shook her head, humbled at last.

Lady Russell said, "Then you will answer Mr. Bacon's questions forthwith."

The defendant nodded meekly.

Francis asked, "Where is he?"

"On a ship called *la Neptune*. It belongs to the du Pins. They will take him to St. Jean de Luz and sell him to the Spanish."

Francis waved the last part away. "We know why they took him."

"Mon Dieu!" She gasped. "You know everything!"

"When do they sail?"

"On Friday. They await a payment from a buyer of wine. And for me to sell the lease at the Savoy."

Two days, not counting today. They must move quickly. "Where are your husband and Monsieur du Pin?"

"They lodge at an inn called the Grapes. It is new and very clean, my husband says."

"Are you certain Anthony is on the ship?"

"I have not seen it with my own eyes. I tell you only what I have heard. I am not part of this insane plan. I implore you to believe me."

Francis met her plea with a stony face. "You set all this in motion, Madame, with your lust for vengeance, pushing Raffe Ridley to spread vile rumors about my brother. Now your friend is dead, and Anthony lies in grave peril. He is not strong enough to endure a voyage across the Bay of Biscay. Your husband will be trading a dead man to the Spanish, and then he will be wanted by my queen — and your king — for his murder."

"You must stop him, Monsieur Bacon!" Du Plessis scooped up her skirts and fell to her knees, clasping her hands before her. "My ladies, my great ladies. I implore you to save my husband from his folly. He is desperate, and so he listens to du Pin with his schemes."

Francis held his tongue, letting his aunt answer. "First, let Anthony be returned to us, unharmed. Then we will consider what justice your husband deserves."

Du Plessis, weeping copiously, raised her clasped hands to heaven and vowed to renounce all vanity henceforward. The judges regarded her with dry eyes and curled lips.

Lady Russell dismissed her with a flick of her hand. "You may go."

Francis raised a finger. "One more thing, my lady, if I may." He turned to Lady Rich. "Do you have a secure chamber where this woman can be contained until we rescue Anthony? She mustn't warn her husband. He might decide to leave early or move Anthony to another ship. Also, she may still be lying."

Lady Rich nodded. Then a chilling smile stole across her lips. "I'll put her in with her former servant. Let them console one another." She tilted her chin at the usher standing by the entry door, who turned on his heel and went out. He returned in a moment with another man in livery. They each grasped an arm of the still-kneeling Frenchwoman, lifting her to her feet and hustling her out of the room.

Silence reigned for a long moment. Lady Russell broke it. She slapped her hands on her black-draped thighs, turned a twinkling smile toward Lady Dorchester, and declared, "Now I want to see that baby."

TWENTY-FIVE

Lady Russell dandled Tom's son on her knees, pinching his plump cheeks and cooing at him as if he were the most amazing baby she had ever seen. What would she think if she knew who the real father was?

Tom hung back, standing at his post by the rear door. He couldn't very well approach and declare his role in the creation of this marvel. Besides, the scene was so far beyond his prior experience of that stern woman he could scarcely believe his eyes and ears. He watched as if she were admiring some stranger's child.

That thought gave him pause. This was how it would be henceforward, watching his boy from the background, standing four feet away like an old family friend. William was the son of Stephen Delabere in all but body. Someday, Tom realized with a sorrowful pang, he would want a child he could claim in public and bring up in his own home.

Lady Russell rose, handing the baby back to his nurse and kissing Trumpet on both cheeks. Trumpet followed the nurse out the rear door, raising her eyebrows at Tom as she passed.

Lady Russell beckoned to her nephew, bidding him to walk with her to her coach and explain to her exactly what had brought the family to this desperate pass. Tom watched Mr. Bacon swallow and nod, accepting that unenviable task with resignation. He would doubtless have to submit to his mother's interrogation on the same subject before too long. Hopefully, they'd have Anthony home by then to mitigate the scolding.

Tom slipped out the door and around to the rear tower. As he expected, he found Trumpet waiting for him in the anteroom.

"Nurse took William back to his cradle. I know you won't have time to visit him today." She stood unmoving, hands folded at her waist, a wary question in her eyes.

He knew what it was. "You lied to me."

"There were reasons. Stupid ones. I should've been stronger. I shouldn't have let Penelope cow me."

Tom's hurt pride shifted in a blink to partisan defense. "She took advantage of you, then. You were distracted by more important things."

Trumpet clucked her tongue. "That's a feeble excuse."

Tom could not sustain one jot of resentment toward this woman, who had created his perfect son within her own body. She'd endured nine long months of discomfort and confinement, ending in those screams that had seared themselves into his soul. He grinned at her. "I forgive you."

"I don't," she said. "But I knew you would."

Two steps and he held her in his arms for the first deep, all-encompassing kiss they'd shared for months. When they broke for breath, they leaned their heads together, letting their heartbeats find the familiar, common rhythm. Tom kissed her fragrant hair and murmured, "You'll tell me when it's time to start the second one?"

"As soon as may be."

He loved her with sinew, blood, and bone. But he knew that one day not too far off — after he passed the bar — he must find a wife who would give him a son he could name after his own father.

* * *

Tom walked up to the gatehouse to meet Mr. Bacon, finding him still deep in conversation with his aunt. Tom stopped where he could see them, but Her Ladyship wouldn't notice him. He turned his mind to the task before him. Best case, he would find the *Neptune* and scale the hull with a blade between his teeth. He'd overpower any poor sea-crab unlucky enough to get in his way, scoop Anthony into his arms, somehow lower both of them into a waiting boat, and row back to Essex House, shooting the rapids under the bridge in an act of breathtaking derring-do.

On second thought, it might be wise to have an alternative plan.

Her Ladyship climbed into her coach at last and drove off. Tom caught up with Mr. Bacon to walk back to Gray's. They crossed the busy Strand with uttermost care and walked up Chancery Lane.

"What do we do?" Bacon asked. "I mean, how do we start?"

"First, I want to go downriver and find the ship. I'll take Lawson. We'll hire a wherry. The boatman should know the Grapes — a new inn on the wharves at Limehouse. From there, we'll just search the river until we find a ship with the name *Neptune* painted on its hull."

Bacon nodded. "Then what?"

"I'd like to get a sense of how many men they leave aboard when they're in port."

"And then what?"

Tom shook his head. "I don't know, Mr. Bacon. I'll make a plan and carry it out."

"What should I do?"

"Pray for luck. Because we're going to need it."

* * *

Tom filled Lawson in on the interrogation of Madame du Plessis as they walked down to the Temple Stairs. That tale pleased the much-injured secretary mightily. Elsa Moreau's confession came as a complete surprise.

"How many versions of Ridley's murder did we hear?" Lawson asked. "First, I was guilty. Then Sir Robert Cecil had it done. Third, the insufferable Madame du Plessis and her henchman Louis Vandame conspired to do it. The funny thing is I would've guessed Sir Robert or Madame before Moreau any day." He shook his head. "She always looked as if butter wouldn't melt in her mouth. And never seemed like anything less than what she claimed to be. They fooled us all, her and that rat du Pin."

Tom had never met the wine merchant, so he couldn't fault himself on that score. But his gut had sadly let him down with respect to Moreau. It seemed to lose its powers when faced with a golden-haired beauty. If Trumpet hadn't been distracted by the little matter of a growing babe, she would've been able to take up the slack sooner. They'd always worked better as a team.

The wherryman let them out at the Old Swan Stairs. They walked to the other side of the bridge and picked up another boat. Tom asked the oarsman, "Ever heard of an inn or tavern called the Grapes?"

"The one in Limehouse? Who hasn't?"

Tom asked him to take them there, just to mark its location, and then move slowly on down the river. He said they wanted to look at the figureheads on the big ships. The wherryman shrugged as if he'd heard stranger requests.

Half a dozen two- or three-masted ships bobbed in the middle of the Thames with their sails furled, towering above them as they passed. Dozens of smaller craft maneuvered between and around the great ships, ferrying passengers, loading and unloading cargoes. It was hard to get close enough to read the ship's names.

"There's your Grapes," the wherryman said, pointing at a three-story house separated from the water by a narrow strip of wharf. The top rungs of the ladder used to reach it at low tide were barely visible. The clean white plaster gleamed, and the green sign across the top looked freshly painted. They couldn't see in the windows from down on the water, but anyone inside could see them.

"Keep moving," Tom said, turning his face away. "We're not getting out here."

They traveled on downstream, rowing all the way around the Isle of Dogs before Tom gave up. "Let's turn back. Stick closer to the south bank this time. That ship must be somewhere." This time he told the boatman what they were looking for. It wouldn't do them much good to be so secretive that they failed in their mission.

They neared Greenwich Palace, which was fronted by a long, wide, well-kept wharf. A barge with a red-and-white canopy lay tied up at the eastern end, doubtless waiting for some noble passenger. Sir Walter Ralegh strode onto the boards and headed toward it. He was dressed for travel in brown serge but wore a red velvet cap with a white plume in the band. Liveried men followed him with bags and boxes, which they stowed on the barge. Sir Walter spoke to one of them, then sprang neatly aboard.

"Pull us up beside that barge," Tom told his boatman. "I'll bet Sir Walter knows where the *Neptune* is."

"Now why didn't I think of that?" the wherryman jeered. "I always give Sir Walter a prod when I'm in a quandary." But he did as he was told.

Tom called out, "Good afternoon, Sir Walter!"

"Mr. Clarady," the captain of the guard replied, standing near the stern. "You seem to turn up everywhere these days."

"Yes, sir. I'm sorry, sir. We're looking for a ship called the *Neptune*. It has to do with the matter we discussed the other day."

"That's upstream, near Rotherhithe. It's one of the du Pins' ships. Beautiful figurehead of the god with his trident.

286

You can't miss it." One of his boatmen spoke to him. "Mustn't tarry. Good luck with whatever you're up to today."

"Thank you, sir," Tom said, half rising from his bench to make an awkward bow. "May the wind be at your back."

Sir Walter signaled his men to cast off. The barge moved into the flow of the river, rolling downstream, when Tom remembered his good news. He rose abruptly, rocking the wherry and making the others cry out. Facing forward, he cupped his hands around his mouth and shouted, "It's a boy!"

Sir Walter threw his cap in the air.

"I'm not going to ask what that was about," Lawson said.

"Good," Tom said, "because it's none of your business." He sat down and told the wherryman to keep going upriver to Rotherhithe. That hamlet lay directly across the river from Limehouse and had little to recommend it, apart from its weathered gray wharf and a road leading south into Surrey.

Tom studied each great ship as they passed, knowing what to look for now. He saw an eagle at the bow of one, then the figure of a woman with streaming red hair. "There it is!" he cried, pointing to a wide-bellied galleon.

The figurehead lashed under the bowsprit was a lifelike carving of a bearded man wearing a loose tunic and gripping a golden trident. The whole ship had been decorated to the same high standard. Arcades painted blue, white, and yellow adorned a full third of the hull, surrounding each window, rimming the gunwales, and enlivening the quarter gallery running around the aft castle.

The prow pointed downstream, as if ready to sail away. But Tom was most interested in the stern, where the aft castle rose high above the main deck. "Take us right around it," he told the boatman. "Not too close."

He and Lawson tipped their hats down over their brows and kept their faces turned down too, studying the ship out of the corners of their eyes. The wherryman watched them with his tongue poked into his cheek. "If there's to be any thievery here, Master, I'll have to charge you double. And I'll want a share."

"No thievery," Tom said. "We want to admire this beautiful vessel, but the sun is getting in our eyes." A few bright beams were slanting between the clouds in the western sky, so it wasn't a complete falsehood.

The wherryman expressed his opinion of that excuse with a grunt.

Let him think what he liked. Tom told Lawson, "Look for faces at windows or movement on the decks. We want to know how many men are left aboard. We should see the pilot at the wheel. The coxswain or someone will be ready to lower the boat when the crew comes back. Then someone has to keep watch."

"And they've got two prisoners to guard," Lawson said. "If I know Jacques, he'll have found a way to make friends already."

"Good," Tom said. "That might help."

"Where's Anthony?" Lawson asked, a note of longing in his voice.

"In the captain's cabin, is my guess." Tom pointed to a small window near the top of the aft castle. "It's the most secure."

He studied the stern carefully. The cockboat bobbed a few yards back, its line made fast to a cleat on the starboard side. That was good. The ship was closer to the south bank, with another galleon on her larboard. Little risk of being spotted from the Grapes if anyone were watching. He could use that line to climb up to the cleat easily enough and then hoist himself onto the quarter gallery. He'd have to climb from there up to the captain's cabin, but he should be able to find hand and footholds aplenty, thanks to the owner's taste in ornamentation.

They came back around to the bow. "See that man by the foremast?" Tom pointed by tilting his head. "He's the one on watch. There'll be a few others in the crew's quarters below, I'll wager, sleeping or playing cards. Especially if they're setting sail in two days."

"I should think they'd all be in the nearest brothel," Lawson said. "Getting in one last bout before sailing."

"Not if they've spent all their money. They must've been here at least a few weeks if they brought du Plessis and du Pin to speak to the queen."

The wherryman interrupted. "Want me to go around again? I'm getting a mite dizzy."

"One more time," Tom said. He wished he could be certain Anthony was here.

As they rounded the stern again, Lawson whispered, "Look!" He turned his face away, pointing with his eyes.

Tom ducked his head and peered up. Jacques Petit walked along the quarter gallery with a large pot in his arms. He tilted it over the side, filling the air with the stench of piss and wet shit. Anthony's chamber pot, and well filled, by the stink of it. He must be all right.

A guard waited at the end of the gallery. Jacques performed his task without looking around and went straight back to be ushered out of sight.

"Thank God for Little Jack," Lawson said. He held his hand against his heart.

"That's all we needed to see." Tom told the wherryman to take them back to Fresh Wharf. To Lawson, he said, "We'll come back at sunset. We'll make our move when the light is trickiest."

"Do you have a plan?" Lawson asked.

Tom grinned at him. "As it happens, I just might."

TWENTY-SIX

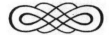

Francis watched Tom and Lawson stride across the yard to the gatehouse. It lacked an hour to sunset, but it would take time to collect some number of Lord Essex's men and travel down the river. They'd use His Lordship's boats and boatmen, which would be both swifter and more discreet. Lady Rich had been eager to offer them anything that might help, clearly seeking to atone for her role in this disastrous affair.

The chapel bell tolled the quarter hour. Francis stared at Anthony's empty chair for a long moment, then shook himself. He couldn't bear to sit idly in his chair, listening to the bells advance the time, not knowing what was happening out there. He grabbed his hat and cloak and hastened across the yard to the stables. Widhope was just harnessing the horses. His part was to drive the coach to Limehouse and wait at the Grapes. They'd decided it would less distressing for Anthony to bring him home that way than up the river against an outgoing tide. It would also avoid a delay at Essex House while Her Ladyship expressed her remorse.

"I'll ride with you," Francis told him and climbed in.

They were halfway there before it occurred to him he might encounter du Plessis and du Pin at the inn. What would he do in that event? He doubted du Pin could be reasoned with. The man described by both Nathaniel Welbeck and Elsa Moreau enjoyed tweaking society's nose.

He made his own rules and clearly considered his own case desperate enough to risk everything on one reckless act.

Du Plessis, on the other hand, had written works of genuine religious devotion. He must have a conscience somewhere deep within his breast. Perhaps he could be persuaded to stop this madness. And, Francis remembered with a spark of hope, they had his wife under lock and key. Perhaps a trade could be effected?

Francis left Widhope with the horses and went inside the tavern. Candles were lit in sconces and holders on the tables, casting their light against the white plaster walls. Coming out of the dimness of descending night, the interior brightness made him blink. He wanted to look out onto the darkening river, hoping to spot the *Neptune* figurehead Tom had described. Perhaps he could find a table by a window and blow out its candle to help his vision adjust.

He mounted the stairs and surveyed the tables along the front. He startled and took a step back when his eyes met those of Philippe du Plessis-Mornay, who sat watching him from one of those tables. He held a cup in his hand as if he'd been about to take a drink.

Francis glanced quickly around the room, but he did not see du Pin. He approached du Plessis and stopped not quite close enough to shake hands. "Where is your friend?"

"If you mean Antoine, he's on the ship." Du Plessis regarded him coolly. "Where is my wife?"

"She is safe. She won't be joining you for a while yet."

"She did not seek the death of Raffe Ridley."

"She is not blameless." Francis would not alleviate this man's evident misery by telling him about Moreau. Du Plessis could have simply left the country, trusting Anthony to keep those old crimes locked in his chest. Instead, he chose to believe the worst of his wife and respond by committing a major crime of his own.

Anna Castle

Du Plessis grunted. "When I went to the Savoy to collect her, the girl told me she had gone to Essex House to meet the celebrated Lady Russell. Hours ago, and not yet returned. I knew at once the game was over. My wife has many virtues, but like me, she also has flaws. She would tell that *puissant* lady everything — the ship, this place, the date of sailing."

Francis nodded. That was precisely what had happened. "Where's my brother?"

"On the ship." Du Plessis gestured at the stool opposite him. "Sit down, Mr. Bacon. Have some wine. You can watch with me."

"Watch what?" Francis asked, his heart freezing. He stared out at the dark waters. Wherrymen were lighting the lanterns that bobbed at the front of their small crafts. More lights danced high above them, hanging from masts on the tall ships. The overall effect was confusing.

"They'll make way as soon as the tide turns," du Plessis said. "I had to tell him. Antoine. I had to let him make his own choice."

Francis sank onto the empty stool, astonished. "In the name of our dear Lord, why? He'll destroy you."

Du Plessis shrugged. "I am destroyed already. I knew you would come, or that tall retainer of yours, with men to take me — somewhere. But I cannot leave without Charlotte."

"Why not help us stop him? You know this is an abomination."

"I owe Antoine too much. We have been friends for many years, you see, as different as we are. We fought together side by side as young men. Antoine cared about politics in those days, if not so much about religion. He brokered my release from the Duke of Guise's prison. In fact, that was how I met my wife." Du Plessis shook his head with a wry smile. "God must have a powerful sense of humor, do you not agree?"

292

"God did not tell you to abduct my brother. There is no humor here." Francis studied du Plessis's pale features. The Frenchman refilled his cup and drank with the air of a man who could see nothing beyond this moment. He'd given up.

Despair was considered one of the deadliest sins for good reason. Through it, a man divorced himself from the world, absolving himself of all responsibility. Francis considered it the grossest form of spiritual sloth. While one had life and reason, one had a positive obligation to act for the good.

"Take hold of yourself, man!" Francis moved the jug out of reach before the cup could be refilled. "The game is *not* over, not until Anthony is safe at home."

"But what can I do? Antoine intends to brazen it out if he is caught before he effects the transfer. He will say he rescued Anthony from the Spaniards instead of the other way around." Another Gallic shrug. "It might succeed. Who will gainsay him?"

"*You* will, Monsieur. You must." Francis clasped his hands on the table and spoke from the heart, mustering all the persuasive power of which he was capable. "You must not sit here wallowing in despair and allow this foul deed to transpire. How will you face your Maker when your time comes, knowing you did nothing while a man you once respected is carried off to be sold to his enemies? It's monstrous. You're a better man than this, Philippe. Reach inside yourself and find the strength. Here and now. You *can* redeem some part of what you've done."

Du Plessis shot him a bitter glance, then turned his sightless gaze to the window. Francis could almost see the man's better and worser angels wrestling for his soul. At last, he returned to the world and met Francis's eyes. "*Eh, bien*, I will go with you. And I thank you for showing me that I am not wholly damned. Not yet."

They got to their feet. Du Plessis dropped some coins on the table. "You have changed my heart, Mr. Bacon. Now what shall we do?"

"We'll get a wherry and row out to the *Neptune*. My man might be there, but his plan depended on a nearly empty ship. If du Pin is preparing to set sail, the whole crew will be aboard. It might be impossible for Clarady even to approach. Worse, he might already have been taken captive as well."

Not hurt, he devoutly hoped. But if du Pin were desperate to escape unchallenged, who knew how far he would go?

They went downstairs and out the riverside door. Du Plessis peered out across the water while Francis scouted about the wharf for a free wherry.

"Mon Dieu!" du Plessis cried. He pointed to a galleon moving slowly down river. "Alas, we are too late! The *Neptune*, she goes out with the tide."

TWENTY-SEVEN

Tom followed the usher through the narrow garden that edged the outer wall at Essex House. He lifted his hat as he passed under Trumpet's window. He had no time to run up and kiss Baby William's chubby cheeks this evening. His plan depending on perfect timing. He wanted to reach the *Neptune* at the very edge of night, when there was still light enough to see where you were putting your hands and feet, but shifting shadows made you difficult to see. Especially in dark clothes against the tarred black hull of a ship. He'd remembered to wear a brown flat cap to cover his fair hair.

He and the head boatman had discussed the plan. They had agreed they could never hope to battle their way through a ship full of sailors. It would create a tremendous tumult, for one thing, which they'd been trying to avoid from the outset. They must depend on guile; in which case, two men to handle the boats and two more to help with the rescue would suffice.

Tom had left Lawson to help choose the men and get the boats ready while he went into the house and begged an interview with Lady Rich. He wanted to borrow one of her prisoners.

Elsa Moreau had proven her skill at playing a part. Tonight, she could play one more. They needed a distraction to lure the crewmen onto the forecastle while he and two Essex men climbed up aft to the captain's cabin. What better distraction than a beautiful woman who spoke the sailors' own language?

Lady Rich objected. "She'll escape. I'm not sure what to do with her, but I can't just let her go. Not after the way she's cozened me."

Tom bit back a laugh. Getting a job under false pretenses was hardly the worst thing Moreau had done. "She won't escape from me, my lady. Not unless she can swim very fast in two layers of skirts. And Lawson will be with her every minute."

Her Ladyship understood the need for haste and granted the plausibility of Tom's plan. "I'm certain she can play the whore well enough."

He went back to the boathouse and jumped into one of the waiting wherries. The head boatman had already sent a swift messenger to make sure His Lordship's Greenwich boat would be waiting for them east of the bridge. They'd hire a humbler vessel for Lawson, Moreau, and one of the skilled Essex boatmen.

A tall servant led Moreau down to the private wharf. When she heard what Tom wanted from her, she laughed. "Do not worry, Monsieur Clarady. I will have every man on that ship leaning over the gunwales to get a better look at me." She eyed the shallow-bottomed wherries with a critical eye, then unhooked her doublet and left it in the boathouse. "My cloak is warm enough. And who knows when I will receive so fine a garment again?"

Off they went. As they approached the *Neptune*, the two crafts separated. Lawson and Moreau made straight for the prow, which was pointed downriver. Tom's team slowed to a halt alongside the cockboat, still tied up aft.

He pulled off his shoes and socks, directing the two Essex men who would climb up with him to do the same. "You get a better grip on the hull with bare feet."

The boatman held the wherry while they clambered into the cockboat. Tom grabbed the line and jumped, his

296

toes dipping into the chilly water before he got his feet planted on a plank. One good pull and he gained the ledge under the blocks anchoring the mainsail ratlines. From here, it would be easier to climb up to the main deck and scurry across to the aft castle, but he'd be visible to the watchman for several seconds.

Nothing for it. He'd have to spider along the hull for about three feet in the other direction. He had a few harrowing moments hanging by his fingertips from a painted arcade while his feet stuttered across the planks, searching for support, but he made it. He swung himself up and over the short balcony around the quarter gallery. The two Essex men followed his lead.

They crouched behind the balcony for a moment to get oriented. Tom's heart pounded, and he had to open his mouth wide to catch his breath without making a noise. This had been a lot easier when he was eighteen, working on his father's ship. Back then, he could scurry up the ratlines with the rope between his toes like a seafaring squirrel. He hadn't grown fat — he kept himself in good trim — but he'd lost that extra bit of youthful spring.

He walked in a crouch to the windows across the back and peeked into the great cabin. This was where the officers took their meals and held their meetings. Candles had been lit around the walls and in the stick on the long table. A man in costly gentleman's garb sat studying an unrolled map. Antoine du Pin, most like.

Tom's blood boiled at the sight of the traitor. What would the man do if he caught them? They'd find out if Moreau failed to keep the sailors busy.

Her sweet, feminine voice rang out from below the prow, carrying clearly over the water. She spoke in French, but her meaning was plain in any language. A man's voice called down to her. Someone whistled. The man at the table flicked a glance at the door, then returned to his map.

Tom crouch-walked away from the window. He kept half an ear on the banter forward while he scanned the upper half of the aft castle, considering their next move. He pointed up to a small ledge outside the highest window and whispered, "Once we reach that ledge, we can climb those lines to the aft deck and come down the steps."

He jumped for the head of the window and got the balls of his feet on the sill. From there, he clung to an upright timber while he pulled his toes up to where his hands had been. Another arcade and his fingers found the ledge supporting the shrouds of the mizzen sail. He granted himself another short rest after gaining that vantage, then raised his head to look into the captain's cabin.

Anthony Bacon lay on the narrow bed, facing the wall, wrapped in a blanket. Jacques Petit sat on a padded chest, playing with a deck of cards. Tom gave a low whistle, and the youth startled, throwing the cards in the air.

"*Mon Dieu!* Monsieur Clarady!" He babbled excitedly in French.

"Wake your master," Tom whispered, pointing at Anthony. "We're here to rescue you."

More excited French. Tom dredged a word in Law French from his memory, hoping Jacques could comprehend his lamentable accent. "*Deliverer vous.*" He pointed at Anthony again, then beckoned toward himself.

"*Dieu merci!*" Jacques turned away from the window and shook his master awake.

Anthony startled to see Tom but quickly recovered. He wrapped the blanket around his shoulders as he shifted unsteadily to lean beside the window. He spoke in a low voice. "You must hurry. Du Pin is here. Below us, I think, in the great cabin, waiting for the pilot. The crew's returning. They mean to sail tonight when the tide turns."

"God's breath," Tom said. "It's already started. Well, get ready. We'll have you out in a matter of minutes. It might be a bit rough getting you down to the wherry."

"We'll manage."

Moreau began singing something scurrilous, to judge by the throaty laughter of the men. There were many more voices than before. Tom hoped the *Neptune* had a lax boatswain. If the pilot was still ashore, the crew might be ready to go, but they were waiting for the command. This was the perfect moment for a last, longing look at a woman.

Tom gestured to the Essex men, who were still on the quarter gallery waiting for his signal. He waved for them to come up to this ledge and then climb the ratlines up to the aft deck. He moved his pointing finger and up and down to show them how to proceed from there. They both nodded. It made more sense to do than to illustrate. And they'd doubtless been aboard ships in the service of the restless Earl of Essex.

He swung over to the main deck and hid behind the steps leading up. A sailor stood less than three feet away, guarding the door to the captain's cabin. But his attention was riveted on the front of the ship. Lawson's voice called out something, and the guard took three paces forward, craning his neck to see what was happening.

A cheer rose from what sounded now like a crowd of men. Tom guessed Moreau had won an invitation to come aboard.

The two Essex men dropped like cats onto the main deck. One of them lunged for the guard, wrapping his hand around the man's mouth. He spun him around toward the other retainer, who slammed his palm up under the guard's chin, snapping his head back. He slumped senseless in the first retainer's arms.

The whole maneuver took only a few seconds. It would appear His Lordship kept able men in his service.

Tom slid out from his hiding place and whispered, "Get him in the cabin and tie him up. Then get the prisoners ready to go. I'll find a rope. We'll have to lower them down from here."

One of the Essex men said, "If Nokes here hops back down to that gallery, I can lower them one by one. Can't be more'n twelve feet all told down to the water, and that gallery's about halfway."

Nokes was Tom's height — six feet — and the other wasn't much shorter. With arms outstretched, they could do it. It'd be hard on Anthony, but it'd be over in a minute.

"Do it," he said. "Get them into the wherry. I'll signal Lawson and then come down."

Though he had one other thing he wanted to do, if he could find a way.

The Essex men set to their task. Tom leaned against the wall, a dark figure against the dark wood, and watched as Elsa Moreau was lifted onto the deck by three pairs of hands. She laughed gaily and scampered up to the forecastle, where she began to sing and dance, flipping her skirts to reveal a snow-white petticoat. Lawson edged his way past the group of admiring sailors.

Tom moved toward the steps leading down to the gun deck. He had one short question to ask the ship's master before he left. But as he stepped across the short stretch of decking, he heard someone coming up and plastered himself back against the wall.

The gentleman from the officer's cabin emerged, staring at the dancing woman. He said, "Elsa?" followed by something else in French, perhaps speaking to the guard who was no longer there. Then he croaked as Tom slipped his knife into the hollow behind his right ear.

"Are you Antoine du Pin?"

"I am. Who are you?"

"Did you sell gunpowder to the Spanish in the summer of '88?"

"What? Who are you?"

"A man whose father died. Answer the question."

Du Pin eyed him as best he could from the strained position. "I know what you want. Oyez!" he shouted toward the sailors forward.

One of them turned around, gaped at them, then turned back and shouted at his fellows. Six men moved toward Tom with their knives out. Lawson kept easing his way toward the stern along the gunwale.

Tom dug his knife in a little deeper and said, "Stop them. Answer my question and I'll let you go."

Du Pin gestured them to stay back. "I sold no powder. There was none to be had. Some fool blew up a whole shipful in Rouen."

That was the *Susannah*. Tom would give a year of his own life to know who the fool had been. "What did you sell to our enemies?"

"Food, drink. Shot, when I could find it. I am a merchant, Monsieur. And we do not have the same enemies."

A shout rose up from below. "All aboard!" The Essex men must have Anthony and Jacques in the wherry. Time to go.

Lawson leapt onto the ratlines and disappeared over the side. Tom walked du Pin forward a few feet, then pushed him hard into the knife-holding sailors. Then he dove for the ratlines and swung down after Lawson. They paused together on the ledge holding the block and tackle. There was nowhere to go from here — not without getting wet.

"Now what?" Lawson asked.

"Now we swim." Tom turned and dove into the cold waters of the Thames. He pulled himself to the surface and saw Lawson's pale face bobbing nearby. They swam to the wherry, which came rowing to meet them. The Essex men hauled them in by their sopping doublets and the seats of their soggy hose.

They lay in the bottom gasping while the boatman leaned to his oars, rowing as if their lives depended on it. Shouts arose from the ship, but no one followed, and no shots were fired. Du Pin must have recognized the folly of attracting attention to himself and ordered his men to let them go.

"What about Moreau?" Tom asked when he'd caught his breath.

"She's staying," Lawson said. "She said she'd rather take her chances with du Pin. We had to get her on board to draw off the men, so I didn't argue."

"Nothing you could've done," Tom said. "Let's get these men to the Grapes. Then we'll come back to deal with du Pin and his doxy."

Anthony huddled in Jacques's arms on the front bench. "I'd hug you both," he said, "but you're a trifle damp."

Tom grinned, though he doubted Anthony could see it. The man would seemingly maintain that wry self-possession in the face of imminent death.

"You seem undamaged," Tom said. Their faces were pale ovals in the failing light. His first rescue mission had gone off without a hitch, thanks to the agile Essex men.

The wherry crested a small wave. The tide had turned; now the river was flowing strongly toward the sea. Tom looked back at the *Neptune* and saw dark figures in the yellow glow of the ship's lanterns hauling at a hand-thick cable.

"They're weighing anchor!" he cried. "They'll get away before we can come back. We've got to turn around." Though he had no idea how they could get Moreau off that ship, much less du Pin. He'd saved the prisoners, but the villains were escaping.

"Let them go," Anthony said.

"After what they did to you?" Tom protested. "Don't you want them to face judgment?"

Anthony chuckled. "They will, never fear. I'll write to King Henry first thing tomorrow. My letter will reach him before the *Neptune* can cross the Bay of Biscay. Du Pin may well find the king's men waiting for him when he steps off that ship. And French prisons are even worse than ours."

"A fair trade," Lawson muttered.

Tom had to agree with that, but letting Elsa Moreau sail away scot-free galled him. "We could catch them if we tried. Or at least alert the harbormaster."

"And tell him what?" Anthony asked. "Think, Mr. Clarady. To punish them here in England, we must have trials. That means more people, including pamphleteers and court gossips, spreading Ridley's slanders far and wide. We've gone to great lengths to prevent that very thing. Better for this whole sad concatenation of events to sink into oblivion." He gave a short laugh. "I earn my bread trading political secrets, but I prefer to keep my personal ones to myself. I thank you gentlemen most wholeheartedly for helping me to preserve that distinction."

TWENTY-EIGHT

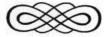

Francis placed his hands on the arms of his customary chair before Anthony's hearth, leaning back against the soft cushions with a sigh. He felt as if he'd been absent from this refuge for months instead of one short, agonizing week. Now once again, he sat contentedly waiting for a hot drink while Jacques hummed over his pipkin at the edge of the fire. Anthony was reading letters from the stack on his portable desk. He'd only been home for one day, and he was already back at work. Life at Gray's had returned to normal, and yet somehow everything had changed.

"Our lord of Essex will be home tomorrow," Anthony said, exhibiting a page. "He lies in Dartford tonight."

"What will we tell him about the hurly-burly of these past few weeks?" Francis asked.

"The truth, of course." Anthony flicked his dark eyebrows. "Or some of it."

"Where shall we start? He'll have heard the Affair of the Hair from my lord of Dorchester."

"I hate to go that far back. But we can't leave Madame out of it since du Plessis is in it up to his neck."

"Not to mention that we have them both imprisoned in His Lordship's house," Francis pointed out.

"That does demand some explanation, doesn't it?" Anthony's smile faded. "But the business with the seneschal and poor little Pierre must be forgotten by one and all."

"Agreed. We'll say Madame's resentment was inflamed anew when she and Ridley came together in London."

"Her lust to discredit me and assuage her pride set the whole train in motion. That's nothing more than the simple truth." Anthony folded the earl's letter and tucked it into his sleeve.

"Lady Rich's ambition drove it forward," Francis said. "She was so eager to deliver you to her brother like a trussed deer that she allowed her servant to play a risky game."

"She should never have countenanced that false story. She'll face a reckoning when her brother comes home."

"Not if we hold our peace." Francis cocked his head. "Shall we?"

Anthony shook his head. "These things have a way of coming out. I've written to King Henry about du Pin. He's liable to tell Essex next time they meet. Then His Lordship will wonder why he didn't hear about it from us first."

"We'll tell him together," Francis said. "As soon as we meet. He loves a good story."

Jacques handed him a wooden goblet filled with spiced wine. Francis held it to his nose, inhaling the voluptuous aromas of nutmeg, honey, and red tinto. He took a tentative sip: too hot. He set it carefully on the arm of his chair to cool a bit.

He turned a rueful smile toward his brother. "I was useless throughout this whole ordeal. Your involvement froze my wits. I would have dropped Ridley's murder the moment Tom showed us Lawson's handkerchief. If he hadn't persisted, and Lady Dorchester hadn't uncovered that maidservant's lies, I would have lost you."

Anthony reached across the narrow gap between them to clasp his arm. "You trained them. You've been their guide and teacher — and more. They acted out of friendship for you, my brother. Which is more than we've ever received from our cousin Robert. I notice that you never asked him for help."

"I was saving that as a last resort. I knew he would regard any assistance as proof of our incompetence. He would never forget." Francis tested his wine again. Just right. He took a sip.

"I had time to think in my little berth," Anthony said, "between the doses of laudanum du Pin gave me to stop me talking to his men. Our lord uncle's days are nearly spent. We should look to him for nothing. Nor will Robert help us, or even use us fairly. You may not have noticed, but while Essex chases armies and Ralegh searches for the City of Gold, our little cousin has been gathering all the power he can reach into his own two hands."

Francis had noticed. "Is it Essex for us, then?"

"It's Essex. He's bold, intelligent, ambitious, and beloved of the queen. He needs our guidance and our gravity. We'll never pry the mantle of Secretary of State from Robert's bony fingers, but we can establish a rival under another roof." He picked up his cup and held it to his nose, closing his eyes to savor the rising steam. His gaze slid toward his brother. "Don't worry, Frank. There will always be time for your philosophical work."

Francis flapped that away. "It can wait." He smoothed his moustache with one finger, thinking about the year ahead. "Easter term begins on Wednesday. I should take a case this year, something worthy. Maybe two. With support from the Earl of Essex, Solicitor General might be within my reach, don't you think?"

They grinned at one another, in perfect accord. The world had changed this spring. Francis had turned thirty-one and finally grown weary of waiting for his kin to show him favor. Lord Burghley had grown weak, while his son grew strong. Lord Essex had gained vital allies at home and abroad. Best of all, Anthony Bacon had come home.

HISTORICAL NOTES

You can find maps of the places we go in this series at my website on a page called "Maps for the Francis Bacon mystery series:" www.annacastle.com/francis-bacon-series/maps-for-the-francis-bacon-series. Some are downloadable, and some are links to maps I don't have rights to, including a delightful interactive map of Elizabethan London.

I collapsed several historical events that occurred in the first half of 1592 (our calendar) for narrative impact. First, Anthony Bacon returned to England on 4 February, coming straight to his brother's house at Gray's Inn. He was much debilitated by the journey. But I had to set this story in mid-March to accommodate Trumpet's pregnancy. As those who have read *Let Slip the Dogs* know, she could not have fallen pregnant before 28 June 1591. So I sent Anthony home to his mother at Gorhambury for six weeks of recuperation. Nothing of interest happened during that time.

Second, Monsieur du Plessis-Mornay (see the list below) was in England in January pleading King Henry's cause. Alas, he left on the very day Anthony Bacon returned. What fun is that? I want my enemies in the same place at the same time.

Third, Raffe Ridley (see below) spread slanders about Anthony in May and June of 1592, but in France, not in

London. Again, how does that make a good story? So I brought him back to England in time to get himself strangled.

If you find Anthony Bacon as intriguing as I do, read Daphne du Maurier's highly entertaining biography, *The Golden Lads*. She is a consummate storyteller and brings that keen insight into character and motivation to this historical work. You'll quickly discover that I didn't invent any part of Anthony's troubles in Montaubon. Who would believe it?

The Affair of the Hair is absolute historical truth, as are the vengeful pederasty charges and Anthony's stint in jail. King Henry really did rescue him. Anthony really did borrow money from the Bishop of Cahors. I doubt he ever paid it back. He also really did write a letter to his uncle about du Pin and du Plessis "sweating into their doublets" about information he had on them in '88. Nothing further survived on that theme, so I made their perfidious treachery up.

Credible threats were in truth made by Spanish agents to capture Anthony Bacon on his way home from France and trade him for Don Pedro de Valdés. Don Pedro had been captured by Francis Drake and imprisoned in Torbay. One of the things I love about this period is that I don't have to invent this sort of thing. It's just there for the taking.

Anthony suffered from gout and the stone (kidney stones) and occasional recurrences of quartan fever (probably malaria contracted on the coast.) In our time, gout is a specific ailment. In Bacon's day, the term was applied more broadly to any severe affliction of the joints, especially the legs. I think Anthony suffered from rheumatoid arthritis, inherited from his father.

One last note: Poor Anthony never presented himself to the queen; or if he did, it was never recorded. Du Maurier thinks he resisted it during this period because he was afraid du Plessis had told her about the pederasty charges. Du Maurier recounts a valiant effort Anthony made in October 1592 to see Her Majesty at Windsor. He got as far as Colnbrook (between Heathrow and Eton) when he had an attack of the stone. He had his driver take him to Eton to beg lodging from a friend. His aunt, Lady Russell, went to visit him there, perhaps to verify his incapacity. She went on to Windsor to inform the queen, who graciously forgave him. More play-acting, or a genuine effort? With Anthony, we can never be certain.

Here are the real people who appeared in this book, including our regular cast, for completeness:

- Mr. Francis Bacon.
- Mr. Anthony Bacon.
- Queen Elizabeth I.
- Sir Walter Ralegh. His son Damerei was born on Easter Sunday, or so it is said. That birth was a deep secret known only to Sir Walter, his wife Bess, her brother and sister-in-law, and of course, the wily Sir Robert Cecil.
- Sir Robert Cecil. Francis Bacon's cousin.
- Lord Admiral Howard.
- Lady Rich (Penelope). The older sister of Robert Devereux, 2nd Earl of Essex.
- Lady Russell (Elizabeth). Francis Bacon's aunt.
- M. Philippe du Plessis-Mornay. Yes, he was real. He was responsible for having Anthony sent to jail in Montaubon in 1586. He was one of King Henry's closest advisors, serving as a royal envoy to England. He did write Calvinist tracts and he did found a Calvinist college. He most certainly did not collude in the kidnapping of Anthony Bacon, though he did retire from court not long after 1592.

- M. du Pin. Also real, but elusive. I searched in vain to find out more about him. Then I surrendered and invented nearly everything, including his first name.
- Mme. Charlotte du Plessis-Mornay was also real, right down to that ridiculous hairstyle. Until du Maurier uncovered the Affair of the Hair, Charlotte was chiefly remembered for writing a pious biography of her husband.
- Thomas Lawson. Lawson lived with Anthony until the latter's death in 1601, though little is known of him. He was a faithful friend and secretary, presumed by Lady Bacon to have also been a lover. He really was arrested at her request and spent those dire ten months in prison. I invented his backstory.
- Jacques Petit. You think I made that name up, but little Jacques was very real. He did indeed join Anthony's household as a page. He attended faithfully upon his master until Anthony's death. As he grew older, Anthony often sent him in the train of some important person; ostensibly to serve, undoubtedly also to observe.
- Henry Percy was Francis's lifelong friend. His mother decried him as a 'coach companion,' (a clandestine lover), but he remained in Francis's circle all his life. And now I've told you everything that seems to be known about that man.
- Raffe Ridley. I would never make up a name like that; it's too much fun. Ridley was real, and he really was the Privy Council's emissary in Bordeaux. His father was a minister in Cambridgeshire and his older brother was the physician to the Muscovy Company. I searched everywhere, JSTOR included, and could find no references to Raffe outside of du Maurier's book.

So I merrily went ahead and murdered him. It's a risky business, being a footnote in the history of an important person.

- Thomas Phelippes was the cleverest and most sought-after cryptographer in Europe. Francis recruited him to the the Bacon~Essex team after Walsingham died.
- The Grapes in Limehouse was and is a real place. You can go there, next time you're in London, and watch the boats on the river. I'm afraid you won't see a three-masted galleon, but it will still be delightful.

If you spot something missing, something wrong, or just want to chat, please write to me at castle@annacastle.com

ABOUT THE AUTHOR

Anna Castle holds an eclectic set of degrees: BA in the Classics, MS in Computer Science, and a Ph.D. in Linguistics. She has had a correspondingly eclectic series of careers: waitressing, software engineering, grammar-writing, a short stint as an associate professor, and managing a digital archive. Historical fiction combines her lifelong love of stories and learning. She physically resides in Austin, Texas, but mentally counts herself a queen of infinite space.

(www.annacastle.com)

BOOKS BY ANNA CASTLE

Keep up with all my books and short stories with my newsletter: www.annacastle.com

The Francis Bacon Series

Book 1, *Murder by Misrule.*

Francis Bacon is charged with investigating the murder of a fellow barrister at Gray's Inn. He recruits his unwanted protégé Thomas Clarady to do the tiresome legwork. The son of a privateer, Clarady will do anything to climb the Elizabethan social ladder. Bacon's powerful uncle Lord Burghley suspects Catholic conspirators of the crime, but other motives quickly emerge. Rival barristers contend for the murdered man's legal honors and wealthy clients. Highly-placed courtiers are implicated as the investigation reaches from Whitehall to the London streets. Bacon does the thinking; Clarady does the fencing. Everyone has something up his pinked and padded sleeve. Even the brilliant Francis Bacon is at a loss — and in danger — until he sees through the disguises of the season of Misrule.

Book 2, *Death by Disputation.*

Thomas Clarady is recruited to spy on the increasingly rebellious Puritans at Cambridge University. Francis Bacon is his spymaster; his tutor in both tradecraft and religious politics. Their commission gets off to a deadly start when Tom finds his chief informant hanging from the roof beams. Now he must catch a murderer as well as a seditioner. His first suspect is volatile poet Christopher Marlowe, who keeps turning up in the wrong places.

Dogged by unreliable assistants, chased by three lusty women, and harangued daily by the exacting Bacon, Tom risks his very soul to catch the villains and win his reward.

Book 3, *The Widow's Guild.*

London, 1588: Someone is turning Catholics into widows, taking advantage of armada fever to mask the crimes. Francis Bacon is charged with identifying the murderer by the Andromache Society, a widows' guild led by his formidable aunt. He must free his friends from the Tower, track an exotic poison, and untangle multiple crimes to determine if the motive is patriotism, greed, lunacy — or all three.

Book 4, *Publish and Perish.*

It's 1589 and England is embroiled in a furious pamphlet war between an impudent Puritan calling himself Martin Marprelate and London's wittiest writers. The archbishop wants Martin to hang. The Privy Council wants the tumult to end. But nobody knows who Martin is or where he's hiding his illegal press.

Then two writers are strangled, mistaken for Thomas Nashe, the pamphleteer who is hot on Martin's trail. Francis Bacon is tasked with stopping the murders — and catching Martin, while he's about it. But the more he learns, the more he fears Martin may be someone dangerously close to home.

Can Bacon and his band of intelligencers stop the strangler before another writer dies, without stepping on Martin's possibly very important toes?

Book 5, *Let Slip the Dogs*

It's Midsummer, 1591, at Richmond Palace, and love is in the air. Gallant courtiers sport with great ladies while

Tom and Trumpet bring their long-laid plans to fruition at last. Everybody's doing it — even Francis Bacon enjoys a private liaison with the secretary to the new French ambassador. But the Queen loathes scandal and will punish anyone rash enough to get caught.

Still, it's all in a summer day until a young man is found dead. He had few talents beyond a keen nose for gossip and was doubtless murdered to keep a secret. But what sort — romantic, or political? They carried different penalties: banishment from court or a traitor's death. Either way, worth killing to protect.

Bacon wants nothing more than to leave things alone. He has no position and no patron; in fact, he's being discouraged from investigating. But can he live with himself if another innocent person dies?

The Professor & Mrs. Moriarty Series

Book 1, Moriarty Meets His Match

Professor James Moriarty has but one desire left in his shattered life: to prevent the man who ruined him from harming anyone else. Then he meets amber-eyed Angelina Gould and his world turns upside down.

At an exhibition of new inventions, an exploding steam engine kills a man. When Moriarty tries to figure out what happened, he comes up against Sherlock Holmes, sent to investigate by Moriarty's old enemy. Holmes collects evidence that points at Moriarty, who realizes he must either solve the crime or swing it for it himself. He soon uncovers trouble among the board members of the engine company and its unscrupulous promoter. Moriarty tries to untangle those relationships, but everywhere he turns, he meets the alluring Angelina. She's playing some game, but what's her goal? And whose side is she on?

Between them, Holmes and Angelina push Moriarty to his limits -- and beyond. He'll have to lose himself to save his life and win the woman he loves.

Book 2, *Moriarty Takes His Medicine*

James and Angelina Moriarty are settling into their new marriage and their fashionable new home — or trying to. But James has too little to occupy his mind and Angelina has too many secrets pressing on her heart. They fear they'll never learn to live together. Then Sherlock Holmes comes to call with a challenging case. He suspects a prominent Harley Street specialist of committing murders for hire, sending patients home from his private hospital with deadly doses or fatal conditions. Holmes intends to investigate, but the doctor's clientele is exclusively female. He needs Angelina's help.

While Moriarty, Holmes, and Watson explore the alarming number of ways a doctor can murder his patients with impunity, Angelina enters into treatment with their primary suspect, posing as a nervous woman who fears her husband wants to be rid of her. Then a hasty conclusion and an ill-considered word drive James and Angelina apart, sending her deep into danger. Now they must find the courage to trust each other as they race the clock to win justice for the murdered women before they become victims themselves.

Book 3, *Moriarty Brings Down the House*

An old friend brings a strange problem to Professor and Mrs. Moriarty: either his theater is being haunted by an angry ghost or someone is trying to drive him into bankruptcy. That would shut down his Christmas pantomime before it opens, throwing two hundred people out of work. The Moriartys can't let that happen! Besides, Angelina is longing to play the lead in a West End show and James needs a bigger challenge than yet another high-stakes game of whist.

But the day they move into the theater, the stage manager dies. It wasn't an accident; it also was most definitely not a ghost. While Angelina works backstage turning up secrets and old grudges, James follows the money in search of a motive. The pranks grow deadlier and more frequent. Then someone sets Sherlock Holmes on the trail, trying to catch our sleuths crossing the line into crime.

How far will Moriarty have to go to keep the show afloat? And will they all make it to opening night in one piece?

CPSIA information can be obtained
at www.ICGtesting.com
Printed in the USA
LVHW091207040421
683393LV00003B/686

9 781945 382239